MAY 7 2010

9/10·7x

The Big Bang Symphony

Also by Lucy Jane Bledsoe

The Big Bang Symphony

A Novel of Antarctica

Lucy Jane Bledsoe

Terrace Books
A trade imprint of the University of Wisconsin Press

Terrace Books, a trade imprint of the University of Wisconsin Press, takes its name from the Memorial Union Terrace, located at the University of Wisconsin–Madison. Since its inception in 1907, the Wisconsin Union has provided a venue for students, faculty, staff, and alumni to debate art, music, politics, and the issues of the day. It is a place where theater, music, drama, literature, dance, outdoor activities, and major speakers are made available to the campus and the community. To learn more about the Union, visit www.union.wisc.edu.

Terrace Books
A trade imprint of the University of Wisconsin Press
1930 Monroe Street, 3rd Floor
Madison, Wisconsin 53711-2059
uwpress.wisc.edu

3 Henrietta Street
London WCE 8LU, England
eurospanbookstore.com

5   4   3   2   1

Printed in the United States of America

Library of Congress Cataloging-in-Publication Data
Bledsoe, Lucy Jane.
    The big bang symphony : a novel of Antarctica / Lucy Jane Bledsoe.
    p.   cm.
    ISBN 978-0-299-23500-0 (cloth: alk. paper)
    ISBN 978-0-299-23503-1 (e-book)
1. Antarctica—Fiction.   2. Man-woman relationships—Antarctica—Fiction   I. Title.
PS3552.L418B54   2010
813'.54—dc22
2009040630

"Me and Bobby McGee," words and music by Kris Kristofferson and Fred Foster © 1969 (renewed 1997) TEMI Combine Inc. All rights controlled by Combine Music Corp. and administered by EMI Blackwood Music Inc. All rights reserved. International copyright secured. Used by permission.

This is a work of fiction. While, as in all fiction, the literary perceptions and insights are based on experience, all names, characters, places, and incidents are either products of the author's imagination or are used fictitiously. No reference to any real person is intended or should be inferred.

The heavenly motions are nothing but a continuous song for several voices, to be perceived by the intellect, not by the ear; a music which, through discordant tensions, through syncopations and cadenzas, as it were, progresses toward certain predesigned six-voiced cadences and thereby sets landmarks in the immeasurable flow of time.

Johannes Kepler, Harmonices Mundi (1619)

The Big Bang Symphony

1

The plane was only half full. Mostly scientists. Few workers deployed to the continent this late in the season. Rosie was glad to be doing a short stint this year. By the time she left in February, three months from now, she would have her down payment. If she managed to not get fired.

Rosie smiled. She couldn't help it. She knew she should hate McMurdo Station, that scattering of debris that passed as a town. All the workers said they did. Everyone said they returned only for the good money you could make in a few short months. But Antarctica was like a vortex that drew you back, season after season. The place was so raw and pure, all seal hide and crystalline iceberg. The fishbowl community at McMurdo intensified relationships, jacked all emotion up to a ten. The trick was to get what you needed and then get out fast.

This was Rosie's third season and she intended it to be her last.

An exceptionally tall man, sitting across the plane from her, thought the smile on her face was for him. He smiled back. Then he raised a camera. A bright flash blinded her for a moment as he took her picture. He was still smiling after he lowered the camera. She couldn't see much of him in the dim light of the plane's interior. A prominent Adam's apple. Good posture. His bearing gave the impression that he'd never had a doubt in his life. He reached into his pocket and took out a pencil stub and tiny notepad. He scratched down a few words.

The loadmaster, a chubby man wearing military fatigues, emerged from the cockpit and pulled the intercom system's mouthpiece to his face. Rosie strained to hear what he had to say. Even with the amplification, hearing anything over the loud engines on these austere Air Force planes was nearly impossible. The loadmaster cleared his throat before announcing that they had passed the point of safe return.

The announcement sent a few quick pulses of fear through Rosie. The Southern Ocean, the roughest patch of water on the planet, sloshed thousands of feet below. Ahead, glaciers and sky, three months of hard work. She looked out the porthole to the left of the tall man's head and saw blue brilliance. Good thing. From here on in the plane wouldn't have enough fuel to turn around and fly back to New Zealand. The point of safe return held a satisfaction, like gambling, all or nothing.

She just hoped that this year she would get the all, not the nothing.

Rosie swallowed, closing her throat against the urge to sing. Always the urge to sing when she felt scared. But that was exactly her problem. Song was like flight. Temporary, impermanent. Yet she treated singing like going home, as if her voice would deliver her somewhere safe and warm. She had turned thirty this past summer. Yet here she was, still in flight, literally.

These LC-130s they used for transporting workers and scientists on and off the continent, crewed by the 109th Airlift Wing of the New York Air National Guard, were ski-equipped cargo planes. Red webbed seats lined the inside hull and a complex tangle of mysterious pipes and hardware covered all the other surfaces. Designed before women were ever deployed anywhere, the women's "bathroom" was a curtain drawn incompletely around a rustic toilet, set up on an unstable crate. A few porthole windows let in a bit of light and views of the sky. She might be riding a tough military cargo plane, but it was still flight. Rosie closed her eyes and let the LC-130's powerful vibrations shake her to the core.

This would be her last landing in Antarctica. She'd leave the continent in February. Hopefully, with a grubstake in her bank account. She'd give up flight of all kinds. She wanted home. She wanted to land somewhere permanent. But it was like she had to travel to the opposite of what she wanted, into the very heart of transience—and then get out again—to get it.

Rosie had come by this lifestyle honestly. Her father had changed jobs every year as he chased each new get-rich-quick scheme. Ironically, that's why she'd left home and never gone back. She'd never wanted to be him, the person who didn't know how to keep two feet on the ground, who thought a wish was the same thing as a bank account. When she left home at seventeen, she knew with a full-body certainty that she was going somewhere concrete and specific. She just hadn't figured out where. She'd lived in Boise, Portland, Durango, White Salmon, Tucson, Lincoln City, Redding, and Fairbanks, and worked as many short order cook and tree-planting jobs. She'd become her father and hadn't even noticed.

Rosie opened her eyes and looked directly into those of the tall, resolute man. He raised his camera slowly and pushed the shutter release button. It felt as if he'd touched her. She closed her eyes again, twisting in the web seat so she could lean her head against the plane's steel hull. Eventually, she managed to fall into a light sleep.

When they hit the first bump, it jarred her awake. Nothing more than a mass of air at cross purposes with the plane, but still, she checked her seatbelt. A series of bumps followed, as if the plane had bounced down a short flight of stairs. She glanced at the photographer. He stared at the camera in his lap, which he was gripping with his two big, capable-looking hands, as if it were a baby. She let her gaze travel up to his face, rest on his mouth. To avoid thinking about the turbulence, she considered what kind of kisser he would be.

When the LC-130 next lurched, he looked up, directly at her again. She smiled. He lifted his camera and, this time, took a series of shots. All of her.

She hand-motioned for him to stop. "What are you doing?" she mouthed.

But he didn't have a chance to answer, even if he had been able to read her lips, because the plane dropped suddenly, and then tipped, as if a forceful gust had slammed under the right wing.

A grizzled guy in the seat next to Rosie yelled, to be heard over the engine's roar, "Is this normal? These bumps?"

A FNG, as in *fucking new guy,* and pronounced *fingee.* Rosie nodded even though so far as she knew the turbulence wasn't exactly normal. She had only experienced smooth flights to the Ice.

The round porthole to the side of the photographer's head now looked like an ominous pearl, glossy with storm cloud. The plane shuddered so hard it felt like her internal organs were getting shaken loose. The loadmaster, who usually milled about the front of the plane, had disappeared. The photographer was furiously scratching notes in his notebook, as if writing would stabilize the plane.

"Mandatory ECW gear!" The loadmaster's voice boomed the three words over the sound system. He gestured at his own clothing and Rosie understood that he was instructing all passengers to suit up fully in their Extreme Cold Weather gear, if they weren't already. Most passengers, accustomed to emergency drills, moved slowly at first, even lazily, tying laces and pulling mittens out of pockets. A few got up to rummage clothing out of duffels. But when the loadmaster grabbed the mike again, this time to announce that he expected everyone to be suited up in ten seconds or less, people began to panic, catching the fabric of their parkas with the zippers or putting their feet in the wrong boots.

The loadmaster made his way through the plane, lurching with each jolt, making sure all the passengers were strapped to their seats. As he bent to tighten Rosie's straps, she felt fear in his fumbling hands. The turbulence caused him to stumble on his way back to the flight deck, and he fell onto the pile of duffels in the center of the plane. Rosie looked away as he struggled to his feet, fell again, and then crawled toward the cockpit before the plane's flight smoothed out enough for him to get up and walk.

The grizzled guy sitting next to her laughed.

During the next few minutes, it felt as if they were slamming into one mountain after another. But they stayed in flight, so Rosie knew they were colliding with terrific crosswinds, masses of air not land. A thick onslaught of tiny snowflakes pasted the porthole window. They would be landing blind.

Rosie so badly wanted to sing. People would think she was crazy. Instead, she watched the tall man, trying to figure out if he felt as calm as he looked. Though he still gripped his camera tightly, his mouth and brow seemed tranquil, almost virtuously so. Rosie wanted to run her fingers across the smooth skin of his lips. He held his knees together and his elbows in close, keeping his very long legs and arms from crowding the passengers on either side of him. She couldn't help wondering what it would be like to wrap her own legs around those lanky limbs.

Another wall of air upended the plane's right wing and they turned on their side, putting Rosie flat on her back with the photographer hanging in his seat belt directly above her. She made eye contact, willing an erotic charge, as if that could save her life, as if locking eyes with this one man would secure the entire flight.

Another major jolt brought her back to her senses. To think of sex while flying in an Air Force cargo plane that was losing its battle against fierce Antarctic winds! Maybe she *was* crazy.

The sun suddenly appeared in the porthole, momentarily liberated from the storm, and a white glare shot into the plane. Someone screamed. The plane shook violently. The tall man pulled his camera to his stomach and leaned his entire body over it. At first Rosie thought he was protecting the camera, but then she realized he was positioning himself for a crash.

They hit the ice, the force of the impact sending shocks of pain through Rosie's body.

2

When the plane slammed into the ice, it sounded to Mikala as if all the musicians in the world had thrown their instruments—horns, pianos, cellos, timpani—off a tall building at once. Music's apocalypse. A simultaneous thud and crunch and crash of uncharted dimension and amplification.

Pain followed, waves of it surging from some point at the back of her head, one swell rolling after another. Her eyes blacked out, and she entered a strange and protracted silence, as if time had stretched. She sat in a large bubble of stillness. She could even think. Her thoughts were infinite kinds of thoughts, like *Where is Sarah?* And, *Am I dead?*

But no, too much pain for death. A long, searing screech propelled her out of the silence bubble. The plane screamed as it skidded across the rough ice, bouncing into the air and smacking back down again. Mikala leaned forward, her hands around the back of her neck, to protect her pounding head. The plane swept a full 360 degrees and then tipped. The centrifugal force thudded her against the body to her left, a pillow of human and parka, and she didn't even try to right herself. Motion slowed, but she stayed slumped against the person. Another moment of calm swallowed her, almost a luxuriousness, as if the end of suffering were in sight. Then, it seemed the plane had come to a stop.

Carefully, she allowed her fingers to travel up the back of her neck until she could touch the epicenter of pain. She expected a sticky mass of blood and hair, but found only a hot, dry tenderness, swelling even as she fingered the spot.

Others began to stir. Mikala didn't dare look up. She listened. Some grunts of fear, people testing their voices, still in too much shock to shout. The sounds of gear being slammed into place. The metallic clicks of seatbelts being undone. She tested her head again. No blood, just a lump. She slowly extended each arm, each leg, and found them all in working condition. The sounds around her muted, softened, and she listened for the possibility of music.

The moment was destroyed by an explosion, a blast that ripped away all other sound and thought. The rest of Mikala's senses leapt to attention now and she looked around quickly. The interior of the plane was still intact, but a dull roar grew in intensity. A dense and rank smell plugged her nose. She saw fire out one porthole.

The loadmaster got the main door and emergency hatches open and he frantically beckoned the passengers to get moving. The rest of the crew shot off the flight deck and helped evacuate the plane, checking for injuries, taking elbows, and carrying one unconscious woman.

"Go! Go! Go!" the loadmaster shouted. When it came Mikala's turn to exit the plane, she felt his hand against her back, pushing her hard out into the storm. Crunch under her feet and blowing snow in her eyes. She blinked, trying to clear her vision, but a cold white grasped everything. The rest of the passengers ran like a frightened herd away from the plane, some scattering in the icy wilderness, others shouting to stay in a group. Mikala began to run, too, but after about ten yards, another one of those quiet pauses overwhelmed her. She had promised herself that she would start living with not just her ears open but her eyes, too, that coming to this continent was the beginning of moving on. From Sarah's death. From the blockade of grief. She would use all her senses here in Antarctica. This, of course, was an extreme situation, a disaster, and surely she could be excused from her intentions in this instance, and yet something deeper than a voice, something visceral, caused her to stop and look back at the plane, just briefly, so she could see what was happening.

Blue and orange flames spiked above the far side of the plane. The crew now wrestled with fire-fighting equipment, their bodies a vigorous dark dance against the bright snow and brighter flames. Two more passengers rushed past her, and one small figure darted away from the plane, disappearing into the thick blur of blowing snow.

Mikala wondered, looked around quickly, and then the intensity of white sucked the moment away. She felt only a dry, very cold fear as she turned and looked for the group. The other passengers were barely visible now, a pale mass of retreating color. She could scarcely hear the loadmaster shouting for everyone to keep moving away from the plane, to move fast. Mikala broke into a run over the hard cold snow and ice, her lungs burning by the time she reached the others.

3

Rosie had no idea if they were on the ice runway near McMurdo Station or if they'd crash-landed miles away. The loadmaster kept shouting for everyone to stay in a group, but that was nearly impossible in these conditions. A blinding snow angled down and she saw only the jacket in front of her. A couple of steps in the wrong direction and she'd never find the group again. Rosie put her hand on the shoulder of the nearest jacket. The bearded man who'd been sitting next to her turned and smiled. He actually *smiled,* as if this were exactly why he'd taken a job in Antarctica, to relish a threat to his life. Rosie reached for another shoulder, but that person moved away and her arm fell through the icy air and back to her side.

When the group came to a standstill, Rosie walked right into someone's back. The loadmaster worked to corral everyone, encouraging them to huddle for warmth like penguins. Moments later, a couple of other crew members began distributing survival duffels they had pulled from a stash on the plane. "Groups of three!" the loadmaster shouted. A man wearing a red jacket grabbed the arm of Rosie's tan Carhartt parka, and then he reached out and snagged another red-jacketed person.

The three stood in a circle, their arms going around one another as if by instinct, bracing themselves against the hard wind and horizontally blowing snow. They paused for a long moment, like a team doing a chant before taking to the playing field. When one of the crew dropped a duffel against Rosie's legs, she and the man stooped to unzip it. They pulled out a tent and wrestled it from its sleeve. Rosie thought he had it and he thought she had it, and the taffeta flapped away from their hands and billowed into the air. Rosie dove for the tent, just barely snatching it from the arms of the storm.

The third member of their team stood hugging herself, her legs buckling. She looked very frightened, so Rosie had the idea of putting her inside the limp tent to keep it from blowing away while she and the man erected it. Once they got the woman slipped between the sheets of fabric, they dug deadman anchors, deep holes in which they buried snow stakes so that the tent would hold up in this wind. They inserted the poles into the tent sleeves and popped up the shelter. Then they shoved the duffel with the rest of their survival gear into the vestibule and crawled over the duffel and into the tent.

Rosie put an arm around the woman's shoulders while the man extracted three sleeping bags from the duffel and unfurled them. After they got into the bags, Rosie and the man inflated the Therm-a-Rest pads.

"Get on this," she told the woman. "The insulation will keep you warmer."

Rosie was glad for the safety of the tent but sorry there was nothing left to do. Taking action calmed her. Now they could only wait to see if they would be rescued.

Each time the wind buffeted the side of the tent, the woman flinched. The man lay motionless. Rosie began humming a hymn she'd learned from a minister she'd had an affair with in White Salmon, Washington, when she'd had the tree-planting gig. It shouldn't have been an "affair." The man wasn't married or even involved with anyone else. He just didn't think Rosie was an "appropriate" date for a minister. He said she was too wild. He didn't want his congregation to know about her. Rosie had laughed when he'd told her that. Story of her life, inappropriate lovers. At least she'd learned this lovely melody.

"I'd prefer silence," the man lying next to her said.

Rosie stopped humming.

The woman on the other side of her said, "What happened?"

That seemed kind of obvious to Rosie, but the woman was probably in shock. Hell, *Rosie* was probably in shock. Conversation seemed like a good development. "Is this your first season?" she asked.

"Yes."

"I don't really know what happened except that the crew had to land the plane blind because the storm came up after we passed the point of safe return."

No response.

"Hey. Are you okay?"

Another quiet and unconvincing, "Yes."

"I'm Rosie. Rosie Moore." She looked over her shoulder at their other tentmate who lay flat on his back, shoulders squared to the ground, eyes open, staring blankly at the tent ceiling. She rolled back to face the woman and asked softly, "What's your name?"

"Mikala Wilbo," said the muffled voice coming from deep inside the sleeping bag.

"I work in the galley," Rosie offered, needing conversation as badly as she needed this sleeping bag and tent. It was all she could do to not hug the woman. "What do you do?"

"I'm a composer."

Rosie laughed, and then regretted the unkindness. But a *composer*? Had the woman thought she was getting on a plane for New York and accidentally boarded one for Antarctica?

Mikala's head popped out of the sleeping bag and she barked a laugh too, short and staccato. Rosie was relieved. Okay, so it *was* funny, a composer in Antarctica. Then Rosie caught on. "Oh, you must be with the artists program."

"Yeah."

"Please," the man said. "I really would prefer silence."

"Who are you?" Rosie asked him. Whether they died or lived, she'd like to know who was on her survival team.

"Dean Rasmussen. Dry Valleys. Climate change." Like he was reporting to a commander.

"Got it," Rosie said. "I'm looking forward to some climate change in the very near future."

Mikala laughed again, which made Rosie instantly fond of her.

The man groaned and rolled over in his bag, turning his back to the two women.

Mikala whispered, "Will they find us?"

Rosie couldn't answer that question. She had no idea how far they were from McMurdo. Storms could blow for weeks. They might be somewhere entirely inaccessible to helicopter or snow-mobile rescue. As the wind howled and the tent poles bent with the strain, Rosie could no longer resist her need for direct human contact, and she scooted up against Mikala and put an arm around her. Mikala didn't ask any more questions, and with the partial comfort of that near-anonymous snuggle, Rosie found herself slipping into a dormant state. She couldn't exactly call it sleep. At all times she was conscious of her tentmates, the fierce storm, the growing ache in her back.

4

Mikala burrowed down as deeply into the mummy sack as she could get. She tightened the drawstring that pulled the bag closed over her head. At first she thought she'd imagined the tune. But no, the woman lying next to her was humming *Te Deum*. Mikala loosened the opening of her sleeping bag a bit to hear better, and that's when the man asked for silence. Just to hear that lovely voice again, even if only talking, Mikala asked what had happened. The woman, who identified herself as Rosie, had a clear, delightful laugh, a song in itself. She seemed so experienced, knowing about deadman anchors and insulating pads. Humming a tune in an emergency camp in the heart of the most desolate wilderness on earth! Clearly this wasn't her first season. Mikala knew what it meant that Rosie hadn't answered her last question. They might die.

Mikala had plenty of experience thinking about death. Her partner, Sarah, had died of lymphoma three years ago. She'd thought about death most every day since then. Strangely enough, it had never occurred to her that she, too, might die prematurely.

Now, in her cocoon of sleeping bag and tent, all wrapped by the strangely insulating effect of the whiteout, Mikala realized how well she'd wasted these last three years since Sarah's death. She hadn't written one useable piece of music. She'd as good as flushed her years of meticulous training, including the expensive educations from Oberlin and Juilliard, down the toilet.

Worse. She'd devised this harebrained scheme to spy on her father. In Antarctica. The father who might not even remember her existence. Wasting three months in this endeavor would be bad enough. But losing her life in the pursuit of that sperm donor, that would be just too stupid for words.

The possibility of death coursed through Mikala. In its wake came another silence, the deepest one she'd ever known. As if everything in the universe came to a brief but profound stop. Then, slowly, it began to spin again, only in the opposite direction. The first thing she came to know, after the bottomless quiet, was the feel of Rosie's body against hers. Mikala felt like a larva curled in this cocoon of nylon, feathers, taffeta, and blowing snow. Life was also a possibility.

5

When a militarily precise voice shouted at the door of their tent, "Is everyone all right in there?" Rosie woke up.

Dean Rasmussen answered, without checking with his tent-mates, that they were fine.

The tent zipper scraped open and energy bars cascaded in the gap, the hard frozen foil-wrapped corners striking Rosie in the face. She couldn't really blame the Air Guardsman for just dumping the bars in the entrance, but the assault jarred her out of her hibernation reverie. She wondered how much time had passed since the landing.

Rasmussen sat up in his sleeping bag and unwrapped an energy bar, and then cursed when his teeth struck the frozen block. Rosie had heard of the geologist, and that he wasn't the easiest person to get along with, especially if you were a woman. After putting a couple bars in her sleeping bag to thaw, she reached for what she thought was Mikala's shoulder. "Hey. How're you doing?"

"I'm all right."

"You really should eat something. Your body needs all the calories it can get."

They all managed to gnaw down energy bars. Then Rosie slept hard. When she awoke, the tent's skin was bright with light and she quickly unzipped the door and vestibule to look out. The sky was a frozen blue and the air was still. A small group stood in the center of the tent camp, all wearing their ECW gear but laughing raucously as if they were on a holiday camping trip. Their laughter rang out one word: *Alive.*

Rosie pulled on her wind pants and jammed her feet into boots. She grabbed her parka and crawled over the duffel to get out.

"Where are you going?" Mikala sounded panicked.

Rosie poked her head back in the tent. "It's cleared! Blue sky!"

"Does that mean they'll find us?"

"Yeah!" Rosie couldn't help shouting. "It does. Hang on, I'll get some news and come back, okay?"

Rosie laced her boots and shook out her legs. A hundred yards away, the steel casing of the LC-130 glared in the sunlight. The black snout of the plane, round and undamaged, was topped by the row of flight deck windows, also intact, as if all that was missing were a pilot. Black lettering on the side of the plane spelled out "U.S. Air Force" in bold capital letters, like an announcement of confidence. The fin on the back of the aircraft jutted toward Mount Erebus and the port wing pointed toward the sky, as if it were in flight, banking a turn in the updraft of a wind current.

But the plane was grounded. It was tipped onto its starboard side, where the wing had severed between the two engines. Spilled fuel blackened the ice, and carbon from the fire had charred that entire side of the plane. The menacingly jagged metal edges around the amputated wing seemed to stab at the blue sky.

Rosie shuddered. The far side of the plane offered the only possibility of privacy for relieving her bladder, but she wasn't going near that steel hulk.

Looking in the opposite direction, she saw nothing but ice stretching in a perfectly flat sheet all the way to Mount Erebus. A curl of smoke eased from the mountain's caldera.

"Hey. Look up."

Rosie turned toward the voice and the photographer took her picture. He pulled off a mitten and held out a hand. "I thought that was you. I'm Larry."

Rosie touched her head, realizing that she wasn't wearing a hat, before shaking his hand. "Hi!" That sounded way too chirpy for a plane crash introduction. She revised, "Uh, nice to meet you. I'm Rosie."

"You're very photogenic. Nice contrasts." He gestured at her face, meaning, she supposed, her dark hair and pale skin.

She had no idea how to respond, so she asked, "Your first season?"

"Yeah. I'm going to be working on the *Antarctic Sun*. The McMurdo newspaper."

Another FNG. "I guess you got your first big story."

Larry laughed. "I guess so. Yeah, absolutely."

"So. Any news about our rescue?"

"Yeah. Apparently we're quite close to McMurdo. They've made contact with the station, and rescue vehicles are on the way."

Relief made Rosie weak in the legs. She wanted to sit down right there on the ice.

"We're incredibly lucky. The crew did a bang-up job getting us on the ground." Larry paused and laughed at his unintentional pun. "And putting out the fire. If they hadn't worked so fast, the whole thing could have blown up. They're in the process now of checking the manifest list. But it looks like everyone is safe."

"Wow."

"Yeah. I know. Absolutely."

Rosie couldn't see much of the man with his sunglasses and ECW gear covering nearly every inch of skin, but his height alone was impressive. He had to be close to six feet five. He also had a beautiful smile, very regulation with its perfectly straight and bright white teeth, yet a slight asymmetrical jauntiness tipped one corner down.

She was about to tell him that he was quite photogenic himself, but was saved by his saying, "I need to get all the shots I can before rescue shows up. But I'll absolutely catch up with you in McMurdo."

Rosie nodded, wondered at his overuse of the word absolutely, and watched him stride toward the cluster of revelers in the middle of camp. She really needed to pee, and she didn't think her bladder was going to be able to wait for the rescue vehicles. Everything on this continent took forever, and even if search-and-rescue showed up in ten minutes, it could be a couple of hours before they were delivered to anything that resembled a toilet.

So she started walking in the direction of Mount Erebus. Not that she'd find privacy. It didn't matter how far she walked, this was Antarctica and you could see forever. Anyone who looked in her direction, including Larry, would know she was urinating. But what was she supposed to do?

She picked a spot in the distance, it looked like a small hummock, unusual in this uninterruptedly flat snowscape, and decided that would be her destination.

As she walked, she heard a tiny roar in the distance. Soon it filled her ears and she turned to see a small posse of snowmobiles heading for the camp. What a welcome sight! Not only did those snowmobiles promise hot food and a warm bed, they meant she had a chance of privacy. Everyone in the emergency camp turned to watch the arrival of the first of the search-and-rescue crew. Rosie trotted the rest of the way to the small mound of snow, and as quickly as she could, threw off her parka so that she could pull down the suspenders of her wind pants, shove them to her ankles, and then push down the fleece and long underwear bottoms as well. Finally, she could crouch and empty her bladder.

It wasn't until she began redressing that she took a better look at the lump of snow beside which she'd just peed. It had a fetal shape, round and curved like a giant lima bean. It also had hair.

Rosie stepped over to the body and brushed some snow off the woman's hatless head. She was very dead.

The yellow hole Rosie's urine had drilled into the snow wasn't three feet from the woman's back. Quickly she scuffed snow over the stain, stamping it down until no trace of yellow could be seen. Then she looked back at the camp where more snowmobiles were arriving to take the survivors to McMurdo Station.

6

In a burst of courage, Mikala climbed out of the tent. Mainly she wanted to see where Rosie had gone. What she saw, though, was the wreckage of the plane, toppled on the ice like a shiny alien creature. It looked strangely intact. It *was* strangely intact, except for its broken wing and spilled, burnt, and toothy guts at the place of rupture.

The sight was unnerving. Just as Mikala decided to reenter the tent, she saw Rosie approach. She walked very quickly, her head down with intent, and didn't look up until she was standing in front of Mikala.

"Help," she said.

"What happened?"

"I found a body."

Nylon and taffeta rustled in the tent behind them as Rasmussen lunged out the door. "You what?"

"A body. Where's the loadmaster?"

"He was just here," Mikala said. "Counting, um, bodies. To see if there was anyone missing."

"Well, there is," Rosie said. "Please come with me."

Mikala wasn't sure if she was talking to her or to the geologist, but he didn't yet have his boots on, so she went. They found the loadmaster crouched in front of a tent a few yards away.

"You have to come with me," Rosie said.

The loadmaster rose slowly from his crouch. Rosie pulled off her sunglasses and said, "Please. It's important."

Then she grabbed Mikala's arm and pulled her along, too.

By this time Rasmussen had caught up. Rosie stopped and said, "Thank you, Dean. But I just want Mikala and—" She turned to the loadmaster. "I'm sorry. I don't even know your name."

"Vernon."

Rasmussen held up his hands as if he were surrendering something and walked a couple of steps backward.

"Do you mind?" Rosie asked Mikala quietly. "I don't even know you."

Mikala minded very much. She didn't want to see "a body." But she didn't want to let Rosie down, either. She shook her head.

The frozen girl lay partially buried in the snow, curled up as if she'd been trying to keep warm. Except for her head, she was fully dressed in ECW gear and her eyes were closed. The exposed parts of the body were covered with a soft dusting of snow. After a long pause, during which the three stood over her silent as a prayer, Vernon knelt down and started brushing the newly blown snow off the girl's face and shoulder. Rosie helped, starting at the feet.

Mikala stood holding herself tightly, trying to watch, and then had to walk twenty yards away. Though she thought she might pass out, she forced herself to remain facing the girl.

The memory hit her like a piece of shrapnel. That straying figure at the end of the exodus. People were shouting and running through the storm. The crew members were putting out the fire. Mikala had seen her. Then instantly forgotten her.

While this girl was wandering, Rosie had pushed Mikala onto the ground in an envelope of taffeta. The clack of aluminum tent poles, syncopation to the howling wind. The warmth of an expedition-weight mummy bag. Rosie's humming and full body next to hers. While this girl lay in the snow and slid across the line.

Vernon found a hand and felt for a pulse. "She's gone," he said in way too loud a voice. "We need to move the body."

7

Vernon asked Rosie if she would wait with the body, and she said she would.

"Go on back with Vernon," she told Mikala. The big handsome girl stood several yards away with her fleece hat in her hands, her head bare to the cold Antarctic sun. She had short black hair and lovely matching eyebrows that arched above her sunglasses. She looked terrified. Rosie felt bad for having enlisted her help. It was her first time to the Ice, after all, and she was with the artists program. Not exactly a group known for their forbearance. She should have brought Rasmussen instead.

"It's okay," Mikala said quietly. "I'll wait with you."

"You really don't have to."

Vernon had already started running back across the snow to the makeshift camp, where everyone was still oblivious to the casualty. A great noise of cheering and hooting rose up in the thin, cold air as the first of the rescue snowmobiles arrived and the survivors gathered around them.

Rosie watched their heads slowly turn toward Vernon as they saw him running in their direction, gesturing wildly. A couple of tan parkas and members of the Air Force crew ran to meet him. His excited voice, but not his specific words, traveled back to Rosie.

She squatted next to the body for one last look. The girl, now uncovered, looked peaceful, as if she'd given up quickly and without a struggle. It was pretty clear that somehow she'd gotten separated from camp and died of exposure. She looked very young, in her twenties, and pretty. Her blond hair was long and straight, her skin now gray but obviously, just hours earlier, had been pink and clear. Rosie had never seen, let alone touched, a dead person. She softly placed two fingers on the girl's frozen lips.

Three snowmobiles, one towing a rescue sled, raced across the ice toward them. Rosie backed away from the body as Martin, head of search-and-rescue, leapt off the lead machine. He ran to the body and checked for a pulse, pulled back the girl's eyelids, tried to straighten an arm. The other man disengaged the sled and brought it around. The two men lifted the rigid girl onto the conveyance and dragged her back to the waiting snowmobiles.

"Wait!" called out the third member of the rescue team. Rosie recognized Megan from last season. Without saying anything more, she started to climb on top of the girl's body. If there was life left in the girl, only the heat of a live body could save her.

"Don't," Martin said. "She's dead."

"Are you sure? What if she's not?" Megan quoted the first rule of hypothermia: "No one is dead until warm and dead."

Martin waved a hand at his colleague, meaning go ahead then, and Megan settled on top of the girl, folding her arms along the sides to maximize body coverage. The other rescue worker glanced at Martin for guidance, but he was already climbing back on his own skidoo, so the man wrapped a couple of sleeping bags over Megan and the body, tucking them in tightly. The tent enclosure that covered the rescue sled wouldn't fit over two bodies, and so he tossed it to the side.

Vernon climbed on the idling machine Megan had been driving and the three skidoos shot away, leaving Rosie and Mikala standing alone on the ice, in the spot where the girl had died.

8

Rosie opened the door to the dorm room she'd been assigned and dropped her duffels. The room was empty. Was that possible? Had she really scored a room to herself this year?

Perfect. She'd embrace solitude again.

That had been the plan when she first took a job in Antarctica. Total exile. Her own personal Siberia. A way to make money, get on her feet, stop giving herself away to anything handsome on two legs.

It had worked out the first year. This beast of a continent had slung her under its arm and set out running. *Take me to your cave,* Rosie had shouted, waving her arms and kicking her legs. What relief it'd been to look only at ice and sky, sleep in the narrow dorm bed, tend the grease-spitting galley grill. For an entire season she'd managed to love no one.

Last year she'd slipped a bit. That wee little affair with the computer tech.

Perhaps she hadn't defined exile precisely enough. The word celibate came to mind now. Really, it came down to sex, didn't it? She used to believe that sex was the closest one could come to truth. It was the biological imperative, right? The urge to reproduce. Though god knew the urge was one thing and the reproductions were another. Let's just say the need to touch. One body touching another body transcended interpretation. Needed no leap of faith. It just was.

But if sex was truth, why did it lead so quickly to lies and abandonment of oneself?

Rosie walked down the hall to the bathroom and took a long, hot shower. When she returned to her dorm room, she unwrapped the towel and scrutinized her steaming body in front of the mirror. Her wide mouth, plumped with the damp heat, and her thick and glossy chestnut hair, the wet ends just touching her collarbone. Her full hips and breasts, the tangle of reddish hair between her legs. She knew that her looks somehow announced her out-sized appetite that attracted people. Her whole life she'd felt its draw on people, even if she didn't fully understand why.

As she looked and wondered, the heat evaporated off her skin, leaving her cool and clammy. How quickly one could go from hot and alive to cold and dead.

Rosie dried her hair and dressed quickly. She grabbed her jacket, ran down the stairs of the dorm building, and pushed out into the icy Antarctic day. She walked around to the back of the dorm building where she could look out across Winter Quarters Bay and then beyond the frozen sea to the mountains. She had another chance to get it right. The girl had died after the crash landing, but Rosie hadn't. That feeling of survival surged through her body like music, as if sorrow and joy were the same thing. Rosie sang to keep from crying. She sang to the bluing glaciers and the biting peaks, to the sea, and to all the orcas and minkes making their way south. As she sang, she made a vow to reestablish her exile.

"Hey, Rosie." Pamela's voice, too soft with sympathy, snuck up behind her. "What a lovely singing voice you have."

"Thanks."

Pamela took the liberty of kneading her shoulders through the thick layers of fleece and down. "I'm so, so, *so* sorry. I heard you're the one who found her."

She sounded excited, not sorry. Before Rosie could think of a way to escape, Pamela snickered, "So, it's your third season, isn't it?"

Rosie knew what was coming and didn't want to hear it.

"You've heard what they say about the third season."

Only about a hundred times.

Pamela spoke slowly, drawing her words out with false sensuality. "The *first* season you come for the adventure. The *second* season you come for the money. *Third* because you no longer fit in anywhere else anymore." Pamela laughed merrily and then said, "Ah, Rosie. Don't take it so hard. We're all family here. Everyone's stuck. Except for the FNGs. They're always trouble. Steer clear of them."

Rosie nodded.

"Coming to the party tonight?" Pamela had managed to hook her elbow with Rosie's. "It'd be good for you. You've had a hard start to the season."

"There's a party?"

"Yeah. At the Heavy Shop." Pamela cocked her head up the hill toward the huge garage and parts warehouse where machinery was repaired.

The opportunity to lose herself in loud music, dancing, and laughter pulled like an undertow. "Maybe." Then, to get away from Pamela, she said, "See you later. I'm going to check my mail."

"I can come with." As if Rosie were a patient needing an attendant.

"No. I'm fine."

"You sure?"

"Positive."

Rosie unhooked her arm, said goodbye, and walked toward the mailroom until Pamela was out of sight. Then, since she was already most of the way up the hill anyway, she went on ahead to check for mail.

When Rosie told people she'd left home at seventeen and never returned, they were usually impressed. Like her independence was something to be admired. What she never told anyone was that she had expected to be apprehended. When she left the note with the number of a post office box in Portland, she figured someone would come looking for her. Instead, her mother had mailed her a hundred dollars cash the next day, like a final goodbye, an endorsement of her leave-taking. Only recently had it occurred to Rosie that maybe her mother had only wanted to help free Rosie from a lifestyle she herself would have liked to leave.

Rosie used to call her family from time to time, but at some point, after she herself had moved a couple of times, she'd tried calling them and found they'd also moved. Now she hadn't had any kind of contact with either parent, or either brother, in over eight years. A couple of months ago, on the chance that they were still somewhere in or near Newberg, Oregon, and that some postal worker would recognize the family name, she'd sent a letter General Delivery to the post office.

"Welcome back, hon," Bea the McMurdo postmistress said, handing her a thin packet held together with a rubber band. People loved sending mail to Antarctica. Today she had a postcard from a waitress in Boise, one from some Dutch guy she'd met on the Oregon coast, and a letter from the computer tech. Bea handed the guy in line behind her a big package probably full of home-made cookies, warm pullovers, clippings from a hometown paper.

Rosie tucked the letters in the inside pocket of her parka and walked back to her dorm room, where she climbed into her sleeping bag fully dressed. She shouldn't go to the party tonight. Jet lag was too soft a word for her state of mind. She was nearly delirious from sleep deprivation, severe geological dislocation, and probably a major case of post-traumatic stress disorder.

Perhaps if she hadn't had to narrate, over and over again to an array of officials, the exact way in which she'd found the girl, she could forget. The image of the frozen lump in the snow might melt away from her memory. But they'd wanted to know an impossible number of details. Her best estimate of the distance between the body and the camp. Was she a mathematician? Her thoughts on the girl's hatlessness. How was she supposed to know why the girl wasn't wearing a hat? An exhaustive description of each snowflake and eyelash associated with the body. As if she were a photograph Rosie had been studying for pleasure.

28 |

Rosie slept through dinner. When she awoke, she blocked out thoughts of her exile resolve and climbed the hill to the Heavy Shop.

Twenty yards away, she stopped and reconsidered. The sky was streaked with clouds backlit by the sun hovering on the horizon. As she watched, the clouds turned from pearly-gates white to psychedelic orange and pink and lavender. That combination of razorblade cold and audacious beauty could bring Rosie to her knees. How could the two exist simultaneously? The extremity of it contrasted so with what she had always known. Her childhood summers had been spent bare-legged and sneaker-clad, picking blackberries beside dusty roads, and her winters had been one long rainfall. She would literally walk to the edge of town and look out, wondering and longing. When the family did leave Newberg, it had been to go to Grateful Dead concerts, either in Portland or some other town within driving distance. Sometimes her dad quit whatever job he was working to do a road trip, following the band's tour for a few months. The family didn't go along on these longer trips—someone had to work, her mother would say—but Rosie soon realized that he still wasn't seeing much more of the world. The close smell of patchouli oil and marijuana smoke, along with the endless and languid beat of the Dead, made its own enclosure, just another small place. Even when she was very little, Rosie saw the absurdity of her father's devotion to that band and the finality of his small-town life. A dead end. No pun intended. So when she was seventeen, she left. What a joke, though, that she just ran away to *other* small towns. Even McMurdo was a small town in its own way, but set on the edge, the very most extreme edge, of the planet.

Looking at that wild sky tonight, she thought she could hear god laughing. At her. She definitely could hear the band inside the Heavy Shop, made up of musicians who, just like her dad, had dreamed their entire lives of being rock stars. These guys had finally found a receptive audience at McMurdo Station. The music was masochistically satisfying, pummeling the air waves with a metallic, decibel-bending rigor. The community here on the Ice was nearly tribal at times. Parties in the Heavy Shop were a ritual.

And rituals could be dangerous as they worked on your private piece of the collective unconscious and sucked you right into the group dementia. Rosie felt something primal in the pull of the music, like homesickness. Who wouldn't feel raw loneliness after finding a dead girl? She should turn right around, go back down the hill to her room, and sleep herself into a sensible state of mind.

But then she thought of the tall photographer. The resolute guy with the big, sensitive-looking hands. Larry. The sight of him would be a lovely antidote to the image of snowflakes on lifeless eyelashes. Sex and death, the two had had an intimate relationship since time immemorial. Why should she be any different from the rest of humanity? She thought she heard god laughing again.

Rosie walked toward the big warehouse doors, the volume of the music growing with each step, and then she was inside. She grabbed a beer from the drinks table and orbited the warehouse, prowling on the outside of the party. With his height, he ought to be easy to spot. She'd say hello and then return to her room for a good long sleep.

That guy who'd sat next to her on the flight, the grizzled one who'd laughed at the stumbling loadmaster and grinned during the plane evacuation, walked toward her with two beers. Obviously a small-town guy himself with his long, scraggly brown hair, poorly fitting pants, a dog grin. He offered her one of the beers. She lifted her own can, showing she already had one, but he grabbed and shook it. Empty. He triumphantly handed her the full one. She nodded her thanks and walked away.

This party was so like the parties in high school, the music threatening to destroy the sound system, guys clustered near the speakers playing air guitars, other guys wandering, searching, sad, dissatisfied with the party, thinking that the big guys with air guitars felt something that they were incapable of feeling.

Larry wouldn't be here. He'd be holed up somewhere with his laptop, tapping out the crash story for the *Antarctic Sun*. She'd gone out with a journalist in Durango. He was always working. When he wasn't actually writing, he was looking for angles and hooks. Or worrying about getting enough sleep so he could work. She let her gaze sweep the party one last time, looking for Larry, and instead caught the eye of that small-town guy who'd handed her the beer. Now he was leaning against a forklift, a contented smile on his face. She looked away. Pamela danced with a small band of women in the middle of the warehouse. They looked so wholesome, arms around each other's shoulders, laughing at their own clumsiness. She envied lesbians that clubbiness, a sense of belonging. She saw her coworker, Jonathan, with his hair playfully spiked, sporting a T-shirt about three sizes too small, his sinewy and tattooed arms dangling and his sunken belly exposed. He looked captivated by a girl with blond dreadlocks.

Rosie got another beer and felt herself settle into the party with a woozy pleasure. Maybe they were right about the third season. Maybe she really didn't fit in anywhere else anymore. At the age of thirty, she'd finally found a place from which she couldn't extract herself—was *that* the meaning of home?—and it happened to be the windiest, coldest, driest, most remote continent on the planet. That lump in the snow. Home.

Then she spied Larry, standing with a couple of women in a back corner of the warehouse. A current of warmth zapped through her. She practically bound in his direction, her approach drawing the attention of the entire group. Too late, Rosie saw that one of the women was Karen, her boss.

Karen smiled her fakey smile and beckoned with big, full-armed gestures, probably thinking Rosie was coming to greet *her*. Rosie smiled up at Larry and, just for a moment, ignored Karen. This was the first time she'd seen him in street clothes, without sunglasses and a hat. His head was shaved clean! Yet the severity of his bald head and exceptional height was offset by the humble way he stood with much of his weight on one leg, one hand holding the other in front of his body. He wore a tidy, white button down oxford shirt and Levis with a shiny brown belt. He looked like an overgrown altar boy. Up close, she could see his eyes, which were the color of stone warmed by the sun.

She forced herself to look away and turn to Karen. It was the politic thing to do. Rosie wasn't exactly on great terms with her supervisor.

Karen had threatened to fire Rosie last year because of a simple practical joke. It'd been a dare. Jonathan said he'd give her a hundred dollars if she tended her grill in an apron and nothing more. So she did. Easy money, right? And a lot of laughs. Besides, the stunt lasted all of fifteen minutes. At 9:00 a.m., Rosie had stepped to the back of the kitchen, stripped, and then put her apron back on. She'd returned to the grill and continued flipping bacon and pouring batter, as if nothing were unusual, her backside buck bare. Jonathan and her other coworkers were literally rolling on the rubber mats of the galley floor, holding their guts with laughter, as diners slowly noticed Rosie's near-nakedness. At 9:15 a.m., Rosie put her clothes back on. No one, she's quite sure, was ever offended by the gag.

But Karen had made herself out like a hero the way she described having had to "go to bat" for Rosie with the National Science Foundation, who reportedly wanted her off the Ice. Rosie had made the mistake of rolling her eyes in that interview. Karen had leaned across her desk and said, "One more slip."

"Are you all right?" Karen asked now, without hugging her hello or even offering a hand. She did take a step to close the large gap Rosie had left between them.

Rosie shrugged. "Yeah. I'm fine." She allowed herself a short gawk at Larry who smiled tentatively.

"I hired her," Karen said, as if that made her responsible for the death. "She was only twenty-four."

Rosie nodded. She really didn't want to talk about it.

Another woman in the group spoke with passion. "They're heroes, the entire crew. I mean, it's awful about the girl. But just one death in that situation? That's pretty incredible."

"It *is* incredible," Karen agreed.

The other woman turned to Larry. "So have they released the official report?"

"No. But I've talked off the record to a couple of people. They think she probably strayed just as we were deplaning. It was the only moment of real confusion. Most of the crew were working on putting out the fire, so the loadmaster had to manage all the passengers on his own. And everyone had to move fast because of the possibility of more explosions. She was really young and had never been on the continent before. Probably scared and confused. Like you say, it's absolutely to the loadmaster's credit that only one person was lost."

His calm and steady voice was like a solid wall Rosie could lean against.

"They say she died really fast," Karen said. "She seems to have walked only about a hundred yards, lay down, and pretty much died within minutes."

"Of exposure," the passionate woman added unnecessarily, as if by unpacking every detail she could spare herself. Then she started to itemize the girl's clothing. "I mean, she had a full fleece layer, her parka, but somehow no hat!"

"How're you doing?" Rosie said quietly to Larry, thinking maybe the two women could continue their conversation while she and he went to get a beer together.

"Great," Larry said, looking directly into her eyes for the first time tonight.

"Oh," Karen said. "I'm sorry I didn't introduce you. Rosie, meet my husband Larry."

The band finished a tune just then. Everything went too quiet, as if someone had shut down the master volume. Larry's voice sounded far away and muted as he reported that they'd already met. Karen explained how thrilled she was that Larry had taken a sabbatical from the paper in their hometown of Pocatello, Idaho, to staff this season's *Antarctic Sun*. The other woman, the passionate one, commented that it must have been difficult, last year, when they'd been separated while Karen was on the Ice.

Rosie tried to think of an escape sentence while the band started up a Grateful Dead tune. *Trouble ahead. Trouble behind.* She could hear her dad's tenor wailing the song while shaving, while changing the boys' diapers, while slow-dancing with her mother. Always wanting the family to share his zeal for the Dead. The song made Rosie's heart hurt.

Someone tapped her on the shoulder. She turned and faced the scraggly guy.

"How's it going?" he shouted in her ear. "Earl." He placed a hand on his chest. His other hand managed to grasp two more cans of beer. She took one, thankful for the excuse to turn away from Karen. And from her husband Larry.

Rosie took a few long swigs and then looked at Earl. She saw everything she needed to know about him. She could tell that, like her, he was a traveler. Maybe ten years older, though, and that extra decade of roaming had changed the traveler into a transient. There was a difference. Rosie hadn't yet morphed into one of those edgy, tough-skinned perennial travelers she met in roadside cafes. Their eyes, like Earl's, were lit from within by the self-given permission to always indulge curiosity. They were permanently unmoored. Not Rosie. She just hadn't found home yet.

When the song ended, Earl leaned in and said, "The guitarist sucks."

He had ringed irises, like the planet Saturn. She asked, "First season?"

"Fuck, yeah. I'm a heavy equipment operator. A *HEO*," he added, proud of already knowing the slang. "I was on your plane. You don't remember me?"

"Sure. You were sitting next to me."

"I'll be working out at Williams Airfield."

"We just call it Willy Field."

"What else should I know?"

Rosie shrugged, wanting to dismiss his provocative grin. "Stay out of trouble. Every year they send a batch of troublemakers back to Cheech right at the top of the season."

"Ha!" he hooted. She'd made the mistake of delighting Earl with the word troublemaker. He said, "I'm already here. If they send me back, I'll still have had a free trip to Antarctica. And New Zealand is fucking paradise. I wouldn't mind being dumped there."

Earl's demeanor swaggered not so much from an overdose of confidence than from an excess of energy. He knew he was too much, he knew he was trouble, and he sought out Rosie. Story of her life.

"What's your last name, Earl?" She meant to put a mental marker on the man, file him under hazards.

"Banks," he said. "Earl Banks." He tapped his chest again, and then said, "Let's explore."

She thought of several good reasons to walk away from Earl. One, the effects of alcohol in cahoots with sleep deprivation. Two, the picture of the dead girl in the snow, curled up like the end of everything. Three, the fact that she very nearly made an all-out attempt to seduce her boss's husband—in front of her boss.

Then she thought of several reasons to walk away *with* Earl. All of the above. He was like a muscle memory of all the men in her childhood. Surrendering to his company was like putting on an old pair of jeans.

Anyway, she liked how he didn't mention the dead girl, as everyone else did.

"Follow me," she said, leaving Larry and Karen and the other woman without saying goodbye or even looking in their direction. She felt all three pairs of eyes on her back—Larry's curious, Karen's disapproving, the passionate woman's perhaps pitying. It didn't matter. Earl was like a train and she was hopping on.

Rosie led the way to the door of the warehouse. As they stepped outside, the cold air slapped her face hard. Both the sea ice and the sky ached with blue now.

"The sun will never set while we're here," she told Earl.

He nodded. "I'd like to winter over after the summer season."

"You have to pass a psych test, you know."

Earl looked at her.

"Actually, antisocial people fare pretty well because you have to be able to deal with being alone for a long time. You have to want to read books and watch the same videos over and over. And be able to live without sunlight for months."

"I'd just play my guitar all winter. I'd be perfect for the job." Earl wore only a T-shirt and he wasn't shivering.

"You know what they say about people who keep coming back, don't you?"

"Nope."

"First season you come for the adventure. Second season for the money. Third because you no longer fit in anywhere else."

Earl kept his eyes on the horizon and smiled. "And this is your what season?"

"I'm cold." Rosie turned and headed back inside the Heavy Shop, deciding to lose Earl as quickly as she'd decided to attach herself to him.

She found her jacket in a pile by the door and then made her way to the back of the warehouse where stacks of boxes and a couple of polar vehicles blocked her view of Larry, Karen, and the rest of the partiers. She'd sit for a moment, sober up. Then she'd go back to the dorm.

When she realized that Earl had followed her, she turned to confront him. With men like this, you had to be very, very direct. But the sight of his manic delight in their surroundings kept her quiet. He was all kinetic energy, touching the boxes, reading their labels, hitching up his jeans, crouching to examine the axle on a van.

"Peaches!" Earl called out, thumping the label on a cardboard box. "This says canned peaches."

Rosie laughed. The screeching music, the futuristic machinery, an increasingly drunk population of Antarcticans on the other side of the warehouse, and here, something as innocent as cans of peaches in heavy syrup. Giving in felt so good. Laughing too hard to remain standing, she leaned her back against the stack of cardboard boxes and slid down until she was sitting on the concrete floor. Earl joined her, grinning his dog grin. He clunked an arm across her shoulders and she let him kiss her. Whiskers, beery tongue, blocky hands. Just like the boys in Newberg.

He wasn't her type. Not really. Not anymore. But god it was good to lose herself in someone else's mouth, to warm herself with someone else's body heat. She knew exactly what she was doing. She was countering the effects of that dead girl in the snow. So what. Right now it seemed like body heat was the only thing in the world that mattered.

The peaches helped. If she'd found herself with Earl behind cartons of salted ham hocks, maybe this wouldn't have happened. The peaches in heavy syrup mitigated the rough edges, sweetened everything. Peaches and a mountain man. The combination worked for the moment and it was an honest moment. But that was always her problem, that saturation in the now. A goal for so many people, but for Rosie a trap.

Earl tugged her shirt out of her pants and moved a hand up along her ribs. She shrugged off her jacket, wanting to feel his callused hands on her skin. But when he grabbed her breast, she flinched. The clumsy gesture reminded her of her whole life, a series of accidental collisions. Even sex was makeshift. She was thirty, not sixteen. What was she doing making out with a man at a *party*? She grabbed Earl's wrist. She could think of no words of explanation, so she simply stood without giving notice, put on her jacket, and left the Heavy Shop.

9

"Close the door."

Rosie gently pushed the door until it clicked into place. Then she faced Karen, feeling as she always did in front of this woman, as if she were reporting to the principal. She was only ten or so years older than Rosie, but she commanded her forty years with a cool composure that was unnerving. Beautiful and athletic, she had a whiff of dominatrix about her.

Rosie threw herself into a chair, too cavalierly.

Karen, sitting behind her desk, smiled too hard. "Hello!"

"Hey." Just start over, Rosie thought. Pretend that little encounter at the party hadn't happened. "How was your summer?"

"*Lovely.*" So emphatic. "We had a huge family reunion on the Fourth of July. Larry and I hosted it. Of course my four siblings, all of whom live in Pocatello, were there with their kids. But we also had forty-eight others—cousins, aunts, uncles, and both sets of my grandparents made it. Can you imagine?"

No, Rosie wanted to say, I can't imagine. She knew that Karen's family had lived in the region for three generations. What would it be like to exist in such a densely layered web of landscape and people?

"How was *your* summer?" Karen asked.

"Good. Fine."

"You had a difficult flight over. I'm sorry."

Rosie laughed at the understatement. "Yeah. Thanks. It was a little rough."

"You looked pretty shook up at the party last night. I was worried about you."

Rosie nodded. She wished her boss would get to the point of this meeting.

Karen cleared the papers from the center of her desk, pushing them to the sides as if making an open path to Rosie. She dropped her hands in the empty place. "I'm going to be frank."

Lots of people in McMurdo liked Karen. She was a brick. You could always count on her. She was so perfect with her lovely long blond hair and high cheekbones, her finely tuned marathoner's body always moving with simple ease. But Rosie didn't trust her perfection. Everything about Karen was a little too carefully arranged, like the smile on her face and warmth in her eyes, as if she forced them there.

"I didn't have to rehire you," Karen said.

"I know."

Karen leaned back in her big boss chair, her hands sliding with her across the desktop. She seemed pleased with Rosie's acknowledgment of her good deed.

"In fact, it was suggested that I don't rehire you."

Rosie couldn't suppress a big sigh. She gave in and said, "Come *on*. It was a joke. A joke that hurt no one."

Karen picked up a stack of papers and tapped their edges on her desktop. She set the straightened pile down again. She wasn't smiling anymore. "Don't push it, Rosie. Everyone is impressed by how well you handled being the first respondent on the casualty. You have everyone's good will right now. I called you in here today to commend you."

Just last night Karen had expressed a personal responsibility for having hired the girl. How quickly she'd been demoted from a girl with a job to "the casualty."

"What was her name?" Rosie asked.

Karen shook her head tightly. "We're not releasing that information."

"Where is she?"

"The body is being held until we can fly it back to the States."

An "it" instead of a "she."

Rosie stood. "Anything else?"

Karen forged another smile. Rosie wondered if Larry really fell for this pretense of grace under pressure. "No. You're excused."

"Thanks. I promise I'll keep my clothes on this season."

Karen cocked her head and pursed her lips.

"I'm joking!"

Karen lowered her eyelids slowly in response. Maybe she started to smile.

Rosie's hand was on the doorknob.

"Oh, and Rosie?"

She considered pretending she hadn't heard. But she turned. "Yeah?"

"You'll have another roommate in a couple of days."

"Another?"

"Oh. Yes. The casualty was meant to room with you."

10

Alice thought that maybe she was, at this moment, the happiest she'd ever been in her life. It was ten o'clock at night and a hard New England rain pelted the roof and windows of the city bus. She should have been home hours ago. She should have spent her last evening with her mother instead of in the lab. She'd pretty much wrapped up everything at school, so it hadn't really been necessary to stay this late. She didn't know what was making her behave so irresponsibly, even unkindly. Yet she felt sure that this show of commitment to her work, in the face of her mother's protest, was the cause of her euphoria.

Euphoria? She'd never once used that word in association with herself. She'd never once used that word, period. Maybe this was what courage felt like.

The levity was frightening, actually, the way her hands and feet were tingling, as if she might float off the bus seat. Even this weather couldn't dampen her sense of . . . yes, *liberation*.

She was leaving her mother. Finally. She was starting her career, the work she'd dreamed of for most of her life. At long last. She was doing it. Alice pressed her palms hard against the vinyl of the bus seat as the tingling traveled up her limbs, threatened to fill her head.

What's more, her professor had set everything up for her, made it easy, or as easy as was humanly possible given the situation. Thinking of her doctorate—and now postdoc—advisor, Dean Rasmussen, helped relieve the invasive euphoric fizzing. He was bedrock. At least compared to the sliding shale of life with her mother.

For the past ten years, ever since she graduated as valedictorian from high school, Alice's mother had thwarted all her attempts to move out. Even though she'd received a full scholarship to the university, her mother wouldn't pay for her to live in the dorms. Alice had tried, during those first couple of years of college, to get a job to pay for the dorm room herself. But the restaurants and copy shops near campus wanted smiley, crowd-pleasing girls waiting on customers, not reticent, serious-minded ones like Alice. Anyway, she didn't try that hard. She wanted every spare moment for study. Besides, she owed her mother so much. Living at home was the least she could do.

Alice's mother had been working on her degree in English literature when she got pregnant. She rarely had more to say about Alice's father than that he was "another student, some good-looking guy." Once, in a fit of temper, her mother had answered the question, "Who is my father?" with, "Obviously, someone brainy and humorless like you." After Alice was born, her mother took an administrative assistant job. In the evenings, she worked on the novel she had always planned on writing. She often complained about how the demands of being a mom kept her from finishing the novel, as well as from ever finding a stable relationship.

When Alice began the doctorate program in geosciences, she announced to her mother that she was going to move into graduate student housing. That's when her mother began having health issues. Alice stayed home.

It took Alice another six years to realize that none of these health issues ever actually panned out. Her mother's health threats were just that—threats. To Alice.

Rasmussen was her ticket out and she was taking it.

Still, it wasn't easy. As the bus neared her stop, Alice's elation began to seep away like steam from a fissure. She was twenty-eight years old. She was leaving home. At last. But she hated hurting her mother. Like tonight, all she'd been doing was corresponding with Rasmussen. She could have done that from her laptop at home. She hadn't needed to be in the lab. She could have kept her mother company in front of the television while she emailed him her questions and received her final instructions.

What she didn't want to admit was that maybe she was going to miss the lab more than she'd miss her mother. Alice loved the geology lab. The cold linoleum floors. The hum of computers. The mix of iron and earth smells emanating from rock samples. Even the other grad students. She rarely talked with them and never went out for beers or sandwiches, but their intermittent presence in the lab was a form of companionship she now realized she prized. Other folks who loved rocks.

No one loved rocks as purely as Rasmussen did. And nowhere was the geologic record as untainted as in Antarctica, where the thick covering of ice and the absence of humans has preserved the earth's crust. The idea of not just visiting but *camping out* on that continent unnerved Alice. But she would be with Rasmussen. He was taking care of everything. He'd even arranged for her to room in McMurdo with a girl he'd met on his flight over, an experienced Antarctican named Rosie Moore who would show Alice the ropes.

Good thing, too, because he'd also written that he was going to be delayed at his first field camp, where there wasn't space or work for her. She'd have to bide some time in McMurdo before flying out to the second work site. He'd offered to find out if he could postpone her deployment. At first she'd thought, yes, definitely, but then realized that changing the date of her departure would only make it harder on her mother. Anyway, Rasmussen advised that she come on along, that a period of acclimatization in McMurdo Station would be the best thing. Especially for her first season. That phrase—*first season*—implied more seasons to come, and she'd felt a mix of thrill and panic at his assumption.

Alice pulled on her hood and stepped off the bus into the rain. Inclement weather had never bothered her. One wore rubber boots and a good rain jacket. Likewise, if August dished up hot nights, one wore sandals and a loose cotton dress. For years she'd made this short walk home from the bus stop, properly attired, and had always felt a sense of impending comfort. But not until tonight, as the rain hit her face like fear, did it occur to her that the word comfort was associated with home. Home had been a notion so deeply a part of herself that she had never even examined its meaning. Severing herself from home was like having a vital organ removed from her body. By the time she reached the front door and let herself in, she felt miserable.

"Mom?"

No answer.

The television was on and a half-drunk glass of white wine sat on the side table next to the couch. Alice checked the kitchen where the counters were clean and the dishtowel folded in thirds over its rod beside the refrigerator. The bed in her mother's room was heaped with clothes, as if she'd been trying on outfits for a date.

"Mom?"

Alice went back to the living room and turned off the television. She dropped onto the couch and, with a mix of worry and impatience, tried to remember if her mother had said anything about going out. She hadn't. Alice rose again and went out to the mudroom to examine the contents of the recycling bin. There were two more empty wine bottles than had been there yesterday. Even for her mother, that was a lot of wine. Alice ran up to the street and was relieved to see her mother's car still parked by the curb.

There was only one more room in the house. Alice descended the basement stairs slowly. Years ago her mother had fixed up the basement with a couch, throw rugs, and a television, but neither of them ever used the room. It had reverted to storage, full of broken chairs and kitchen appliances, stacks of paperbacks, Alice's untouched childhood toys, and a stuffed coyote, a gift from a taxidermist her mother once dated. Even as an adult the coyote scared Alice, but not as much as the room's disorder, and she avoided the basement as much as possible.

She found her mother lying on her back across two giant unopened packs of toilet paper from Costco. She wore a deep burgundy silk dress and matching heels, an outfit she bought last year for a date she had with a local high school teacher who'd arrived wearing sneakers and paint-splattered blue jeans and suggested they stay in for the evening. Tonight the dress, which still looked new, was arranged dramatically about her legs as if she was posing for a femme fatale magazine shoot. Her silky, honey-colored hair was clean and brushed, and the ends dangled off the side of the toilet paper package.

She was breathing.

"Mom. Get up."

No answer. Alice nudged her mother's calf with the toe of her sneaker. She got a weak moan in response. How like her mother to drink the right amount of wine to pass out but manage to get herself into a theatrical position for discovery before doing so.

Alice dug around the basement until she found an old blanket. She billowed this over her mother and watched the pilled and stained fabric settle onto the burgundy party dress.

Alice thought, there is no way I can leave tomorrow. At the exact same moment she also thought, nothing could stop me from leaving tomorrow. The moment was excruciating for Alice. She so rarely experienced contradiction in her own will.

11

Just two days after the crash landing near McMurdo Station, the National Science Foundation expected Mikala Wilbo to board another LC-130 and fly to the South Pole. She asked if she might recover for a day or two at the much bigger station on the edge of the continent before she was sent to the planet's cold heart. The answer came back no. She was expected to get over that episode and move on.

Moving on was not exactly Mikala's forte. But then wasn't that why she'd come to this godforsaken continent? To get on with things. To put grief behind her, start writing music again, and well, maybe get a look at that man who'd been the shadow across her entire life.

The morning of her flight, Mikala stopped in the galley for breakfast and found Rosie behind the grill. The night before, in the coffeehouse, someone had told her about Rosie's stunt last year, flipping eggs and pancakes wearing only an apron. She was fully dressed this morning, though, and singing "Piece of My Heart," trying to imitate Janis Joplin's rasp. The grease hissed and popped on the grill. Her coworkers were laughing at her souped-up rendition.

When Rosie saw Mikala, she broke off the song right after the word "feel" and right before "good." Neither woman smiled for a moment as they silently acknowledged what they'd gone through together a couple of days ago. Rosie looked like a glorious animal to Mikala, trapped behind a sheet of Plexiglass and the hot steel grill, her roan hair caught in a ridiculous cafeteria-style paper hat.

Suddenly, though, the girl smiled her big, opened-mouthed smile. Rosie stood on her tiptoes and leaned forward, keeping her belly from touching the sizzling grill, and reached a hand over the Plexiglass. "Hey," she said.

Mikala squeezed her fingers, feeling awkward, and said, "Hey."

Rosie rocked back on her feet and shook her head. "Surreal, isn't it?"

Mikala nodded, knowing exactly what she meant. Here was the loud clank of flatware hitting plastic trays, a buzz of group dining chatter, the spitting hiss of batter on the hot grill. The making of food, lots of sweet, fried, doughy food.

It *was* surreal. Compared to that other reality that had lodged so deeply in her memory. The hush of taffeta rubbing against itself. The clack of tent poles. The howling wind. The crunch of snow under her boots. The soft hiss of sled runners transporting an unspeakable load. And finally, the roar of the snowmobiles overriding all other sound. Atop the sled a woman riding the body of a dead girl. Sliding across her mind, over and over and over again.

Yet out of the cold finality of the girl's death came some new feeling. Sailing like a bird through all that noise was Rosie's voice. Not just any bird. A song bird. Lilting and free.

There was a line behind Mikala, and anyway, she felt tongue-tied. So she managed a silly little wave and moved on, taking only a box of cold cereal. At the milk machine she looked over her shoulder at Rosie, who was laughing at someone's joke. The milk overflowed Mikala's bowl and sloshed onto the floor. She mopped up the spill with some napkins, hoping Rosie hadn't seen.

A couple hours later she was flying to the South Pole. She sat in her red webbed seat like some kind of refugee, hugging herself tightly. She was scared. About the flight, yes. And with good reason. But even if she made it to the South Pole safely, she had a hell of a three months ahead of her. The NSF expected her to do something she'd been virtually incapable of doing since Sarah died: write music. What they didn't know was that she'd applied for the fellowship with ulterior motives. She intended to write the music. But she also wanted to have a look at, maybe even get to know, Marcus Wright, the principal investigator on the South Pole Telescope. Without his knowing who she was.

That wouldn't be difficult. They had different last names. They'd never met. He'd never have to know she was his daughter. Still, most people who go in search of a biological parent find them somewhere like Flagstaff, Arizona, and are horrified and charmed in equal parts to find them eating Spam and smoking Marlboros. Or at best find them surfing and living in a shack in Hawaii, skin tanned to leather and brain adrift due to a lifetime of smoking pot. Most people plan extensively with counselors, buy plane tickets with great care, book motel rooms strategically, rehearse scripts with friends. "Hi. Remember the baby your ex-girlfriend told you about when you were twenty-three?"

But oh no, *her* father had to turn up at the South Pole. Not that it was a secret. He spent most of the year in Chicago, only a month or two each winter at the Pole. She'd known this pretty much her whole life and had never contacted him stateside. He did know, or had once known anyway, that she existed. Her mother had written him thirty-five years ago to say that she was pregnant, and in that letter she'd absolved him of any responsibility, saying only that she thought it was his right to know he'd be a father. He did write back—Mikala had the letter—that he was sure Pauline would be an excellent mother. Pauline said she'd sent him a picture when Mikala was born, but he'd never acknowledged it.

Mikala could have just gone to Chicago and found him. She could have just called him. His number was listed. His email address was posted on the University of Chicago physics department's website. But then what? There really was nothing to say.

This way, by traveling to South Pole Station, she could observe without interacting. She'd be undercover. Meanwhile, she hoped the South Pole would shock some music out of her.

At the end of the three-hour flight, Mikala stepped safely onto the polar plateau. She drew a breath of the thin air and immediately felt light-headed. Though flat as any other desert, the altitude here was as high as the American Rockies. Only a bit of precipitation fell each year, but nothing ever melted, so the mass of snow climbed toward the sky, incrementally, over the millennia. Her limbs felt heavy as she lugged her two duffels toward the station. The sun glared off the top of the big silver dome. Beyond it was the new station, still under construction. A handful of other outbuildings dotted the landscape. But this was no small town like McMurdo Station. This was one brilliantly cold desert on the bottom of the world.

12

"S orry," Larry said when Rosie answered the knock on her dorm room door. "I tried calling, but you didn't pick up." He ran a hand over the top of his freshly shaved head and opened that beautiful, asymmetrical smile of his, now apologetic. "So I thought I'd just stop by."

Her shift had ended an hour earlier and she had just begun to drift off in her customary afternoon nap. She considered pretending that he was just a dream. Anything could happen, without real life consequences, in dreams.

Larry looked past her to the bed on the far side of the room, the one with the bare mattress. He said, "She was going to be your roommate."

Rosie nodded.

"You okay?"

Every time she looked at that bed she felt cold. But she smiled as she said, "Everyone wants their own room. Before I knew whose bed it was, I thought I'd won the lottery."

"May I?"

"Sure." Rosie opened the door wider and stepped aside.

He walked directly to the empty bed and sat on it. "There," he said, smiling.

It did help, seeing a very alive man on that ghost's bed. Rosie considered sitting down on the mattress, too, and leaning against him.

Your boss's husband, she reminded herself and remained standing. "So. What can I do for you?"

"I'm doing a story on our flight for the paper. I was hoping I could interview you." He touched the camera that hung from a strap around his neck, as if offering proof of his legitimacy.

Rosie nodded, embarrassed by her relief. She hoped it didn't show. Of course he was here on official business. Anyway, besides her vow of celibacy, besides his marriage to her supervisor, she knew these feelings—were they actually *feelings?*—had been crash-induced. Something about sharing a near-death experience with someone can inject emotions as artificial and powerful as drugs.

"That was a week ago." A long week, too, during which she'd only glimpsed Larry once, due to their offset work schedules and maybe, she guessed, to his avoiding her.

"I know. They've only just released the official statement and I've finally been given the go ahead to write it up for the paper."

"Okay. Do you feel like a walk? I need some air."

"Absolutely."

She changed into boots and grabbed her hat and mittens. He took her parka off the hook by the door and held it open for her.

Then, as they headed down the dorm stairs, "I bet you don't really want to talk about it anymore."

"Well, I guess that's true."

"I don't need much." She knew he meant for the story. But his modest demeanor lent the words a larger meaning.

They left the dorm and walked around to the back side of the building where they took the long road down the hill to Winter Quarters Bay, the small harbor where later in the season the Coast Guard icebreaker and the resupply ship would tie up. It was a lovely day, in the high twenties, and perfectly clear. Beyond the bay, the sea ice soared toward the horizon, eventually meeting the sky. Larry stopped every few yards to take pictures. It seemed to Rosie that he shot almost randomly, photographing anything in his field of vision, and yet he did it with such single-mindedness, as if looking through that lens was his only way of seeing. She wanted to ask *what* he saw, but somehow thought that too personal a question.

Larry suffered no such shyness. "So. Tell me everything. Why are you here?"

Rosie laughed at the blunt question. "You mean in McMurdo?"

"Yeah."

"Money. Adventure. Same reason anyone else is here."

He shrugged. "I'm not sure why I'm here. Karen is hoping the experience will spark some ambition in me. But I don't know. Almost dying in our plane landing kind of did the opposite. It made me want to cut all ties, forget about goals for the future, live every single second fully. Know what I mean?"

"Sort of," Rosie said, knowing exactly what he meant. She thought of the empty bed in her room. Allowing any kind of intimacy with her boss's husband was a bad idea. But his invocation of their shared survival popped the cork off what little sense of propriety she had. She couldn't help asking, "What does she want you to do?"

"I work for her dad in Pocatello. He owns the paper. Her brother is second in command. So basically, there's no future there for me, and she wants me to have a future. She doesn't think I should be satisfied being a reporter my whole life. She hopes this job in Antarctica will be a stepping stone to my doing something else. To my advancing in some way."

Rosie could imagine that Karen would be the kind of woman who was never satisfied, that *advancing* was a very meaningful word for her. Still, she was surprised. Larry seemed such a boy scout, so stable and steadfast, the perfect partner to Karen's perfect life. What about the forty-eight cousins, aunts, uncles, and grandparents at the Fourth of July family reunion in Pocatello? He and Karen seemed like the heart of a virtual ecosystem.

"Just wait," she told him. "This continent will change your perception of everything."

"That's what I'm afraid of."

When they reached the water's edge at the bottom of the road, they walked past the ice pier and out the peninsula toward Hut Point. They didn't even pause in front of Robert Falcon Scott's hut, built in 1902 during his *Discovery* expedition. The big structure resembled 1960s architecture with its pyramidal roof and overhanging eaves. The British explorer had purchased the whole thing in Australia where that style of bungalow was used by outback settlers. Typical of Scott's poor planning, the building was completely unsuitable to Antarctic living—far too drafty and cold—and he used it only for storage. His crew lived on the icebound *Discovery*. Rosie wondered at what a fool he'd been. Bringing ponies to the continent! Taking an extra man on his trek to the Pole. He flubbed so many decisions—they all *died*—and still he was revered. As if crossing over that final frontier made him brave. We *all* die. Figuring out how to live right was what made someone courageous.

Maybe by definition explorers were people who ran away. People who craved the furthest reaches. People who didn't understand homes, even houses, and certainly not families.

Rosie said, "Cutting all ties isn't all that liberating. You're lucky to have such a big, close family."

Larry stopped walking and said, "But I can't live up to her expectations of me."

Rosie picked up her pace, left him standing alone. She barely knew this man. He shouldn't be talking to her about his marriage.

He caught up with her on the tip of the point, and they stood for a moment looking out at ice and mountain. He breathed, "Wow. Yeah, absolutely this place will change me." Then he slipped his arm through hers and she let him. She couldn't help it. This beauty, his touch. She felt that one word again: *Alive.*

Two Adélie penguins waddled along the edge of the ice, like an old couple on its way to the market, catching their notice and breaking the tension. Larry laughed and left Rosie to photograph the birds.

"See," Rosie called to him. "You're falling in love with Antarctica already. Come on. I'll show you something else."

Rosie led the way, climbing the hill above Scott's hut. She didn't stop for a rest until they had reached the shrine at the top of the ridge. This was Rosie's favorite place in all of McMurdo Station. The Our Lady of the Snows shrine stands atop a huge rock pile and within an iron grid arch, which gives her the nickname "Roll Cage Mary." The four-foot-tall statue wears a high-gloss coat of paint, her gown a creamy white with a gilt gold belt, and her veil and robe Antarctic blue. The hardy saint commemorates a man who drowned in 1956 when his thirty-ton tractor broke through the sea ice.

Rosie sat in front of the rock pile at the shrine's base and spread out her legs. Larry knelt a few feet away, shooting pictures. He jumped around, changing positions and angles, moving in closer and closer, until he was doing close-ups of Rosie's face. He finally lowered the camera and gave her one of his gorgeous smiles. Then, using his hands to shield the camera monitor from the sun, he clicked through the images and grunted several times with satisfaction.

"Look." He sat beside her to show his work.

She was in every frame, looming in the foreground, looking wild and free at the foot of the statue. In the best ones, the saint hovered behind her like an aura, its piety juxtaposed with Rosie's irreverence. The close-ups made her look unleashed.

"What about you?" he asked. "Do you have someone at home? Or here on the Ice?"

His shoulder leaned against hers and she couldn't move away. Nor could she think how to answer him. She had forgotten to settle down. She had forgotten to get married. Or maybe she should just splay the truth. Claim it. She liked trains and sex, loud music and mountains. Finally she just said, "I guess I'm missing the domestic gene."

Larry laughed. Then he said, "Seriously."

So she told him far too much. She talked about her father's quest for the Grateful Dead, her mother's resignation, the rainy winters and dusty summers, leaving home on the bus at seventeen, and the hundred dollars cash. She told him about the minister in White Salmon and the journalist in Durango, how she'd been looking for home her whole life and hadn't even known it. She told him about the letter to General Delivery in Newberg, Oregon. "I haven't seen my family in thirteen years. If I can find them, I'm going to go see them this spring, when I get off the Ice."

He nodded solemnly. She had the feeling when talking to Larry that he considered every word carefully. "What will you say to them?"

"I don't know."

"Maybe 'hello'?"

Rosie laughed. "Yeah. I guess I'll start there."

Then Larry said, "I think I'm going to leave her."

Rosie shook her head vigorously. But she could think of no appropriate words. The cold early evening air, a transparent lavender, infused her with a keen and dangerous longing.

He said, "I told her I'd do this Antarctica thing. But . . ."

"But what?"

"I need more. More love, not more achievement."

After too long a silence, Rosie said, "What questions did you want to ask for your newspaper story?"

"Ah." Larry waved a hand through the air. "Actually, I have everything I need. I mean, I pretty much will just print the NSF report."

"Oh."

"Wait. You're right. I should at least get a quote from you."

"I don't have anything to say."

"That's all right," he said softly. "I really just wanted to spend time with you."

She slid off her sunglasses to visually level with him. He took his off, as well. Those basaltic eyes.

She asked, "Where will you go?" Meaning, when he left his wife and the huge family in Pocatello.

He leaned in and kissed her on the mouth.

Rosie shook her head, but couldn't find her voice.

"I'm sorry," he said. "That was an accident."

"You better go," Rosie said. "I'll stay here for a while."

Larry stood right up, but then paused, looking down at her. She knew she should look away but couldn't. She felt a great void beside her, where he'd been sitting.

"One more," he said, kneeling. This time she gave in to the kiss.

He slowly stood again, put a hand on the top of her head briefly, then turned and took long strides to the edge of the ridge. A moment later, he was out of sight.

She twisted around and looked up at Our Lady. The shrine ought to have scolded her, or at least have warned her, but she only looked back at Rosie with sad eyes. She seemed to understand Rosie's longing perfectly. Our Lady never came out of the cold. She never sat down. No one ever held her. She endured her solitary post.

Rosie remained at Our Lady's feet until she could no longer stand the cold. Then she got up and tromped back to the dorm.

13

The room frightened Alice. It was full of another woman's stuff: a map of the United States was tacked on the wall over the one small desk, a pair of jeans were crumpled on the floor at the foot of the first bed, which was strewn with a sleeping bag, no linens at all, and an open tube of toothpaste oozed next to the sink.

Rosie Moore lived here. Her Antarctic mentor. Rasmussen had hand-picked her. Alice knew all that. She'd been issued a key to the room, too. But still, she felt as if she were entering someone else's home uninvited.

She set her duffel on the bed farthest from the door, the one without the sleeping bag, and then hung up her parka on one of the four wall hooks. Then, not sure if she had a right to one of the hooks, she retrieved her jacket and tossed it on her duffel.

Carefully, she pulled aside the wool blanket duct-taped across the one window and looked out onto the plaza between the row of dorms and the rest of the buildings in town. The sky blazed blue, as if it were 70 degrees outside. Alice turned and surveyed the room again. Two twin beds. Two tall wardrobes. The little desk. The sink. A ratty brown carpet. She had never lived any-where other than home. Once she and her mother had gone to a resort in Hawaii for a week, but Alice's fear of the steady supply of ultraviolet rays, which lead to skin cancer, as well as her clinical approach—her mother's phrase—to the resort cocktail hours, had caused her mother to make subsequent trips to Mexico, Tahiti, and the Bahamas alone, which suited Alice just fine. In junior high school, she'd stayed overnight at a friend's house once, no, twice. But that had been it: in twenty-eight years, a total of nine days in a bed other than her own.

Alice considered unpacking. She opened her carry-on and took out her journal. She squared this on a corner of the desk. Rosie Moore wouldn't be the kind of woman who read someone else's journal. She found her Cross pen, too, and set it against the top edge of the journal. She hadn't made an entry since leaving New Zealand.

She unzipped her duffel, but it felt impossible to stay in this room another second. The messiness, the inhabitedness, the not-hers-ness! Alice grabbed the huge red down parka the NSF had issued to her. She shot out the door, took the stairwell two steps at a time, and popped out of the building into the shocking cold. She knew right away that the prudent thing to do would be to return to the room. This was Antarctica, and not only was the cold life-defying, there was in fact a hole in the ozone directly overhead and her chances of soaking up ultraviolet radiation were far greater here than in Hawaii. But then the truly prudent thing to do would have been to stay home in the first place.

Deeply jet-lagged from her flight from Christchurch, which locals called Cheech, Alice walked halfway across the plaza before choosing a destination. The need for a goal, even a tiny one, lodged in her throat. She turned in a full circle, trying to see the cluster of buildings that was McMurdo Station. The chapel. Perched on the top of the bank that led down to the frozen sea— painted white with blue trim, complete with a bell on its roof— the little building was friendly and inviting. Alice had always taken comfort in people of faith, as if they had an ability to enter a fantasyland that her scientific mind denied her. Left out in the cold harsh reality of this planet, its history and terrible future, she occasionally liked to bask in other people's dreams of places of perfection, joy, and complete comfort. The idea of heaven.

Though only one hundred meters from her dorm, Alice was very cold when she reached the chapel. Antarctic cold is altogether different from the kind in Massachusetts. Here it numbed her instantly. She stepped inside the chapel to warm up before trekking back to the dorm.

"Hi!" A chirpy voice greeted her. Blinded by the dark chapel, Alice stopped and waited for her vision to return. The girl said, "I just love it in here, don't you?"

The people in Antarctica were alarmingly friendly. She began to make out rows of wooden chairs, set up in place of pews, with an aisle down the center, a simple cross at the altar. "I don't know. I've only just arrived."

"Really? That's exciting!" Alice saw the figure slide out from the middle of a row and emerge in the aisle, and she stepped backwards as the girl approached her. "Another sanctuary in McMurdo is the greenhouse. It's lush there and truly restorative when you absolutely must see green. Wait: in a couple of weeks you'll think you're going crazy with gray and white. That's all we have here."

"The sky is blue."

"Wow." An intake of breath. "Yeah. Wow. You're right. I need to stay open to the blue."

Alice could see her now. She was quite young and dressed like some of her undergraduate students. Her fleece top was torn at the shoulder and elbows and didn't match her equally ratty warm-up pants. Alice knew the girl was dressed as intentionally as anyone else but her mother would have thought she was impoverished, either that or "too self-hating to do something about herself." Up close Alice realized that the pair of green plastic-rimmed glasses and several child's barrettes in her purposefully messy hair made her look younger than she actually was.

"You've come kind of late in the season. Where are you working?"

"In the Dry Valleys."

"You're kidding."

"No. I'm not."

The girl stared for a long time and then, "This is *such* an amazing coincidence." She stretched out her arm, palm facing out in the halt gesture. "Wow. But no, obviously, it's *not* a coincidence at all." The arm now swept out to indicate all of the chapel. "I mean, this is a spiritual place. I *came* here looking for an answer. Not that I'm Christian or anything. If I had to say I was one religion, I guess it would be Buddhist or something, but honestly, I don't believe the Great Spirit distinguishes between a church and a temple and a synagogue or a mosque. Know what I mean? That's what I believe, anyway. I'm Jennifer."

Alice nodded.

"What's your name?"

"Alice Neilson."

"Cool. Hi Alice. What's amazing is I was just saying a prayer—a spiritual request, an affirmation, a whatever-you-want-to-call-it—about the Dry Valleys. And you walked in! Thank you, goddess! Do you believe in the goddess?"

"No." Alice needed sleep badly. The chapel interior was beginning to swirl. She stepped over to the small window, a square of white radiance, and put her hand on the bottom of the window frame to balance herself.

"Wait," Jennifer said and skipped back to the row of chairs where she'd been sitting. She picked up her knapsack and brought it over to Alice standing next to the square of Antarctic light. Jennifer unzipped the pack and drew out an irregularly shaped object, about the size of a soccer ball, wrapped in tissue paper. Jennifer plunked down in the straight-back chair next to the window, cradling the object in her lap. "Can I share something very, very important with you?"

That kind of question short-circuited Alice on a clear-headed day. Today she tried to examine each word as if it were a factor in an equation. Before she could answer, Jennifer took a deep breath and forged on.

"The Dalai Lama has made a number of very special vases. They represent ecological healing. He has also located places all over the planet that are ecologically sensitive and has sent out people to bury these vases in those places. The Dry Valleys might be the most pristine place on Planet Earth, know what I mean? I can't even tell you how awesome it would be for one of these vases to be buried there. I mean, the *power* it would have. It would probably be worth *fifty* vases buried in other places. I totally believe that this continent is spiritual, know what I mean? This vase here"—she gently bounced the tissue-wrapped object on her knees—"came into my hands via an incredibly beautiful journey. I am *so* honored to have been entrusted with it. The thing is, I haven't been able to figure out how to get it out to the Dry Valleys and I have my heart set on burying it there. I'm a GA—you're new, you might not know that means general assistant—and I've worked every angle I can think of to get to the Dry Valleys. But I've resigned myself to the fact that it's not going to happen. Those jobs are totally plum and they go to people more senior than me. Not to mention higher up in the caste system. You'll find out: there's a big class system here on the Ice. Beakers—that's what we call the scientists—on the top. GA's definitely on the bottom. But what do I care? I'm only here this year. I don't plan to come back. In other words, this is my one chance for placing this vase."

Alice did not think of herself as the kind of person who lost control of her senses, and yet this situation was quickly slipping from her grasp. Jennifer's goofy sincerity was disarming. Alice felt as if she were in a dream, enclosed in the dark chapel, next to the window she was unable to look out of because of the glaring ice. Countless times students had sat across from her desk at the university and tried all kinds of tactics for talking her into a better grade or to retake a test, and Alice never had any difficulty in saying no. Furthermore, unlike with her students, she had no obligation whatsoever to Jennifer. And yet, when the girl placed the tissue-wrapped vase in her hands, Alice took it.

"You walked into this chapel the moment I was praying for an answer to my dream for this vase. That is so amazing, don't you think? Would you bury it in the Dry Valleys for the Dalai Lama?"

Alice held the object slightly out from her body, but her fingers probed gently, feeling for a shape beneath the tissue. She did want to know what the vase looked like. Was it an actual vase with a bulbous base, a thin neck, and a fluted opening, or was it just a symbolic vase? Had the Dalai Lama himself handled this package? Did he himself or some disciple choose the Dry Valleys? Would he understand the contradiction in burying an object from where—Tibet?—in "one of the most pristine places on Planet Earth"? That pristineness was the whole point of doing science here on the Ice, the fact that this continent is relatively uncontaminated by humans. Every drop of human urine in the Dry Valleys is caught in a bottle and flown back to the United States. Depositing this foreign object, this icon of faith, in the Dry Valleys would run against everything Alice knew and believed in.

"I can show you a map that comes with each vase that shows where vases have been buried so far. It's in my room. Want to see it?"

"No. That's okay." Alice immediately regretted the word "okay" because Jennifer might interpret it to mean assent to her request about the vase.

"When do you leave for the Dry Valleys?"

"I'm not sure." Rasmussen had said a couple of weeks.

Jennifer wrapped her hands around Alice's holding the vase. "This is so important. Antarctica is the one place on earth that all countries share cooperatively for the good of humankind. This vase represents the healing that has already begun on this continent. Just wait until you meet some of the scientists here. They are such cool people."

"I *am* one of the scientists." Alice was used to this. Her pale, freckled skin and slender frame gave her a tentative look, as if she weren't quite there. Now that she'd cut her thin, auburn hair to a length of five or six centimeters, she could practically pass for ten years old. Only when people saw her jade eyes did some realize her intelligence, although others read the bright eyes in the pale face as some weird mental state. Her mother was always telling her not to stare so intently, as if she could soften her gaze at will.

"Oh." Jennifer withdrew her hands. "Shit. I mean, I know the NSF wouldn't exactly approve of the Dalai Lama's idea. Maybe you have reservations about doing this? I meant what I said about scientists—I love them—but some are a little bit . . . What am I saying? Look, the most amazing scientists throughout history were highly spiritual. Like Einstein! He said amazingly spiritual things."

Alice knew what scientists, including Einstein, said. "I'll take care of the vase."

"Oh, thank you!"

Alice knew she'd misled the girl about her intentions for the vase. But she could think of no way out of the situation, other than taking it. Anyway, now she could dispose of it properly. Alice ducked under the vision of colorful barrettes and green glasses coming toward her for a hug and, with the tissue-wrapped blob under her arm, made her way out of the chapel. The cold shocked her again, even though this time she'd zipped up her jacket and thrown the hood over her head. Still, when she reached the midway point between the chapel and the dorm, she stopped and once again turned a full 360 degrees, looking at this place she'd come to. She was afraid of the cold—and especially of the prospect of camping in the Transantarctic Mountains for a couple of months—but these were physical challenges that could be met with the correct gear and practices. What truly scared her was this dreamlike state, as if she had wandered into a myth on this continent over which no one had jurisdiction. And now this vase—surely a symbol?—put into the hands of someone who had no capacity for symbolism.

One day when she was eight years old, Alice's mother had entered her bedroom and swept her neatly categorized rock collection off the bookshelf. She opened every drawer in the dresser and stirred her hands through the contents until the clothes were unfolded and jumbled. She tore the blankets off the crisply made bed and threw the toys from the toy chest all over the room. "This," she said, "is a child's room. Mothers are supposed to argue with their children about straightening their rooms, not the other way around. Loosen up, Alice. If you don't, you'll never create a thing in your life."

"But I *like* things in order," she'd protested.

Slumping onto the messed bed, already looking ashamed of herself, her mother said, "Fine. Okay, fine. If the shoe fits, then wear it."

It being a hot summer afternoon, Alice was barefoot at the time. So she looked around her newly disheveled room for her shoes, found only one, but decided that would do since her mother had said shoe, singular. She slipped it on and tied the laces, and then, perplexed, looked up into her mother's face, hoping she had accommodated the compromise: It was okay if her room was orderly, but she'd have to wear the shoe—if it fit. It did.

Alice has never forgotten the look on her mother's face, as if just in that moment she realized that something was dreadfully wrong with her child. Her mother stood, gently touched the top of Alice's head, and went speechlessly back to the kitchen table where she was working on another draft of her novel.

When Alice was twelve years old, she found a copy of *The Concise Dictionary of American Proverbs* in the library and felt as if she had found the key to her mother. She read it cover to cover and then ordered her own copy from the bookstore. She loved how the dictionary not only translated the proverbs but also provided the source and history of their usage. Eventually, she began to understand that language was similar to geology in the ways it evolved incrementally, and so very slowly. By uncovering ancient texts, language scholars could determine important meanings and their significance to humankind. Proverbs were like fossils, anomalies lodged in the language and then covered over by years of word evolution.

The most alluring and puzzling proverb in the dictionary was a declarative statement which gave Alice the impression that it should be easy to interpret. *Seize the day* was a direct command, seeming to offer some kind of stunning opportunity. But what exactly? She saw how you could seize money or the best cookie on a plate or even a chance at something, like entering a sweepstakes. But how, she had wondered her entire life, do you seize a *day*?

A sharp pang of affection for her mother changed Alice's course and, rather than returning to the dorm, she walked quickly to Crary Lab, the big building in the middle of town where all the scientists, including Rasmussen, had offices to use when they were in McMurdo. Her key card let her into the building and she asked directions from a big, clownish man to Rasmussen's office. She entered the windowless room and closed the door behind her, feeling as if she were crawling into a familiar den. Not that there was anything at all cozy about Rasmussen's style: the room contained a computer, a pile of rocks on the desk, stacks of geology journals on the floor, and a few reports posted on the walls. She wasn't surprised that there wasn't a single photograph in the office, no hint of a wife, daughter, or even beloved niece or nephew. He seemed utterly self-contained and solitary, which made his recent—What would she call it? *Interest* in her?—all the more of an honor.

She sat in his office chair, a bare bones non-ergonomic seat, and pulled herself up to the desk. First she turned on the computer and then, while she waited for it to boot, she reached for the phone.

"Hi, Mom."

"Alice. Are you still in the lab?"

"Well, I'm in the lab, yeah, but—"

"Coming home soon? I'm lonely."

"I'm not at the university, Mom."

"Oh. Of course." A dry laugh. "You're at the North Pole. I didn't forget, honey. I'm just distracted."

"South Pole. Actually, about thirteen hundred kilometers from the South Pole. I'm at—"

"North Pole, South Pole, whatever. Same difference. Anyway, why do you insist on saying kilometers? It makes you sound odd. You're American. Use miles."

"How are you feeling?"

"Obviously not well." A long pause and then, "I may have to go in the hospital."

Alice double-clicked on Rasmussen's email program and then, seeing that it wasn't password-protected, quickly exited again.

"The CAT scan showed nothing. Why would you go into the hospital?"

"Exactly. The CAT scan showed nothing. So more tests are in order."

"Did the doctor say that?"

"I'm frightened, Alice. I don't want to be alone if anything happens."

"I'll be home in a couple of months."

"A couple of *months*! Who knows what—"

"Mom, I'm calling you from McMurdo Station in Antarctica. Isn't that pretty amazing?" Surely this qualified as dramatic enough for her mother. "It's like I've walked into a myth."

"There must be lots of men."

"I guess."

"Maybe you'll meet one."

"I have." Alice instantly regretted the concession. Yet she searched for a way to describe Rasmussen to her mother. There wasn't a single detail that would appeal: not the perennial outfit of denims that were not so much dirty as dusty, as if he had just come in from the field, and navy blue T-shirt; not the too-lean build; not the boyish haircut, parted on the side with a short shelf flopped over his forehead; certainly not the fieldwork-toughened skin.

Her mother was silent for a long time, confronting, Alice guessed, what she had always said she wanted for her daughter. "How could you have met a man already?"

"I only meant there are lots of men here, like you said."

"But are you *interested* in them?" her mother asked with relief. She wanted Alice to be desperate for a man, like herself, and never find one, like herself.

"I've come to Antarctica for the rocks."

"Of course. I know that. But I also know you have a few human desires mixed in with the academic ones."

"Mom, remember the time you asked me to wear the shoe if it fit?"

In the following silence, Alice tried to picture what her mother was doing. Reaching for her wineglass, holding the phone receiver away from her face as she took a sip? Or maybe she'd become momentarily absorbed in a particular piece of her jigsaw puzzle. She would stand with a hand on her hip, cradling the phone in her neck, holding the frustrating piece over one section of the puzzle and then over another.

"I know you remember. You were angry that my room was so neat. Remember how I took you literally and put a shoe on?"

"Alice, what are you talking about?"

"You've always wanted me to understand metaphor and symbolism. You've always wished I were an artist. But you see, I'm in my own story now. I thought that might interest you, my being here in Antarctica."

"My headache is too strong tonight to follow you."

Was this a French headache or a Napa Valley headache? "Mom, why don't you take this opportunity while I'm gone to get back to your novel. Maybe if you were writing, you wouldn't get headaches."

"Don't harass me. I had to stop writing to raise you, you know that."

"I'm twenty-eight years old. I'm raised. Now you have time."

"Why did you call?"

"To see how you are."

"I told you: not well."

"All right. I'm sorry. I'll try calling again in a couple of days. I won't be heading out to the field camp for a while."

"Try to have some fun, Alice. Men like cheerful women."

Alice found a database of crystal images on Rasmussen's computer and began clicking through the pyrites.

Her mother's voice softened, "I love you, honey. Maybe this will be an opportunity."

Alice clicked out of the database. "It *is* an opportunity. I've been trying to tell you. For a geologist, doing fieldwork is . . . it's like the best thing."

A deadened pause—her mother's call-waiting function—interrupted Alice's sentence.

"I understand that, honey. Truly. I'm so glad you're getting what you want. Gotta go."

"Bye, Mom."

Alice explored the icons on Rasmussen's computer desktop, opening anything that looked interesting. It felt a little like rummaging through his apartment, a liberty she wouldn't have dreamed of taking at any previous moment in her life, but now she was in the field, or almost in the field, and she had left her mother. Everything was changed, different, and she had no idea what the new rules were.

Alice had had opportunities to do fieldwork before, once in Montana and once in England, both of which she'd turned down, ostensibly because they hadn't jibed with her academic interests, but really because her mother believed that she couldn't live alone. When Rasmussen offered the Dry Valleys in Antarctica, Alice knew that she had a simple choice: take the opportunity or give up rocks. She had worked with him the last couple of years, dating and analyzing his Antarctic ash samples, and had come closer with him than she had with any other scientist to taking sides. Fieldwork, she knew, invariably meant choosing a hypothesis and setting out to prove or disprove it. Most scientists will tell you that they remain strictly objective in their fieldwork, that they would be equally thrilled to discover that their hunches were incorrect as to learn that they were correct. That's a lie. Behind many of the intellectual disputes in academic science are highly competitive human beings who want, more than anything else in the world, to justify their life work by being right. Loyalty, especially of graduate students to professors, is legendary. When it's breached, like when a student switches camps, the effects reverberate throughout the geological community.

Other graduate students complained that Rasmussen gave Bs, unheard of in graduate programs where everyone is assumed to be working at the A level, and also that the man never smiled. But

Alice viewed those Bs as Rasmussen's respect for the field of geology. Everyone knew that the students who got them deserved them. As for smiling, Alice didn't do it much herself. There was a falseness to most smiles, a manipulation that Alice had no use for. The deep silences in Rasmussen matched the one in Alice perfectly.

The night he told her, she was reading in the geology library at about eleven o'clock. A bar of dark chocolate, broken into chunks, sat on its wrapper on the library table next to her book. She was allowing herself a chunk for every ten pages she read, as if she were a lab animal. He had always referred to her, as he did to all the graduate students, by her last name, but this evening as he strode toward her in his denims and navy blue T-shirt, he said, "Alice." The library was dark except for the one lamp over her book, the light from its translucent green plastic hood glowing up on his face. She pushed the chocolate down the desk into a darker section, closed her book, and waited for what he had to say.

"You're coming with me to Antarctica this year."

She had three consecutive thoughts: Leaving her mother was impossible. Saying no to Rasmussen was unforgivable. Her career in rocks would be dead.

He squatted beside her chair so that he was actually looking up at Alice. She felt as if he were touching her when he said, "I know you haven't worked in the field. I know you'd rather stay right here in the library. I'm going to say this only once: you're the smartest grad student I've ever had. You'd be throwing your brain in the garbage if you stayed home the rest of your life."

In that greenish light, as a smile softened his face, just for that quick moment, he looked as though he thought Alice was beautiful. Then he let his eyelids fall and though he remained squatted next to her, one hand on the back of her chair, the other on the desk, he gazed only at the floor. He waited for her to speak. Alice was amazed to hear herself say, "Okay."

A couple of days later, he handed her a sheath of paperwork to complete for the NSF. Alice searched for a way to tell him she couldn't go, but she never found one. Slowly over those months, she came to realize she *wanted* to go. Even when the worst happened, a few weeks before Alice's deployment, she didn't waver. Her mother had managed to talk the doctor into sending her in for a CAT scan, apparently hoping for a brain tumor.

In the end, all that happened was that the doctor prescribed stronger pain meds, but both Alice and her mother were astonished that Alice hadn't buckled. On the morning of Alice's flight, her mother sat at the kitchen table taking bracing sips of a sauvignon blanc, an antidote to her headaches, as Alice set her duffel by the door.

"I'm sorry," her mother said. "I just don't get it. If you were a concert pianist going on tour . . . Or going into the Peace Corps, even . . ."

Alice thought resolve ought to feel a lot better, not as if her heart were a dry, cold rock. But if she let herself think about this cliff she was stepping off of, she could never do it.

"Mom. Please." Alice covered her mother's hand with her own. They had both been adults now for so long. "Getting to do fieldwork is a really big deal. I want to be the best geologist I can be. And I want for you to understand. This opportunity is amazing. I'm very, very lucky to be asked to do this."

"Pride comes before a fall."

Alice imagined tripping and falling, right there on the kitchen floor, all because she had mentioned that Rasmussen's offer was an honor. Even at the last moment, when the airport shuttle driver honked, Alice saw in her mother's face the hope that she'd wave the van away and stay home.

After she looked at everything there was to see in Rasmussen's office, she punched her mother's number again, but the answering service picked up, meaning that whoever had been calling earlier was still entertaining her mother. There was relief in that. Alice made sure she hadn't left anything out of place, picked up the package the girl had given her in the chapel, and shut the office door. The clownish man was coming down the hall and he smiled a big, loopy smile.

"You working with Rasmussen?"

She nodded.

"Tall order."

"Meaning?"

He reached out a hand the size of a small shovel and Alice gave him hers reluctantly. He must have been used to shaking hands much smaller than his own because he managed to find a grip on hers without crushing it. "Meaning that I would think Rasmussen would be a difficult master." He jutted his neck out and placed an ear next to the doorjamb, then hammed distress with his eyes and hands. In a stage whisper, "He's not in there, is he?"

"He's in the field."

"Ah. He does climate change, right?"

Alice nodded slowly, tried to let it lie, but couldn't resist sharpening the point by adding, "As evidenced—or not—in glacial moraine."

"Ah." He paused a moment. Then, "Glad you asked. I'm a biologist, working with Weddell seals. Considerably less, shall I say, esoteric than the health of the planet. Nothing goofier than a Weddell. Mainly they just lie around on the sea ice and I count them. The interesting part of my project is that it's a cooperative one with the New Zealand seal biologists. So when I'm not in the field I stay out at Scott Base."

His light brown hair was dry and mussed, and one shirttail dangled over his belt. There was something pleasantly optimistic about him. His large, slightly protruding ears gave the impression of his being a dedicated listener, and his rounded stomach seemed to announce laughter. Though his khakis and shirt were unironed, they imparted the agreeable scent of Tide laundry detergent. He had clear, dark tawny eyes that seemed to want to look at everything at once—Alice's face, the hall behind her, the hall behind *him*—not so much evasive as visually voracious. An urge to describe this man to her mother motivated Alice to ask, "What's your name?"

"Jamie MacKenzie. Yours?"

"Alice Neilson."

His eyes lit and he opened his mouth, as if to make a joke about her name. When meeting her, men often sang a bar or two from Arlo Guthrie's "Alice's Restaurant." But if Jamie had been on the verge of doing so, he thought better of it, and said instead, "You already have a prize rock to send back to the lab, huh?" He nodded at the wrapped vase.

"Oh, um, no. This is just . . . something someone gave me." The less said about the vase the better.

"I'm starving. Are you hungry?"

"More like hallucinating from extreme jet lag."

Jamie guffawed like a big bear, as if she'd been very funny. "Come on then. Food first. Sleep second. Actually, as a biologist, it's my duty to tell you the full story of life: sex first, food second, and sleep third. But I don't know you that well, so how about dinner?"

Alice's mother would be hooting with delight at his sense of humor. Instead she thought of how comforting Rasmussen's complete lack of nonsense was and she didn't even acknowledge the joke. But when she considered her alternative to dinner with Jamie—entering the galley alone and choosing between the two mortifications of eating alone or asking to join someone—she agreed.

The galley was just as she imagined it: a big, noisy happy crowd of people eating with friends. Jamie was solicitous about helping her find the flatware and giving advice on which dishes to avoid. They carried their trays to an empty table, where Jamie took a break from talking to polish off half his plate of food. Then he asked questions, listening in the same style in which he ate. He wanted his information in one huge serving. What did the volcanic ash trapped in the Dry Valleys moraines look like and how did its existence support Rasmussen's stablist view of the ice sheet? Jamie wanted the full explanation of Morrison's dynamic view of the ice sheet, too, and he wanted to know which point of view Alice thought the evidence supported. She told him she hadn't decided.

Jamie grinned. "And Rasmussen? How does he feel about your being undecided?"

"He knows it's scientifically correct." Jamie lifted an eyebrow. "You sound like you know Rasmussen."

Jamie said, "Only of him. He's sort of an Antarctic legend, isn't he? A contemporary one, anyway."

"I guess," Alice said, remembering her mother's cautions about men and modesty.

"You must be an ace geologist to have been invited to assist him in the field."

"I love my work."

"I've heard he's kind of a, well, let me just say I'm surprised he's allowing a woman in his camp."

"I guess I'm the first."

"Hopefully not the last." Jamie wiggled his eyebrows.

"He's not so bad. He lives for science, is all."

"You too?"

"Me too, what?"

"Live for science?"

The question felt like a trap, so Alice didn't answer.

Jamie took several big bites of mashed potatoes and gravy. Wiping his mouth, he said, "I wish you the very best of luck in the Dry Valleys. It's bound to be an experience of a lifetime."

"Thanks."

"What else? Tell me about home. A boyfriend? Big family, I bet."

"No. Just me and my mother."

"And your boyfriend?"

"You sound like my mother."

"What do you mean?"

"About the boyfriend."

The big moo-cow laugh again. She checked his hand, saw that he wore no wedding ring, which didn't mean a thing.

"I'm a world-renowned dessert architect. Will you allow me to design your final course?"

Again she imagined her mother's cascading laughter and knew that she should manage a facsimile of it, but the guy's cornball tone rubbed her the wrong way.

"Shall I go the *chocolat* route or the *faux fruit* route?"

"*Faux?*"

"No freshies. It's all compotes and preserves. Or wait, maybe you're able to handle the complexity of *fruit avec chocolat*. The full treatment?"

She'd brought her own supply of chocolate to the Ice and the thought of it still unpacked in her duffel brought her to her feet.

His face did a little collapse, as if he'd embarrassed himself. "You must be exhausted."

"Sorry. I am. Thank you for dinner. The conversation, I mean."

"Right. I'll let you go. But I have an idea. Tomorrow I'm making a quick trip—just half a day—to check on my Weddells out at Hutton Cliffs. I have to be back in the afternoon for a meeting so I won't be staying in the field. Come with me. It's quite spectacular out on the sea ice, with Mount Erebus looming over everything." When Alice didn't answer, he said, "Look, you have a couple of months of Rasmussen ahead of you. A little fun with seals might put you in good stead."

"I like Rasmussen."

"Ah. I didn't mean to say anything against him. I'm just trying to talk you into coming out on the ice with me. Just half a day, nothing too taxing. And anyway, no one is allowed to travel off station alone and I haven't yet found a companion. You'd be doing me—and science!—a favor."

She surprised herself by feeling slightly hurt that he'd asked her only because he needed a partner. At the same time, this information freed her from worrying about his excessive friendliness.

"I'll come get you at seven." He checked his watch. "That gives you twelve hours of sleep."

Alice heard herself say, "Okay."

"Excellent. Sleep tight. See you tomorrow." As she shook his hand, she thought of sex first, food second, and sleep last. She gathered up the Dalai Lama's vase and returned at last to that foreign bed.

14

Mikala had been at South Pole Station for five days—and written no music at all—before she laid eyes on her father. He spent all his time in his lab out at the Dark Sector, getting ready to launch a new telescope. The word "dark" did not refer to light rays, which were impossible to avoid during the southern hemisphere's summer, but to noise and radiation. To protect the astrophysicists' probing of the universe from any stray, human-caused energy, the Dark Sector—a small enclave of shacks and outsized instrumentation—was situated a half-mile away from the rest of Pole Station. The South Pole Telescope was a high-profile project this season. When, or if, they got it working, Marcus Wright and his team expected to be able to detect the universe almost all the way back to the Big Bang.

Polies, as the community affectionately called themselves, revered Wright. They said he worked like a dog. He didn't even take time for interviews with the press. His grad students delivered his meals to the lab. He cared only about investigating the origins of the universe.

Mikala found his reputation irritating. If they only knew what she knew.

Besides, she hadn't traveled all this way to hear rumors about the man. She had no intention of revealing her identity to him, but she *had* planned on seeing him, observing him, probably even meeting him. She'd gone so far as to tell the NSF that she intended to musically represent the Big Bang, leaving open the possibility of even interviewing him. That seemed unlikely now. No doubt he viewed music as unworthy of his time as media interviews.

Then, on Friday, Wright showed up in the galley. Mikala knew what he looked like from a picture on the university website. But that afternoon she heard him before she saw him.

"Listen to that guy's laugh," Jeffrey, the other artist-in-residence, a painter, said over his heaping plate of macaroni and cheese. "He sounds exactly like you."

Mikala stopped spooning her potato-leek soup and listened.

"It's Marcus Wright," Jeffrey said, jabbing his fork in the direction of the laughing astrophysicist who sat a couple of tables to Mikala's back. "Do you know who he is? He's the principal investigator for that big telescope they're building. The one that looks all the way back to the Big Bang."

"I know who he is," Mikala said. She wouldn't turn and look, not yet. "And the telescope looks back to about three hundred thousand years or so *after* the Big Bang. It's a big difference."

"Aren't we touchy today."

Mikala tipped her bowl, scooped up the last of the soup. Then, slowly, she pivoted on the dining bench.

Another blast of *Ha!* from the astrophysicist. Just like Mikala's, his laughter came out in one staccato note, backed by the force of a big expulsion of air from his lungs. The familiarity of his laugh unnerved her, and she turned back to face Jeffrey without having allowed her gaze to travel all the way to Marcus. She was actually shaking.

"What I'm thinking," Jeffrey persisted, "is that chatting with him might jumpstart your muse, know what I mean? Talking to him might give you some ideas. He's reportedly very charming. You need to get going on your project."

"Go to hell," she said, getting up and shoving in her chair.

She couldn't believe she'd just said that. She barely knew Jeffrey. In front of an entire table of Polies, too. Several guys in Carhartt overalls looked up at her with bland, expectant faces.

She wanted to march out of the galley and pretend it hadn't happened. But this community was a lot like the one at Redwood Grove, the northern California commune in which she'd grown up, in that it was too small for indulging her temper. Mikala put her still-trembling hands on the back of the chair and said, "I'm sorry, Jeffrey."

"You should talk to Marcus Wright," he said around a mouthful of macaroni and cheese.

"You're a relentless sonofabitch."

Chuckles from the guys in Carhartt overalls.

"Artist to artist. Just trying to be helpful."

"What I'm trying to tell you," she said, "is that you're not helpful."

Jeffrey shrugged. "Talk to him. I hear he's a great guy."

Mikala again turned her back to Jeffrey and searched out Marcus. There he was, her father. He sat with a group of young people, probably his graduate students, leaning forward on his elbows, gesturing with his hands, entertaining the table with a funny story. Marcus had thick black hair, like hers, though his was longer, tousled, and shot through with gray. With his prominent brow and square jaw, also just like hers, he might have been handsome, but his eyes bagged and his cheeks sagged. He wore a pair of slightly too big, serviceable glasses. She knew he was exactly her height, five feet nine inches, but rather than having her fit build, he was dumpy.

He looked like a man with a mission, a rocket about to take off. Even at this distance, Mikala felt something like heat radiating off him.

She sat back down on the bench, facing out, and watched. Him. Her father. The bank bomber. The revered astrophysicist. Of course the grad students had to laugh at his jokes. They had to pretend he was hilarious. Their careers depended on him. To look at him, you'd think he was any hard-working sixty-year-old university professor.

Mikala took a deep breath. She tried to imagine him at Redwood Grove more than three decades ago, how the place had been when she was conceived. The adults had been much younger than she was now, the men and women both long-haired and painfully earnest. They had bought the land in the Santa Cruz mountains with someone's grandmother's money and proudly called themselves a commune. In the summer of 1968, they built the longhouse, four sleeping cabins, and the sweat lodge. They never cut a single tree, still haven't. A gorgeous redwood with its feathery rust-colored bark soars right up through the north end of the longhouse. According to Mikala's mother, Marcus arrived that fall, just as the construction work was completed. Typical, Pauline liked to say, that he showed up just after the manual labor and just in time for the talking. Even as a young man, he wasn't buff or grand in any physical way. His glasses then were as out of style—thick black plastic frames—as the ones he wore now. But he could think, and he could talk. That winter was famous in the commune's history; they spent long hours trying to decide if anarchy could be a guiding principle, or if the question itself—linking the word "anarchy" with "guiding principle"—was a contradiction in terms. Marcus's voice was a persistent and passionate one in those discussions. By the following summer, when they built two additional cabins on stilts, straddling the creek, Marcus was gone.

Mikala was the only one of her generation who still loved and visited the place. Most of the original Redwood Grove community members now lived conventional lives as librarians, software technicians, even bankers. She knew that. But it didn't prevent her shock in actually seeing Marcus Wright, the man who split the commune into two factions. He looked extraordinarily ordinary.

She stood up and left without looking at him again. Outside the galley, Mikala stopped to take her bearings. She could still get lost under the big silver geodesic dome that covered the cluster of orange trailers and temporary buildings. The dome's entrance was open to the outside, so long icicles hung from its ceiling, and a hoary coat of frost clung to most surfaces. The light under the dome was always dim and murky. Mikala shivered hard.

Jeffrey was right. She had to get to work. The first couple of days here she had told herself she was recovering from the plane crash. Even when she put on headphones and listened to Mahler, with his swelling symphonic climaxes, she couldn't drown out the sounds of those twenty-four hours. The explosion. The wind. The rescue snowmobiles. The runners of the sled carrying the one dead and one live body. Sometimes she even imagined hearing the dying woman's last words, mumbled to herself as she lay in the snow.

But those sounds were just noise. Noise that prevented creativity. She'd heard something else during those twenty-four hours: the song of Rosie. Just thinking of her smile, like a visual shout, was music.

That's what she needed to concentrate on—not Marcus, not the noise—but that hum in her heart.

Still, even knowing that, she had wasted another couple of days exploring South Pole Station, looking for a good place to work. She was housed in a Hypertat, a glorified tent with a semi-private cubicle, situated a couple hundred yards away from the dome. The big, barrel-shaped structures slept about twelve people in separate berths. Mikala was pleased with the privacy of her curtained-off space where she had a twin bed, a shelf for books, a mini-desk, and a chair, but there were no outlets for her keyboard and laptop. Barney, the station manager, had suggested she work in the galley during off-hours, but the steady stream of folks looking for snacks and coffee was too distracting. Valerie, the science manager, proposed asking Marcus Wright if he could spare a corner of his lab, but then took back the idea, since the telescope was just days away from receiving first light. He couldn't afford any disturbances. Mikala was relieved. That would have been way too close for comfort.

Finally, Jeffrey had shown her the Sky Lab, a small glass room perched tower-like above the silver dome. Mikala made her way there now, wending through the temporary buildings to the back of the dome, and then climbing the long rickety route of stairways that led up to the Sky Lab. In spite of the long climb to the room, the Rapunzel effect had been diminished by years of blowing snow that had piled up around the station, threatening to bury it. The surface of the snow was now just a few feet below the tower windows. The Sky Lab had evolved over the years into a makeshift music studio and a motley set of instruments was left there for all comers. Jeffrey had helped Mikala carry and set up her keyboard. She had hoped the 360 degree view of space and ice would inspire her work.

She sat now and tapped the piano keys with painful randomness, hitting an E and listening to the sound extend, thin, and eventually disappear. Then an E flat. When she became disgusted enough with her inability to compose a single bar of music, she played scales. She pretended she was punishing herself, but in fact Mikala had always loved playing scales. She never tired of hearing the precision of each note and appreciating the perfect relationship of the notes to one another. It was soothing and reminded her of the hours she'd spent as a small child with her stepfather Andy, carefully listening to the river, the wind, the clatter of summer insects. He'd insisted that each had a melody that they could discern if they listened hard enough.

"There!" Andy would say, nodding at the river. "That was the theme again. And now—" Holding up a hand, he'd go back to listening.

The June she was five years old, he claimed that it was possible to build a "piano" from river stones. He and Mikala painstakingly selected "keys" and then a "knocking stone." He swore that once in Japan he'd seen such a "keyboard" made of hanging pieces of shale, each of which had a different tone. But his and Mikala's river stone piano never worked. The sound was always *clunk*.

Even so, Andy viewed the failed river stone piano as an indispensable step in uncovering Mikala's gift. Later, the entire Redwood Grove community would claim a role in nurturing her talent, but Andy was on his own in those early years. He was also hell-bent. He lied, cheated, and stole to give his stepdaughter music.

Later that same summer of her fifth year, Andy took a job clearing brush for a local property owner. For over a month he swung a scythe and wielded a chainsaw in the hot northern California sun. The community frowned on the work. Accepting wages from a would-be developer? Denuding the earth of its vegetation? Anyway, where was the money? All wages earned from the outside were supposed to be turned over to the community, but Andy came home each week empty-handed. He claimed he would be paid at the end of the job.

On the last Friday in August, Andy drove onto the land with an upright piano in the bed of a borrowed truck. He told the community that the property owner had stiffed him and so he'd taken the man's piano instead of money.

Andy wasn't a good liar. But five-year-old Mikala took his story at face value. She saw her stepdad as mightily heroic, single-handedly carrying an entire piano out of the property owner's house and hefting it onto the truck bed. Surely the adults in the community had asked questions about the piano and truck. Surely no one believed his story. But everyone loved Andy. Not only did he do far more than his share of community work but he could charm anyone, from the local Baptist minister to an IRS bureaucrat. Redwood Grove needed Andy. After a few moments of shocked silence, which the child Mikala read as awe, several of the Redwood men helped Andy carry the piano to the longhouse. A few days later, Andy announced at the Friday night meeting that his stepdaughter had perfect pitch.

Not long after that he stole a turntable and amp from a high end stereo store. He said the heist had been ridiculously easy. He took the boxes off the shelf and carried them out the door. He built the speakers himself.

Andy's thieving was controversial since the community had long been under surveillance because of Marcus's alleged involvement with the bank explosion. But even more touchy was the whole idea of personal property. Andy insisted that he hadn't taken the listening equipment solely for his stepdaughter, that he'd intended it to benefit the entire community. A few remained stubborn about the agreement that music at Redwood Grove be found in nature or performed by live people, but others argued that a fiddle was simply an earlier form of technology than a stereo.

Thereafter, Andy always volunteered to be the one who hitch-hiked to the library in town for everyone's books so that he could also borrow record albums of Bach, Beethoven, Mahler, as well as every contemporary composer the library stocked. Mikala spent the rest of her childhood, when she wasn't at school or playing the piano, on her back in the longhouse listening to music. Sony came out with the Walkman in 1979, when Mikala was ten, and Andy lifted one of those, too. That allowed her to loll on the forest floor during the summer months listening to music for hours at a time.

It didn't take long for the community to make full use of the stereo and speakers. The voices and guitars of Joan Armatrading, B.B. King, Bob Dylan, and Jimi Hendrix became staples at their parties. Still, they maintained a fierce pride in Redwood's experi-mental lifestyle. If there were outside guests at a party, the equip-ment would stay in the back shed, and they danced to the piano or banjo. This led to some awkward situations, later in life, for Mi-kala. Once someone told a reporter that all of her musical talent had come from instruments she and Andy had made from gourds, shells, hollowed wood, and of course stones. This story had been repeated, in print, too many times already to bother correcting. Anyway, Andy's mythology hadn't hurt her career any. Still, it could be awkward when she admitted to the years of lessons from the most renowned piano teacher in San Francisco, as well as tickets to dozens of chamber music and symphony concerts.

Mikala left her keyboard and went to kneel at the Sky Lab window, staring out at the field of white, hoping the tabula rasa would somehow inspire music. From nowhere, a man appeared, coming around the bend of the dome, pushing through the snow drifts! He held his arms aloft and used his chest to shove the powder aside. He wore a purple fleece hat, his own puffy down parka, and the government-issued white, insulated, rubber boots, called bunny boots. Who was this person arrogant enough to think he could pit himself against snow drifts at the South Pole?

It was him. Marcus Wright.

Mikala grabbed her parka and hat and descended the stairs quickly. Once on the floor of the dome, she hesitated, but before she could question what she was doing, she hurried through the passageways of the old station until she emerged into the freezing bright sunshine. Marcus was just coming into view, now tromping along a worn path, moving quickly toward the entrance of the dome. But he didn't turn in. Instead, he continued on past her and disappeared around the dome. It was as if he were doing laps for exercise!

Mikala followed him, rounding the bend of the dome in the trail he'd blazed. Though he didn't look particularly fit, Marcus was fast. She couldn't quite catch up and he didn't seem to notice that someone was tailing him. This didn't surprise her. If someone were following her—even in such an unusual course as laps around the old silver dome at the South Pole—she might be as oblivious as he was. Her obliviousness had driven Sarah crazy, the way she'd fall into musical musings at stoplights, not noticing when the red turned to green. Sarah would say, "Green," with barely suppressed annoyance. If she were by herself, without Sarah to prompt her, and if no one honked, she sometimes sat through entire green lights without noticing.

Even though the gap between her and Marcus widened, Mikala pushed forward. The idea of facing him on the backside of the dome, totally alone on the polar plateau, appealed to her. Strip the thing down to basics: ice, sky, daughter, father. But his form became smaller and smaller as the distance between them lengthened. She felt as if this stretching gap were symbolic of the relationship she'd had with him her whole life. Finally, she lost sight of him as he rounded the dome.

She stopped, out of breath, to rest. The freeze-dried air felt as if it were scrubbing her lungs. Her face and feet were very cold. Mikala wore only her hiking boots, which weren't insulated like bunny boots, no goggles or neck gaiter, and it was 30 degrees below zero. She needed to keep moving to keep her blood circulating. Actually, she needed to get back inside. She was dangerously underdressed.

Mikala turned around and started walking in the opposite direction, figuring she'd meet him coming the other way. But when his fiercely determined form, topped by that purple hat, came into view, she knew she wouldn't stop him. He seemed deep in thought, and she could tell just by the set of his mouth and shoulders that he was working out some complex problem. It was exactly how she looked when she was deeply involved in a composition. She might have even spoken and he wouldn't have noticed her.

Marcus did indeed walk right by and said nothing. She let him pass and didn't look over her shoulder.

Alone on the backside of the South Pole dome, Mikala dropped to her knees, suddenly missing Sarah with an acuteness that felt unbearable. She'd intended this journey to Antarctica to be a way to travel beyond that grief. She'd thought that by meeting Marcus Wright, she could dispel and free herself from the legend of him. Instead, it seemed that by putting herself within spitting range of her father, she'd traveled to the very heart of grief.

Mikala could no longer feel her feet. Worse, no one knew where she was. The *sssss* of the sled runners brushed her thoughts.

Still, she remained kneeling in that cold white place. It would be so easy to fall back in the snow, just lie there. It'd take minutes, maybe only seconds.

Then she heard the hum. Wild Rosie's voice. Quiet and deep and distant, but she heard it. Mikala rose to her block-like feet and stumped back toward the entrance of the old station.

By the time she got there, she felt as if the cold had seeped into the folds of her brain.

She made her way under the dome and fumbled toward the galley. Thank god it was empty. She didn't want to have to explain anything to anyone. She poured herself some coffee and slumped into a chair.

How stupid she'd been. Charging outside without dressing properly. Chasing Marcus like some kind of stalker! Sure, she'd wanted to get a look at him. But at a distance. Just a bit of surveillance.

The problem was, now she'd seen his thick black hair and steel gray eyes, just like hers. She'd heard his single-blast laugh—*ha!*—also like hers. She'd witnessed the identical way in which his distraction could be yanked away to total concentration. These things made him astonishingly familiar. They changed everything.

15|

Alice sat on the edge of her bed holding the lump of tissue that allegedly wrapped a vase from the Dalai Lama. She was considering walking it down the hall to the bathroom where she could deposit it in the trash bin. But what if Jennifer lived on this same floor in this same dorm? She might see that Alice had just dumped it. Instead, she would take it over to Crary Lab, where only scientists were allowed, and dispose of it there.

The dorm room door flew open and slammed against the wall. The entering woman let out a hushed, "*Fuuuck.*" Then, startled at seeing Alice, "Jesus. Who are you?"

"I'm Alice Neilson."

The woman ran a hand through her hair and again breathed, "*Fuck.*" She peeled off her outerwear and flung herself on the other bed with a loud groan.

Confused, Alice said, "Am I in the wrong room?"

"Oh, probably not. I mean, I knew I was getting a roommate eventually, just not . . ."

This wasn't right. Rasmussen said he'd picked Rosie Moore specifically because she was knowledgeable and skilled. This woman appeared distraught and whacked. Maybe she *was* in the wrong room.

"My advisor, Dean Rasmussen, said I'd be rooming with Rosie Moore."

"That's me, I'm afraid." The woman's face finally softened and she propped up on an elbow. "I'm sorry. What a poor excuse for a welcome. Please, make yourself at home. And welcome, really. I'm sorry you caught me at a very, very bad moment. I just did something really stupid."

"What did you do?" Alice wanted to take back the words. You weren't supposed to ask direct questions when you first met someone.

But Rosie's sudden, big, generous smile was evidence that she didn't mind the question. She looked like someone who played hard. The kind of person who, as a child, would have intimidated Alice on the playground. She could see her commanding squadrons of other girls, not because she was overly pretty or clever but because she had the most vigor. Alice liked her.

Rosie spread out her hands, looked at the backs of them, and then flipped them over and looked at her palms. She said, "I just kissed a married man. Can you think of anything more stupid?"

Alice shook her head slowly.

Rosie barked a surprised laugh at Alice's agreement.

Alice hugged the wrapped Dalai Lama vase. Should she have said that kissing a married man wasn't stupid? That would have been dishonest.

"Look. I gotta sleep. I work from five in the morning until two, so I usually take a nap in the afternoon."

Alice nodded but couldn't stop staring at Rosie. She was beautifully feral, the kind of woman who did exactly what she wanted to do.

Rosie shoved into her sleeping bag and turned her back. "Good night. Please do make yourself comfortable. I promise I'll be more civil when I recover."

"Good night," Alice said and reached for her notebook. On the top of a fresh page, she wrote, "Rosie of the Antarctic." Below that she made a list of observations.

Deep chestnut hair.
Totally comfortable in her body.

Very big smile.
Musical laugh.
Kissed married man.
Survivor.

16

When Alice woke up the next morning, Rosie was gone. She checked the clock. Jamie the seal biologist would be showing up soon. She'd said yes to his invitation! The extreme cold must have addled her brain. Alice had read about it on a science poster in Crary Lab. The environment caused the release of a rogue hormone that screwed up a person's judgment and memory.

Alice had come to Antarctica to do geology with Rasmussen. She couldn't think of one good reason to spend the morning on the sea ice with a biologist. She could think of several good reasons to not do so, such as preserving her energy and not risking her life.

She pulled her journal into her lap, opened to the first blank page, and drew lines for a chart. On the top she wrote, "Sea Ice with Seal Biologist." Then she headed the first column "pros" and the second column "cons." She began devising a system for weighting each entry, a simple scale of one to ten, one being a weak reason and ten being a strong one, so that her decision could be mathematical.

The phone rang. Alice stared at the old-fashioned handset as it rhythmically *brrred*. Maybe it was Rosie. Maybe they could meet later on for coffee. Alice could use an official briefing on how to conduct oneself at McMurdo Station.

"Hello?"

"Hey! It's me."

"Oh."

"Jamie," he clarified. "Look, I'm behind schedule. Can you do me a big favor? There's really no point in my coming into McMurdo to get you because we're heading out my way anyway. So listen. Right in front of the dorms there's a stop for the shuttle out here to Scott Base. You can't miss it. Looks just like a city bus stop, with a bench and everything. Catch the shuttle. By the time you get here, I'll be ready to go."

Alice stepped to the window and pulled aside the blanket. The day was brilliant, the sky a rock hard blue, as if she might be able to knock on it.

"Alice?"

"Okay."

A few minutes later, as she bounced along in the van that ran between the American and New Zealand bases, she couldn't quite believe herself. It was her usual habit to say no. She *felt* the no but was acting the yes. She wished she had her proverb book with her. There must be something along the lines of: She who walks through open doors . . . what? The ending could be about either opportunity for taking risks or punishment for greed.

The van dropped Alice off behind Scott Base where Jamie was throwing two survival gear bags into the back of an orange tracked vehicle that looked like it was designed for travel on Mars.

"Morning. Climb in. I'll be right there."

Alice hoisted herself up into the passenger seat and slammed the door shut behind her. Jamie returned with two cups of coffee. He handed her one, clutched the other between his knees, and turned the key in the ignition. The Spryte didn't start up until the fourth try and Jamie was cursing. When the ignition did engage, the roar of the motor so startled him that he squeezed his knees together, popping the lid off the cup, and hot coffee erupted onto his lap. "Shit." Leaving the motor running, he jumped down from the Spryte and disappeared inside the station again.

Moody man. Bizarre vehicle. Sea ice. A sane person would get out of this thing and head back to the American station.

Jamie returned with a fresh cup of coffee and his loopy smile. "Do you mind holding this for me? I'm not exactly a morning person. Sorry. Got up late. Couldn't find my notebook. But I'm set now. How are you?"

"Fine."

"Ready to go?"

Alice nodded and they lurched toward the ice road leading out to Willy Field where her LC-130 had landed just yesterday. Jamie steered the vehicle by means of two brake levers, looking like someone at a slot machine. He didn't attempt conversation above the loud Spryte engine. From time to time, he reached over for his coffee cup, took a gulp, and handed it back for her to hold. She couldn't drink hers for all the cream and sugar he'd added, so she offered it to him when he'd finished his own. He pantomimed disappointment at her rejection of the coffee but polished it off just the same.

As Alice looked out at the relentless ice, she worried. She imagined a dozen frightening scenarios for her mother involving cars, stairs, the kitchen range, the shower. But—Alice had to admit— the evidence didn't support these fears. Her mother didn't make stupid mistakes. She forced herself to imagine something different: Wasn't it possible that with Alice gone, her mother might rally, harness her own resources, even thrive? Hadn't she always said she had quit doing what she loved because she had to raise Alice? Maybe that had become a habit she could now break. Maybe her mother would spread her novel out on the card table in place of the jigsaw puzzles. Maybe she would unplug the phone, like she had done when Alice was little, and disappear into the world of her story, her hand cradling a pencil, a small smile releasing the tension in her face. When she was a child, Alice had railed against those evenings, wanting to bring her mother home to her. She regretted that now, how she had yanked her mother from her writing, insisted on attention, not understanding how an adult needed to do her work. If only she had understood. And now she herself had left because she wanted to do her own work. She might be the most selfish person on the face of the earth.

When Jamie stopped the Spryte and shut off the engine, the silence slammed into her thoughts. Jamie waited to speak until she looked at him. "Okay, Sunshine. From here we walk. It's not far. About an hour. Is that going to be okay?"

Sunshine? She thought she ought to be offended but his tone was more self-mocking than presumptuous. She nodded.

"Have you ever used crampons?"

"No."

"Nothing to them. Jump out. I'll show you how to put them on your boots."

Once they were both outfitted with metal spikes on their boots and had stuffed survival gear into their knapsacks, they walked toward a great jumble of building-sized blocks of sea ice that had been pushed up against the continent by the tides. The ice glowed a translucent blue.

"There's a good route through the pressure ridges to the left here, and then we'll be on the sea ice."

"It's like a city of ice," Alice said as they made their way through the blocks towering over their heads. She stopped abruptly, realizing she'd made a simile. Maybe when the rogue hormone released by the extreme cold decreased one's ability to reason, it also increased one's facility for figurative thinking.

Jamie guided her to the edge where water sloshed up through a split in the ice. Alice stepped over the gap, the spikes in her crampons biting into the slick surface. Sea ice. A slab that stretched for miles and miles. Beneath the ice lay dark, deep, and extremely cold saltwater. Overhead the intense sun beat down but provided no warmth.

That was scientifically incorrect, of course. The sun must be providing warmth. But Alice felt nothing that she would have called warmth on the small part of her face that was exposed to the air.

They walked for about a hundred paces before Jamie stopped and put an arm around her shoulders. "You're the first person I've brought out on the sea ice who didn't ask, right away, if the ice would hold our weight."

"Obviously we wouldn't walk out on it if it wouldn't hold our weight."

"Obviously," Jamie smiled. "But you have no reason to trust that I know what I'm doing."

Alice realized that was true. Yet, something about him relaxed her. His funny-lookingness was pleasing, comfortable.

"Okay, you didn't ask. But it's a few meters thick in most places. Early in the season, I actually camp out on the sea ice and while I'm lying in my tent at night, I can hear the seals swimming and vocalizing right below my bed."

Alice imagined a fat, fur-clad seal swooping through the sea beneath her feet.

"You're not scared?"

"No." Though she had no idea why not.

"How *do* you feel?"

"Feel?" she said, not wanting to admit the answer. She felt free.

They walked on toward Erebus. The mountain looked much huger than it had yesterday, its haunches long and graceful sloping down to the sea, a plume of steam rising from its caldera like a wish. Another simile!

"Rasmussen is kind of a scary guy," Jamie said, picking up their conversation from last night. "Not that I know him personally. But what I hear about him. I heard that he doesn't think climate change is an issue. I mean, no one denies that the climate is warming, but he says it doesn't matter. The earth changes. Species die. It's happened before. It's not ours to control. There's a kind of relief in that message, I guess. We can throw our hands up."

"He's interested in the evidence, not in relief or what people should *do*."

"Ah, the correct scientist. No emotional investment. I'll tell you a secret. I've named my seals."

"Like Jane Goodall and her chimps."

"Just like that. I talk to them when I'm alone."

"Lots of biologists have challenged the objective paradigm."

"I've petted them."

"That's going a bit far."

"Yeah, I know. But if I'm interacting with the seals by tagging them, counting them, taking their blood, is a bit of love going to interfere with whatever 'natural' processes I'm trying to observe?"

"This isn't a problem with rocks."

Jamie laughed. "I guess not. I hope you won't judge me harshly for petting a few Weddell seals."

"I'm in no position to judge anyone."

Jamie stopped again and looked at her. She guessed she'd made her usual mistake of responding too seriously to a light comment.

But he picked up her tone and said, "I'm curious. I want to know how you would judge me. If, that is, you thought you were in a position to do so."

"Maybe I chose rocks so I wouldn't have to ask those questions. There's no way I can hurt rocks." He nodded slowly, silent for once. An urge to not hurt his feelings made her add, "I don't think you're bothering the seals by petting them."

He smiled. "But I might be doing bad science."

"You might be."

He rocked his head from side to side, satisfied. Then, "Hey, Sunshine. Look. See that rectangular-shaped cliff? And the black things on the ice in front of it? My seals."

The Weddells barely lifted their heads as Jamie and Alice approached. The big slugs lay about in mother and pup pairs, blinking their long lashes, scratching their tubular bodies with their fins. They had faces like dogs, more pug than other species of seals, and big pleading eyes. They seemed particularly comfortable lying on the ice, amazingly at peace with their environment. Jamie explained that the animals in Antarctica had never learned to fear humans. He took a pair of binoculars out of his pack and studied a seal just five meters away. "I'm reading the number on her tag."

"You already told me you touch them. Why not just go read it?"

"I don't make a practice of touching them. Only in weak moments. And never in front of anyone. Try to bust me and I'll deny everything." He lowered the binoculars and smiled at her. "Come have a look at one of their breathing holes."

As he explained how the Weddells cut the holes with their teeth, and that old seals die of starvation when their teeth become too worn from ice-gnawing to catch fish, she looked down into the window of slosh.

"I wish I could enter their world," he said. "Up here I'm only observing a fraction of their lives."

"I had an affair with a married man once. That's how it felt, like I was seeing his life on just one plane."

The silence let Alice know that her scientific observation was also a social faux pas. She knew one didn't casually mention affairs with married men. But it was exactly what Jamie's comment about the seals made her think. "Sorry," she said, but only half out loud because she didn't know if an apology were appropriate, either.

He didn't respond, and they walked another half-mile, stopping each time Jamie needed to peer through his binoculars and record a seal's tag number. It was only eleven o'clock when he asked if she was ready for lunch. She was starving.

Jamie spread out a space blanket near another seal's breathing hole and pulled out sandwiches of cheese, pickles, mayonnaise, and mustard. He ate half of one before asking, in a voice that sounded nearly involuntary, "Are *you* married?"

Alice wanted to laugh at the way he choked the question. "No."

"Why not?"

"What does 'why not' mean?"

"You seem so purposeful. Like it would be a conscious choice: career over marriage."

"That's so 1950s."

Jamie laughed. "I guess so. But *you're* sort of—"

"1950s?"

"Uh. I guess that's what I was going to say."

"Are you?"

"1950s?"

"No. Married."

"No."

"Why not?"

"Hell if I know. Want to?"

Alice said, "Sure. There's a chapel in town."

Jamie laughed out loud, not so much at her joke as at the fact that his serious companion had made one, and tossed her a plastic-wrapped cookie. "I hand-carried the chips from the States. Top of the line organic bittersweet chocolate."

"You baked these?"

"Yep. The chewy kind."

"I have a weakness for chocolate."

"I know."

"How do you know that?"

"You quivered last night when I said the word."

"I did not."

"I thought you did. Maybe it was just my company."

Flirting usually annoyed Alice. It was like fencing, these little forward pitches and backward retreats. A series of silly jokes. But right then, eating Jamie's cookie, she felt happy, just plain happy.

A sleek gray head shot up through the breathing hole. The round eyes surveyed the scene and seeing no leopard seals, only a couple of humans, the seal heaved itself out of the hole and onto the ice. It lowered its eyelids drowsily, wriggled into a comfortable position, and appeared to fall instantly asleep. The urge to touch the wet pelt shot through Alice like adrenaline. The seal's eyes flew open and held Alice's stare. The connection was too raw. "Wow," she whispered.

"Yeah," Jamie said. "I know."

As they walked back to the Spryte, Alice considered her current circumstances. She was in the most inhospitable environment for humans on earth. She walked next to a man who seemed best described as a big mammal. Every second of this day had seemed spontaneous, a condition she normally found distressful. Yet she felt elated. Yes, that was in fact the right word. Elated. Again.

After they traversed back through the city of ice blocks and removed their crampons, she said, "Let me drive."

"Okay, Sunshine. Hop in the driver's seat."

It was simple, once she got the hang of using the two brake levers for forward and backward movement. She drove down the hill and turned onto the ice road. "Won't this thing go faster?"

"You in a hurry to get back?"

"No, I just thought faster would be fun."

Jamie stared in surprise. Alice kept driving, more surprised than he was. Maybe she had some of her mother in her, after all.

"Ah," he said. "I'll give you a tour then. See that intersection ahead?"

"Sort of." All she saw ahead was ice.

"The path in the ice forks. Go left. You'll see it when you come upon it."

A few minutes later, Alice drove the Spryte toward a cluster of bright yellow Scott tents, the kind that look like circus tents with steep points and canvas stretching to the ground, held out by guy lines. On the edge of the camp was one pale pink tent with two lines of Tibetan prayer flags radiating from its tip to stakes in the ice. She managed to stop the vehicle and they got out.

"This is where I stay when I'm not at the station. The pink tent is mine."

Alice thought of sex first, food second, sleep third. This feeling she had, it was probably just a survival response, a physical reaction to the severe cold and wild geography. She was scaring herself.

"Want to look inside?" He held open the canvas tube door to his tent and gestured for her to enter.

"That's okay. I better get back, actually."

Jamie let go of the tent fabric.

What was she doing out here in the middle of the ice continent with this man who seemed more creature than person? This man who was so different from reticent Rasmussen?

"I could show you the cook tent," he said.

"Would it be okay if we went back?" Alice walked quickly to the Spryte and got in the passenger's seat.

"Are you okay?" Jamie asked as he climbed into the driver's seat.

"I didn't realize how late it was."

"It's only one o'clock."

Her excitement had fizzled. She longed for home. Her orderly bedroom and predictable evenings with her mother. Even more, she longed for the geology lab at the university where the only unknowns were the outcomes of her research.

Jamie drove the Spryte back to Scott Base and when he turned off the engine, he reached for humor. "I thought we were going to get married."

Alice tried to manufacture a laugh but emitted something that sounded more like a groan. "Thanks for the morning." She jumped down and headed toward the road.

"Alice!" he called after her. "Come warm up with a cup of coffee. You don't have to walk. The van will take you back to MacTown."

He was a big golden retriever, too friendly, too rambunctious.

"Thank you!" she called over her shoulder. "I'll walk. I want to."

Jamie ran to catch up. "Don't be silly."

"It's only two kilometers."

"I know. But the van can take you." He took her hand out of her jacket pocket and kissed it, then looked as if he had startled himself.

"I can walk," she whispered, but wondered if it were true. She felt entirely unsteady on her feet as she weaved her way along the road to McMurdo. She didn't know if he watched her because she didn't turn around, but she felt him at her back all the way into town.

A bad case of pheromones, she told herself, a chemical situation that she had no time for. She needed to get up to the Dry Valleys, to Rasmussen, to work.

17

Alice went directly to Crary Lab and let herself into Rasmussen's office. She'd be with him soon. Though the mountains were bound to be more daunting than the road between McMurdo Station and Scott Base, she'd have work. Work was salvation.

She sat in Rasmussen's chair and laid her fingers on his keyboard. This was where she belonged. Not walking across a frozen sea with an overzealous biologist. What had she been thinking?

Relieved to have righted herself, Alice punched her mother's number.

"Oh, Alice. This isn't a good time. Can I call you back?"

"No. I can call out but we can't get calls in. Unless it's an emergency."

"Believe me, it is."

"Now? Right now an emergency? What's wrong?"

"I can't believe you didn't leave a way for me to get in touch with you. You don't know what I've been through the last few days."

She felt as if a vacuum were sucking her heart out through her feet. "We talked yesterday, Mom. You were fine."

"I don't want to alarm you."

"*What?*"

"You know what. I'm not well. You knew that when you left."

"The doctor said you were fine."

"He said the CAT scan showed nothing. He didn't say I was fine. I know fine and this isn't it. Could you come home, just for a few days?"

"I'm in Antarctica."

"Antarctica . . ." Her mother exhaled the word, as if Alice had said she was in the gulag.

"Do you have a headache?"

"You know I do."

"Well, what about the Percodan?"

"If it were only the headache, I could deal."

"What else then?"

"I can't do this."

"Do what?"

"Life."

Alice didn't mean for her voice to come out in a whisper, but it did. "I can't come home."

She heard the fridge door shutting, the clink of the bottle being set down on the ceramic tiles of the kitchen countertop, the pop of the cork, as if her mother were exaggerating the sound effects for her benefit. A moment later, a full body sigh that probably followed a long drink. "Of course you can't come home. But you're so good to call. Tell me. How's Rasmussen treating you?"

"I haven't seen him yet. He's in the field."

"He sounds like such a character. Taciturn. Rough." A low chuckle.

"Not really rough. He's exacting. He's very focused on his work."

"Married?"

They'd had this conversation before, but if it comforted her mother, they could have it again. "No."

"An affair with some young thing in the department?"

"I don't think so."

"Oh, come on now. Don't tell me you spend all those evenings in the lab and *nothing* happens. Even scientists have libidos."

"I think he's very shy."

"Well, then, what about his scientific rival—does he have a wife?"

"You mean Morrison?"

"Whoever. Sure, Morrison. Does Morrison have a wife?

"I think so."

"Maybe Rasmussen fancies Morrison's wife."

"I don't think so." Why'd she call her mother? To stop the free-fall she'd felt in her morning with Jamie. It was working.

"But you *told* me they have a fiery dispute."

"About geology. Morrison basically believes that the earth has warmed and cooled, the ice sheets melted and frozen, several times in recent geological history, but Rasmussen—"

"Trust me. Their dispute is about more than rocks. You do know it's not about rocks, don't you? There has to be something else there. Something in their personalities, if not their personal lives. What makes them so opposed to each other? The real fire in every dispute is always something deeply human, utterly personal. Tell me you know that."

"No one is sleeping with anyone's wife."

"Then Rasmussen got turned down by the other's university. Or—what about this?—one of them has published more prestigiously than the other."

So many evenings her mother had tried to engage her in this kind of speculation, longing for Alice to tell her something juicy, and she often wished she could make something up. But Alice was not good at inventing stories. She could only examine the evidence, all of which, in the case of Rasmussen and Morrison, pointed to the dispute being about rocks and ice, just rocks and ice.

"Maybe," Alice told her mother. "I don't really know the history of their relationship."

"What about you then? Is there something between you and Rasmussen?" When Alice didn't answer her mother said, "Ah hah! You could do worse than a college professor."

Alice hesitated. She knew it was pointless to remind her mother that Alice herself was a college professor. Or would be soon. If she made it through these couple of months of fieldwork. To do that, she had to placate her mother. So she conceded, "I don't know yet. Nothing has been said."

"What does he look like?"

"He's maybe fifty."

"You should introduce him to me!"

"Not your type."

"Oh well. So maybe you'll meet some handsome man your own age in Antarctica."

"Age doesn't matter that much."

"You don't want to be alone in your old age, like me."

"You're not even fifty."

"Trust me, Alice. *Thirty* is old for a woman."

"I better go."

"Don't worry about me. Study your rocks. Look for a man. Have a good time."

Hanging up felt so much easier than Alice thought it should. She sat in Rasmussen's office for another half an hour, surfing the net and flipping through familiar geology texts, grounding herself in his mineral world.

18

Every single morning, when Rosie's alarm went off at 4:30, her first thought was of kissing Larry, sitting against the pile of rocks supporting Our Lady of the Snows. The sensitivity of his mouth, the briefest of moments when his tongue touched hers. The sad kindness in his eyes.

She annoyed herself, this not moving on. Enough already.

Rosie swung her feet off the bed and looked at her new roommate. The woman's freshly washed hair spiked out from her head in thin wisps on the pillow and two red patches bloomed on her otherwise pale cheeks. Her fair complexion and perfectly smooth skin made her look untested, incongruent with this continent. They hadn't really had time to get to know one another, but it was a relief to see that bed filled by a live person. Alice. She took up so little space, filling just a small corner of the desk with her neatly stacked composition book and Scharffen Berger chocolate bars. A tissue-wrapped lump on top.

Rosie left the room as quietly as she could and stumbled across the ice to Building 155, which housed the galley, some offices, including that of the *Antarctic Sun,* as well as Karen's, more dorm rooms, an ATM, a barbershop, and a bank of public-use computer terminals. In the galley, she poured herself a cup of coffee and tied on an apron. She cracked dozens of eggs into a vat and used a broom-sized whisk to mix them. She stirred pancake batter and retrieved the morning's rations of breakfast meats from the refrigerator.

An hour later, Rosie started taking orders at the grill. The workers were first in line, folks who shoveled snow, fixed machinery, hauled garbage, and sorted recyclables. They ate eggs, sausages, french toast, and potatoes. A handful of beakers started their days that early, too, like the guy who studied penguin feces and the woman who was discovering the history of the earth by reading ice cores. They generally passed by her to scoop out bowls of oatmeal, which they dolloped with canned fruit.

Earl's pioneer hands, gripping either side of a tray, stopped right in front of Rosie's grill. She made herself busy with some eggs, pretending to not see him. It had been two weeks since the party in the Heavy Shop and she'd worked hard to forget that incident against the crates of canned peaches. It had been a mistake, a big mistake. Thankfully, since he worked at Willy Field, he took most of his meals in the small galley out there.

The hands and tray didn't move on, even as customers piled up behind him, and she was finally forced to look up. "What'll you have?"

He looked at her dead on, very rugged. "Good morning, Rosie. How's it going?"

"Good. What'll you have?"

"Not a morning type?"

"Just doing my job. Omelet?"

"You don't remember my name, do you?"

Of course she did, but she shook her head.

"Earl."

"Omelet, Earl?" Rosie shoved her spatula under a partially cooked amoeba of egg.

"What are you doing this evening?"

"Sorry. Busy." Even as she made a grand effort to harden her words and blank her face, something soft slumped inside her. She glanced back up at him and saw his smirk. He knew she was resisting, that she wasn't entirely neutral. It was a misstep, allowing him to see that. Earl Banks was the last person she needed. He was a bundle of crazy and trouble. Not the specific kind of trouble Larry was, but a random and chaotic kind of trouble. Trouble for its own sake. She forced herself to shift her eyes to the next in line, but Earl remained in her peripheral vision, just standing there holding his tray, and she feared some sort of outburst, a confrontation. She flipped two sunny-side overs and toyed with the bacon.

"You," Earl said, cocking a finger at her like a toy gun. He moved on at last, but she realized she'd blundered. She should have humored him. She knew those small-town boys. Slights festered. You always had to pay.

At the end of her shift, Rosie cleaned up the grill and left a few minutes early. She walked slowly up the hill to the mailroom.

Bea wore a smock printed all over with pastel butterflies. Her sensibly short hair and comfortably full figure, as well as that ever-present dimpled smile, seemed to promise a stack of mail. But Rosie had just one letter, from the Dutch guy who'd returned to Amsterdam and wanted something postmarked from Antarctica. He didn't even pretend to care about continuing contact with Rosie. It was her exotic locale that interested him. That, and the fact that there was nothing from her family, filled Rosie with a moment of profound loneliness.

She hurried back to the dorm, sorry that the new roommate was out. The woman had seemed so grounded, so focused, and Rosie could use that kind of influence. She lay down and slept for several hours. When she awoke, she stayed in bed another hour and wondered if she should go to the party Pamela was having in her room.

Karen was a friend of Pamela's. It was probable that she and Larry would be at the party. Rosie ought to go. Larry would be with his wife. Karen would be with her husband. It would be a corrective measure. Wife, husband, folksongs, popcorn. Pamela's parties were as wholesome as pillow fights. The situation with Larry would right itself automatically, just by virtue of the context. She would leave the party cleansed of her desire for him.

"Whoa," Rosie said out loud, realizing that she was actually buying that absurd line of reasoning, just because she wanted to see Larry. She needed something bracing, something hard and cold. An Antarctic stroll. She dressed in expedition-weight long underwear, fleece pants and a sweater, her wind suit, a thick down parka, and a hat and mittens. It was quite late and she'd slept through dinner. She could get something later at mid-rats, short for midnight rations, the meal served for nightshift workers.

Rosie stepped out of the dorm and breathed in the cold, dry air. She stared across the sheet of ice that spanned the distance between Building 155 and the brown box dorm buildings. Neither Karen nor Larry would be in their offices. They'd be at the party. Where Rosie wasn't going.

Rosie walked down the hill, past the coffeehouse, past the Chapel of the Snows, and continued to the shore. She passed below the desalination plant and helo pad until she came to the base of Observation Hill, a perfect cone that sat on the edge of town. Taking the path that traversed the slope, she walked far enough around the hill so that she could look out at the frozen sea without seeing the ugly buildings of McMurdo. There she stopped and faced south. Just across McMurdo Sound, the Royal Society Range graced the horizon with endless peaks. White Island and Black Island sat like fraternal twins, one truly black and the other all white, with a narrow strait between them that led the way due south. When you could see a front moving through that strait, katabatic winds from the polar plateau slamming weather north-ward, it was a matter of twenty minutes before the storm hit McMurdo Station. However, this evening the air was still and a comfortable 10 degrees Fahrenheit, the sky clear and creamy blue.

That girl—that's all anyone ever called her, as if she hadn't had a name—never once saw that the continent could be beautiful.

At the sound of boots crunching on the red volcanic rock, Rosie looked up to see Earl navigating the slope. "I saw you leaving the dorm. I followed you."

"You shouldn't have."

"Well, shit."

"Look, I can't really, you know, go out with you. I'm sorry about the other night. At the party. It was a mistake."

"I didn't ask you to 'go out' with me. I asked what you were doing this evening."

"Yeah. Well. I'm heading back to the dorm."

Earl crouched, picked up a piece of red volcanic rock and tossed it from one hand to the other. He wasn't wearing gloves or mittens. "You didn't even remember my name. Girls remember your name if they're into you. So, like, I got the idea. Besides, I'm not really into you, either. Not in that way." A slow smile.

"I guess that makes it nicely mutual."

"I wanted to show you something," Earl said. He tossed the volcanic rock toward the sea.

Rosie followed the path of the airborne rock. Then she looked back at Earl.

He said, "Cool. Come on."

There was a contained thrashing in Earl that drew her. She gave in and went with him back to his dorm room where he grabbed a guitar case. Then they walked toward the outskirts of town where a cluster of fuel tanks crouched like an enormous drum set. Earl stopped in front of a dull green one and turned to Rosie. "Ready?" Grasping the guitar case in one hand, Earl began climbing the metal rungs of the exterior ladder.

Rosie climbed after him, each frosty metal rung sticking briefly to her leather mittens. At the top, she swung her leg over the rim and found a toehold in the ladder leading through a small opening into the interior of the cistern. She waited there, fearing a pool of oil or water, until she heard Earl's feet drop to the floor. As she reached the bottom she heard the scratch of a match, smelled the puff of sulfur, and then a moment later, marijuana smoke wafted her way. She walked carefully toward the glowing ember at the end of Earl's joint and sat next to him with her back against the curved interior wall. Without speaking, they smoked the marijuana cigarette, shoving their hands into pockets while the other was taking a toke. Earl extinguished the roach between his thumb and forefinger. If any vestige of fuel lingered in this monster receptacle, it could have ignited with a spark. *Poof.* They'd explode in one infernal blast.

"But I don't smell oil," Rosie said out loud, her voice having the quality of a round canyon.

"Shh," Earl said. "Only water. Don't worry. Don't talk."

Colors swirled in the blackness, like those in pools of oil, glossy lavenders, pinks with sheen. Earl shifted. Something snapped, metal on plastic, his guitar case. What if it was full of drugs he'd smuggled into McMurdo? What if he wanted her to help with his pharmaceutical business?

Rosie stood up to go. Or thought she had. But then realized that her behind was still planted on the tank floor. She was very high.

The first low note sent out long shallow waves of vibration, gave new meaning to the word acoustics.

"Oh, my," Rosie said.

Earl tuned another string, listened to the last four, and then played a classical riff. Here inside the holding tank, it was as if each note of the song were a dancer moving through inky darkness. She heard some of the notes far above her head, others bounced off the metal cylinder, and a few pierced her like darts. Then she heard all the notes at once, and it was as if Earl had taken the lid off a pot of fairies. Surely all of McMurdo could hear the classical guitar music coming from the drum on the hill.

"Oh, my," she said again and then traveled deep into the moment. There was nothing but cold metal, black space, and the vibrations of guitar strings spinning round and round the interior of the fuel tank. With relief, Rosie let the music draw her away from thoughts of Larry. The tank was like a black hole and she spun deeper and deeper into Earl's world. Swallowed, gone.

Too soon, Earl said, "I can only play for a couple of minutes before I have to warm my hands." He set the guitar in its case and shoved his hands into his pockets. "Yesterday I played for too long. I thought I'd frozen my fingers for good."

"I didn't know—" she started to say, and he guffawed, recognizing the end of her sentence. That he knew classical music. That he was capable of such tender beauty. It made her want to touch him.

Earl said, "So, like, when you found that dead girl, were her eyes open? What about her hands? Clenched or relaxed?"

So he was going to talk about that after all. "She looked like she was asleep."

"Did you like gag or what?"

Rosie shook her head, though Earl couldn't see her.

"Do you think it could've been suicide maybe?"

Rosie sighed. "Why would you go to all the trouble of getting a job in Antarctica and then kill yourself here?"

"Because it'd be easy. A few minutes in a storm and poof, you're gone. She had a good death."

"She was probably terrified. She probably had a horrific death."

"You don't know. She might have been totally at peace."

That's exactly what she'd seen when she discovered the frozen girl, that the line between terror and peace, as well as the one between life and death, was mathematically thin, existed only in theory.

To change the subject, Rosie said, "It's like a black hole in here."

"Are you saying it sucks?"

"Don't laugh so loud. We'll get caught. No, I mean it's like we could time travel in here."

"Smoke much dope?"

"No."

"Didn't think so." He rubbed his hands together hard and then lit another joint. Inhaling, he asked, "So everyone here seems to have a plan for their Ice money. What's yours?"

Loneliness engulfed Rosie again, but she resisted the urge to lean against Earl. Instead, she pressed her back against the steel wall.

Earl said, "I'm gonna travel, but in style, until it runs out. You know, no youth hostels or early bird specials. Real hotels. And pretty women. I'm going to take pretty women out to dinner."

"Maybe I'll find a home." The word home conjured Larry, that clear gaze of his, the way his tall body looked like rest.

Earl tapped the heels of his boots together and spoke in a falsetto. "There's no place like home. There's no place like home."

"Fuck you. Just wait. People like you are always looking for places to crash. You'll be begging for a night on my couch."

"Don't know where I'll be next year. I like to live in the moment."

"What if the moment sucks?"

Earl laughed too loudly again. "Like a black hole?"

"Moments can be like that sometimes."

"Deep."

She was too high, and too lonely, to endure being mocked. She stood up to go. It was pitch black, but if she walked forward, surely she'd find the ladder. After a few steps she'd come to nothing. She took a few more steps and still found only black space. Was she inadvertently walking in a circle?

"Earl?"

No answer. Why'd she smoke marijuana?

"Earl!"

Nothing. A pure vacuum. "Earl. Answer me."

A few beats later he spoke in a quiet bass. "I'm here." His voice seemed to swirl around the interior of the cistern.

"Where's here?"

"Ah. That's the question, isn't it?"

"Cut it out. Look, I'm not a philosophical dope smoker. I'm the visceral kind. I like food and sex when I'm high." Did she really say that?

He said, "Then let's go to mid-rats."

Had he just rejected her? She said, "One more tune."

"You like guitar?"

"My dad used to play."

"He doesn't anymore?"

"I don't know. He probably still plays. Badly, though. He was never any good."

"What kind of music?"

"He's a Dead Head."

Earl laughed. "Okay. You want some Dead?"

"No. Something sweeter."

"Okay. This is for you." When he started playing "Somewhere Over the Rainbow" she knew he was making fun of her. She sang anyway. She thought she heard his surprise in the way his hand faltered on the strings, a slight knock on the box of the guitar where his knuckles slipped, but he didn't say anything. In fact, he played more softly, following her voice.

She was high, but who cared? Her voice warmed the iced air, billowed to fill the space, and though she knew he'd never stop teasing her for impersonating Judy Garland, the acoustics in this place were like a narcotic and she couldn't stop. It felt too good letting her voice fill the void. The music counterbalanced Earl's craziness, that wild energy that drew her.

"You can sing," Earl said after the first verse when he stopped to warm his hands.

"I like to sing sometimes. Let's go get something to eat."

"You said you liked food *and* sex when you're high."

Match to dry kindling. What the hell. Rosie knelt down and kissed him, his mouth and tongue so much rougher than his guitar-strumming fingers, but she could still feel the song in her throat and she let that move her. He wrapped his arms around her, too hard, and pulled her onto the floor. She threw a leg around him, wanting to disappear in this black container, into his woodsy kisses. Too much tree bark, too much resin, but they were like medicine. A remedy to make her forget those true sky kisses of Larry's.

"If we take off our clothes here, we'll die," Earl said and laughed.

Maybe dying of hypothermia while fucking in a fuel tank wasn't such a bad way to go. Sex and death. She was about to suggest it when Earl pulled away from her. "My roommate might be out," he said.

Rosie climbed first. She could hear Earl's boots coming up on the rungs below her. When they reached the ground on the other side, Earl whooped and held up a hand for a high five. He said, "I'm starving. Let's go to mid-rats."

"Okay," Rosie said hesitantly, feeling a mix of disappointment and relief.

Walking down the hill with Earl reminded her of sitting next to him during their flight to the Ice. His laughter and delight in their near-death experience. Flight and danger. Danger and flight. Maybe the crash landing was a message, a strong message for a girl who needed her information in a big whopping dose. She remembered the series of hard shocks the crash had sent through her body. The screams of other passengers. The ice under her boots as she stepped off the burning plane. Landing. Earth. That's what she needed.

In the galley, she helped herself to two pieces of pizza and made a sundae with strawberry frozen dessert and marshmallow cream. Earl heaped a plate with beef stew and hovered in indecision over the tray of pastries. If she hadn't had the marijuana-induced afterthought of going back to toss a scoop of crushed pineapple on her sundae, she would have entered the dining hall ahead of Earl. She would have steered him away from the big round table where the remnants of Pamela's party quietly conversed.

Earl dropped his tray on the table and yanked out a chair. "Howdy," he nearly hollered. He undid the leather strap holding back his long brown straggles, shook his head, and retied the strap.

Rosie pulled out the last chair at the table, next to Larry, and sat. He turned slowly and looked at her.

"What?" she said, too familiarly, as if they were simply continuing a previous conversation.

Karen, who sat directly across the table from her, didn't even say hello. She just sat there, so calm, with her lovely blond hair pulled back in a loose ponytail. A few stray locks fell to the sides of her face, in a perfect display of casual.

"Soooo," Pamela said in a tone intended to convey that she knew exactly what was going on and would come to the table's rescue. She winked at Rosie. "Who's your friend?"

"Earl," Rosie said, waving a hand in his direction. God, she wished she wasn't so high. Pamela's long bouncy curls looked serpentine and her mouth like a sticky red candy. Earl looked like a picture of Early Man in an illustration of human evolution.

Earl said, "What up, everybody?" and dug into his beef stew.

Rosie longed to look at Larry. Instead, she made herself look across the table at Karen, who held half a green apple in her left hand and a paring knife in her right. Carefully, she cut the core out of the apple and then sliced it into wedges. Rosie waited, wanting to see the woman place something, anything, in her mouth, but Karen laid the wedges on her plate and wiped her fingers on a napkin.

"You should dip those apple slices in the hot caramel they have by the frozen dessert machine," Rosie said. "It's really good."

A bit of color rose on Karen's cheeks, but she didn't respond. Nor did she eat an apple wedge.

When Larry's knee brushed hers, Rosie felt her entire body respond. She wanted to crawl onto his chest, wrap her legs around his. This desire felt so much more authentic, an organically essential part of her life, than the escapist kind she'd briefly felt with Earl.

No one had spoken since her comment about the caramel, as if she'd said something explicitly erotic. Had she? Rosie knew she should just not talk. She was too high to trust herself. Still, she pressed on, turning to Pamela and saying, "I'm sorry I missed your party tonight."

Pamela laughed too frothily and looked knowingly at Earl.

Larry's gaze followed Pamela's. Then he turned to Rosie with an expression of pained curiosity. He immediately lowered his lovely long lashes.

"Good story," she said to him, meaning his follow-up article about the plane crash and the dead girl that had appeared in the *Antarctic Sun* this morning. She knew that she'd brought up this taxing topic of conversation, her least favorite, only because she wanted to cover up the even less agreeable subject of her apparent connection to Earl.

Larry nodded slowly and held her gaze for a moment. Rosie allowed her knee to graze his again.

Earl, the only one at the table who didn't feel tension, was tapping the butt of his knife on the table in some private rhythm. He dropped the knife on his tray with a clatter and said, "Man, I'm stuffed. Gotta hit the sack." He stood, pushed in his chair, and looked at Rosie. "Rain check?"

Earl swaggered off. Pamela raised her eyebrows and pretended to be suppressing a smile. Karen did suppress a smile. Larry sat perfectly still beside Rosie, wondering.

19

Mikala stood at the exact geographic South Pole. A simple stake marked the spot. It had to be moved a few yards every year due to the shifting ice sheet. A sign, quoting the journals of the two men who had raced to be the first to stand in this place, announced the results of their competition. Roald Amundsen had won, and on December 14, 1911, he wrote, "So we arrived and were able to plant our flag at the geographic South Pole." A devastated Robert Falcon Scott got there three weeks later, on January 7, 1912, and he wrote, "The Pole, yes, but under very different circumstances from those expected."

Now, nearly a hundred years later, Marcus Wright had come to plant not a flag but a telescope. Mikala had come to write music.

The pursuits of humankind had evolved, maybe, but not the place. It was still a godforsaken frozen desert. Other than a small jumble of buildings, there was nothing for hundreds of miles but a field of ice topped by a field of sky.

And endless silence. The awful kind of silence that accentuated noise. The syncopation of hammering. The hushed roar of generators. The searing mock violins of power tools. An underlay of that free South Pole wind, so liberated by space that it flowed by in silky sheets, making a sound too thin to be called a whisper.

Now, insinuating itself into the cacophony came the grinding, soon to be bludgeoning, engine of the LC-130. A moment later, Mikala saw the day's plane coming as a speck into the field of blue sky. The speck became a winged being, then a hard gray thing. And finally, its red fins sliced the sky like some kind of aerial fish.

An orchestra might express the plane's approach with growling tubas and an atonal harp. But why would she compose that? Music should transcend mere expression. It needed to be beautiful. Nothing about that approaching plane was beautiful. It filled Mikala with a cold fear. She knew that the crash landing of her first flight had been an aberration, a highly unusual event, but she still expected to see every plane break on the packed snow runway and burst into flames. She didn't want her music to convey fear or devastation. She'd already written *The Sarah Songs,* her sonatas on grief, and she wanted to be done with that topic, too.

So why had she thrown herself into this new vortex? The proximity of her father induced a kind of riotous confusion that merited nothing musical whatsoever. Coming to this place had been a vast miscalculation on her part. Days had passed and she hadn't written a single note.

Jeffrey, who did photorealistic paintings, did not have her problem. His project, called "Extreme Machine," was already signed with a gallery in New York, with the exhibit scheduled for the fall. He was, at this very moment, out on the runway snapping pictures of the Air Force plane as it skied to a stop on the ice runway. He had been producing nearly a painting a day, setting his alarm for all hours to capture images in perfect light and then holing himself up to paint from the photographs. After sketching and laying down the first layer of color, he again visited "the living site of his subject," as he called it, and corrected for true light. The acuteness of his discipline, his stellar work ethic, was matched only by the intensity of his depression.

Mikala watched him hopping from location to location, shooting dozens of pictures, hoping to get the harshest light, the sharpest angles, the dullest colors. He flopped onto his belly to shoot up from the ground. Now he was running—running!—as if he could beat an Air Force plane to the end of the runway. He gave up, slowed, slumped. Mikala watched him hit his forehead with the heel of his hand, imagined the muffled thump of that self-abuse.

She thought Jeffrey should be a choreographer for how expressively his body moved, except that there was no joy. Someone should put the guy on antidepressants.

Mikala sighed. Who was she to talk? She began walking back toward the dome. She would get a plate of food for supper, so she could eat alone, and then, she promised herself, she'd write a bar of music, just one bar, an achievable goal.

In the galley she found a pan of leftover lasagna and cut herself a square. She carried the covered plate to her cubicle in the Hypertat. Mikala stretched out on the bed and let her mind drift, trying to think about the one bar of music she would soon compose in the Sky Lab. One bar, one bar, one bar, she repeated as a mantra until she fell into an oblivious sleep.

When she awoke, she ate the cold lasagna, though it was only four o'clock, and dressed for the trek back to the Sky Lab and her waiting keyboard. As she entered the station, she realized that the daily sitting meditation would start in a couple of minutes. Going to that would only delay her for half an hour, and anyway, it would be the perfect preparation for concentrating on work. Mikala was the first to arrive in the tiny gym that was equipped with a basketball hoop, a volleyball net, and a few free weights. She unfurled a yoga mat and began stretching.

Jeffrey came in with the station chef. Betty had been working on the Ice for twenty-three years, having put in time cooking at all three American stations. At fifty-three, she was like a stick of dynamite that had long blown its explosive power. What was left was an incredibly strong and compact body, bright cinnamon eyes, and a fearless verbal capacity.

"For crying out loud, crushes are fun! *Enjoy* it," Betty exulted.

"They aren't fun with extenuating circumstances," Jeffrey whined, banging his forehead with the butt of his hand. *Thamp!*

"Ah, the little complication of your marriage. Hey, Mikala. How's it going?" Betty asked. "Your work going well?"

"It's okay."

"Making music," Betty sang, doing a little dance step on the wooden floor with a pretend partner. "When do we get to hear the work-in-progress?"

"As soon as it progresses. I wish I had Jeffrey's discipline."

"Discipline," Jeffrey echoed. "It's all I have. If you don't have talent, you have to work." He shrugged apologetically.

Betty widened her eyes at Mikala and shrugged.

"You know what, though?" Jeffrey said, perking up. "I've been having all these insights about my work. Painting is like the most elemental way possible for a human being to interact with the world. I've been thinking about how everything deconstructs down to lines and color."

Betty nodded at the clock. "I don't think anyone else is coming. Jeffrey, you lead us."

"Me?"

Betty gave Mikala another exasperated look.

"Okay, okay," he said. "I don't really have anything to say though."

"That's fine. This is a meditation not a lecture. Just give us a start."

"Okay. I suggest we each choose one line to meditate on."

"Too intellectual for me," Betty said. "I'm meditating on my bellybutton." She closed her eyes.

Mikala closed hers, too. The South Pole ought to be the easiest place on earth to meditate. A landscape couldn't be more uniform. The endless sky attached to the sea of ice by an invisible line. That's it: sky, line, ice. But the line that divided the sky and ice wasn't an actual line, it didn't take up space like a strand of Jeffrey's paint. How could she concentrate on something that didn't exist? But then again, Sarah no longer existed and she thought about her constantly. She was like the line between Mikala herself and the rest of the world. Irrevocably a part of herself and yet a border she had to cross each time she wanted to get beyond herself. A kind of impermeable skin. Truthfully, in real life, near the end, Sarah had been more like a barrier. There was nowhere, geographically speaking, they both wanted to be. All those fights they'd had in the last few years about where to live.

How about the South Pole? Mikala suppressed an out-loud laugh. She bet Sarah would have liked it here. In many ways it was so like Redwood Grove with its small, interdependent community living in isolation. But here the community was made up of edgy eccentrics, many of them loners, rather than folksy communal hippies. Here the highest levels of technological sophistication reigned, while at Redwood Grove technology was scorned. On new moon nights, Mikala and Andy would sit outside for hours looking at the stars. Here, Marcus used a massive telescope to look *through* the stars back to the beginning of the universe.

Mikala realized with a start how much she was awed by her father's extraordinarily long-distance vision. She realized, too, that she'd have never come to Antarctica if Sarah were still alive. It occurred to her that she had slid right out of that impermeable skin that had been Sarah. She had come to this place she couldn't recognize, where there were no tethers whatsoever, where everything meaningful had to be discovered anew.

For someone who had been raised on meditation, had been doing it literally in the womb, Mikala was not very good at it. It was painful sitting here with the void. She tried to focus on the idea of line, but that was just another kind of infinity. Finally, she let herself sink into the memory of Rosie humming *Te Deum*.

Someone else was restless. She heard shuffling. Then the sound of sneakers meeting the wood floor. She opened her eyes to see Jeffrey easing his thin body up from his meditation position, moving like a cat, slowly and gracefully. He crept toward the door of the gym. Mikala glanced at the wall clock. They'd only been meditating for twelve minutes.

"Hold it right there, buster."

Jeffrey winced at Betty's voice.

"That's right, this is the Buddha speaking. Who said you could sneak out of meditation?" Betty spoke from her crossed-leg position, pooching her belly out to better imitate Buddha.

"I can't tonight. I just can't. I'm really sorry to interrupt the two of you. My knees hurt too much."

"Ah, you're just stuck on the lady carpenter."

"That's part of it."

"I have an idea. Wait. Are we disturbing you, Mikala?"

"No."

"Let's take a bottle of wine out to Hotel South Pole, aka The Love Shack."

"*Now?*" Jeffrey asked.

"No, check your calendar. I'm free on the twenty-eighth. You?"

"I just meant that it's almost suppertime."

"I already ate," Mikala said.

"Good girl. Look, I'm off tonight and I feel like having an adventure. I'll stop by the kitchen—I should anyway to make sure those food anarchists who are supposed to be working for me haven't staged a complete coup—and grab some food. Mikala, you get a radio and check us out of the station. We'll all meet at the dome entrance in thirty minutes."

"I should work," Mikala said.

"Come on," Betty said. "Don't leave me alone with Jeffrey." She winked at him. "The solstice is near. All good pagans should celebrate."

"It's only December second," Jeffrey said.

"Yeah, right. That makes the solstice just three weeks off."

Mikala liked the pronounced smile lines around Betty's eyes. She also liked the way her short, hennaed hair, with half an inch of gray roots, was always hat-mashed. An evening hanging out with her might loosen up Mikala's chops.

A half an hour later, as the three began walking away from South Pole Station, Jeffrey asked, "Is this a good idea? I mean, how far away is this place? Is it safe?"

"Yes, it's a good idea. The place is awesome. It's not far, maybe a mile. And yes, it's safe. That's the whole point. Some folks built it a few years ago as a retreat. A place to go when you need a little space."

"Ha!" Mikala laughed. The idea of a retreat from the most remote place on the planet was a bit absurd.

"You laugh just like Marcus Wright," Jeffrey observed yet again. He turned to Betty, "Is the hotel warm?"

"Relax. God, you're a worrywart."

"I know." A big sigh.

"So what'd you paint today?" Betty elbowed Mikala gently, like Jeffrey was a toy they could play with together.

"I'm working on a series of the LC-130. Right now, close-ups. Like the fin and nose and tail. I have a really cool one straight down the spine, the wings cut out of the frame, so all you see is this steel gray bullet shape. It's very lethal looking."

Mikala stopped for a moment and looked back at the station, which from this distance was no more than a thin disturbance on the horizon with a glint marking the silver dome. Another few yards and it would no longer be visible at all. They were dressed in multiple layers of clothing and each carried a pack full of survival gear. Still, Jeffrey was right. They should be frightened leaving the safety of the station.

"People are *obsessed* by machines," Jeffrey nattered on. "They dominate our lives. *Totally.*"

Mikala said, "Maybe I should write a piece to accompany 'Extreme Machine.'" She heard growling horns, sheering strings, rhythmic turbines. "It could play at your opening."

"Oh, I don't know."

"It was a joke," Mikala said, annoyed by his territorialism. "But seriously, Jeffrey, machines have little to do with being human. Look where we are now, entirely out of their domain."

She wanted to say, out here there is no mediation between the living and the dead. Sarah, dying of lymphoma, with the help of a full arsenal of machines, had taken days of painful struggle to cross the line. That girl from the plane no doubt slipped effortlessly from alive to dead in a matter of moments. The hush of the sled runners carrying her away.

"Just the opposite," Jeffrey argued. "Nowhere on earth is our dependence on machines more obvious. You'd freeze to death without the generators. You'd be stuck here for life without the planes. You couldn't even eat without Betty's stove." He paused. "That's a good idea. I'd like to paint your stove."

"I think you're missing something here," Mikala said.

"And that would be?"

It was the same thing she was missing. At least she was looking. "The beauty."

"I don't do beauty. Art is about truth, not beauty. They did beauty a couple of centuries ago."

"Ugly has been done, too."

"True. But doing ugly *well* is another thing. What interests me most here at the Pole is the absence of color, the shades of gray and white. And the way I feel assaulted by the color that *does* exist."

"Assaulted?" Betty asked, nudging Mikala with her elbow again.

"Yeah, like the Hypertats. They're such a blue-blue. It's not sky-blue. It's not midnight-blue. It's not robin's egg-blue. It's the essence of blue itself. I mean, it's impossible to deny or compromise its blueness. It's *obscenely* blue. *Plastic* blue. To me, that's fascinating. The way color invades our space."

Betty said, "It's bad form to criticize shelter in this environment. I like the Hypertats. They have a pleasing shape. The blue is rather jolly."

"The Hypertats are like creatures!" Jeffrey was thrilled by his own ideas. "With those arching ribs holding together the blue skin. Supposedly there's no life at the Pole, but there are these manmade *Hypertat* creatures. And then when you consider that at night they're filled with breathing humans, sleeping breathing humans, then it becomes incredibly potent. So how do I paint that? The aliveness of a polar hut? It's all in the blue. That blue just kills me. Against the deadness of white."

"Okay, fine," Betty said, as if she were still more interested in her bellybutton than his artistic notions. "Look." She raised a mitten.

Mikala saw a black dot on the horizon. As they approached, the dot grew into a dark box. The plywood structure, about eight feet square, was painted black and wrapped in plastic to absorb the sun's warmth.

Mikala knew the place wasn't an actual hotel, but she had expected something a bit grander. At least cheerier. From the outside, Hotel South Pole loomed like a large, crude coffin.

Betty mimed a hotel doorman as she opened the door and bent at the waist in a sweeping bow. Warmth enveloped Mikala the second she stepped inside. The black paint and plastic wrap did an amazingly good job at trapping heat from the constant sunlight. The shack was equipped with a metal-framed cot, a small table and chair, and a Coleman stove. There was one window at the foot of the bed. The space under the table was stuffed with emergency provisions, including tea, canned soups, packets of nuts, and dried fruit. A retreat? Hotel South Pole was more like a spot of survival on the harsh polar plateau.

Mikala pulled off her hat, neck gaiter, jacket, and fleece sweater and tossed these in a corner of the hut.

"What if a storm comes up?" Jeffrey asked. "We wouldn't be able to see the track back."

"Open the wine," Betty said, throwing herself onto the bed. She drew up her feet and motioned for Mikala to share the mattress. Jeffrey sat in the straight-backed chair and uncorked the wine.

"We could even stay the night," Betty said.

"And sleep where?" Jeffrey frowned.

"I guess you're right. The cot is a bit small for three."

Jeffrey found some chipped ceramic mugs and poured each nearly to the brim.

"To meditation," Betty said.

Mikala took a mouthful. The red wine tasked sour and old, like it wasn't of high enough quality to be aged but had been anyway. She took another bracing gulp and it tasted better. She leaned back against the plywood wall behind the bed.

"Mind if I put my feet in your lap?" Betty asked.

"No problem."

"She's so pretty," Jeffrey sighed and looked sorrowfully at his own feet. With his pale skin and black hair, feet crossed delicately at the ankles, he could be a male Madonna.

"Who?" Mikala asked.

"That new carpenter. The one they just flew in last week."

"He likes her," Betty said.

"You haven't mentioned her to me."

"Yeah, well. What's the point?"

"The point is," Betty said, "that you find her attractive."

"Understatement." Another long sigh.

"So have an affair. You're at the South Pole, for crying out loud. If all bets are ever off, it would be here."

Jeffrey gave her one of his long-suffering looks. "I'm married."

"Yes, you've explained this to me already. But you're also: one, unhappy; two, at the South Pole; and three, entranced by a comely carpenter. Have her!"

"We have a two-year-old."

"Trust me. If you do it right—and I'd be happy to counsel you on this—the two-year-old will never know. Neither will the wife."

"Annie."

"Ah, yes, let's grace her with a name before we fuck another woman."

Jeffrey smiled, enjoying the attention. "What about you?" he asked, nodding at Mikala.

"What *about* me?"

"You must have a crush on someone here."

Over the past couple of weeks, Mikala had tried over and over again to reconstruct the visuals of what she had mainly only heard. Lying between the deflated membrane of the tent and listening to the snow stakes being pounded in. She could imagine that big beautiful girl, legs spread and mallet raised. The *poof* sounds as the tent poles were bent and the cavity formed. The *shhh* of sleeping pads being inflated. Even as the wind screamed, Rosie had put together a nest. The rustle of taffeta. The puff of warm goose down. The melody of *Te Deum*. A tiny current of music in the heart of the storm.

Survival isn't love, though, is it? Rosie had called their experience surreal. Not real. Beyond real. But to Mikala, the sound of that clear voice, the picture of that wild smile, the memory of that full-body warmth lying next to her, were all too real.

She closed her eyes and shook her head.

Jeffrey read her response as pain. He softened his voice, too much. "Your partner died, what, three years ago?"

"Really?" Betty asked.

"Yeah."

There was that awkward death silence. Then Jeffrey nudged, "So you haven't seen anyone since then?"

"Nope."

"That's a long time." Betty took another gulp of wine.

Mikala shrugged, glad to be back on familiar ground. "I just haven't felt like it."

"Too bad. It'd be easy for *you*," Jeffrey said.

"Meaning?"

"You know the joke. About dating in Antarctica."

Mikala shook her head.

Betty rolled her eyes, but went ahead and deadpanned the setup question. "How do you get a woman in Antarctica?"

Jeffrey waited, his eyes feigning innocence in his pale and bony face.

"I give up."

"Be one!" he crowed.

"Funny."

"It's a joke. But there *are* a lot of lesbians here. Fact."

"Let me at 'em," Mikala said in her own deadpan.

Betty hooted.

Jeffrey groaned. "How do women stay so, I don't know, satisfied?"

"Women just stay quieter," Betty said. "I hesitate to say this to you, but you don't know, Annie just might be taking this opportunity to have herself a dalliance."

"Never. Not my wife."

"Having had many dalliances with married, or otherwise committed, people in my life, I'm here to tell you that it's those you'd least expect who are having the most fun. Good girls—or good boys, for that matter, look at yourself—get the most thrill out of transgressions." Jeffrey shook his head. "I'm serious. It's the best cover, the good girl cover or sincere guy cover."

"Trust me. Annie is home with Ben every second. She's devoted to both of us. Like, totally. It's suffocating sometimes."

"Another dad at Ben's daycare? A neighbor? Someone in her yoga class? Someone she met at Lamaze? Right under your nose. I'm telling you, Jeffrey, you might not know anything about the woman you married. A surprising number of people don't. I've been the other woman enough times and I've seen that to be the case more often than you'd like to think. People save their darkest secrets for someone they don't have to live with."

"I'm sure you know what you're talking about. But not Annie. Look, I'm an *artist*, Betty. I see hidden stuff."

"Drink more wine," Betty said, getting the bottle and refilling all their mugs. She put on an exaggerated poker-face. "Tell us about the hidden stuff you see."

"You're patronizing me." Jeffrey cocked a defensive elbow on the back of his chair.

"No, I'm not. I'm truly interested."

"Betty wants entertainment. Why don't you tell her your real name, Mikala."

Mikala laughed. "I'm the designated clown? At your entertaining service!"

"It's not Mikala Wilbo?"

"My legal name is Mikala Moonshine Williams-Borowitz."

Jeffrey snorted.

"You're lying," Betty said.

"Nope."

Betty sat up straight. "Look. I'm from Indiana. No one there, and I mean no one, not even in the sixties or seventies, would have named their kid that. Are you serious?"

"Very."

"At least it's just her middle name," Jeffrey said. "The Moonshine part."

"Your parents are hippies?"

"It gets worse." Mikala finished her wine and Jeffrey uncorked the second bottle. She waited for him to pour before continuing.

"We're waiting!" Betty yelped, beating her feet on the tops of Mikala's thighs. "Tell me what's 'worse.' I'm sorry, Jeffrey, but this *is* more interesting than your 'hidden stuff.'"

"Fuck you."

"Maybe after Mikala's story. Go on, honey."

"I was born on a commune."

"She was," Jeffrey verified, as if he'd been there, as if he had known this for years, rather than been told himself a couple of weeks ago.

"More!" Betty clapped her hands. "You're so straightforward. I mean, you don't use hippie language or anything. It's hard to picture you that way."

"Well, for the last fifteen years I've been living mostly in New York and San Francisco."

"It's still functioning? The commune?"

"Only five people live there now."

"Like aging hippies?"

"Yep."

"That's insane. That's so totally insane. Did you like it? Growing up that way?"

"I loved it. But Sarah hated it."

"Who's Sarah?"

"Her partner," Jeffrey said.

"The dead one?"

Mikala smiled, liking the matter-of-fact way Betty could say that, realizing maybe for the first time that it was just that, a fact. Sarah was dead.

"That's so hard," Jeffrey said solemnly, shaking his head slowly, gazing at his wine. Mikala almost laughed at his dramatic display.

"How long were you together?" Betty asked.

"That depends on what you count. A couple of decades."

"Wait. You're how old?"

"Thirty-five. We grew up together."

"No way."

"Yep."

"On the commune?"

"I'm afraid so."

Betty clapped her hands and laughed.

"When I was born, there were eighteen adults and a whole bunch of kids living at Redwood Grove. Sarah and I were insepa-rable from the age of eight."

"And you're thirty-five, so . . . ?"

"So if you count from when we were eight, we were together twenty-four years. When we were fifteen, we decided we wanted to be together for life, so Redwood Grove had a commitment cer-emony for us."

"No way."

"I don't think I could make it up."

"When did you leave the commune?"

"Sarah and I left together when we went to college."

"You went to college together?"

"Oh, yeah. Definitely."

"Unbelievable."

"I know. The thing is, she hated it there. My childhood memo-ries are full of the cool shade of the redwoods, warm summer days with my feet in the creek, everyone telling stories in the longhouse on winter nights. *Her* memories are all about dirty old hippie men feeling her up under the cover of being loving, adults who smoked too much homegrown pot and drank too much blackberry rot-gut, how cold she was on those long winter days when the solar panels didn't generate any heat. She talked about getting away from about the age of twelve on. I tried to protect her, keep her happy. I never really could, though."

"Why'd you stay together?" Betty asked.

"I loved her." Her fierce temper and razor-sharp wit. Her winsome face. A soul like a willow, luminescent and bendable. The way she floated through life on impatience, an impatience so intense Mikala sometimes thought she willed her own early death.

Jeffrey scowled into his mug before asking, "So do you ever feel like you have this other chance now?"

"What do you mean?"

"Like a whole new life. You can do whatever you want. You don't have any ties."

"The upside to your partner dying," Betty observed.

Mikala laughed.

"No, I'm just saying," Jeffrey persisted. "So many of us . . . make choices. You know, before we're ready to make them."

"You said you married Annie when you were twenty-six," Betty said.

"That's young," he said desperately. "And fifteen is *really* young. So I'm just asking."

"Sometimes I do feel that way," Mikala said. "About having another chance. I don't think Sarah and I would have lasted much longer. We were having really big conflicts by the time she got sick. Neither of us had ever been with anyone else."

"So, like, in your life, she's the only person you've ever had *sex* with?"

"You're drunk," Jeffrey told Betty.

"Like you're not. She doesn't have to answer."

"It's true. I've never been with anyone but Sarah."

"Get out."

Mikala smiled.

"No, seriously. Tell me that's not the truth." Mikala shrugged. "So you, what, spend all your time composing music?"

"Sort of. Why? Do you spend all your time having sex?"

"Sort of."

"It probably takes a while," Jeffrey said, too sympathetically, "after your partner dies, to even want to have sex."

"Three *years*?"

"I met this woman on my flight over."

"What happened?" Betty's lively expression begged for intrigue.

Our plane crashed. She sheltered me. She fed me. She comforted me. We almost died together. "Nothing happened. I don't know why I mentioned her."

"Because you like her," Betty prompted.

She's beautiful. And sturdy. Maybe fierce. "I guess so. But she seems sort of like a cowgirl type."

"Oh, I *love* cowgirls. And cowboys."

"Yeah, well, I think she likes cowboys, too. Probably exclusively. She was sort of with this guy at a party the next night."

"What do you mean 'sort of with'?"

"Nothing. Never mind." Why did she bring this up with prurient Betty?

Jeffrey said, "She's in McMurdo?"

Mikala nodded.

"You're going back to McMurdo for Icestock, right?"

"Yeah."

Betty's cinnamon eyes brightened. "There you go!"

Mikala waved off Betty's cheer. "Let's change the subject."

"Betty's pansexual," Jeffrey offered. "She doesn't understand shyness."

"I don't like labels," Betty said, "but practically speaking, that's true."

"She's had hundreds of lovers."

"As you could too, my boy, if only you'd leave off the self-pity." Betty stretched out, putting her feet back in Mikala's lap. She wiggled her toes. "Will you rub my feet?"

"Should I leave?" Jeffrey asked.

"Oh, you want to participate? You could do my shoulders."

"Fuck you."

"Nah," Betty said. "Tell us about your carpenter and we'll counsel you." She wiggled her toes at Mikala again.

Mikala pushed her thumb along the instep of Betty's left foot.

"She's so pretty," Jeffrey said. "She's real slender and her eyelashes are a foot long. I haven't even talked to her yet."

"Yet. So you *are* planning on it."

Mikala massaged between Betty's toes.

"Neither of you has a clue what marriage means."

"Excuse me? Didn't you hear Mikala tell us a few minutes ago that she was married for, what did you say, pretty much her whole life? You and Annie have been married for less than five years. That makes her the expert in this crowd."

Jeffrey opened his mouth but suppressed whatever argument he wanted to make.

"It's really not that different," Mikala said to help him out. "It really isn't. Everyone gets bored. Everyone struggles."

"Okay. So how did it work all those years? Didn't you want other people? Didn't you feel tied down? This is what I'm saying. It's different for women."

"Sarah felt tied down. Near the end of her life it got really bad because I was working so much and she thought my work was a yoke. Then, when she got sick, we had to leave New York and go home where we could get help from my parents. She hated dying at Redwood Grove. But we really didn't have a choice."

"Geez," Jeffrey said. "What if my wife got seriously ill?"

"Christ, boy," Betty said, "you are so self-obsessed."

"We're talking about marriage, aren't we? And what can happen? So that's what happened to Mikala. Why can't I apply it to my own situation?"

"It's very honest," Mikala said. "It's what anyone would be thinking. Most people just wouldn't say it out loud."

"Annie is very healthy," Jeffrey concluded. After another moment's thought, he added, "And I love her."

Betty rolled her eyes. "For the sake of our enjoyment the rest of the season, I hope Jeffrey gets laid. Otherwise, no more meditation on red wine with him."

"Okay," Jeffrey said. "Who's the most exciting person you've ever slept with?"

Betty's big laugh rolled out again. "I find brains sexy."

"So?"

"Years ago, before he married Margie, I had a one-nighter with Marcus Wright."

"No way!" Jeffrey squealed.

"Yeah. He's not, like, that physically attractive. But he'd gotten a MacArthur that year. Ha! I tried to convince him to not use birth control. So I could have a chance at a genius baby."

Mikala pushed Betty's feet off her lap. She thought she might throw up. The words pounded in her ears. *One-nighter. No birth control. Not physically attractive. Genius baby.*

Betty sat up and straightened her spine. "Shit. I'm drunk. I know better than to talk about who I've slept with."

"No problem," Jeffrey said and he made a zipping motion with his fingers across his lips. "Your secret is safe."

"It better be."

"He's an asshole, anyway," Mikala said with way too much passion.

"Marcus Wright? He's a total sweetheart. Everyone loves him. I shouldn't have talked about his business."

"I'm going back," Mikala said, getting up from the cot.

"What's wrong with you?" Betty asked. "You okay?"

"I'm fine. I'm going back."

"No. We're too drunk to walk back. With wind chill, it's pushing 50 below out there. We have to stay here tonight."

Jeffrey was already unfurling a sleeping bag. "Okay. Enough show and tell. I'm wiped out. I'm sleeping."

"Looks like we're sharing the bed," Betty said. She wiggled

under the scratchy wool blanket, keeping herself close against the wall. "Get in."

Mikala started collecting her gear. Anything but get into bed with a former lover of her father's.

Betty flapped the wool blanket. "Come on."

Mikala shoved one leg and then the other into her wind pants, pulled the suspenders over her shoulders.

"I'm very serious," Betty said. "You can't leave now."

"I'm going out to pee. I'll be right back." She took a long look at her pack of survival gear, but left it in the hut. The instant she stepped outside, she knew Betty was right. She couldn't go back on her own. She'd just walk a bit to clear away the picture of Marcus making a genius baby with Betty. So she paced toward the horizon, listening to the rhythmic crunch of her footsteps. The wind made a nearly imperceptible whistle. She needed to compose *some*thing and get off of this massive block of ice that passed as a continent. If only she were a modernist. She could throw together some environmental replicas, insert a lot of self-serving silence that she'd explain in her liner notes to make her sound profound, and she could call it a day. She could claim, like Jeffrey, that beauty in art was just accessible drivel.

Music. She ached for it.

Mikala sat down on the ice, cross-legged, and let the cold seize her. As if it could take the place of her grief. But, she realized all at once, even it, her grief, was gone. She'd lost it somewhere on the way here, flying across those continents, crash-landing on this one. As if it had exploded and gone up in flames with the plane. Or been extinguished with that girl's life. Sarah was gone. That enormous, blinding planet of grief was gone, too. Even its underpinnings, the lifelong absence of her father, had been removed. Marcus was about a mile away as she sat. A man many people loved. A man who looked through all the planets, all the stars, who saw the beginning of the universe. She felt even her contempt for him burn out and die. She was utterly alone.

"Mikala!"

The faraway voice sailed on a sheet of wind. Mikala held still and listened. "Mikala!" A clarinet in its buoyancy. She got up slowly and waved at Betty, the size of an ant, jumping up and down at the door of the hut, waving her arms.

"Come back!" Betty yelled. "Too far!"

Jeffrey appeared at her side. He called, too, his voice bellowing so much louder than Betty's. In spite of his litheness, he had a big voice box, one that produced trombone-like depth.

Mikala shook out her limbs. They still had feeling. She walked briskly back so that Betty and Jeffrey wouldn't have to stand outside for long.

Betty scolded, "You were barely visible. Which means that *we* were barely visible to you. If you'd lost sight of the hut, you wouldn't have had a clue which direction to go in to get back."

She had a point. It would be so easy to disappear here. To completely vanish.

"Get in bed," Betty ordered, getting back under the covers herself.

Mikala slowly stripped off everything but her long underwear and looked for a place on the floor. The sprawled Jeffrey left no option. So Mikala lay on her side, as close to the edge of the cot as she could get.

A few moments later, Betty said, "Oh shit. He snores." Then, "At least he's asleep."

Mikala felt a finger trace the outer rim of her ear. Betty whispered, "A composer's ears. A lot of magic must happen in here."

The bad red wine churned in Mikala's stomach. She couldn't hold still enough to pretend she was asleep. Betty's hand trailed down her neck, her spine, massaged her lower back. "You okay, honey?" Betty asked again as her hand slipped around to Mikala's hipbone.

Mikala held her breath. She felt as if her brain was swirling inside her skull. Betty's tenderness made her feel as if she might disintegrate on the spot. She had lived so long in her sorrow, without touch. But this touch was intolerable: Betty had slept with her father. She moved the hand away and scooted so that she was teetering on the edge of the cot. There she lay as still as she could while the hours went by. She didn't sleep.

At four in the morning, Betty sat up and announced that she had to be at work in an hour, and that they all had to walk back together for safety. Jeffrey, who'd thrown off the sleeping bag, wouldn't budge, even as Mikala stepped in the spaces between his legs and arms and torso to dress herself.

"He has to come," Betty said. "Take an arm."

The two women hauled him into a sitting position and still he slept. Betty stepped outside and made a snowball. She brought it back and held it to his face.

"Fuck. Shit." Jeffrey pushed her away. He got to his feet and Mikala handed him his clothing, piece by piece.

Then they all stepped out into the stunning cold and followed the track back to the station in silence. When they reached the entrance of the silver dome, Betty took hold of both sides of Mikala's head. She said, "Composer's ears" and kissed her on the mouth. Then she turned and trudged to her galley. Jeffrey said, "Coffee," and followed.

Mikala stood, once again only a few yards from the geographic South Pole, and watched them go. Then she walked over and read Robert Falcon Scott's words again. "The Pole, yes, but under very different circumstances from those expected."

She had read his journals. He'd said many other desperate and true things, including, "It has always been our ambition to get inside that white space, and now we are there the space can no longer be a blank."

He was right. She too was now inside that white space. It could no longer be a blank. Mikala closed her eyes and listened.

20

Rosie worked. Every day for three weeks without a break. She worked to avoid thinking about the way it felt to kiss Larry. She worked to forestall walking into the office of the *Antarctic Sun,* just down the hall from the galley. She worked to forget the look on his face, that night at mid-rats, as he considered the idea of her with Earl. She worked to steer clear of using Earl as a default, as a preventive measure.

Anyway, the way she felt about Larry was absurd. One plane crash. One walk. Two kisses.

It was just that he was so stable, so sure, so clear. His gray eyes, so serious and intent. His height and shaved head like an explanation mark of purpose. She'd been in flight her whole life. It'd taken a crash landing to ground her. And when she did slam into the earth, there he was, like home.

But of course he was someone else's home.

Since the walk and kiss, he'd hardly been in McMurdo at all. His job took him all over the continent, doing stories on the penguin colony at Cape Royds, on the climate studies at Byrd Camp, on the molten bowl of bubbling lava on the summit of Mount Erebus. A few times, when he'd been in town, they'd passed on the icy paths around McMurdo or met eyes across the galley during dinner, but they hadn't talked, and those times of not talking had been more potent than if they had talked. He avoided her, as he should. And she avoided him, as she should. Yet so little had happened between them that all this avoiding somehow heightened their connection.

Before the crash, she had vowed that this would be her last season on the Ice, that she would save as much money as she could, and that she would buy her land. Make home. With herself at the center. But finding that dead girl had yanked her out of herself, threatened to unleash all the longing she had been trying to harness.

Work would hold her to her vow. Only a couple more months.

Still, the enduring smells of melting lard, artificial maple flavoring, and fried onions became so oppressive she sometimes gagged. She burned herself on the grill, two times, once badly. Yet when Jonathan complained about needing a day off, she took his shift.

On the morning of the solstice, Rosie took her place behind the grill and wielded her whisk and spatula. After prepping the eggs and breakfast meats, she tossed on three big scoops of home fries. The cold potatoes hissed and spat as they hit the hot greasy steel.

"Rosie." Someone's hand on her shoulder startled her so much she dropped the spatula. She stooped to pick it up before looking to see that it was her boss.

Karen took the spatula out of her hand and tossed it into a dishwashing basin.

"You're not on today."

"I told Jonathan I'd work for him."

"You know that has to be arranged through me. Anyway, you need a day off." Karen touched Rosie's arm just above the bandage. "A burn?"

"No big deal."

"Did you go to Medical?"

"It's nothing."

"I called Jonathan and told him to come in."

Rosie picked up a fresh spatula.

"I mean it. You know . . ." Karen paused and considered. "The chaplain has been meeting with a lot of the folks on that flight. It might help."

"Working helps."

"Take your day off." Karen spoke as one might to a mental patient. The concern in her eyes was tempered by a clarity about boundaries.

Rosie nodded and stripped off her apron. Before leaving the building, she sat down at one of the computers in the hall. She rarely checked her email because there was always a line for the machines, but at this hour she was the only one signing in. There were two messages from Mikala Wilbo, that composer who'd shared her tent after the crash landing. Rosie smiled thinking of her, the way she'd looked so tough with her short dark hair, parted on the side, her bold eyebrows and defined jaw and cheekbones, but how frightened she'd been by everything, including the storm. She had not even been able to get near the dead girl, had stood several yards away, looking as if she might collapse. The first email just said hi and that she had arrived at the Pole. The second email said that she would be in McMurdo for Icestock and that maybe they could meet for a cup of coffee or have lunch together.

Rosie typed a quick note saying she would like that. Then she started deleting all the junk mail, until she came across a message from Larry. It gave her a start. His appearing in her email program was a bit wraithlike, disembodied communication.

He wrote that he'd been deployed to South Pole Station where he was doing a story on the new telescope. He chattered on at length, quite charmingly—after all, he was a writer—about his impressions of that southernmost post. Then, near the end, he wrote, "I know it's none of my business. But are you involved with that Earl guy? It kind of seemed like it in the galley a few weeks ago. 'Rain check?' Again, not my business. Just wondered."

Two hands covered Rosie's eyes and she heard a gurgly laugh that could only belong to Pamela.

"Don't," Rosie said, reaching up and grabbing hold of the two wrists. Pamela resisted the removal of her hands for another couple of seconds, like some kind of eight-year-old prankster.

"Ha!" Pamela said when Rosie finally freed her face. "How are ya, sweetie?"

Rosie clicked quickly out of Larry's message and closed down her email.

"Any good mail?" Pamela asked, peering over Rosie's shoulder at the screen.

"No." Rosie felt a wash of guilt about the email from Larry. The feeling made her be extra polite, even in her annoyance. "Nothing at all. How are you?"

"Fantabulistic!"

Rosie nodded.

"Let's have tea soon."

Rosie nodded again, and then found her voice. "Sure. That'd be great."

Pamela saw someone else in the hall she wanted to accost and flounced off. Rosie opened the email again and finished reading Larry's message. "I know we've been sidestepping each other. I'm sorry about what happened, up at the shrine. I was absolutely out of line. It's just that, I don't know, I felt such an immediate bond with you on our flight.

"Anyhow, on another note, Karen and I have decided to split. It just isn't working. I'll spare you the details. But when we leave the Ice, we'll be going our separate ways.

"That's all. I hope all is well with you. Write me, if you feel inclined.

"Yours, Larry."

Yours? Rosie clicked out of her email again, got up, and pushed in the chair. By now, several more of the computers were being used, though there wasn't a line yet. She hoped someone sat right down in her chair so she wouldn't be tempted to answer Larry's email. She left Building 155 and walked slowly up the hill to the mailroom.

"Merry Christmas, Rosie," Bea said cheerfully. "How's it going?"

"Fine. Great."

"Let me check." Bea began pawing through the bin that held letters for workers whose names began with M. She paused, backed up a few letters, and then went forward again. "Moore, right?" she called over her shoulder. Bea stuffed the letters back in the bin and without looking at Rosie moved slowly, as if her feet hurt, to the big crib holding the packages. One by one she lifted them, read the labels, and pushed them to the side. She finally returned to the window with a cookie wrapped in cellophane and tied with a red bow, Rosie's consolation prize. Bea winked and wished her happy holidays.

"Merry Christmas," Rosie told her and left the mailroom, nothing in her hands but the cellophane-wrapped cookie. It was silly to hope for a response from the letter she'd sent General Delivery to Newberg. The chances of it reaching anyone in her family were infinitesimal. As for other mail, even her far-flung acquaintances were too busy this time of year to drop her a line. She paused at the top of the hill, tore off the crinkly paper, and took a big bite of the cookie. She'd come here to flash-freeze her longings, to deprive them of nutrients. She'd hoped for air so cold it knifed away hunger. But it wasn't like that at all. Instead desire worked overtime, swelling to fill the frigid vastness.

"Fuck it," she said out loud and walked right back to Building 155. The same computer was still vacant and she sat down in the still-warm chair. She opened Larry's message and hit reply, and then typed, "Hell, no, I'm not with Earl. What do you think I am, crazy?" Then she tried to think of some words of condolence about his marriage, but she didn't feel sorry. She'd want to leave Karen, too, with her ramrod spine and frosty demeanor. So she just left it at that. She didn't type "yours" or "love" or even "cheers." Just "Rosie."

21|

Rosie regretted answering Larry's email the second she tapped the send button. There ought to be a delay of ten seconds—call it the remorse pause—so that a correspondent could retrieve a message. Email was way too fast, spontaneous, dangerous. It was high time to renew her vow of celibacy.

Of course writing an email wasn't exactly the same as having sex, now was it? Still, she'd announced her availability. She'd done so baldly. In reply to *his* declaration of *his* availability. But he *wasn't* available. He was still married, if unhappily. An unhappy marriage did not equal available.

Rosie stood in the cold, wide space in the center of town. She stretched out her arms and spun around, wanting to scream, to express *some*thing with her voice. Anything as civilized as singing seemed out of the question, given how crazy she felt. An entire day yawned before her. She could hunt down Pamela and get that cup of tea over with. No, she'd never be able to sit through it.

Rosie ran up to her room and stuffed a pack full of clothing, a water bottle, and energy bars. She plowed back out into the tumult of buildings and sky and snow and dirt, and started walking the road that passes Scott Base and goes on to Willy Field. A light snow fell, flurrying about in random swirls, like flocks of tiny white birds that couldn't make up their minds. Rosie laughed out loud. Each step of the six-mile walk felt like a step toward crazy. But she didn't care. At least they were steps away from Larry and his wife and the idea of home, an idea that would never materialize in her life. She'd embrace crazy. She'd accept her feral nature.

Earl, indeed.

When she arrived at the airstrip, she scanned the expanse until she located the blurry yellow shape of his bulldozer. It was lurching forward, scooping up snow, lurching backward, and then racing to dump its load on a berm a few yards away. Rosie walked slowly toward the dozer, waving her arms to be seen through the snow flurries. He sat at the gears, yanking them harder than he needed, his entire body an expression of carnality. There was relief in his rough tree bark honesty. She hauled herself up into the passenger seat and kissed him on his cheekbone. Earl grinned as he drove the monster machine back to the garage.

"Coffee time," he said jumping down from the dozer.

"Who gets to use these skidoos?" Rosie asked pointing to a small fleet of snowmobiles parked near the garage entrance.

Earl shrugged. "Dunno. Want to go for a ride?"

"Sort of, yeah."

"Coffee," he grunted.

They walked out the big mouth of the garage and headed for the galley until Earl stopped abruptly and said, "You look sad."

That planetary aspect to his eyes touched Rosie. But she said, "Me? Are you kidding?"

He crouched, wrapped both arms around her upper thighs, lifted her off the ground, and then turned in slow circles, his big boots stomping the snow. Rosie arched her spine, leaned back, and threw out her arms as he twirled her faster and faster. Her hat flew off her head. She yelled, "I'm not sad!"

Earl dumped her in the snow, retrieved her hat, and yanked it down over the crown of her head.

"Gentle!" she said.

At this mid-morning hour, the small galley that served the airstrip workers was empty. Earl dropped into a chair and thumbed a rhythm on the tabletop, nodding his head in time.

"What, I'm the waitress?" Rosie asked as she poured two cups of coffee and snagged a leftover cinnamon roll.

"Yeah, guess so," he said. "Thanks, *honey*."

"Fuck you."

Earl looked at the door and then his watch.

"Expecting someone?" Rosie joked.

He grunted.

"It's the solstice," she said.

"Yep."

"I have an idea. I think we should celebrate."

"Yeah?"

"Let's take a couple of those skidoos out to the plane." Travel to the heart of the matter.

Earl laughed. "You can't just *take* the skidoos."

Rosie laughed, too. "Why not?"

"Good point."

"Come on," she said, thinking of Karen's suggestion she see the chaplain. "It'll be *healing*. The *trauma* and all."

"You know. There just might be a way to do this."

"I knew I could count on you." She reached over and squeezed his hand between both of hers. He didn't withdraw his hand, but he left it lifeless, like a chunk of wood.

The door to the galley swung open and a girl came in. She walked right up to Earl and kissed him on the mouth.

"Howdy!" he practically yelled. The rings around his pupils brightened another shade.

"Hi! I'm Jennifer." She held out a hand to Rosie. Small and twinkling with dimpled cheeks, the pixie girl hardly looked old enough to work on the Ice. She wore green plastic glasses and a rainbow of barrettes in her catty-wonk hair.

Earl's eyes followed her as she went to fill a mug and jounce a peppermint teabag in the water. She sat in the chair next to Earl and leaned against him.

"Whoa," Rosie said, looking at her watch. "I didn't realize how late it was. I need to get back to town."

"Not so fast, sister," Earl said. "I thought we were going on a little therapy run. Jennifer might be able to help out."

"What's up?" Jennifer asked, resting her chin in her hand.

"Forget it," Rosie said. "It's a crazy idea." She stood up and pushed in her chair.

"Wait a second. We've hardly had any quality time since the fuel tank." That evil, slow-dawning grin.

Rosie smiled to cover up the onslaught of despair. She felt like a schoolmarm next to perky Jennifer as she said, "We couldn't go out there in this weather, anyway."

"It's clearing," Jennifer said. "Is someone going to tell me what we're talking about?"

"Taking the skidoos on a little adventure. Out to the plane."

"Cool!" Jennifer yelled. Then quietly, conspiratorially. "You know what?"

"What?" Earl asked, melting in her presence like some teenage paramour.

"I gotta go," Rosie said. "See ya."

Earl jumped up and grabbed Rosie's elbow. "Just—hold—on—one—second. Will you?"

"This will work," Jennifer said knocking her knuckles against the tabletop. "Two things. For one, I just finished working on a couple of the machines that weren't doing so hot."

"Back in the states Jennifer's a mechanic," Earl said proudly.

"I'm just a GA here," she told Rosie. "But when they need stuff fixed, I do it."

"Meaning," Earl said, "they're getting skilled labor for un-skilled labor wages. It's fucked."

"Relax, Earl. So we take a little back now and then, know what I mean?" Jennifer scooted to the edge of her plastic chair. "I say we just go. Probably no one will ever even notice. But if we *do* get caught, I can say I needed to test the machines on a longer run. And that you two are helping me out."

Must be a FNG, Rosie thought. That excuse would never fly.

"But here's the best part," Jennifer said, turning to Earl. "That guy Nick? The Air Guardsman who plays the drums? The one I've been making friends with so he'll play in our band? That's his job—he's stationed out at the plane. He won't mind if we make a wee little visit."

"Don't you both have to work the rest of the day?" Rosie asked.

"Theoretically," Earl said, sitting back down and pulling Jennifer onto his lap. She kissed his nose. Earl told her, "You're brilliant."

Rosie stepped outside. She stood still for a moment, listening to the arrival of the day's plane, a high whine deepening to a roar. She watched the black nose of the plane pierce the clouds and land on the airstrip. The plane skied up to the passenger terminal and came to a gliding stop.

Such ease and grace, in spite of the cloud cover. Who were the lucky passengers on *that* plane?

The memories ripped through her. The momentary glare of sunlight zapping through the porthole window. How the plane tipped so steeply that Larry hung in his seat above her, only the seatbelt keeping him from falling directly onto her. He had looked directly into her eyes, as if he knew her. Maybe that moment would have passed uneventfully from her memory, if next the plane hadn't shook fiercely and then collided with the ice, jarring her so violently she felt as if her bones were still vibrating today. In her memory, she couldn't unlock her gaze from Larry's. She couldn't detach that primal eroticism from its twin, the girl's straying cold death.

So Earl had moved on, found himself this pert girlfriend. Rosie knew it was ridiculous to feel abandoned. He'd said, that evening he followed her around the side of Observation Hill, that he wasn't interested in her. Even after she'd practically mauled him in the fuel tank, he preferred a meal to going back to his room. Rain check, he'd said. A polite rejection. It was stupid to feel hurt. She hadn't wanted Earl, either. She'd only wanted escape. She'd wanted wild.

The site of the crashed plane lured.

When Earl and Jennifer came out the door of the galley behind her, she said, "Let's go."

In the garage, Jennifer snagged two sets of keys and tossed one to Rosie. She dangled the other set before slowly closing her fist around it. "Sorry," she told Earl, "but you'll be the biker chick this ride."

"The better to fondle you."

Jennifer cinched survival duffels onto the backs of two snowmobiles. She patted the seat of one and said to Rosie, "Yours."

Rosie straddled the seat. As she inserted the key in the ignition, a feeling of risk filled her like lust.

"Ladies," Earl said, "start your engines."

They eased the snowmobiles out the garage door and onto the road, driving slowly at first, side by side, like cops on a freeway. A sticker on Rosie's machine said to not exceed twelve miles an hour, a speed so slow it practically hurt, a speed that could hardly be called a speed. Until they were out of sight, though, they needed to look purposeful, like they were on an official work mission. As they passed the airstrip, Rosie looked straight ahead but in her peripheral vision she could see a couple of people walking between buildings. She had no idea if they were workers, managers, or beakers, but it was too late to worry about who saw them now. A minute later, Willy Field was behind them, diminishing to a cluster of boxes and then a dusting of black specks and finally just a tiny hitch in the horizon.

The horizon! The clouds had vanished.

Never mind Larry. Never mind Earl. Rosie needed only this machine and the horizon before her. She opened the throttle and drove the skidoo up to twenty, then twenty-five and thirty miles an hour, the speed obliterating any vestige of common sense she had left. Her body seemed to evaporate as wholly as the clouds had, everything one clear blue note singing through pure space.

The appearance of the plane, a long hot glint on the ice, was sobering. It rested like some mythic sky creature, once a flying menace and now an inert cylinder of steel. To its left, Mount Erebus reigned quietly, the plume of volcanic steam undulating upward. Seeing the two together, the disabled cargo plane and the active volcano, gave Rosie a sharp pang of foolishness. What an absurd species people were with their flying and continent-taming schemes. She drove her skidoo right into the shade under the massive nose of the LC-130 and cut the engine.

Jennifer parked next to her, hopped off, and walked toward the polar hut that'd been erected since the crash. Eventually a field camp would be built to shelter the crew who would repair the plane. But first parts had to be built, delivered to McMurdo, and somehow conveyed out here to the crash site. A runway would have to be built, too, so that the repaired plane could take off. In the meantime, the Air National Guard stationed people at the site to keep an eye on the plane.

"Nick?" Jennifer called. "Hi! Nick?" She knocked on the door to the polar hut. When no one answered, she carefully opened it. "No one here," she called over her shoulder.

"Woo hoo!" Earl yelped. He pulled a joint out of an inside pocket and lit up, still straddling his skidoo. "Mood enhancer?" he called to Rosie. "She don't smoke," he added, nodding to Jennifer who wrinkled her nose on cue.

Rosie ignored Earl and climbed off the snowmobile. Slowly she circled the plane on foot, dragging her hand along the steel belly. When she got to the wing, she made a right turn and walked under its reach until she came to one of the propellers. She grasped a blade between her mittens. A hard shiver coursed through her. She was very cold. Keep moving. Rosie made her way to the other side of the plane. From there she looked out toward the place where she'd found the girl.

She felt a tug so distinct and physical it was as if there were a rope tied around her waist pulling her in that direction. She followed the search-and-rescue skidoo tracks until she came to the spot where the body had been. The snow was badly churned and scuffed, from the boots of the few dozen officials and investigators who had visited the site. She checked the mountain, its visibility reassuring. But she wouldn't need a storm to die here. If she lay down in this spot she'd be dead of exposure in a few hours at most. Only the heat generated by moving her body kept her alive. Such an incredibly thin line between life and death.

Then she did lie down on her back, arms and legs spread, as if she were going to make a snow angel. Looking straight up, she saw nothing but sky. She fanned her arms and legs, pushing them hard against the surface of the snow, trying to break through the icy rubble.

Rosie heaved herself up and looked at the imperfect angel. The ultimate symbol of flight. Like an animal that needed to locate itself geographically, Rosie kicked at the snow around the rough angel, working out in circles, until she found the place where she'd peed, a pale yellow patch. It was like returning to the scene of a crime. When they had questioned her, she had had to tell about urinating. They would have seen, anyway. She hadn't killed the girl. No one thought she had. But she felt implicated by the presence of her own bodily fluid and now by the fact that she had come back.

Beyond the chewed-up place, the ice twinkled with color, and Rosie walked toward the sparkles. She walked away from the mountain, away from the plane, away from the snow angel. In the direction of nothing. She had the feeling she could walk forever, or at least until she dropped from thirst, hunger, or exposure. The only thing on this continent to stop her was herself.

Just as she had that thought, she came upon something other than herself, after all. A set of tracks. Penguin tracks. Wide fanned feet, with a tail drag between them. But she was miles from the sea! And there was only the one set of tracks. What was a lone penguin doing way out here on the ice shelf? She searched the expanse of snow, looking for another bird, another creature of any sort. Nothing. Just this evidence of a solitary penguin on the southern summer solstice.

Rosie half-walked, half-ran, moving as fast she could on the snow and ice, back to the airplane. She was breathing hard by the time she arrived, the dry ice air burning her lungs. She circled the plane, looking for Earl and Jennifer, but they were nowhere in sight. The two skidoos still sat under the nose of the plane. How could they have disappeared? Entering the plane would be impossible: there were no stairs up to the hatch.

Then she heard Jennifer's giggles and Earl's grunts emanating from the polar hut. She stood still for a moment, immobilized by the idea of their intimacy. The shelter of a hut, warm skin, laughter. Compared to her snow angel and lost penguin.

Rosie threw a leg over a skidoo and started the engine. She accelerated quickly, taking it up to twenty-five miles an hour. The machine's skis skimmed along the snow as if it might take off into the sky. The idea of flying through the atmosphere soothed her. A moment later she heard the other skidoo gaining behind her. Then Earl roared past, grinning too hard, long hair flying beneath his fleece hat. Jennifer, riding in back this time, circled a fist above her head as if she had a lasso. Rosie cranked the throttle on her machine, driving it up to thirty and then thirty-five. The skidoo bounced on snow hummocks, soared over smooth patches. Time collapsed and she completed the ride in that vacuum.

22

Mikala sat at her keyboard and allowed herself a Bach riff. If she couldn't write, at least she could play. The keyboard felt especially silky today, her hands loose and fluid, and she played Bach's C minor Prelude with her whole body. To be perched in a glass room over the South Pole, warmed by the sun pouring in the windows, letting her fingers run free, was lovely. She closed her eyes as she played and imagined what it would have been like to have composed that herself. Did the notes flow, all in a stream, from his heart to his fingertips, and he said *Aha*? Or did he write each note separately, laboriously, dragging melody from his musical core, bit by bit, until one day there was a score?

At Juilliard, her fellow students always seemed so full of purpose as they described the ways in which they figured out the time, colors, dynamics, pitches, and orchestrations of their compositions. Back then, she'd had to fight the stigma of Redwood Grove, of being a nature girl, as if the only music she had ever heard was birdsong and snow falling off branches. She'd never claimed to be mystical. Yet even when she got the highest scores on music theory tests, even though she could name the composer and performers of just about any classical piece she heard, she'd been aware of a certain distrust toward her methods, which weren't so much unorthodox as nonexistent. Each piece she composed came to her in a different way. Of course after her post-graduate work had been so successfully performed and recorded, fewer people voiced their misgivings about how she came to her music. But she'd never been able to shake the feeling that she didn't really know how to compose, that each piece of music she happened to write was a gift, maybe her last one. This had never felt more true than now.

It was all so confusing. As a trained musician, Mikala knew that much of what Andy had taught her was goofy, but still she longed to recapture that innocence. Because it *had* been meaningful, the way he had her listening to the layers of wind tearing through the forest, one along the ground, hushed and mellow, another through the canopy, complicated and loud, and a third freely over the tops of the trees, flying at a high pitch. He would hold a hand up at the sound of the first drops of rain on their tin roof and say, "*Shh*. Listen." He would tell her that the wind and rain were the Great Mother's music. As a child, this worldview was utterly magical. She, Pauline, and Andy would sit with mugs of fragrant green tea and listen. They still did, when she was home.

She felt guilty when she found herself discounting Andy's lessons. He and Pauline had made so many sacrifices for her. The Redwood Grove community had split up not once but *twice* because of Mikala. True, the first time, when Marcus had the FBI swarming all over the property, she was still in the womb. But the second time, when Andy insisted on the special piano teacher in San Francisco, she was eight years old. The collective argued for three months about whether anyone deserved a bigger share of the resources just because of an alleged greater natural gift. The conflict ended with a group of five adults and four children leaving Redwood Grove. The remaining members agreed to pay for Mikala's music lessons as well as season tickets to the San Francisco Symphony. They also bought an old car to accommodate these excursions.

Even though the adults, and some of the other children, took turns accompanying her to the concerts, and even though these outings became favorite bartering commodities in the commune's economy, Mikala felt as if she still owed the community for the years of privilege they'd afforded her. Sarah used to get so angry at Mikala's feelings of guilt and always argued that she'd more than paid them back through hundreds of free concerts and years of free piano lessons for anyone who wanted them.

Still. There was the very fact of her birth, which caused the necessity of sheltering Marcus's guilt, which in turn put the entire community at risk for years. About that, Sarah would point out—with great exasperation at the obviousness of her point—that Mikala really had no control over how her life had been used when she was still unborn.

It was as if Marcus's guilt were planted in her very fetus and had grown with her into adulthood. She still felt so much pressure to be worthy of the sacrifices that had been made for her.

Mikala slipped off her keyboard bench and lay down on the floor next to it. God, she missed Sarah's correctional arguments, even the way they sometimes had been delivered harshly and impatiently. Sarah had been right about Marcus. He'd never paid for his breaches. He'd walked away, unscathed, leaving Mikala to carry that burden. Fact: if she hadn't been in Pauline's womb when he blew up that bank, Marcus would no doubt be in prison. She had been raised to not wish prison on anyone. But the craving in her fingers, the way that right now the loveliest music she had ever composed rested just below her sternum, too far from her ears to hear, out of reach, was his fault. She had managed so much up until Sarah's death. The *Times* predicted she would be one of the top composers of the twenty-first century. Now this, three years of nothing.

She thought she had spent her life protecting Sarah. But maybe it had been the other way around. With her life partner gone, she had to face not only *her* absence but the absence of her father. The permanence of death, the irretrievability of Sarah, highlighted his loss, a loss she never had thought mattered, maybe because he was, theoretically, retrievable.

The thing was, she really did want to write music about the Big Bang. She knew this was no accident, just as it was no accident that she looked and laughed exactly like Marcus. Unfortunately, the impossible composition was in her genes. The music would be released when she made him take back the burden he'd given her.

As she lay on the floor, a faint metallic echo touched her skin. The sound grew incrementally, morphing into reverberating footsteps on the stairway. Someone was ascending to the Sky Lab. With each flight of stairs being a bit different in its material composition and construction, the quality of the sound changed in segments as it approached. Mikala moaned softly, feeling an intense but unspecific need, as if she were spiritually starving. She got to her feet, sat back at her keyboard, and tried to look like she was working. She hit the note of her moan, an A flat.

"Hey girl." Betty looked around the tiny tower studio, then threw herself in the beanbag chair. "Am I interrupting you?"

Mikala meant to say yes, but shook her head no.

"Hot up here." Betty kicked off her Tevas. She wore a periwinkle sundress under an oversized, man's white dress shirt. She took off the shirt and said, "Phew."

Her freckled arms matched the henna tips of her disheveled hair. She smiled at Mikala. "You look upset."

"I can't work."

"It's no wonder with three years of celibacy."

"What?"

Betty laughed. "You heard me. Come sit in the beanbag chair with me?"

She couldn't be serious. Didn't people talk first?

Then again, Mikala had no idea how romance—or sex—happened. Often, on those occasions when she was out for drinks with some renowned conductor or a group of musicians, in some sophisticated big-city bar, she would listen to the melodies of voices as attractions waxed and waned, entire sonatas of subtle rhythms and not-so-subtle crescendos. The orchestration was what caught her attention, the wash of feeling among people. But occasionally, especially since Sarah's death, it would occur to her that she ought to pay better attention to the actual transactions, to the words said, the arrangements made. The gulf between her musical sophistication and social ineptness was mighty.

Unlike those conductors and musicians with whom she occasionally had drinks, Betty knew of Mikala's staggering inexperience. What things one finds oneself confessing on this continent! Perhaps Betty's plain-speaking was intentional. Perhaps this was exactly what Mikala needed. A way forward. A way out of herself. A bridge to the rest of the world. Perhaps that bridge would lead to music.

Nevertheless, Mikala stayed where she was on the keyboard bench.

Betty said, "You're a big handsome girl."

It would be like practice, a warm-up act. After all, the woman had had hundreds of lovers. She was like a professional seductress.

Betty captured one of Mikala's feet with both of hers and tugged. "Don't be afraid. Come here."

Mikala slid off the keyboard bench onto her knees and sat back on her heels.

"Closer." Betty held out a hand.

Mikala leaned forward and took her hand, kissing the knuckles.

"How courtly."

Mikala felt foolish. She wished she could scoot back to her keyboard bench. But Betty weaved her fingers into the short hair at the back of Mikala's neck and pulled her forward. Mikala tumbled onto the beanbag, throwing herself to the side so that she didn't fall right on Betty.

Betty laughed and, as if reading her thoughts, said, "Don't you think you need some practice? In case you do attract the interest of your friend in McMurdo?"

Mikala wished Betty wouldn't talk. Especially not about Rosie. If she was going to go through with this, she'd rather invest it with as much genuineness as she could muster. Betty did smell good, like pie dough and apples.

Betty kissed her. "For someone so out of practice, you're a nice kisser."

"Thank you."

Betty started unbuttoning her jeans. That fast.

"Maybe we had better shut the door."

"I like it open."

"Someone could come in."

"We'll hear them coming up the stairs. Don't worry so much."

Mikala never would have dreamed that this would be the way she ended her lifelong faithfulness to Sarah. Not that she hadn't had opportunities. There was that painter in New York a friend had introduced her to. She had asked Mikala over to her place on what seemed like a date. But the excessive neatness of the woman's apartment made Mikala so uncomfortable that she made an excuse to go home directly after dinner. How could a painter, any creative person, be that neat? Then there was the executive director of a foundation that had given Mikala a grant. The woman had initiated a long dialogue about whether or not it would be inappropriate for them to get involved, because of the fellowship and the possibility of future fellowships. If any attraction had ever existed between them, that conversation sort of killed it. They did hold hands, briefly, and the woman's bird bones gave Mikala the heebie jeebies. So she used the excuse of their professional relationship to get out of further involvement, which the executive director accepted with what looked like relief.

Rosie was the first woman she had met since Sarah's death who seemed to exist in four dimensions, who billowed in her imagination. Rosie had finally answered her email, too, saying she would like to get together when Mikala was in McMurdo next week. Just the thought of her brought on that purr of music, quiet and deep and hidden. If only she could find a way to nurture it.

A little worldly experience might help. Engage her senses, ones other than hearing. That lovely apple pie smell. Touch.

Mikala put a hand on Betty's hip, round and soft through the jersey fabric of the sundress. Betty smiled. Mikala leaned over and kissed her mouth, her clavicle, the top of her breast. When Betty sighed, it sounded more like an exhalation of getting through something rather than pleasure, and Mikala looked up, alarmed. But Betty didn't meet her glance. Instead, she reached over and pulled Mikala on top of her.

Mikala's face smacked into the beanbag chair, to the side of Betty's head, but Betty didn't seem to notice that, either. She pushed herself against Mikala's hipbone, rocking gently. The beanbag chair crunched beneath their combined weight.

Mikala panicked, not knowing what she was supposed to do, but then, feeling Betty's hands on her ass, holding her in place, she realized she didn't have to do anything at all. Without any action on her part whatsoever, things happened. Betty's periwinkle sundress rode up on her waist. She wore no underwear. Her head fell back and the ice hot Antarctic sun poured in the tower windows, lighting her face.

Then it was over.

Betty scooted to the side of the beanbag and laughed. "You're something else," she said. Then she tried to put her hand in Mikala's jeans. Mikala shook her head.

"Oh, don't be like that," Betty said, persisting.

Suddenly it felt like a sex workshop, but Mikala gave in to that, too. She had always thought more about love than technique, but had to admit there was something to the latter. She came a few moments later, surprising herself and making Betty laugh again.

"You're so sweet," Betty said. "And sincere."

Mikala felt neither. She felt empty. She thought of how Betty had noted Marcus's brains and how she said she'd begged him to not use birth control. Betty had also noted, two times, her composer ears. Perhaps she should apologize for being unable to give Betty's offspring a shot at musical genes.

Betty pulled down her dress and sat up. She looked at her watch. "Uh-oh. I was supposed to be at work five minutes ago. I was on my way in when I had the idea to visit you for a sec."

Mikala wondered if she had planned the seduction as part of her visit. Sex in a sec. "So how many people have you been with, anyway? Do you know? Exactly?"

"There's a rock back home where I make hash marks. I'd have to check it."

"Really?"

"I'm joking, girl."

"It didn't sound that far-fetched."

Betty cocked her head. "There's edge in your voice. You okay?"

"Do you ever fall in love?"

Betty pushed herself out of the beanbag chair and sat on the keyboard bench. "I'm human."

"Then what?"

"Then I'm mind-bogglingly faithful until they dump me."

"Or you dump them."

"Hasn't happened. By the time I fall in love, I don't fall out. I've always been the dumpee. Three times."

"Men or women?"

"Two men, one woman. Is that important?"

"What kinds of people do you fall in love with?"

"Not sweet and sincere ones."

"Huh." Was that a warning, and if so, was she supposed to thank her for it? "Maybe that's your problem. I mean, why you're always the dumpee. You fall for insincere people."

"Yeah, well, that's obvious. I can't help it, though." Betty slid her feet into her Tevas and pulled up the heel straps. "I gotta go."

She stepped out the door and headed down the stairs.

"Wait," Mikala called, running to the door of the Sky Lab. Betty was already down a flight and a half. "What are you doing after work?"

Betty shook her head. Meaning no, but to what?

"Want to have a glass of wine later, or something?"

Betty climbed back up the stairs. "You lesbians are all the same," she teased, and Mikala felt the hair on the back of her neck stiffen. "Such sweeties. But don't do this. Don't get attached."

Mikala didn't feel even remotely in danger of that. She had suggested the drink to offset the emptiness she felt, the vacuity of the encounter. "I know. You only fall for cowgirls."

Betty missed the sarcasm. "Yeah. Or cowboys."

Mikala listened to her footfall all the way down the sets of stairs. She listened until there was no trace of Betty left. She had heard no music, not one lovely sound, while with her.

Where *was* the music? She walked to the window and looked out. Just the polar plateau. An endless stretch of frozen desert.

And, coming into view, a bobbing purple hat. Marcus Wright, her father, doing his laps around the dome. He too had succumbed to Betty's wiles, if that word even applied to someone so benign. Like father, like daughter. He, at least, was doing his work. He was reportedly on the verge of a major cosmological breakthrough.

Mikala returned to her keyboard and laid her fingers on the keys.

"The first movement," she said. "The Big Bang."

23

On New Year's Eve, Alice waited for Rosie. She'd be leaving for the Dry Valleys in two days. Finally. But she didn't think she could spend another evening alone in this dim room. She had a plan. Surely Rosie would be going to the party out at Scott Base. She would invite herself along.

While she waited, she tried to work out the tangle in her head. Understanding her life in any quantifiable way was becoming increasingly difficult. She resorted to making two frustratingly vague and short lists in her journal.

Facts:
Jamie hasn't contacted me since our day on the ice over a month
    ago.
Rasmussen is waiting for me at his field camp.
Probabilities:
Jamie will be at the party.
Rasmussen continues to assume whatever it is he assumes about
    me.

The door opened at 7:30. Rosie said hello as she tore off her hat, scarf, and jacket. She sat wearily on her bed and said, "How's it going?"

"Someone named Earl called you about two hours ago," Alice said. "He said you were supposed to be at rehearsal."

"Yeah. Right."

"Are you playing in Icestock tomorrow?"

"Earl thinks I'm singing with his band. He's been haranguing me all week. But the answer is no, I'm not." Rosie ran her fingers through her hair and sighed. "What are you doing tonight?"

Alice took a deep breath and silently practiced, *I thought it'd be fun to go out to that party at Scott Base. I bet you're going.* She said, "Oh! I guess I'll stay in and read."

"It's New Year's Eve."

You're right. Let's party. "I'm not the kind of person who likes to party."

Rosie nodded and ran her hands through her hair again. She looked sad. "Yeah. Maybe I'll do that too. Stay in and read. It's sort of a radical idea staying in on the biggest party night of the year."

"People are very active on New Year's Eve."

Rosie laughed.

Alice ducked her head in that flinching way that Frank had told her was annoying.

Rosie said, "It's just that you said that so scientifically. Like, 'Gerbils become more active in warm weather.'"

Alice nodded. "I see the world that way, scientifically."

"Yeah? So why geology specifically?"

"It's like a jigsaw puzzle. There are actual pieces, the rocks, that fit together and eventually give an entire picture. Other sciences, like cosmology, have such huge margins of error."

Rosie said, "Cool," and started to get up.

Alice took a breath and said, "You mentioned, when I first arrived here, that you had just kissed a married man."

Rosie looked like a lab rat stunned by a quick injection. Before she could recover and change the subject, Alice continued, "I've been involved with a married man, too."

"Yeah?"

"Yeah. His name was Frank."

"Actually, I'm not *involved* with a married man. I just kissed him."

Alice nodded, a little disappointed.

"But tell me what happened with Frank." Rosie pulled off her boots, drew her feet up on the bed, and crossed her legs. It looked as though she genuinely wanted to hear.

Alice put her journal aside and also crossed her legs. "I don't want to burden you with my story. It's just that, I don't know, you seem like someone who knows how to do everything."

Rosie shook her head. "No. I don't know how to do anything."

"But you don't seem afraid."

Rosie looked puzzled.

"I know. I don't know you at all. But I'm very observant. That's my job, as a scientist, to observe."

"But I'm not a rock."

Alice laughed. "True. But Rasmussen told me you're a very skilled Antarctican."

By the look on Rosie's face, Alice now knew for sure. He'd never spoken to Rosie at all. He'd just arranged for Alice to room with her and figured they'd connect. That was so like him, to make silent assumptions about human beings connecting.

Rosie said, "So. Frank."

Alice nodded. "I've only ever had two boyfriends. The first one was in high school, my junior year. His name was Frank, also. I'm a very cautious person—straight As and all—but I guess some sort of adolescent hormones kicked in. Made me crazy."

Rosie laughed.

"I know. Me crazy. Not exactly an easy thing to picture." Even if Rasmussen hadn't arranged for Rosie to be her Antarctic mentor, her warmth made Alice want to tell everything.

"Frank was a year older, a senior. He smoked and went to keggers every weekend. He flunked his academic courses and spent all his time in the auto shop building engines. He had what they call bottle-bottom glasses, so thick his eyes looked distorted. Rectangular metal frames. Silver. When he took them off, his eyes were so soft you just couldn't imagine him doing anything bad. We had to meet secretly because my mother forbade me to see him. She's always accused me of being asexual, even when I was a little girl, but when I finally got a boyfriend she couldn't stand him. I live alone with my mother so sneaking out to see Frank was really difficult. Mainly we saw each other at school. We only had sex one time, the night before he left. I know he loved me, but the sex wasn't like that. He just, you know, did it. I was glad to have it over with. My virginity. We did it in our driveway, in a car he'd just stolen, though I didn't know that yet. He'd come over to tell me he was leaving. My mother was enough out of it that night that I could sneak out for a little while. Long enough.

"Next day they showed the car on the news. He took a turn too fast and missed it. He went into the opposite rock outcropping and the car flipped."

"God. I'm sorry."

"He's fine. So far as I know. The police found the car empty. He'd walked away. Maybe he stole another car, I don't know, but he got away. No one ever caught him. He called me once, a week after the accident, to tell me he was okay. You know what he said?"

Rosie shook her head.

"He said, 'I thought I should call you because I know you love me. I didn't want you to worry.' I thought that was really sweet."

"Alice."

"You're thinking he should have said he loved *me*. But that's as close as he could get. He did love me. When his glasses were off, you could see pure innocence. It really was there, in spite of the bad grades and cigarettes and keggers and stolen car. Now? Well, now he knows what it feels like to crash and roll a car. He knows what it's like to be homeless. On the run. Anyone he ever finds to love again will know him amputated from his first seventeen years. That's never quite enough."

"You think childhood lovers are the only true ones?"

"I'm saying that continuity is very important. I'm the kind of person who needs to know the whole story.'"

"So I'm guessing that the story of Frank Two is related to the story of Frank One."

Alice allowed herself another grin. "My second boyfriend hardly deserves the nomenclature. That lasted for a year, the year I wrote my doctoral dissertation, and ended two years ago. Frank was doing a postdoc in geology. He had curly black hair and a kind of angelic face. I didn't find him nearly so attractive as I had found the first Frank, but he had a kind of delicacy that felt safe. He would come up behind me in the lab and stand very close, speaking softly about whatever he was working on." Alice paused. "Sometimes I get very lonely."

Rosie pulled her knees in more closely and folded her arms, what humans do when they're feeling lonely. That Rosie could be lonely, too, surprised Alice.

"I've never told this to anyone before. I'm sorry to burden you."

"Don't apologize. You're not burdening me. It's the Ice."

"What do you mean?"

"Capital I: the Ice. This place transforms everyone. Splits your heart right open."

"Oh! I don't know if transformation is necessary."

Rosie laughed. "Just inevitable. Tell me what happened with Frank Two."

"The first time was in the lab. Actually, every time was in the lab. It was fun. It really was. The lab worked fine for me, living with my mother and all."

"She didn't approve of him either?"

"She never knew about him. He's the married one. He thought I didn't know about his wife. I hated that part, how people felt sorry for me. They thought I'd been bamboozled. *He* thought I'd been bamboozled. But I knew all along. Married guys are obvious. They don't ask you out. You never see their homes. They have cleaner clothes and bag lunches. They treat you a little extra nice because they feel guilty and also so you won't ask questions. I mean, sex in the lab. The evidence was all there. I hated people thinking I'd been fooled, but I'd hate it worse for them to know I'd willingly had an affair with a married man. I'm the kind of person people often take for a victim."

As Alice said the word victim, the dorm room door flew open. A man who looked like he'd stepped right out of the most recent Ice Age, entirely Neanderthal, burst in.

Rosie screamed. Alice picked up the first object at hand, which happened to be the tissue-wrapped Dalai Lama vase, and prepared to hurl it.

The man raked his fingers through his ice-crusted beard before bellowing, "She's fucking the drummer."

"Shit, Earl," Rosie said. "Most people knock. What the hell?"

"All I wanted to do was play music tomorrow. You know? Show these fools what real guitar-playing sounds like."

"Alice," Rosie said with mock formality. "Have you met Earl?"

The man scraped the desk chair across the floor, placing it next to Rosie's bed, and sat down. "Did you hear me? Jennifer is fucking the drummer."

The man's eyes had a swirling quality. Alice hoped this wasn't Rosie's married man.

"I'm sorry," Rosie said softly, trying to calm him.

"I thought we had something. I thought we had fun."

"She's very young."

He reached into his pocket and withdrew a bag of marijuana. He looked around, appearing lost, and then dragged his chair back to the desk where he started to roll a joint.

"Uh," Rosie said. "Alice is a geologist, a grantee."

Alice didn't like the implication that she was of a different class than the two of them, someone who might tell, but nevertheless, smoking in this temporary building was a very bad idea. She said, "Fire hazard."

"I wasn't going to light the building," Earl said. "I was going to light the joint."

"Still," Alice said.

"She's right," Rosie agreed.

"Shit." Earl dropped the papers back into the plastic bag with the weed, sealed the plastic zipper, and threw the bag in the wastepaper basket. Then his whole body slumped. He said, "Do you ever think you want something different?"

Rosie said, "All the time."

"I feel like this place is breaking me. Not physically. Shit, I just ran the six miles from Willy Field here. More like this is the end of the fucking road. The last fucking continent. Here I am: ice, sky, mountains. This is it. I have to admit this is all there is to me. Now what?"

"You're asking the wrong person," Rosie said.

Earl pounded a hand on the desk top and Alice jumped. He turned and looked at her, and then, as if he were sorry he'd startled her, he lowered his voice and addressed her directly. "Do you know what I want?"

She knew her eyes were wide as she shook her head no.

"I want a woman and kids. It's that simple. Sometimes, some-times before I go to sleep I lie back and think about waking up to three little munchkins jumping all over me, squealing and kicking me accidentally in the balls and smelling of pee. Some woman who looks like shit in the morning with circles under her eyes and ratty hair from too little sleep. I *want* that. All the other guys in the world want what I have and I want that. Is that crazy shit or what?"

"There's rarely any correlation between what people want in love and what they get," Alice said, locking her calm eyes with Earl's wild ones.

He looked at Rosie, cocked a thumb at Alice, and said, "What the fuck? I don't want a *correlation*. I want a good woman."

"Go get your guitar," Rosie said. "Let's take Alice in the fuel tank."

A slow smile overtook Earl's face. Alice set the Dalai Lama vase on the floor at the foot of her bed and then walked to the waste-paper basket. She retrieved the bag of marijuana and handed it back to Earl. He stuffed it in his pocket.

Ten minutes later, they were walking up the hill to the giant drums.

"Hey, Dr. Rocks," Earl said. "Are the ice caps melting?"

"Yes. They're melting. The questions are why, how fast, what's the relationship of this period of warming in comparison to other periods in the planet's history, and the role of humans in the change."

"Are you talking about core-eee-lations again?" When Alice didn't respond to his mocking, he said, "I really want to know. What do *you* think?"

"I need more data." Then Alice laughed out loud at her own caution. Walking between Rosie of the Antarctic and Ice Age Earl, heading for an illicit adventure, she felt as if a seismic shift were shearing her very core. Recklessly, she said, "It doesn't really matter whether the ice caps are melting or not. We'll be wiped off the face of the earth by something else before the flooding. The demise of the human race is imminent."

Earl barked something between pain and amusement.

"Disease probably," Alice said. "But maybe nuclear or biological warfare."

"Now here's a girl who can cheer a man up," Earl said, throwing an arm around Alice's shoulders.

A low rumble on the road behind them caught Alice's attention. The shuttle to Scott Base was running every twenty minutes tonight, due to the party. Even with the van's windows up, she could hear the New Year's Eve revelers inside the vehicle. She stopped walking and took Rosie's arm. She wanted to say something about continuing their conversation. She had heard nothing about Rosie's married man. Nor had she gotten even close to asking the questions she wanted to ask about Rasmussen and Jamie. Now there was no time.

Alice let go of Rosie and flagged down the van.

24

"Let her go," Earl said.

"But I'm worried. She seems like she's on the brink of something."

"We're all on the brink of something."

"She already told me tonight she's not a party type. What's she doing?"

"Changing her mind. It's everyone's prerogative." Realizing the implications of his words, with regard to Jennifer, Earl sat down in the middle of the road and dropped his face into his mittens.

"Get up," Rosie said. "This is Antarctica. You'll die."

"That girl was lucky. The one who died."

"Shut up. And *get* up."

"Half the women I fall for are free spirits. The other half are too young. Jennifer is both." He unsnapped the latches on his guitar case.

"Come on, Earl."

"You were both, too."

"You didn't fall for me. Get up."

He tuned the strings, then played a blues riff, bending the notes in full circles, rich and succulent. Rosie looked up and down the road, and then up at the sky. A gray haze. It was damn cold.

"I could have fallen for you," Earl said pulling off a string and letting the note thin. "But I could tell you weren't interested, not really. You just wanted sex. You haven't found your heart yet."

"Excuse me?"

"You know what I mean." He played a couple more slow notes in a blues scale. Then shook his hand out. "Frozen already."

"Come on, Earl."

"That's why you travel," he said. "Looking. Not me. I travel because I'm pissed off."

Rosie gave up and sat down in the middle of the road next to Earl. She picked up his mittens and held them out to him. "At what?"

"Everything. Absolutely fucking everything. It's like a fuel, anger. I love it, really. It's great. Like this big old diesel engine in my bowels. But you know, I'm beginning to feel as if I've journeyed it off. I've walked enough, talked enough, fucked enough. You'd think that was a good thing. But what's left? What's left now that I've run out of fuel?" He spread his hands in front of himself to show her his emptiness. Rosie took one hand and guided it into a mitten, as if he were five years old, and then did the same with the other. He said, "I'll tell you what's left. An empty man. Nobody sees home when they look at me. They see a parking space."

"Come on." She took the guitar out of his lap and put it back in the case.

"They might be right."

"You said you wanted a woman with circles under her eyes and three stinky kids."

"I do. But that doesn't mean I'm capable of it."

"I hear the van coming back. Let's get out of the road."

"He looks like a professional baseball player."

"Who?"

"The drummer."

"You mean beefy?"

"I mean all-American. Orthodontist-enhanced smile. An overgrown Boy Scout."

"It won't last."

"She'll marry him. They all do. As soon as they meet the boy who will inherit Quaker Oats."

"What do you expect when you go after girls half your age. You're a cliché, Earl. And it brings you only pain."

"I don't understand what she sees in him. He's so *normal*. A drummer. There's something pedestrian about all but the cream of the crop drummers and he isn't even a fair drummer."

The van bore down on them and Earl slowly stood. Rosie dragged him by the arm to the side of the ice road and they watched the van roll by. She said, "I'm freezing. Literally. Let's go back to the room."

"I feel like doing something extreme. Something extra extreme."

"Come on. I'm going." Rosie started walking back toward McMurdo, leaving Earl beside the road.

He yelled after her, "I feel like finding them. I want a confrontation. I want an answer."

Rosie turned and yelled back, "You don't even know what the question is. Come *on*."

"I'm so sick to fucking death of this continent. It's like a wall."

Rosie walked back to Earl and extended a hand. "I would never have taken you for a whiner."

He batted her hand away. "I *am* a whiner. That's just it. I'm a whiner who wants a fucking picket fence."

"Oh, Earl."

He tore off his mittens again, retrieved the bag of weed from his pocket, crouched down, and began rolling a joint, using the top of his thigh as a table. She rested her hand on the top of his head. "Put that away. You can't be a bad boy and have a picket fence both. They're mutually exclusive."

Earl licked the seal of the paper and thumbed the joint closed. "I don't notice you living inside any picket fences."

"I never said I wanted to."

Earl lit the joint. "But you do."

After three hard tokes, he dropped the joint and mashed it with his boot. He pressed the guitar case into Rosie's arms. "Take this back to the dorm for me?"

"Where're you going?"

Earl did an about face and started to trot down the road toward Scott Base. She yelled his name once and then gave up, standing still until the lumbering man was out of sight. Then she walked slowly back to the dorm room. She shoved Earl's guitar in her wardrobe and put on flannel pajamas. Bed. She'd sleep in the new year. She reached for her wadded sleeping bag and gave it a few good hard shakes to fluff the down loft. An envelope fell to the floor.

"Rosie," a note scrawled on the white envelope read. "You didn't come by the mailroom today, so I've been carrying this letter around thinking I'd run into you. It came yesterday. Bea."

She sat down in the desk chair and examined the envelope. Return address: Newberg, Oregon. She broke the seal and slowly pulled out the single piece of lined notebook paper.

> Dear Rosie,
>
> Got your letter, though it was pure coincidence. Mom's working for a caterer, whose son works at the post office. He recognized the name and asked Gigi—that would be Mom's boss—if it was the same Moore. We figured not. But when Gigi showed Mom the letter, it was you. She said she nearly passed out.
>
> We had no idea where you were. Dad's been sort of missing, too. We just kind of thought he'd gone off on another Dead tour, but he's been gone since March.
>
> Antarctica? I guess you wanted to get as far from home as possible. Mom said to tell you hello. She's doing okay. She's kind of lonely, though. I think. Max is the same as ever. Insane. Full tilt righteous. I've been in a bit of trouble. So what else is new, ha ha. Remember Daryl? Dad used to work on his crew sometimes. He's hired me, which is

pretty nice of him, given my record. But I'm not letting him down. Do you have email there? I'm at Jed1000280@hotmail.com. You know—I miss you. We all do. I think.

Jed

25

The van came to a stop, and someone slid open the door, but the driver shouted above the voices of the party-goers that she didn't have room for another passenger. "Unless you're in physical danger," she said. "I need to ask you to either walk or wait for the next van."

Ignoring the driver, a number of hands reached out of the packed van and grabbed Alice, hauling her up onto a bed of laps. Someone tugged her feet inside and someone else slammed the door shut. The van groaned on down the hill toward Scott Base.

This, Alice thought as she jostled along on the human nest, swallowed up in the drunken laughter, must be what fate feels like.

"I'm going to my fate," she said out loud because no one could hear her anyway. Her mother would like those words: my fate.

When the van came to a stop someone managed to unplug himself from the interior and he turned and wrapped his arms around Alice's waist. "Let go of her!" he shouted to the others in the van as he pulled, and she slid free, the release of her weight knocking them both to the ice. *I've been born*, Alice thought, *and my mother is a van.* The man was laughing and she found herself laughing, too. He helped her up, without looking at her, and joined the rest of the party guests who were crowding into the entrance of Scott Base.

Alice stayed outside, listening to the ice creaking. Inside at the party, Jamie was undoubtedly chatting up some woman who was not only much prettier than she was but also much better at conversation. She had no idea why she was even thinking about him. He'd made no attempt to contact her since their day on the sea ice. If her life hadn't depended on taking shelter, she would have abandoned this madcap party plan. But the climate forced her to open the door and enter the main building at Scott Base.

Loud music and party chatter assaulted her. An avalanche of cheer. She tried to listen for Jamie's voice, but of course hearing any particular voice would be impossible. There were dozens of people at the party. As panic tightened around her, the noise dimmed and then seemed to go completely silent. She felt as if the entire room was dark except for a spotlight on her.

"Looking for someone?" asked a chubby man with pink skin and thin brown hair.

Was it that obvious? "Yes. No."

"Wait here."

Alice did, wondering if she'd said Jamie's name out loud, expecting the man to return with him. What would she say then?

Maybe her mother had been right all along. Now that she'd left her, she wished she could take the lessons she'd shunned for so long: how to converse socially, which clothes to wear for which occasions, what tone of voice to use with men.

The chubby man was back. He handed her a plastic cup full nearly to the brim with a pink drink. Little pieces of citrus pulp floated to the top.

"Try this. Looks nasty but it's our specialty." He spoke with that jaunty New Zealand accent, much more mountain and sea in it than a British accent.

Alice took a sip. It tasted like vodka laced with lemonade. She took a few more swallows. Then the man touched her elbow and led her through the maze of rooms at Scott Base until they were in the small library, tucked on a top floor, with a view out over the sea ice. He gestured toward one of the cushioned benches and Alice sat.

"You okay?

"I'm not the kind of person who goes to parties much."

"You picked a doozy of a one for experimenting." When Alice didn't answer he asked, "Been here before? Scott Base?"

"Only briefly." This would be a good time to ask the man if he knew Jamie.

"I always think it's good to have a bailout room at a party. So I thought you'd like to see the library. Guess I'll go back to the party."

"I'll come too."

He looked pleased.

"I think I need my drink freshened," she said, using her mother's expression, as if having another vodka were the same as washing your face.

He glanced at her cup, obviously surprised at how much she'd already drunk, and said, "Sure. Follow me."

They both got new drinks and went to sit in a lounge where other pairs were talking quietly, away from the main body of the party. Alice realized she didn't even know his name. She appreciated that he wasn't big on social skills either.

After they talked for a few minutes, exchanging basic information about where they were from and what kind of work they did, he shyly slipped an arm across the back of the couch behind her.

A slow, vodka-soaked signal limped to her brain with a message about caution. "Wait," she said. "Do you know a guy named Jamie?"

"Yeah. He's that American seal biologist."

"Is he here?"

"I don't think he's back yet. I heard he's been out at his camp all month. Hard worker, that chap. Friend of yours?"

She nodded and his arm dropped off the couch and onto her shoulders. She thought she should move away, but she didn't want to hurt his feelings. Anyway, she liked his comprehensive descriptions of his tasks as a lab tech. She knew most people would consider him a complete bore, but she found the long explanations of debugging subsystems, design implementation, and phenotype analysis soothing. Even after finishing her third pink drink, they engaged in lengthy calculations and problem-solving, huddling closer as they talked, as if the scientific jargon were an aphrodisiac.

"Show me your lab?" she asked.

Alice held onto him as they walked unsteadily down the narrow hall. It was well past midnight. At some point in the evening, she'd heard an uproar of cheer coming from the main room of the party, and she'd deduced that the new year had begun. By now most of the guests had gone home. However, coming down the hall toward them were three men, and the one in the center was Earl.

"Alice," he said. "My friend Alice. Dr. Rocks."

The men on either side of Earl forcibly took his arms. "Come on, guy. The last shuttle is leaving. You're on that van."

Earl yanked his arms away from them. "Let go. I want to talk to my friend Alice. I want to hear more about the ice caps."

Alice and the lab tech pressed their backs against the hallway wall as the two men carted Earl, now thrashing and beginning to shout, past them.

"You know him?" the lab tech asked.

"He's a friend of my roommate's."

"Uh, do you think you should get on that last shuttle to McMurdo?"

"What about your lab? I haven't seen it yet."

He put his hands in his pockets nervously. "Uh. Okay."

The hallway was close, painted green, and poorly lit. As they passed the doorway to the galley, Alice saw Jennifer, the woman who'd given her the Dalai Lama's vase, holding an ice pack on the face of a handsome, clean-cut guy. Another five meters down the hall, the lab tech said, "Here's my lab." He pulled a ring of keys from his pocket and opened the door.

Alice entered the room after him and shut the door behind her. The sinks, beakers, seismographs, and power washers began to swirl. Yet the cool and rational environment calmed her. It didn't matter that she was drunk. She was in a lab. She ran a finger along the steel end of a pick and then walked to the window. She placed her hand flat against the pane. It was ice cold.

When she turned she saw that the lab tech still stood just inside the door. She walked back to him and started unbuckling his belt.

"I don't have a condom," he whispered.

"It doesn't matter."

It had been a lot like this with Frank Two, as Rosie called him. The linoleum floor was cold on her back and the computers in the room hummed overhead. Only the lab tech was much more nervous than Frank Two, less smooth, and bigger. She wished he were even bigger than he was, that he could swallow her whole, take her somewhere much farther away than where he took her. She held onto the mounds of flesh at his hips and tried to concentrate on the feeling in her groin. But she was too drunk to care about how sex felt. So she let go, let it spin, let him finish. Afterwards, he held her too tightly.

"I should get back," she whispered and twisted out of his arms.

She very much wanted to walk back to McMurdo alone, but he insisted on accompanying her, so they walked together in silence. She was now perfectly and miserably sober. So much for her fate. The idea of fate, after all, is only a human construction, a cheap way to patch up confusion about causal relationships. Science is full of mysteries, but with enough investigation and evidence, all questions can be answered. Eventually. Cause and effect rule the universe. That's the beauty of science: the unknowns are only unknown because we don't have all the data. Fate is just a short answer for the lazy.

That's what she'd like to tell Earl about the ice caps, the fate of the planet. Yes, of course the ice caps were melting. Everyone knew that. It was on the front page of every paper, every day. No serious scientist doubted the impact *homo sapiens* were having on climate change. But what she couldn't abide was humankind's hunger for drama—the cravings for a quick disaster, or even a quick fix, either one, tragedy or comedy, but spectacle, a show. The flooding of major cities. Mass extinctions. Lots of human suffering. Or conversely, a superhero to sweep in to right the biosphere.

She wanted to tell Earl what she knew, as a geologist, about the planet's extreme fragility and deep resiliency, both. How the two states existed simultaneously. How truth lay in an infinite number of tiny actions made by an infinite number of factors, including human ones. There is no such thing as fate. There is only cause and effect, and the human endeavor to understand the relationship between the two.

"Maybe we can have dinner or something later in the week," the man said in front of her dorm.

"I'm sorry," she said, meaning it, liking him, wishing she hadn't been such an idiot. "Day after tomorrow I'm going into the field for the rest of the season. Good night."

26

Jed had been thirteen when Rosie left home. He'd already burned down a state park shed, been caught stealing money from a teacher's desk, and could chug a pint of whiskey. Max, a year younger, was busy making a vocation out of being good. It was painful watching his confusion as even adults recoiled with contempt at his good boy antics. They were so obviously false, so blatantly driven by something other than genuine benevolence. He seemed to actually squint in his desperation for approval. It was years before Rosie realized he probably just needed glasses, that his fear was, at least in part, a simple inability to see. Had his vision been corrected when he was a little boy, Max might have had more courage.

The night before she left, Rosie stood on the floor between the boys' twin beds. Asleep they looked like children still, their limbs twisted in the sheets, their hair fluffy and soft. She leaned over Max first, pushed back his hair, and kissed his forehead. It felt odd kissing her twelve-year-old brother, neither man nor boy, and she neither mother nor lover. He smelled faintly of shoe polish.

The sight of Jed asleep had made her heart hurt. His hands twitched as if they longed to caress or hit, either one. She slipped her arms under his thin shoulders and hugged him, fully expecting him to awaken, but he didn't. He whined a bit and rolled over on his side.

Holding his letter now, she could remember perfectly the heat of his thirteen-year-old skin, the delicacy of the muscles in his shoulders. It was almost impossible to believe that by now he'd be taller than she was, a man, twenty-six years old.

As Rosie read the letter again, she thought of the hundred dollars her mother had sent when she first left home. How she had felt that money like a door slamming behind her. But maybe it had been the opposite. Not a shove. Rather, a helping hand. A sacrifice. Maybe that cash had been an act of love.

She could pay it back. The money and the love. She'd get her place where they'd all be welcome. A big place. A spread. For the first time, she started to imagine the particulars: a view of mountains, open meadows, maybe even a stream.

A single, quiet knock on the door. After several seconds, another single knock. Then four more evenly spaced ones. Rosie sat very still on her bed, ignoring the thumps, and wishing she had locked the door. Hopefully, he'd decide she was out and just go away. She couldn't take any more of Earl tonight. She could tell he was remorseful by the quietness of the knocking. At least he'd returned from his mission of revenge. Earl with his tail between his legs.

The knob turned and the door eased open.

"Rosie?" he whispered.

Larry stepped into the room, the lank of him like a whip. Rosie took a quick, short breath and stared as he grabbed the crown of his hat and yanked it off. He seemed to bring his own weather, an invigorating lash of cold tang.

"I'm in my pajamas," she said, as if that explained or solved something.

"Okay if I come in?"

"It's New Year's Eve." Another nonsensical remark.

"Yeah. Happy New Year."

She'd meant that it was a significant evening, and therefore that he ought to be with someone significant. But his beautifully sculpted mouth eased into a smile, which in turn hitched up his finely formed ears. The smile, the fact that the year would be over in a couple of hours, the letter from Jed, still in her hands, created a soup of intensity that overwhelmed every "ought." Rosie's entire being shrugged. She gave in. She didn't even care that she was wearing flannel pajamas. "Can I offer you a cup of tea?"

"No, thank you."

Rosie motioned to the desk chair and Larry sat in it. He pulled his camera strap over his head and gently set the camera on the desk. He said, "Thanks for your email." Paused, then, "Brief as it was."

"What else could I have said?"

"True. I know I shouldn't have asked about Earl. But I was glad to hear you're not with him. He's a bit beastly, isn't he?"

Rosie laughed. "Yeah. I guess so. He has a good heart, though. Awesome guitar player, too."

As tall as he was, Larry sat on the wooden chair with a childlike posture, slightly hunched, his folded hands dangling between his thighs. The smile was gone. He didn't look so much sad, though, as passionately resolved. He looked at her with the same intent gaze he'd had on the plane.

Rosie said, "I got a letter from my brother."

"Hey, that's great."

"Yeah. He wrote me back."

"What's he say?"

"Not much. My mom's working for a caterer. My dad's not been around. Jed's been in some trouble." Rosie waved the letter in the air. "It's like a gash cut through me. I feel like I abandoned them."

"Oh, Rosie." Larry started out of his chair, and then sat again.

"I told you that I haven't seen my family in thirteen years. But actually, I sort of saw them about nine years ago. I was twenty-one, living in Portland, taking a couple of classes, bagging groceries for money. The Dead came to Portland and I knew they'd be there. My dad wouldn't miss a Dead concert for his own mother's funeral. It was like religion for him. And we were all supposed to follow suit. We went even when the boys were in diapers.

"Anyway, I bought a ticket. It felt like a pilgrimage, even down to the fact that I walked to the concert that night. That whole long walk—it was way out at the racetrack—I tried to figure out what I'd say if I ran into them. Part of me thought that if I *did* see them, I'd just get in the car after the concert and go back home.

"Portland Meadows is huge. But the four of them were seated only about ten rows away. Down to my right. I could see them perfectly. Dad's hair was cut in the same ridiculous shag and he was talking too much, all happy to be there in the patchouli and marijuana fumes. Mom was nervous, biting her nails and straightening everyone's jackets. It was wrenching seeing them, how much they'd changed in a couple of years and how much they hadn't changed. Mom had put on a bunch of weight. That was surprising. Max was bigger, but not much. He was pretty much the same, that way he has of fidgeting, as if he's bursting with desperation for attention but at the same time doing everything in his power to corral that desperation. But no, he'd changed, too. It was like the desperation had shifted to a kind of arrogance. He had put his arm over the back of Mom's chair as if he were in charge of her.

"Jed had grown a lot. He looked really handsome, too. He has these big blue eyes. Once he turned around and I swear he looked right at me.

"I felt like my behavior was kind of shameful, spying on my family like that, and at the same time, I felt sorry for myself. Alone, abandoned. It's taken me all these years to realize that I was the one who left them, not the other way around."

She added, "This was right before Jerry Garcia died."

Larry smiled the saddest smile she'd ever seen. The planes of his face looked so soft, deflated. Maybe she'd been wrong about that resolve she thought she saw in him. Maybe his purposeful bearing was just a container for fear. Like Max.

She asked, "Is what you told me true, about you and Karen?"

He nodded.

"She's my supervisor."

"I know."

"I should ask you to leave."

"Please don't. I know this is crazy. *Pure* crazy. I hardly know you. But Rosie, that's the thing, I'm so tired of being safe. You're so . . . so beautiful. And grounded. Watching you on our flight over here, it's like you saved my life, even before anything happened. The way you are. I just . . . I just want you."

Rosie repeated herself, whispering it this time. "I should ask you to leave."

"Please don't."

Outside, the extreme cold. The revelers at private parties in dorm rooms and out at Scott Base. A host of random heartaches.

Inside, a pale light in a quiet room. The sweet surrender in his posture. The ridiculousness of her baby blue flowered flannel pajamas.

He stood and moved to the foot of the bed. She'd never seen him separated from his camera, which he left on the desk. The literal lens through which he viewed so much of his world, left behind, making the space between them thin and raw. It was as if he'd already undressed. He took off his sneakers and folded his legs, like hers. He said, "Thank you for telling me about the Dead concert and your family."

"You're leaving yours. I'm returning to mine."

He blinked, as if her words had been too bright a light, too harsh. Needing something soft, right away, he reached out a hand and brushed her cheek with his knuckles. Rosie caught his hand and put the knuckle of his middle finger in her mouth. Then she drew it out and said, "What will you do, though, when you get back to the States? Where will you go?"

His kiss sent her directly into the freefall of the LC-130, when their eyes had caught, before they hit the ice. The long cold bivouac. The discovery of the dead girl, who knew nothing anymore about a mouth on her breast, warm skin over tired muscles, the core of desire that pushed Larry's body into hers. That night Rosie made love to him as if only that act could protect her from her own death.

27

Alice knew there'd been a man with Rosie last night. She could smell him. Also, Rosie slept naked, her pajamas on the floor beside the bed. Then there was the white T-shirt she clutched under her chin as she slept.

Rosie groaned, rolled onto her back. She pushed her face into the T-shirt, then flung it away. She sat straight up and declared, "Oh, boy."

Alice had been waiting for her roommate to wake up. Rosie wrapped herself in the sleeping bag and went out to the bathroom. When she returned to bed, she rolled on her side, and said, "You're up."

"Yeah."

"I was worried about you last night."

"I went out to Scott Base for the party. It was the stupidest thing I've ever done in my life."

"What happened?"

"I had sex with a lab technician."

Rosie shook her head like the information was a glass of cold water thrown in her face. "Uh."

Alice waved the confession away with her hand. "I'm not really as naïve or innocent as I look."

"I know," Rosie said, but her voice was tentative and Alice figured she was thinking, *two Franks do not make for sophistication.* "I need coffee. I'm going down to the lounge to make some. Be right back."

Rosie swaddled herself in the sleeping bag and left the room.

A few minutes later, she returned with two cups, the sleeping bag dragging behind her, and handed one to Alice. "Are you okay?"

Alice said, "You're a people person." Rosie looked dubious. "Can I ask you for some advice?"

"I guess so."

"It's about men."

"Oh, my area of expertise."

Alice knew that was a joke but couldn't manage a smile. "You seem so easy with people, like you know what to do."

"I never know what to do."

The sleeping bag, the man smell, Rosie's nakedness suddenly made Alice shy. She tried to drink some of the coffee. At least it was black, if weak.

"So," Rosie prompted. "Does the advice you want have something to do with what happened last night?"

Alice nodded.

"New Year's Eve is a brutal holiday."

"What'd *you* do?"

"Tell me what happened," Rosie said, deflecting the attention away from herself.

"I don't know how."

"What do you mean?"

"It's just so . . . complicated. There are so many factors and causes for what happened. I can't sort them out. I'm not good at people stuff."

"Pretend you're a scientist—"

"I *am* a scientist."

"Right. I know. So I'm saying, just tell me what you observed. As a scientist. Last night."

"Okay." The idea cheered Alice. "First I would have seen a woman board a van on the road between McMurdo Station and Scott Base."

Rosie laughed. "I can vouch for that part of the story."

"The woman gets out of the van at Scott Base where there's a big party happening. She stops just inside the door and listens. Oh darn."

"What?"

"You see, this is precisely the problem with science. What I need to tell you next is what the woman was thinking, but a scientist observing an organism can't know that, or even know if the organism thinks."

Rosie made a small exasperated sound.

"I *know*. But if I were to try to tell you, just as a person, as *me*, what I was thinking, that's where my story gets all balled up."

"Okay, fine. So stick to observation."

"Okay. So she's looking around the party at Scott Base. A careful observer might be able to tell that she's looking for someone in particular. In fact, a man walks up to her and guesses, 'Looking for someone?' She says, 'Yes. No.' He says, 'Wait here.' He returns with drinks."

"Uh-oh," Rosie said.

"Should I describe what he looked like?"

"Is it important?"

Alice considered. "No."

"Go on."

"They sit on a couch in some room and talk for a couple of hours. She likes him. He gets more drinks. She lets him lean into her and she leans into him. She—" Alice broke off her narrative. "This is the last thing you want to hear, isn't it?"

"Actually, I'm quite engaged. But I have a question."

"What?"

"Who was she looking for?"

"An observer couldn't possibly know the answer to that question."

"But *you* know. Alice the woman knows."

She ducked her head, but quickly forced herself to look up again. The gesture didn't work anymore, anyway, because she had cut off her hair and it no longer fell in a protective curtain over her face.

"Go on," Rosie said.

"By all appearances, the woman was quite interested in the man. She listened intently. They touched more. Just stuff like his hand on her forearm. Then later, even though there were other people in the room, on her thigh. She let him. She even moved toward his touch."

"She wanted him," Rosie said.

"By all appearances. And it was becoming rather apparent that he wanted her, too. She asked to see his lab. The party was thinning out by then. It was about two in the morning. I know that because the last van of the night was leaving. He took her to his lab and was very courteous. She unbuckled his belt. The rest was pretty straightforward. All animals mate."

"Ha."

"What?"

"'All animals mate.' Like that's all there is to it."

"That's the point. That's all there *is* to it. We're animals. The closer to that truth we live, the easier it is to accept . . . life."

Rosie watched her face closely. "You mean that, don't you?" Alice nodded. "So then. What was the problem?"

"He wasn't who I was looking for."

"Who were you looking for?"

"I came here to be a geologist. To focus. I'd prefer to stay uninvolved. I thought I could choose rocks, just rocks."

Rosie harrumphed softly. "It must be nice to know what you want to choose. I've spent years looking for something to choose. I think I came here to quit looking. The last continent. The windiest, coldest, severest continent."

"Do you think so?"

"Everyone thinks so. I'm only quoting brochures. The encyclopedia."

"But that's just it. Even given those characteristics—windiest, coldest, severest—people here are still thrashing around in the same way they always do. We should be able to live like the seals out on the sea ice. They're fat and happy. This place sustains them. No drama. Just eating, breathing, keeping warm. That's all they have to do."

"Ha. How can you know what the seals are feeling? 'This is precisely the problem with science,' to quote you. Maybe the seals feel extreme angst. Jealousy."

Alice liked Rosie. A wash of affection prompted her to ask, "Who was here with you last night?"

Rosie picked up the white T-shirt, wadded it in her hand, and then unfurled it. She said, "I think I love him."

28|

After Alice left to call her mother from Crary Lab, Rosie threw off the sleeping bag and sat on the edge of her bed, naked as the day she was born, while a feeling of tremendous well-being dawned on her.

Anything was possible. Her letter had reached her family. Jed had written back. Larry was leaving Karen.

Earl strode into the room. "Good morning. Where's my guitar?"

Rosie grabbed her sleeping bag and draped herself. "I've told you. Knock first."

"Whatever. I've seen naked women before. Anyway, why aren't you dressed? Haze is on in half an hour."

"Haze?"

"Where's my guitar?"

Rosie pointed to her wardrobe. "You're in a foul mood."

"I'm good. Never been better." Earl gently lifted his guitar case out of the wardrobe and leaned it against the door. He walked over to the window and ripped down the duct-taped blanket. "Look. Beautiful day. Concert's already started."

Rosie squinted against the light. "Okay. I'll be out there to see you. Break a leg."

"Rosie. You aren't in the audience. You're in the band. How many times do I have to tell you?"

With that brilliant light in her face, she again felt a welling of possibility. As if all obstructions had been cleared. As if finally she could see the path forward. Singing would feel so good. "What the fuck. Okay."

"That's my girl. Get dressed. Something sexy."

"I'll meet you out there."

"I'm waiting for you right outside your door, in the hall. Hurry up. You have three minutes."

Rosie dug through her wardrobe until she found that purple satin miniskirt she'd packed for whimsy. Bare legs were out of the question, so she pulled on a pair of black long underwear bottoms. She laughed out loud when she found the sparkly silver tube top and wiggled into it. She checked her effect in the mirror. She needed jewelry. She couldn't find a matching pair, but put on one dangly earring that looked like a fishing lure and one sapphire post.

Shoes were a problem. Hiking boots or sneakers? The hiking boots would look more intentional. They'd also be warmer.

Standing in front of the mirror, enjoying her own image, she sang that minister's hymn to warm up her voice. Outside her door, in the hall, Earl was tuning his guitar. Anything was possible. The simple joy of a welcome future.

"Very nice," Earl said, when she opened the door. "Let's go."

"Yeah, well, I'll last a couple of minutes on stage in this ensemble." She pulled her down parka off its hook and followed Earl down the stairs and out into the glittering day.

The stage for the New Year's music festival, set up next to Building 155, was framed by a huge painting of ice, penguins, mountains, blue sky, and the word *Icestock*, looking a lot like a grammar school set. Pamela was onstage, wielding an electric guitar, belting out the lyrics to an Irish folksong. Her voice sounded especially strident with the amped up guitar.

When she finished the song, Earl said, "We're on. Move it."

A crew of techs swarmed on stage, stringing cables and plugging in more amps for Haze. Rosie climbed the stairs at stage right, while Earl leapt directly up, front and center. Jennifer used the back stairs, with the drummer, looking as though she were trying to be discrete, but bubbling over in her excitement anyway.

"You look cute!" she told Rosie. "Just like a singer."

"At least the visuals will work."

"Have you met Nick?" Jennifer flung her hand at the guy arranging the drum kit. He did look like a Major League baseball player with his short hair and big white teeth. The classic effect was ruined, though, by a wicked cut and magenta-deepening-to-purple bruise on his left cheekbone.

Nick made a little salute and said, "Howdy."

Earl directed the sound tech to boost the amp on his guitar before even playing a note. He slung the strap over his head and swiped at a loud, dissonant chord, his greeting to Jennifer and the new boyfriend.

"Is there a song sheet or something?" Rosie asked anyone on stage.

"You're gonna have to improvise," Earl said. "Mainly blues."

"Right. Sure. Improvise."

"Rock-influenced blues," Nick corrected.

"Jimi," Jennifer said. "Mainly Hendrix, right?" She smiled her pixie smile at Nick. Rosie kind of hated her for betraying Earl. Free spirit or not, it was fucked up to make an ex-lover witness the new glow.

"Sure," Rosie said. "Hendrix. Right-o." The impact of her impulsiveness caught up with her, too late as usual. She'd let the expansive feeling she had this morning heft her right up on stage. To sing. Publicly.

"Don't worry," Jennifer encouraged, pushing the green plastic glasses up her nose. "Until two weeks ago, I hadn't touched a bass since grammar school."

Earl said, "Shut up, ladies. We're ready. One, two, *one two three*—"

Rosie nestled into her jacket and slunk to the back of the stage while he handled the vocals of "Purple Haze" by himself. The lyrics fit Earl's moment so well, how lately nothing worked anymore, and though he tried to hide his anguish, it came through. When he finished that, he segued right into "Voodoo Child." His insinuation of Jimi Hendrix was impressive, in spite of the grungy layers of shirts instead of a psychedelic tunic, the messy mane instead of a giant Afro. The music—Earl's music, anyway—was spot on, luscious Hendrix. Nick, on the other hand, manipulated the drum set like it was a piece of gym equipment, and Jennifer plucked tentatively at the bass.

When he couldn't take it anymore, Earl waved a hand behind his head, silencing them for his solo. He squeezed his eyes shut, held the guitar low across his crotch, and rendered a devastating performance, soloing with languid nuance, as if the guitar were an external soul. The audience roared its approval.

Rosie stood in the far back of the plywood stage, hiding behind the unoccupied keyboard, plotting how she might sneak off. When Earl finished his solo, the bass and drums joined in again, sounding like a riot. The stairs off the front of the stage were close, but she'd feel so foolish bailing out in plain sight. So she edged her way behind Nick and the drum set, heading for the stage's back stairs. She'd almost gotten past him, when he reared up his hand for a particularly enthusiastic beating of the cymbal. The drumstick hit her on the bridge of her nose, and the pain was so acute she almost burst into tears.

Rosie crouched down, right there beside the drums, and held her face.

"Ladies and gentleman," she heard Earl shout into the mike. "Joining me now on vocals is Ms. Rosie Moore."

Rosie stood up unsteadily. She looked out over the heads of the audience, beyond the dorm buildings, to the ice sitting heavy and gray on the sea. The sky, in contrast, was a blue so fragile it seemed to levitate above the frozen earth. The pain eased from the bridge of her nose.

Anything was possible.

Earl didn't wait for her. He began the first ballad of the afternoon, Hendrix's "Angel." And the thing was, Rosie did know the lyrics.

She walked around the drum kit, ducked past Jennifer brandishing the bass, and stepped over cables until she reached Earl's side at the front of the stage. She took the other mike off its stand

and sang about that rescue angel from heaven. The song tells a story, about the moon and the sea, and Rosie lost herself in the easy swing of it.

Earl grinned fiercely, first at her and then at the audience. He stepped back from his own mike and let her carry the vocals, following her with the guitar, just as he had in the cistern. As Rosie sang, she felt her sorrows take flight, the snow angel winging away with the dead girl. She sang for her joy, for her survival. She sang for the springtime with Larry. She sang like it was prayer.

Rosie shucked off her parka, kicked it to the side of the stage. The audience howled and she sang harder. The angel spreads her wings to fly on home.

Someone in the audience whooped, "Yeah, Rosie baby, *sing* for us!"

Rosie did. She sang and sang, pulling the song up from the soles of her feet, giving it her whole heart. She had a chance. *Anything was possible.*

Then Earl came in again, his voice blending with hers to finish the song. The crowd yelled for them to do it all over again, and so they did, Earl and Rosie looking over their shoulders at the band, cracking up at Jennifer and Nick's hyped zeal. Rosie felt as if she were taking flight with Hendrix's angel, spreading her own wings. Going home.

"Next, ladies and gentlemen," Earl hollered into the mike, "please welcome on keyboards, the talented Mikala Wilbo."

The composer hopped up the stairs and onto the stage. She didn't acknowledge Earl or even the audience. She went right to Rosie and said, "You were stunning. Beautiful."

Rosie laughed. "Thanks. I didn't know you were playing with this band."

"Me neither. Earl only asked me this morning."

Earl swung around and hissed at them, "Girls! Let's go. *One, two—*"

Rosie laughed again. It was as if by singing about angels and death and going home she'd summoned this woman who'd been her silent companion during those long post–crash landing hours. Seeing her tall, solid stance and butch-short black hair, that shy smile and intelligent gaze made Rosie simply happy. A full circle. Everything coming around. Anything. Possible.

"You're shaking," Mikala said, ignoring Earl's count-off.

"I'm surprised I'm not dead." Rosie gestured at her outfit. "I mean—"

"I know exactly what you mean. Hold on." Mikala fetched Rosie's jacket off the stage floor and held it open for her. Rosie was shivering so hard by now that she couldn't even weave her arms into the sleeves. Mikala took one of her hands and helped her work it in, walked the jacket around behind her and over her shoulders, and then helped with the other hand and arm. Then Mikala stood in front of her and zipped up the jacket. The audience cheered wildly at Mikala's chivalry. She turned and took a deep bow, and then sat at the keyboard. She rocked back and forth, shook out her hands, and nodded at Earl.

The two played a couple of duets, elegantly dreamy, as if they'd been waiting their entire lives to converse musically. Rosie paced at the back of the stage, again scheming how she might quietly slip away. Surely they didn't need her anymore, and she'd rather watch and listen. But she was trapped on the tiny space with Mikala and the keyboard to her right, and Jennifer now blocking the exit stage left. She'd have to jump straight off the front of the stage if she went.

So she gave up trying to escape, and instead scanned the audience, looking for Larry. He said he'd be here today, taking notes. and shooting pictures for the paper. The memory of his touching her, the way he'd held her feet and slid his hands up her legs, dissolved every other thought in her head. The soft hairs on the backs of his hands. The quiet and eager way he talked throughout lovemaking. How, after the ridiculous flannel pajamas had come off, he'd marveled at all of her, touching such innocent places like her kneecaps and ribs as if they were precious.

When Earl gestured for the rest of the rhythm section to come back in, Nick pounced on his snare, startling Rosie and clobbering everything lovely about the music. She decided to leave boldly, just walk off the stairs at stage right, as if her exit had been planned for this moment.

She made it to the front of the stage as Earl grabbed the mike and purred, "Ladies and gentlemen, before we get into our next number, I want to apologize for subjecting you to this asshole bashing on the drums." Nervous laughter rippled through the crowd. Earl improvised a short, comical riff.

Nick stopped drumming, laid his drumsticks, side by side, on the snare. He stood. Jennifer shook her head at him, motioned for him to sit back down and ignore Earl.

Earl shouted into the mike, "As for the little twit on bass, I can only say this—" Rosie jumped back to stage front and tried to grab the mike away from Earl, but his grip was tight.

That's when Mikala started improvising. Her aggressive entry surprised Earl, and he stopped talking mid-sentence. He turned and watched her solo. Rosie put an arm across his shoulders, held him, and willed the music to lure him off his downward spiral.

Nick glanced around, unsure what to do, and finally sat back down at the drums. Apparently unaware that Mikala was soloing, he picked up his sticks and resumed his hammering.

Earl spun in his direction and said, "Shut up, asshole."

Nick kept drumming, his spine straight and his chin high. He hadn't a clue that he wasn't in the same league musically as Earl and Mikala.

Earl laughed and shouted into the mike, "On drums, Nick the Man." He signaled for Mikala to stop and swept his arm toward the drum kit. Nick pounded out a solo, clearly believing his performance was a triumph rather than a humiliation. The audience shouted and applauded when he finished, responding to the theatrics—and their increasing blood alcohol levels—rather than to Nick's ability, but he stood anyway and took a bow.

Earl's grin was maniacal and the rings around his eyes lit as he played the first notes of "Hey Joe." He shouted, "Welcome, once again, Rosie Moore on vocals."

Rosie said, "No, Earl," and the mike broadcast the words.

Nick said, "We didn't rehearse this one."

Earl smiled as he sang the opening lines about Joe heading out with a gun in his hand.

The tune has a soft, hammocky feel, a dreaminess that lies to the hard lyrics about a man shooting his girlfriend. Earl slowed the tempo way down, teased the song along with a demonic intensity.

Within range of the mike, Rosie said, "That's enough, Earl. Stop now."

The audience shifted, a few people started to shout for them to just play music.

Nick dropped his drumsticks and touched his bruised cheek. He said, "This guy's insane." He stood and took Jennifer's elbow with one hand, slipping the bass strap over her head with the other. He gently set the bass in its stand, holding his hand out from the neck for a moment to make sure it didn't fall, and tried to lead her off the back of the stage.

"What are you doing?" she demanded, looking back and forth between Earl and Nick, asking them both.

Mikala fumbled along on keyboards, trying to accompany Earl, looking over her shoulder, clearly confused.

Nick and Jennifer argued about whether or not to leave the stage, and Earl half-turned so that he sang to the couple. Rosie was afraid to touch him again, afraid that the coil might spring loose. But she had no choice. She interrupted the song by stepping between him and the mike, her back to the audience. She put her arms around his neck, her nose practically touching his. She said, "I did this for you. Sang with your band. Now you do this for me. We're finishing our set with 'Me and Bobby McGee.' Just pretend it was planned. Ready?"

"I'm easy, baby. You know that. Whatever you want." He shook her arms off his neck and played the introduction. Rosie twisted her mike off its stand.

"Busted flat in Baton Rouge, waiting for a train. And I's feeling nearly as faded as my jeans."

Earl lowed easy on backups, giving her full rein, and she took it. "Feeling good was easy, Lord, when he sang the blues. And feeling good was good enough for me."

Nick and Jennifer jumped off the back of the stage and Earl made more dramatic stage turns in the direction of their retreat, shrugging and grinning at the audience, as if he'd won some victory.

But it was a false victory, Earl knew that, and the harder he tried to project his control, his calm, the more Rosie felt his brimming desperation. It was hard to bear the sound of Earl tearing his life apart, and so she sang her heart into the song about friendship, about the blues, about love being the only freedom worth anything.

When Rosie sang, "One day up near Salinas, I let him slip away," she put her arm through his and pulled him against her. She sang out beyond the town, beyond the audience, the whole while holding Earl close.

In the distance, the mountains were white teeth biting into the blue sky.

If only she could show him: Anything was possible.

29|

Rosie was a miracle.

No musical training. No inhibition. No affected phrasing. No coddling of precious vocal cords. Just out there in the frozen air, belting her heart out. Just raw voice. A natural diva. She tore up Hendrix's "Angel."

What Mikala would give to find her way back to that kind of musical innocence.

Not to mention the woman's getup. That shiny purple miniskirt and the sparkly tube top outlining perfect breasts, showing lovely arms.

All that was thrilling, but what really got Mikala was the way Rosie averted the mysterious crisis on stage, using the music to defuse Earl. If her interpretation of "Angel" made Mikala want Rosie, her rendition of "Me and Bobby McGee" made her love her.

Mikala knew it was crazy to say love. They hadn't exchanged more than a few dozen words. But music was the language Mikala understood and Rosie sure could speak it. Anyway, how many people their age even knew those songs?

At the end of the set, Rosie jumped off the stage and nearly ran back to the dorm. Mikala stopped herself from going after her. Clearly Rosie needed to warm up and put on some real clothes. Still, Mikala didn't want to miss her chance to set up the date they'd emailed about. So as she listened to the bluegrass trio that took the stage, she kept an eye on the door to Rosie's building.

Following the bluegrass trio, a brass quintet played a rousing set, and after that Mikala heard her name being called from the stage. Rosie still hadn't emerged from the dorm, but it was time for Mikala to play a couple of compositions. She didn't want to. The previous performers had played lively music that met the rustic stage and polar climate head-on. Even if her fingers survived another few minutes on the piano, she was sure her classical musings would not. She had planned to play *The Sarah Songs,* and it was too late to switch gears now, but those sensitive melodies would be instantly killed by the harsh cold and bright light.

Mikala climbed the stage stairs, deciding to not say anything into the mike. She'd sit down, play, and get it over with. From the height of the stage, she took one last look out over the heads of the audience to the dorm building entrances, just in time to see Rosie bound out of hers. Now dressed in polar clothing, she headed right for the crowd surrounding the stage, but before she got there, a woman stepped in her path.

The emcee repeated, "Welcome, Mikala Wilbo, South Pole composer-in-residence!"

Mikala sat down at the keyboard and played *The Sarah Songs,* feeling entirely out of synch with their sadness. She wanted to stay under the influence of that purple-skirted, angel-voiced muse.

30

After taking a hot shower and changing into warm clothes, Rosie set out to find Larry. It was puzzling that she hadn't seen him at the concert. With his height, he couldn't hide in a crowd.

Once outside her dorm, she stopped briefly, wondering where to look.

"Nice performance." The woman's voice came from behind, as if she had been waiting to waylay her from under the dorm building stairs.

Rosie said, "Thank you" before seeing that it was Karen.

"I didn't know you could sing." Her voice held no trace of kindness.

Rosie stuffed her hands deep in her jacket pockets and nodded toward the stage. "I'm going to go listen to the rest of the concert." She tried to step around Karen.

"You're being transferred."

"Excuse me?"

Karen forced singsong into her voice as she delivered the information. "Of course you've heard about the flu epidemic at Pole Station. They're incredibly short-staffed."

"I'm sorry. I can't do that."

"You don't have a choice."

"Sure I do. I took a job in McMurdo, not at Pole. Anyway, lots of people are dying to work at Pole. Send someone else."

"They need a line cook."

"Send Jonathan."

"Don't even try to tell me how to do my job, you little shit."

So she knew. Rosie stared brazenly, her pair of sunglasses facing off with Karen's.

"Where's Larry?" Rosie asked, becoming suspicious about his absence today.

"You leave next week." Karen managed to look regal, even in this exchange.

"He said you split up."

"Our relationship is none of your business."

"I think it might be. If you don't want him, you can't control—"

"Hi Rosie! Hi Karen!" Pamela grabbed Rosie by the shoulders. "You were *hot*. I mean, hot, hot, *hot*." She whirled around to face Karen. "Did you know she could sing?"

"Rosie is a very talented woman," Karen said.

"Okay." Pamela clapped her mittens. "New Year's resolutions. Rosie?"

She slowly shook her head. "I don't have one."

"You're no fun! Karen?"

"Oh, yeah," Karen said, looking at Rosie. "I have a doozy of a one." She turned and walked toward Building 155, as if she were going to work, even on New Year's Day.

"Whoa," Pamela said. "Bad moment?"

"Happy New Year, Pamela," Rosie said quietly and patted the woman on the arm, using kindness to diffuse further curiosity. Then she turned and walked quickly past the chapel and down the hill to the sea.

How could she have been so stupid? Larry said that he and Karen had agreed mutually, that both were resigned to the breakup. But that didn't mean she had to step smack in the middle of their disentanglement.

She'd been impulsive as usual. She'd indulged her appetite when her brain knew better. Larry might look like some version of home. But he was still married, and his wife was her boss.

Rosie walked, listening to the ice shards chime as they loosened along the shore. The seals loafed on the bigger chunks of ice, their seemingly complacent bellies pressed to the bergs. All animals mate, Alice had said. Rosie sat down in a patch of volcanic rock and put her face in her hands. Alice was right, obviously, but surely all animals didn't mate so stupidly.

Even so, Rosie couldn't take back what had happened last night. She didn't want exile anymore.

31

The next morning, Rosie got up at five o'clock to go to work. She dressed in an exhausted blur. She almost didn't see the well-sealed envelope that had been slid under her door some time in the night. It was from Larry. He wrote that he had confessed to Karen because he thought honesty was the best policy. He'd be away at Siple Dome camp, doing a story on the ice cores, for the next week. He also said that, "under the circumstances," email wasn't a safe mode of communication.

Rosie looked up from the note and considered this assertion. It was true that all workers signed a statement acknowledging that no email message could be assumed to be private, and most workers believed all their mail was perused by higher-ups, but Rosie thought he was being a wee bit paranoid. Or making excuses.

Larry concluded his note by saying that he hoped he could find a way to get to South Pole Station so that they'd have more time together before the end of the season.

So he knew about Karen's banishment of her.

Rosie read the note, written in a journalistic, just the facts ma'am style, over and over again, looking for a subtext. She couldn't decide if he was superbly honorable with his straightforward truth-telling, or if he was using a list of facts to cover up cold feet. Even his handwriting—bold, blocky printing—was strangely ambiguous. A big strong hand, but was it holding her to him or pushing her away?

Rosie felt tired, deeply tired. She had been balancing on one precipice or another her entire life. She didn't intend to do it any longer. Yesterday she had felt that surge of possibility, springtime, survival in song. She didn't need Larry for that. She needed only her voice, a stretch of land and a ribbon of water.

She tore Larry's note into confetti and tossed the pieces into the wastepaper basket. Then she walked slowly in the cold early morning light to Building 155 to start work. As she was hanging her parka on a hook outside the galley, Jennifer grabbed her arm.

"Rosie! I've been waiting for you. I didn't know what dorm you were in, so I couldn't come get you. They're sending Earl back. I didn't mean to make that happen. I'm so sorry. Can't something be done?"

"When?"

"Now. This morning. He's on the first flight."

Sometimes people spoke to Rosie as if she were the teacher, the camp counselor, as if even though they knew she didn't have official power she had some other kind of authority of the heart. She didn't. But she wasn't going to let Earl go without saying goodbye.

Rosie ran back to the dorm and pounded on the door to Jonathan's room. He opened it in his boxers and a T-shirt, squinting his eyes in sleepiness. The spikes on the right side of his head were smashed flat.

"Please take my shift this morning. I've done it for you a bunch of times."

"But," he said, rubbing his face with the palm of his hand, "Karen had a fucking fit last time."

"I don't care."

"I do."

"Jonathan, it's important. She won't fire you. She can't. She's sending me to Pole because of the flu there, so she's going to be short-staffed here."

"What? The Pole? How come *you* get to go?"

"Look. You work for me this morning, and I'll do everything in my power to get Karen to send you instead of me." This was a bit deceitful, since Rosie knew that Karen wouldn't do it. Still, it was true that she'd try.

"Okay."

She waited as he pulled on jeans and a flannel shirt. He didn't wash his face, straighten his spikes, or brush his teeth. He grabbed his jacket and followed her out the door.

Rosie caught the shuttle to Willy Field. She found Earl sitting in the flight passenger waiting area, slouched in a plastic chair, knees as far apart as possible, eyes closed. He looked way too skinny in his baggy pants. His face, behind the beard and all that frizzed hair, was more gaunt than it'd been earlier in the season. Rosie took the seat next to him and touched his temple. His eyes flew open. She doubted that Earl had cried in years but a tremor ran through him.

"I heard they're sending you home."

"Home?" he said, as if she'd spoken a language he didn't understand. His clenched fists rested on his thighs. "Will you tell Jennifer something for me?"

Rosie nodded.

"Tell her she better watch her back. That asshole will turn her in the minute she stops fucking him. I thought she was smarter than that. She got herself messed up with a twisted one and I'm sorry for her. I really am. I cared about her. I really did."

"I'm sorry, Earl."

"Are you kidding?" A jolt of adrenaline seemed to shoot through him. He sat up straight. "A free ticket to New Zealand. Tan babes, white sand beaches, big gaudy tropical flowers. While you all freeze your butts off here another month."

"Sounds nice."

"Nice? Fucking paradise."

A member of the 109th Airlift Wing of the New York Air National Guard opened the door to the passenger terminal. His black boots and green camouflage uniform looked kind of silly against the stark white backdrop. He spoke gently to Earl. "Let's go, dude."

Earl hoisted his guitar in one hand and his carry-on duffel in the other and he swaggered out the door without so much as saying goodbye to Rosie. She watched him cross the ice toward the plane, remembering how a couple of nights ago he'd sat in the middle of the road and said, "I could have fallen for you. But I could tell you weren't interested, not really. You just wanted sex. You haven't found your heart yet."

She jumped up and ran after him. "Hey, Earl!"

He turned, cocked his head, grinned that evil grin.

"You're wrong about me, you know," she shouted across the expanse of ice. "I do have a heart. I just put it in the wrong places a lot."

"Ah, babe. I know that." He strode back to her and set down his guitar and duffel. He cupped her cheek with his big pioneer hand. "You know I know that."

Rosie moved forward to hug him, but Earl turned away, grabbed his things, and boarded the plane.

32

Alice awoke feeling refreshed. She was going to Rasmussen at last. She thought of his lean cragginess, his leathery scent, his capable hands with a feeling of homecoming. Nothing truly disastrous had happened in McMurdo and now she could get on with the plan. *A clean slate,* her mother would say.

"You're late," the helicopter flight coordinator told her when she arrived at the helo pad.

"I am?"

"Yep. You were supposed to fly out on the second."

"What's this?"

"The third."

She had slept through an entire day without realizing it.

"No worries." The flight coordinator weighed Alice and her gear, and then fitted her with a helmet, chatting the whole time. "We can run you over there. We have a pick-up in the Dry Valleys, anyway. In fact, there's your ride now."

Alice heard the low whine of a helo, looked out and saw it zipping over the sea ice toward McMurdo. It hovered and then touched down.

"Let's go," the helicopter coordinator shouted to be heard above the engine. "I'm loading you hot."

Alice followed her out to where the helo, the propeller a blur, and its pilot waited. They ran in a crouched position, their heads tucked low, and for a moment she flashed on the Dalai Lama, as if she were humbly approaching him. But as she stepped under the whirring propeller all her attention was focused on avoiding decapitation. She loaded her sleep kit and survival duffel in the cage, clamped it shut, and opened the passenger door.

"First time on the Ice?" the pilot asked conversationally as the helo lifted off.

She nodded, gripping the door handle so tightly her hand hurt. Then it occurred to her that she might accidentally unlatch the door, so she drew her hand into her lap.

"We're going to tip a little," the pilot said, and suddenly her body was parallel to the frozen sea. Only her seatbelt held her in place. On the sea ice below, a quartet of black and white Adélie penguins speed-waddled toward some distant destination. Once they got going fast enough, they flopped to their bellies to toboggan for a bit, then popped back to their feet for more hustling. She also saw Weddell seals lounging around cracks in the sea ice. The sight of them chewed at the calm she was trying to maintain. Maybe Jamie had tagged some of those very seals. Alice closed her eyes and kept them closed until the pilot said, "We've just crossed McMurdo Sound. We're leaving the sea ice now. This is the beginning of the Dry Valleys."

The Transantarctic Mountains were a 2,900-kilometer-long range of peaks that offered unaltered sedimentary deposits more than five hundred million years old. The exposed layers, multicolored stripes of red, tan, brown, tawny, and cream, swirled through the rocks, layers of earth laid down over the millennia. Maybe she could make sense of the men in her life if she thought of them as layers in a pit she had dug into a mountain. Even if they were hopelessly scrambled layers, having endured multiple upliftings, volcanic overlays, even human intervention, even then, with the tools of a geologist, she might be able to understand their relationship to one another. There would be the lab technician on the surface, overlaying Jamie, and Rasmussen, all laid down upon the bedrock of the first Frank, and that thin layer of the second Frank.

Alice and the pilot flew up the valleys between peaks more perfectly striated than the Grand Canyon, passed over Lake Fryxell, and then over the Canada Glacier where the pilot pointed out two tiny human figures walking across the glacier surface. He said that they were biologists studying microorganisms in the ice and that he would be picking them up on his flight back to McMurdo. The beakers waved when the pilot hovered over their heads and gently wagged the helicopter from side to side. Next was Lake Hoare and Lake Chad, and then Mummy Pond where the pilot passed down close to the earth and pointed out the mummy seals, animals that had been dead more than three thousand years, perfectly preserved by the dry, cold climate. No one knew how they'd gotten so far inland in the first place, but there were their bodies, curved among the rocks where they had died. The pilot shot up and flew over Nussbaum Reigel, over Lake Bonney, and up the Taylor Glacier. They passed in front of Knobhead Mountain to reach the Ferrar Glacier, of which Alice had heard so much about from Rasmussen, and then flew southwest to a peak in the heart of the Transantarctic Range.

A pressure built behind Alice's eyes, her vision began to tunnel, and she thought something had gone wrong with the air pressure in the cabin. When she opened her mouth to speak, she couldn't form a word. Finally animal instinct kicked in and she drew a sharp breath. The pressure behind her eyes was immediately relieved and she realized that she hadn't been breathing. Alice took a few long, deep inhalations to pay back the oxygen debt. She had not spent so much as a night in a tent in her life and she was going to camp for six weeks in the Transantarctic Mountains.

Out of the frying pan, into the fire. Did that work in this situation? Alice wished she had her mother's ability to wrap experience in a phrase. The tidiness would be comforting. She should have brought her proverb book.

"That's funny," the pilot said.

Alice waited to hear what was funny.

"That's Pivot Peak right there. According to GPS, we should be directly over the camp. I don't see a thing. Do you?"

Alice looked out the front window and then the side window of the helicopter. Pivot Peak, though 2,450 meters high, didn't look like much in this landscape of such enormous scale. Below was a wide windswept basin that, from this altitude, appeared smooth and gently sloping. There was no sign of a camp.

"No," she croaked.

The pilot circled a couple more times, consulted the flight plan on his clipboard, and then, as if whatever he read there was absolute and unquestionable, despite observable evidence, he descended to the basin. *A miss is as good as a mile.* If Alice understood that one correctly, it would never be more true than here. If the pilot left her in the wrong basin, she would be done for.

"There they are," the pilot said, dropping dramatically in altitude. Alice saw three bright yellow Scott tents. "I'm not going to turn off the engine. You'll be okay?"

The alarm on Alice's face registered on his. He looked at the tents and then at his watch. "You'll be fine," he decided, reaching across her to open the door. "Leave the helmet." Alice, feeling almost shoved, got out and crouched low as she started to scuttle away from the helicopter, the rotary blade slicing the glacial air above her head.

The pilot shouted.

"What?" she yelled back.

She saw his mouth moving but couldn't make out the message. "*What?*"

She never did hear the words but realized that she had forgotten her gear. Practically crawling to avoid the blade, she made her way to the cage hanging on the side of the helo, managed to open it, and hauled out her survival duffel and sleep kit. She slammed the cage shut again and dragged the gear a safe distance away from the helo, which lifted off even before she stopped retreating. Alice stood with the two orange duffels on either side of her and watched it bank and zip toward Table Mountain, already looking like nothing more than a mosquito.

Except that out here, in the Transantarctic Mountains, there were no mosquitoes, no life whatsoever. The camp was deserted. The canvas skins of the three Scott tents trembled in a light, frigid breeze. A mess of crates, shovels, and picks cluttered the area between the tents. The silence, other than the occasional flap of canvas, was numbing.

Alice stood in the Antarctic enormity and felt herself begin to disappear. If she didn't move, just stood there, how long would it take for her to expire? Would her body lie among these tents, perfectly preserved for thousands of years like the mummy seals?

A whinny, thinner and more distant than a whistle, brushed the air. Alice looked around, knowing that there were no other creatures out here, none at all, but feared one just the same. The whinny again, sailing high above her head. Then she did see some creatures, two of them, high on a ridge above camp. Two human figures, the size of ants, waving their arms, Rasmussen and the graduate student, Robert. Alice stuffed some survival gear in a small pack and changed into a light jacket for climbing, then set out for the ridge, knowing that Rasmussen would monitor not only her pace, but the style of her gait and how winded she was when she arrived.

"You're late," were his first words as she crested the ridge, completely out of breath. She looked at her watch, thinking she'd climbed pretty quickly.

"You were supposed to be here yesterday," Robert said, grinning. Her mother would have been able to interpret the grin, but Alice couldn't tell if it was too personal, critical, friendly, or all three. She decided to keep her own face blank.

"You're here now," Rasmussen said, and she may have detected an embryonic smile. He handed her a shovel and pointed at a shallow pit that either he or Robert had begun digging in the ridge. "Any questions?"

Alice took a quick survey of the terrain. Obviously this ridge had been formed originally as a moraine. The two men had pocked it with holes. They looked like Klondike miners leaning on their tools, eyes ice hard and bodies visibly aching from the labor. She answered his question by shaking her head no. She didn't expect any special treatment from Rasmussen, and she knew these six weeks weren't about comfort, but she could have used a *hello* or maybe a *welcome to Pivot Peak*. She shrugged off her daypack and, as forcefully as she could, attacked the bottom of the pit with her shovel. The tool's blade bounced back, sending waves of pain though her arms and shoulders. She made the mistake of glancing at Robert, who glanced at Rasmussen. Again she couldn't read the look but guessed it to be something like, *See what we have on our hands? A girl who can't even dig a pit.* Graduate students begged Rasmussen to be allowed to come as field assistants. She knew one guy who actually worked out in a gym in the hopes that sheer strength would win him a spot on the team. Alice applied her foot to the top of the shovel blade the next time and managed to sink it in about three centimeters. She scooped the rock and tossed it to the side of the pit. Rasmussen had already returned to digging his own pit. "Try this," Robert said, balancing a pick on its head by her side.

Alice grabbed the handle and heaved the tool over her head, bringing it down on the compacted and frozen rock and soil. After loosening the bottom layer of the pit, she could more easily shovel out the loose rock. She noticed that Rasmussen, who was working not far away, didn't manage more than a liter of rock at a time. He worked without looking at her, as if she were no more than a new tool that had just been delivered. Whatever hint of affection that had infused that night in the geology library, when Rasmussen first told her she was coming to the Ice, was invisible or gone. The team rested only when they examined one another's pits, checking for possible samples, confirming or rejecting the presence of ash. It would of course never get dark and Alice wondered what might prompt Rasmussen to call it a day.

When he finally did, at six that evening, the two men filled their backpacks with samples to carry back to camp.

"Tomorrow," Rasmussen said, "you need to bring a full-size backpack."

As she tripped down the ridge, behind the men so they wouldn't see how tired she was, Alice wondered which of the three tents was hers. She wanted only to lie down. Her hands were blistered and shooting pains stabbed at her back. In camp she saw that she had left her sleep kit and survival duffel sitting on the ground, fully exposed to the wild southern sky.

"Which tent is mine?"

"Dinner first," Rasmussen said, ducking into a tent.

"The kitchen," Robert said, holding the flap open for her.

The kitchen? That meant there were only two tents for three sleepers.

The kitchen was furnished with two cots, parallel to each other, and at the back a small bench supported a green Coleman stove. Two tin pans sat on top of the stove, and the area under the cots was stuffed with rolls of paper towels, cans of food, dog-eared paperbacks. Robert threw himself down onto one of the cots. Even at the university, he wasn't exactly a clean-cut kind of guy, with his boyish hair curling at his ears and over his eyebrows, but now his face was covered with a blond stubble, his cheekbones were raw red and his eyes bloodshot. Thin to start with, he looked as if he'd already lost a good ten pounds out here, as if he lay down on the cot because of a endemic exhaustion, an inability to *not* lay down.

"Sit up," Rasmussen said. He pulled a bottle of bourbon out from under the cot and poured a healthy drink into a tin cup. He set this next to the Coleman stove and retrieved the First Aid kit, also from under the cot. He shook out three ibuprofens and handed them to Alice, along with the tin cup of bourbon. She wanted to not look at him, but couldn't help doing so. He nodded almost imperceptibly, and at once she was grateful to him for not speaking of her greenhorn status. She took the pills and drank. He poured himself a tall shot, then primed and lit the stove.

Robert ducked out of the tent to fill a pan with snow, and then put this on the stove to melt and boil for tea. "So what do you think of your first day?" he asked.

The enclosure of the tent was surprisingly comforting. Rasmussen pulled out a paperback—she saw the words *natural history* in the subtitle—from the same place he kept the bottle of bourbon and, with it propped open on his knee, read while he stirred the rice and beans. His cooking and reading, that condensed intensity, spoke to her body like a painkiller. She took another sip of bourbon.

"We got here two days ago," Robert offered, passing her a mug of a strongly scented anise tea, "and set everything up. The sleep tents, the cook tent, the toilet. You know where that is, right?"

Alice poured the bourbon from her tin cup into the hot tea. She shook her head. Earlier today she had found a big boulder which she used to shield herself while urinating into the bottle issued to her in McMurdo for that purpose. The experience had been mortifying.

"You won't get any information out of this guy," Robert said, nodding toward Rasmussen who was absorbed in the book and dinner preparations. "I'll give you the tour after dinner. The toilet, though, is just beyond the last tent, in that depression. Since we now have a coed camp, we might want to work out a system for letting someone know it's occupied. A flag or something."

"There's no enclosure?"

"Open air seating," Robert said.

Alice nodded and wondered what Rasmussen would do if she leaned against him.

"So how was your flight over?" Robert was clearly starved for conversation, but he was barking up the wrong tree—Ha! That one worked, didn't it?—if he thought Alice was going to be more talkative than Rasmussen. She was relieved that her natural reticence had returned. With Jamie, and then over New Year's with Rosie, she'd certainly been chatty enough. This continent splits your heart right open, Rosie had said. Maybe that's why Alice had gone to sleep for two days, as a kind of defense against such drastic possibilities.

After serving the plates of rice and beans, Rasmussen melted another pot of snow and emptied a package of powdered chocolate pudding into the water. He ate, read, and stirred, and then, when the pudding thickened, served it right onto the savory dinner plates. Finally setting down his book, he pulled a can of whipped cream out from under the stove where it had been thawing, and aimed the nozzle at the mounds of slick brown pudding. "Glacier on the mountain," he said, doing hers.

"What's the occasion?" Robert asked.

Alice closed her mouth around the first forkful of chocolate and wished for silence. The proximity of Rasmussen's bony shoulder was enough just then, along with the chocolate, and she wanted to be quiet, completely silent as they ate the pudding.

"Your flight okay?" Robert asked again.

"Yes."

"What did you think of McMurdo?"

"It was fine."

"Were you there for New Year's Eve?"

The pudding seemed to suddenly lump in her stomach. Had they heard something?

Rasmussen sat on the edge of the cot, elbows on his knees, spooning pudding into his mouth.

"I wish I could have seen Icestock," Robert said when she didn't offer an answer.

Rasmussen made a disgusted sound. "We're here for geology."

"I *know* that." Robert looked chastised.

Rasmussen glopped more pudding onto Alice's plate and gushed more whipped cream. She wasn't even close to full.

Robert said, "Guess I'm going to hit the sack. I'll give you the tour tomorrow, Alice. Welcome to the authentic Hard Rock Café." He shoved his dirty plate under the cot and ducked out of the tent.

Alice finished her second helping of pudding and retrieved Robert's plate. "Where do we do dishes?"

"We don't. There's nowhere to dump dish water. Mop yours as best you can with a paper towel. Leave Robert's. He does his own."

Alice wiped off her plate, threw the paper towel in the garbage bucket, and stood. "I still don't know which tent is mine." She regretted that the sentence came out in a whisper.

"I'll show you. First let me see your hands. Sit down."

"I'm fine." She tucked her hands under her folded arms.

He reached up, untangled her arms, and grasped her wrists, holding her palms up. There were five hot blisters. He opened the First Aid kit and found disinfectant and a needle. Holding first one hand and then the other, he popped each of her blisters, smeared the skin with disinfectant, and then applied ointment. He wrapped her hands with clean bandaging.

"Didn't they issue you leather gloves?" he asked.

She nodded.

"Keep the bandages on tomorrow and wear the gloves over them."

Nothing in his manner or the way he spoke indicated that he thought he'd made a mistake in bringing her to the Ice. The silences between his sentences were like places of rest.

"Thank you," Alice said.

"You better get some sleep." He stood and bowed out of the kitchen tent. He pointed to the one furthest away. "That's yours."

She tried to not ask the question, but involuntarily glanced around the camp anyway.

"I sleep in the kitchen," he said and gave her one of his rare smiles. Alice smiled back and then walked, doing her best to not limp, to her tent. She crawled in the tube entrance only to find nothing inside. She stood in the center, dismayed, until she realized that she would have to crawl back out and get her duffels, which remained in the middle of camp.

Rasmussen was still standing at the entrance to the kitchen tent, looking at the mountains and then at Alice. Without acknowledging him, she tried to lift the duffels, but tonight she couldn't even get them off the ground, so she dragged them across the rocky basin floor to her tent, where she stopped and looked out one last time.

The Dry Valleys were so-named because the fierce polar wind had swept vast parts of them free of snow, leaving a landscape of rock. There was no fat on this land. Nothing at all that would divert her attention from earth's crust. This was her life: rocks. Alice shoved her duffels through the tent opening, an effort that seemed even more difficult than digging pits in the moraine. She believed that she was the most fatigued she'd ever been in her life, despite her two-day sleep in McMurdo.

Once she had all her gear inside the tent, Alice opened the sleep kit and found, wrapped in her sleeping bag, the Dalai Lama vase. She tossed it to a corner of the tent and assembled her bed by blowing up the two Therm-a-Rest pads and fluffing the sleeping bag. Her sleep kit also contained a thick fleece liner for the bag, and she inserted this carefully before crawling in herself, fully dressed, and falling into a bottomless sleep.

33|

Mikala had lots of experience cooking for groups at Redwood Grove, but the South Pole galley was cramped and futuristic compared to the big, funky kitchen in the longhouse. Here all the pots and implements hung from steel racks, which in turn hung from the ceiling on chains. Dangling above Mikala's head was every size and shape of pot, colander, ladle, sifter, beater, and spoon. She had the feeling it was very important that she reached for the correct vessel or implement, whereas at Redwood, one was admired for making do. She leaned against the butcher block countertop and waited for the meeting of volunteer kitchen hands to begin.

Betty breezed in and assessed the help. She sighed heavily. Her entire workforce was out sick, and for the past week she'd had to work every shift herself. She'd given up on aprons. Her shirt was splattered with tomato sauce and her jeans looked like they had been dredged out of the scrap bucket.

"All right, gang," Betty began. "I know that half the station is out with this virus. But that doesn't mean that the other half has to be made nearly as sick with the food they're being served. Someone called this morning's pancakes 'wheat slabs.' Okay? And whatever the crew cooked up last night—let's be generous and call it a cornmeal-tofu-chickpea casserole—closely resembled what penguins feed their young."

"I liked it," Mikala said.

"I admire you, babe. But we all know where you came from. You were raised on groats and yak's milk."

The radio on Betty's back hip hissed and sputtered. Then a scratchy voice demanded, "*Kitchen. Betty. Kitchen. Betty.*"

"Yeah," Betty said, snatching the radio off her hip and speaking into the receiver.

"Can you spare anyone?" Barney, the station manager asked. "We have a situation over in the shop."

Betty dropped her hand holding the radio as she said, "Shit." Then back into the receiver, "Not really."

"How many you got there?"

"Four. And we have to make lunch for a couple hundred people."

"Send two."

Betty clicked off her radio and jammed it back onto her belt. "Mikala, Jeffrey, you two stay and help me." She looked at the other two volunteers and jerked her head toward the door. "Barney wants you in the shop." They scuttled away, seeming glad to escape Betty's frazzle.

She did look as though she were about to go toast, an Antarctic term for someone who has been working way too many hours for far too many weeks. She was having trouble giving a shit. She rubbed her brow as the radio on her back hip continued to hiss and sputter.

"Lunch," Betty said and paused as if she were waiting for the true meaning of the word to sink in with her helpers. "We're not going to get fancy, okay? I'm suggesting a hearty soup and a variety of sandwiches. But the thing is, the food has to look and, well, *be* appetizing, okay? That means, *Jeffrey,* that when you spread peanut butter on the bread, just for an example, spread it *evenly* and only up to the *edges* of the bread. Got it?"

"Why are you singling *me* out?"

Betty stared at Jeffrey as if the answer to that question was obvious.

"You'd think the sheer number of hours I've volunteered in this hellhole of a kitchen would get me a little gratitude," he whispered to Mikala when Betty moved off to start the soup.

"Come on. You and I aren't exactly the gourmet types, that's all."

"And the South Pole is not exactly Paris."

Mikala laid out as many pieces of bread as would fit on the counter. She pushed the mega-sized jar of peanut butter toward Jeffrey.

"Hey." Betty was back, leaning against the butcher block and folding her arms. She looked so tired with those dark circles under her eyes, and the way she propped herself against the sideboard, as if she couldn't quite stand on her own. "I just found a few #10 cans of mushroom soup."

"What about your little pep talk?" Jeffrey said. "I thought we were going to make a *special* lunch."

Betty flapped a dismissing hand at him.

"Good," Mikala said. "You need a rest. Let them eat canned soup."

"So. How was Icestock? Did you see the cowgirl?"

Mikala's chest warmed, but she kept her mouth shut.

"Come on, big sincere girl. Speak up. How'd it go?"

Mikala knew Betty longed for lascivious details like some people longed for caffeine. What she wanted to tell her, though, was how it felt to play keyboards to that voice, the way Rosie sang as if it meant physical survival, how she had tried to save Earl. As it turned out, she hadn't gotten much time with Rosie, but they'd had a quick dinner together the next night, and Rosie had told her all about the triangle between Earl, the bassist, and the drummer. Betty would probably like that story.

But before she got started, Jeffrey jumped in with, "I finally talked to Bobbi the carpenter."

Betty sighed. "I thought you decided to leave that alone."

Jeffrey shrugged. "We're going for a walk tonight."

"Congratulations."

"You think I should, you know, maybe kiss her?"

Mikala shook her head no as Betty said, "Hell, yeah. And more. When's the last time you had sex?"

"Uh. Like months ago. Well, Annie and I had sex once before I left for the Ice. But it was, like, rote. You know?"

"Rote?"

"A couple of dry kisses before the deed. I don't think she even came."

"Whoa, lover boy. Sounds like you need some sex education."

"It wasn't me! She was doing it totally out of duty. Because I was leaving."

"So what exactly are your plans with Lady Carpenter?"

"God, she has the nicest ass."

"And?"

Jeffrey put down the peanut butter knife and looked at Betty, checking to see if she really wanted more details. Mikala looked, too. Betty shifted her own ass on the butcher block and waited.

Jeffrey swallowed hard. "I spend a lot of time fantasizing . . . *you* know."

Betty snorted. "You got it bad, don't you?"

"I guess I *am* a little obsessed. What about you?" Jeffrey asked Betty. "Any flings lately?"

Mikala flushed. Would Betty talk about that? Here, in front of her, with Jeffrey?

"Obsessed," Betty repeated Jeffrey's word quietly. "Yeah. Ever since I told you about fucking you-know-who, I've been thinking about him again. They're on the verge of this big breakthrough out there in the Dark Sector. Like, they're about to discover the origin of the universe. I just find that terribly, um, compelling." She laughed her mischievous laugh.

Jeffrey squealed, "Would you do it?"

Betty shrugged. "Then there's this hot new girl who came in on yesterday's plane. She's a line cook in McMurdo. I heard she sang the fucking bejeezus out of Jimi Hendrix and Janis Joplin at Icestock. She's sleeping off the effects of altitude. She'll start tomorrow."

"Isn't that, like, unethical, sleeping with someone you supervise?"

"I said she's hot, Jeffrey. I didn't say I'd fuck her. But she *is* hot."

Mikala set down the ice cream scoop she'd been using to glop tuna on bread slices. "I gotta go."

"Babe! What do you mean you gotta go? I need help here. Lunch is in"—Betty checked the kitchen clock—"less than an hour." Then she made an exaggerated pout. "Hon, you're not—"

"No, I'm not." Mikala turned to leave the galley and Barney, the station manager, practically bowled her over as he came in.

"Turn off your radio!" he roared.

"What?" Betty asked, not unfolding her arms, not standing up straight to face her boss.

"Your radio," the station manager enunciated with cold fury.

Mikala didn't know if Betty moved in slow motion or if she only perceived the following in slow motion. Betty pushed herself off the butcher block. Swiveled her torso so she could reach the radio attached to her belt at the hip. Unhooked the radio and looked at it. "Yep," she said. "It's on."

Jeffrey slammed his forehead with the heel of his hand.

"Turn—it—off," Barney said.

Click. "There," Betty said. "It's off."

"Let's be real clear what just happened," Barney said. "Anyone carrying a radio throughout the entire station—we're talking the supervisors out at the construction site, Johnny in the shop, Roberta out at the Dark Sector—they all heard your entire conversation."

"That's unfortunate," Betty said. Mikala watched her struggle to overcome chagrin, to find the place inside herself where she didn't give a flying fuck.

"You'd be so fired if we weren't having a staff crisis."

"Come on, Barney. You know—"

"No." Barney held up a hand. "I don't want to hear another word out of you. I want you to make food. Period. That's *all* I want you to do."

"It was a *mistake,* for Christ sake," Betty said in a tone of voice she might have used if she'd accidentally made the chili too spicy.

"Look. Watch." She returned the radio to its place on her belt at the hip and leaned back against the butcher block. "See. I think the *on* button got pushed inadvertently."

"One more fuckup and I'm willing to let the whole station starve," Barney said and left the galley.

Jeffrey had become a statue of regret, his whole head in his hands.

Betty looked at Mikala. She said, "It'll be all right. He, of all people, can't fire me."

"What," Jeffrey said, looking up, "you did him, too?"

Betty shrugged.

34

Jeffrey ditched the galley, probably retreating to his berth in the Hypertat, the only place it was possible to hide, so Mikala made herself stay to help finish preparing lunch. Well before the meal officially began, folks started streaming in the galley to gawk at the disaster. Given the tiny staff, Betty couldn't disappear and she probably wouldn't have anyway. She stood right on the serving line and batted back every jest that came her way. The word *relief* didn't come close to doing justice to how Mikala felt about the bout of shyness that had prevented her from voicing her feelings about Rosie. Even after the last dish was washed, she was still feeling lightheaded.

She poured herself a cup of coffee and stacked a couple of cookies on top of a sandwich. Only two diners remained in the galley, Marcus conversing with a neutrino scientist. The two physicists yakked amiably, apparently unaware of the drama that had just rung out across the station's radios, even though Marcus had been one of the subjects. He must not have been listening to the radio, and Mikala doubted anyone would relay what had been transmitted.

She sat down at the far end of their table, sipped her coffee, and eavesdropped.

"It's brilliant," Marcus said to his colleague, shoving his glasses up his nose with a knuckle and, in the same motion, flicking the graying black hair off his forehead. "If it works, it'll be the best visual display yet of the temperature variants in the cosmic microwave background."

"Who wrote the program?" the neutrino physicist asked.

"Couple of my grad students." Another *shove, flick* in his excitement.

Mikala marveled at the fact that he had no idea Betty had just broadcast to the entire station that she'd like to sleep with him. Again. She wondered if he'd care if he did know. He moved in his world with such ease and power. Making and breaking the lives of his grad students, depending on his assessment of their work. Announcing quite conversationally that he might well have the key to the origins of the universe. Moving on, leaving wreckage in his path, seemed to come naturally to the man.

Pauline had told her the story a hundred times. In 1968, during that first summer of building at Redwood Grove, everyone had been so high with hope. They were going to transform culture. They were on the forefront of an historical paradigm shift. They really could design a new world powered by love and sunshine. The original collective members meditated, talked, planned, and sometimes argued about how they were going to accomplish this, but harmony and respect had reigned throughout all their differences.

Until, late that fall, when Marcus showed up.

He was both a hothead and a genius, a compelling combination for a bunch of young people. He believed there was no time to waste. He believed that making love and blackberry wine in the woods of Northern California would change absolutely nothing. Some say he joined Redwood Grove to recruit.

In the end, a bunch of folks agreed with him and the community split. His group went off to San Francisco where they would be "participants in the revolution, not backwoods quitters." Marcus returned to Redwood Grove several times that winter, against the wishes of most of the people who had remained at the commune, to visit Pauline. He told her in confidence that he'd been responsible for the bomb that went off in a San Francisco Bank of America that November. She kept the secret for twenty-one years. When Mikala came of age, Pauline thought it her birthright to have as much information about her father as possible.

"I *loved* your father," Pauline told Mikala. "He was right about so much. I can't deny that it felt really good to have someone like him, so passionate and smart, see something in me. But . . . he was a maniac. What he did. There's no right to that, none. When he left the Bay Area that spring I was so relieved."

Marcus headed east where he attended graduate school at the University of Chicago. There he blithely studied physics and acquired a PhD. Now he was a big muckety-muck cosmologist, speaking at international meetings and winning prestigious awards.

"I don't wish prison on anyone," Pauline had said more than once. "I'd never be a rat. But he just walked away scot-free. I doubt he ever felt a moment of regret."

"We *let* him walk away," Andy would remind her quietly.

"Yes, for our baby."

Those lines had enraged Sarah, who had challenged Mikala to not let them make her responsible for their secret-keeping. When Mikala would argue that they truly didn't want her to be saddled with a daddy in prison, Sarah would argue back that they were only protecting Redwood Grove from having any connection to the bank explosion. They didn't want to cooperate with the FBI. It wasn't, Sarah had been emphatic, about their concern for Mikala. *That,* she would say, was just a ploy to keep her in their emotional debt.

Watching Marcus now, it was hard to see him as a felon, even an unconvicted one. He looked tired with the gray streaks in his hair and the good-sized paunch pressing the edge of the table. He held out his pinky when drinking coffee.

"So my wife called the kid's mother," Marcus was telling his colleague, "and told her straight out that Devon pissed on Jerry's notebook. Devon's mom goes right off the deep end, saying that Margie was a pervert for even suggesting such crude behavior and hung up on her. Hung up on her! So the next day Margie—Did you ever meet my wife? She worked on station from '90 to '93— she marched over to talk to the principal. The principal literally shrugged and said, 'Kids got to work out their playground conflicts.' Margie told her that that wasn't acceptable, and the principal said she would have to accept it nonetheless." A couple of laugh shots from Marcus in obvious admiration for his wife's cheek. "So we took Jerry out of the school. I mean, we're paying thirty grand a year to let our sons be pissed on? I don't think so. Both of my boys are in public school now and it's much better. Regular people. I don't know what we were thinking."

The neutrino scientist chuckled and shook her head. "You must miss your sons."

"Oh yeah." Marcus's voice softened. "I miss my boys and my wife. Too much. I've had it with this continent." He laughed again. "Jerry is already seven and Robbie is five. I've missed too much of their lives. This is definitely my last season."

"Really?"

"Yeah. The telescope will be up and running by the end of this season. I have dedicated, talented grad students. They can do everything. There's nothing I need to see that can't be sent to me in Chicago. I'm ready to be home with my family for the holidays."

Mikala was a blip on this man's past, a moment he might not even remember, a moment that had been followed by two marriages, at least two more children. Biology was her only connection to Marcus, a random single sperm among the millions he'd released into the world. The rest was just a story, one that had been told over and over by her mom and stepdad, a story that had become part of the mythology of her life. But face to face with the protagonist of that story, she realized that stories aren't real. Maybe that's what this continent had to teach her: biology rules. Science is the knife that slices away the fat of stories.

Maybe she could forget Marcus Wright. Maybe he had nothing at all to do with her music. With the rest of her life. Maybe she needed to stop looking backward. She could look forward instead. The forward story of biology was survival, and didn't survival depend on desire?

Rosie Moore, who could sing the fucking bejeezus out of Jimi Hendrix and Janis Joplin, was on station, sleeping off the effects of altitude.

35

Rosie felt wretched at the South Pole. The altitude. The crystal desert. Not one penguin or seal. Just an eternity of ice, two miles thick.

The only spot of relief on the entire station was the computer lab, to which she retreated after every interminable shift in the galley. She spent hours browsing real estate sites, looking for home. The options were so varied and vast that it felt like looking for the proverbial needle in a haystack. Still, she clicked through pictures of cabins, castles, ranch houses, yurts, and Airstreams. She searched a dozen states and sampled deserts, high tundra, coastlines, and bogs. She lusted for plant life, flowing water, the freedom of warmth.

"Dear Jed," she wrote on her third day at Pole. "The Antarctic landscape. White, blue. Ice, sky.

"My biggest accomplishment since leaving home: I've made it to the end of the earth, the last continent."

She deleted the message. It felt thin, whiny, inadequate. She had so much more she wanted to tell him.

She opened another window. "Dear Earl."

She deleted that, too. She had hoped to hear from him by now, about the tan babes and tropical flowers, about being in fucking paradise.

Larry hadn't written, either, but of course he had said he wouldn't.

In fact, she had no messages at all in her inbox. The big zero. It was the classic case of being careful about what you wished for.

She had wanted exile, hadn't she? She should write Karen a thank you note. The South Pole, where nothing lived. Where astrophysicists exulted in exploding heavenly bodies.

The computer screen blipped. A message appeared in her inbox! It was from Mikala Wilbo, suggesting she visit her in the Sky Lab, if she needed a distraction.

Mikala had come through the galley line Rosie's first day on the job, and shyly suggested they get together, but so far Rosie hadn't been able to do anything when she wasn't working, other than sleep and digitally explore landscapes. However, "under the circumstances," as Larry would say, a distraction sounded like exactly what she needed.

So the next day after work, she asked for directions and made her way up to the Sky Lab where she found Mikala sitting at a keyboard in the tiny, hot bright room, playing scales. Mikala swiveled on her bench and looked startled.

"Hey," Rosie said. "What's up?"

"Oh. Hi!" Mikala held out her hands and spread her fingers, staring at them as if confused by what she saw.

"You look busy. Should I come by another time?"

"No, no. No!" Mikala got up and pushed in her bench. "That's okay."

"Nice place you got here."

A long but not uncomfortable silence followed.

Finally, Mikala said, "Um, do you have some time?"

"Yeah, sure. I just got off work."

"I want to show you something really cool. If you're into a walk. It's about a mile." Mikala's smile revealed a devastating stability. Those granite eyes. Those strong hands. Creating music seemed like such an elusive endeavor, like catching snowflakes without melting them. Yet Rosie sensed that Mikala had a monolith of a story that would remain standing in the worst storm.

Rosie said, "You can leave this place? Hell, yes. Let's go."

After gearing up and checking out, they followed a track through the snow, away from the station. The track led nowhere, toward oblivion, but Mikala walked confidently, filling the void with a stream of stories. She told Rosie about the commune in northern California where she'd grown up, making her laugh with tales of a failed goat herd that had denuded their forest floor and the guy who got kicked out of the collective after slipping LSD into the children's afternoon snack. She told Rosie that she now had her own cabin on the land, where her mom and stepdad still gardened and collected rainwater and harvested honey from their own bee hives, though the mom also wrote environmental books for kids and the stepdad taught music at the community college. She told Rosie that her partner had died three years ago, but how just before that a composition of hers had been performed by the famous pianist Yvonne Beauchamp. How the music received excellent reviews and resulted in an overwhelming number of commissions. How her feelings of success became inextricably tangled with her grief. How she had written almost nothing since then.

"Look," Mikala interrupted herself and pointed. "Hotel South Pole."

The sight astonished Rosie. A black box sitting on the ice. Shelter in exile. A respite from oblivion. The tiny building was like a punctuation mark to this wild infinity. Rosie ran to reach it. When she got there, she grabbed the door handle.

Mikala called out, "Wait!"

"What?"

"Let's keep walking."

"We're not going inside?"

"Not yet. I want to show you something else."

Rosie let her hand fall to her side with great reluctance. The desire to enter that tiny building felt something like love. Or maybe lust. Shelter, warmth, the embrace of four walls.

Mikala had already begun trudging toward the horizon, leaving the well-trod route and hut behind, so Rosie followed, stopping several times to look over her shoulder. The hut shrank, became nothing more than a speck, dangerously small, and then disappeared altogether. For 360 degrees, just waves of ice and a bank of blue sky. Rosie could see so far into the distance that the horizon arced, the actual curvature of the earth.

When Mikala finally stopped walking, she crouched and drew a circle in the snow with her mitten. She said, "Thanks for coming out here with me."

"We can't see the shelter anymore."

"I know."

Their tracks leading back to Hotel South Pole were nothing more than feathery indentations in the snow. One gust of wind and the footprints would be wiped away.

Mikala said, "I wanted to tell you something."

Rosie knew that it would be about the dead girl.

"I saw her leave the group."

"What do you mean?"

"As we were all getting off the plane. The loadmaster was shouting orders, telling everyone to stay together. And I saw this person, I'm sure now that it was her, kind of shoot away from the group. I saw her step away, into invisibility. But then I didn't really think about her again, until you took me out to her body."

Rosie put a hand on Mikala's shoulder.

"I could have taken three steps and retrieved her. That's all it would have taken. But it didn't occur to me that she was lost, or on her way to lost."

"How could you have known? It wasn't your job to keep track of people."

"The thing is, I don't feel upset by it. That's what scares me. That's why I haven't told anyone. The NSF asked anyone on the flight who thought they had information to come forward. I guess I should have. But you know what? I wanted to leave her in peace. All I've been able to think is, lucky girl. I can't help it. That's how her death feels to me. She stepped quietly into a whiteout and expired. I'm not saying I want to die. I don't. But everyone comes to this continent for a reason. And everyone expects her reason to be met by the continent. That girl saw the heart of Antarctica in a way you or I never will. I wonder if she heard its music, too." Mikala barked out a laugh. "I'm jealous! Isn't that crazy?"

"No," Rosie said. "It's not."

"The thing is, I can *see* the music: the gorgeous swirling mass of temperature variant energy just after the Big Bang, just after the singularity of time and space exploded. I get a picture of such aching beauty. But I don't know how to create *sound* with that."

Rosie gaped at Mikala. All this time she'd not been able to think past that cold, dead, end-of-the-road human body. But Mikala saw past, *way* past the dead body to some extraordinary place it had gone. Rosie had no idea what a gorgeous swirling mass of temperature variant energy was, but it sounded like the only place anyone should ever want to go. She threw her arms around Mikala and hugged her hard. "You'll figure out how to write the music."

Mikala nodded briskly, as if already embarrassed by her passionate outburst. Rosie took her hand and pulled her back along their faint tracks. Soon the little black mystery package came back into view. Again Rosie was powerfully drawn. But she wanted to savor what Mikala had shown her in the pure polar wild. She'd hold Hotel South Pole in reserve. She could always come back. For now, they walked right on by, without so much as peeking in the door.

36

Alice craved a hot shower, to warm her bones and to wash the cold grit off her skin. The physical pain of the labor was, at times, almost unbearable. And she could not get accustomed to the plain air toilet, which was shielded from view in camp by a slight rise of land, nothing so definite as to be called a ridge.

Yet, in spite of these discomforts, the landscape of rock and ice awed her. Even the work awed her. These mountains held perfect records of earth's history, and she loved Rasmussen's intense focus and exacting methodology.

Robert was less appreciative. At times he seemed nearly crazed by the seriousness of his coworkers, their contented silences and indisposition to laughter. Sometimes Alice thought that he detected something a little more than professor and graduate student between Rasmussen and herself. Not that Rasmussen ever favored her. He rarely even spoke to her alone. When he did, it was to reveal a piece of geological information, like a precious stone delivered just to her. She received these communications like the gifts they were. Alice and Rasmussen shared a love of earth's crust, and at times, that mutual love seemed to hold a greater potential.

It didn't make sense—given all that Rasmussen had to offer— that she couldn't stop thinking about Jamie. She had shared one dinner and spent one morning with the man. He was a big goofy creature, all feet and hands and smile. So why did he feel like an *Aha,* as if he were a scientific hunch for which she only needed to find the verifying evidence?

She would have thought that the hard work, the exhaustion she felt out here, would void all desire. Instead, the harsh environment seemed to heighten it. Sometimes, walking from the kitchen tent to her sleeping tent, simple lust would stop her in her tracks, a full-body memory of the way his mouth had felt kissing her hand. She would look out at the bare rock ridge, the fields of snow, and beyond to the glaciers, and wonder what it would be like to feel him inside her. There was no data, no spreadsheet, no telescope, no instrument on the face of the earth that could help her get a handle on the gravity of that longing. It didn't make sense. Alice was used to life making some kind of sense.

Over and over again, she tried to train her mind on the facts. To find evidence. To review what was known so far.

She worked for Rasmussen. Her job was to help him gather data that would prove or disprove his stablist view of the planet's climate. Which was that the ice sheet is firmly fixed on high ground and that it's been that way for millions of years, surviving several periods of global warming. His evidence lay in the ash samples. All over the earth, ash weathers into clay within about fifty thousand to sixty thousand years. But the Antarctic ash has never weathered into clay. It's still ash after being at the ground surface for eleven million years. What that meant, according to Rasmussen, was that the cold, desert conditions that exist in Antarctica today have existed continuously for eleven million years. The planet's climate has remained stable.

Rasmussen's reasoning was sound. She'd never doubted it in the three years she'd been working with him at the university. And yet, out here, when Alice tried to picture this fixed, stable planet, something felt wrong. But science wasn't about how a picture or model *felt*. It wasn't about *hunches*.

So she corrected her thinking, steered it back to analysis. Of course she was fully conversant with Morrison's dynamist view that insisted that the eastern ice cap had melted as recently as three million years ago. Morrison had discovered plankton, leaves, and twigs in the Transantarctic Mountains, and he believed that the only way they could have gotten there would be for the eastern ice to have melted, raising the sea level and turning much of inland Antarctica into a beach.

This, strangely enough, Alice could picture perfectly. The earth's solid white scabs of ice melting. Seas sloshing up around the peaks of the Transantarctic Mountains. Then freezing up again into the ice caps we have today. If they melted again, New York and San Francisco would be underwater cities. The world awash.

The earth changes. People change.

Rasmussen didn't like change. That much was obvious. Was it possible that his stablist view of the earth's climate might be as much personality-based as evidence-based? Certainly he would never fudge data. But Heisenberg demonstrated that it's impossible to observe something without affecting it. Wouldn't this apply to rocks, too? So far as she knew, no one had written a paper on the effects of love, doubt, and sorrow on rocks.

Alice was truly losing her grip on everything she knew to be true.

And yet. And yet. Why *shouldn't* love be a factor in looking at the evidence?

At the beginning of the third week, Robert came down with a serious stomach ailment. First he vomited violently for a day and then started in with diarrhea. Rasmussen decided to send him back to Medical in McMurdo, and he radioed for a pilot to come retrieve him. That evening, after Robert left, Alice and Rasmussen didn't speak a word in the kitchen tent as they prepared and ate their supper of beef stew and Oreo cookies. There had not been a night yet without chocolate.

The following morning after breakfast, Rasmussen said, "We're taking the day off. I want to show you something."

Alice was shocked. This had to be the first day he'd taken off in his entire life. They packed lunch as usual and stuffed their survival gear into two packs. Then, because the temperature had dropped well below zero, they put on their big red National Science Foundation parkas. Alice didn't overheat as they climbed one ridge, dropped into a shallow valley, and climbed another. Rasmussen seemed even more remote than usual, though he didn't push their pace as he did on work days. Today he walked either at Alice's side or just behind her. She wished they were working.

"The Ferrar Glacier," Rasmussen said as they descended the second ridge and headed toward the biggest field of ice Alice had ever seen. "My favorite spot on earth."

Standing still in that moment felt like a ceremony. Rasmussen pulled his pack off and found the Ziploc bag of M&Ms, nuts, and dried fruit. Alice took off a mitten and scooped a handful.

"I don't mind if you pick out the M&Ms," he said.

A wave of tenderness washed through her. That he was acknowledging his attempts to please her made him seem vulnerable. But then she felt guilty because the M&Ms just didn't seem that important to her, as important as he was making them. Finally, a pang of anger at his grammar school idea that chocolate, an unending supply of chocolate, was somehow enough.

Alice scolded herself. Obviously he was offering more than chocolate. Here was the Ferrar Glacier, his favorite place on earth. She looked unsmilingly into his face and tried to see him. The eyes behind the goggles were, she thought she remembered, blue. Plain blue. Neither bright nor gray. Just denim blue. A straight nose. A surprising cluster of smile lines on either side of his mouth—did he accrue those by grinning happily while alone? His face was like a good sleep. Alice reached into the Ziploc bag again and picked out half a dozen M&Ms.

They took a complicated route along lateral moraine deposits, looking up at the side of the glacier, which was nearly vertical and perhaps two stories high, a huge wall of ice. After walking for an hour, they came to a place where the moraine piled right up next to the top of the glacier. They stopped to put on crampons and then walked out on the surface of the ice. Unlike the glaciers in the United States, which are heavily crevassed and often blackened by soil and rubble, the Ferrar was as slick and smooth and free of debris as a skating rink. Gently curved, like the back of a beast, the huge glacier presented an endlessly receding summit. Alice and Rasmussen walked and walked, disappearing into the land of pure ice, a white so intense it glowed blue, glittering with dots of gold in the sunlight. When they finally stopped, the only land Alice could see was that of distant mountain peaks.

That morning, with her calloused hands healed and her back strengthening in spite of the nightly soreness, Alice saw Antarctica through Rasmussen's eyes.

"What do you think?" he asked.

"It's beautiful."

"Do you really think so?"

"I do."

"It's a geological Shangri La."

She knew that and nodded.

"I will undoubtedly be coming back for many more years."

Alice suddenly and inexplicably yearned for home. The blue ceramic dishes, the chenille afghan on the couch, the area rugs her mother bought on shopping whims, making their own kind of puzzle on the floor. Even the television and procession of wine bottles. She felt so unworthy in the face of Rasmussen's unflinching integrity.

"Do you know," he continued, "that there are tiny pockets of air that have been trapped in the ice of the Ferrar Glacier for thousands of years? Sometimes I chip ice off to bring back to camp. As the ice melts in my bourbon, the ancient air is released, mixes with my drink. It pops and fizzes like Rice Krispies."

Alice loved the idea of ancient air as much as Rasmussen did, yet all she wanted in this moment was to return to her tent, crawl into her sleeping bag, and sleep.

"I know you're about twenty years younger than me," he said slowly.

He looked across the surface of the ice, not at her, so he didn't see her shake her head. Inanely, she heard herself say, "My mother is alone."

"We'd be a perfect team."

He was right. She had chosen rocks. She had already decided, had even told her mother as much. "I need to think."

Since she wasn't looking at him, his hand came as a surprise. Awkwardly, because of the gloves, he tucked some loose hair into her hat. Then he rested his gloved hand on her shoulder. "Think then," he said.

When they got back to camp, Alice thought he might decide that they should work the rest of the day, but he poured himself a bourbon and spent the afternoon organizing their boxes of rocks. Alice busied herself in the kitchen tent, catching up with the camp log, though she wanted more than anything to retire to her own tent. How she would have loved to just lie in her sleeping bag and stare at the yellow canvas. Not read, not record anything in her journal, just lie there. The conversation on the Ferrar Glacier brought out a bone tiredness like none she had ever felt, even after a ten-hour day digging pits in frozen glacial moraine.

When finally he came into the kitchen tent and began cooking dinner, she stepped out to visit the toilet. After, she detoured by her tent where she flopped down on top of her sleeping bag, gulping the moment of solitude. Rolling over on her belly, she surveyed this space where she spent so little time, almost none of it conscious. Her pee bottle, strewn clothes, and there in the corner, the tissue-wrapped bundle that was the Dalai Lama's vase.

37|

Dear Alice,

I'm glad you're getting a few days reprieve in McMurdo, even if you do have to sort samples all day. It means email for me! Thanks for writing.

I hope your feelings won't be hurt if I say my first reaction to your spreadsheet was to laugh out loud.

So down the first column we have the three men (in the order of your acquaintance): Rasmussen, Jamie, Science Tech.

Okay, without looking at another cell in the spreadsheet, I have to say that if you don't know a man's name, he's not in the running. Okay?

Next, the "Attributes for Consideration" across the top row. Oh, Alice. "Emotions" as a category? I mean, it's absolutely true that passion does not necessarily make for a reasonable partnership. On the other hand, a reasonable partnership without "Emotions" is like . . . well, eating brown rice and tofu and kale your whole life because they'll serve your body's functioning best.

All animals mate. Yes. But some pairs of animals mate with a helluva lot more pleasure than other pairs.

But maybe I don't have to tell you my analysis of your "Spreadsheet of Three Men." You know what I'd say, right? Maybe that's why you sent it to me.

Rosie

Dear Rosie of the Antarctic,

If I knew what you'd say, I wouldn't have sent you the spreadsheet. Please be explicit: do you think the chart supports one man more than another? If so, why? (Other than the Science Tech, who you did disqualify already, but I'm not sure your reason is valid. When a geologist discovers a new mineral in the earth, she doesn't assume it's worthless just because she doesn't know its name. It might, in fact, be key to the entire geological story of the region.)

I don't think you read the spreadsheet carefully. I *do* have feelings for Rasmussen. Maybe bigger ones than I have for Jamie. They're just different. Maybe more solid. Maybe more enduring. I know that when we talked earlier I advocated for accepting our animal selves. But if we lived according to biology alone, wouldn't the world be reduced to a chaos of . . . um, you know.

Love,
Alice

Dear Alice All Animals,

A chaos of gorging, sex, smelling the flowers? Maybe. But isn't that truly the way of the world already? Throw in a healthy dose of murder and plunder.

Love,
Rosie

Dear Rosie of the Antarctic,

The thing is, I haven't seen Jamie since our day on the ice. Thinking about him is highly illogical. But being here in McMurdo, knowing he's just down at Scott Base, is distracting. To say the least. Why?

By the way, you never told me about your married man.

Love,
Alice

Dear Alice,

When you first called me "Rosie of the Antarctic" it made me laugh. Then it made me sad. I've had it with this harsh place.

I've recently had a vision of home. That it could be defined by an actual *place*. Where friends and family would visit. All these years I've been looking for a symbolic home. Then it hit me: home could sit on a piece of soil, within a set of walls.

Look at the attached file. Twenty-one acres with breathtaking views of the Bitterroots. Forest and meadow with wandering elk and bear. Northern lights in the winter.

I could wire them the down payment tomorrow.

The married man? I'd rather have the piece of land.

Your distraction is no mystery. Remember, all animals.

Love,
Rosie of the Bitterroots

Dear Rosie,

It's beautiful. But don't you think you should wait until you can see it in person?

Alice

Dear Alice,

I bought it. Twenty-one acres in Montana. I'll go directly there when I leave the Ice.

Love,
Rosie

Dear Rosie,

A habitat. An ecological niche. A place where plants and animals interact with earth's crust. Your impulsiveness terrifies me. But it seems that you seized the day and for that I congratulate you.

Alice

Dear Alice,

Look. This trailer is only a thousand bucks. I could get it hauled onto my land. It's a little rundown, but it's a container that would hold me. Can you picture it in the tall grasses under my big sky? Standing in front of it, outside, I could see North America's spine. In the late fall there'll be a dusting of snow. In the early spring, a zap of green.

I can already smell the coffee brewing inside, on my tiny stovetop. The hot strawberry-rhubarb pie coming out of the tiny oven. See my brother out on the range. He always needed a range. Like a wild horse. I could give that to him. I could give my mom a field of wildflowers.

Will you come visit too? You can bring Science Tech/Professor/Big Mammal, whichever one you like. Bring all three!

Your friend,
Rosie

Dear Jed,

My friend Alice says we're all animals, that biology pretty much explains us to the planet. I like that. Sleep and food. (Okay, and sex.) I've bought some land in Montana. A place to lay my head and at least figuratively to grow my food.

I think I've found home. I'd like you to visit.

Love,
Rosie

Dear Mom,

I'm sorry I've been out of touch for so long. I'd like to come see you this spring. I get off the Ice in March. I could come to Newberg for a few days. Let me know if that'd be okay with you.

Love,
Rosie

38

Rosie came up to the Sky Lab to show Mikala pictures of the land she'd bought online, sight unseen. She sat on the piano bench next to Mikala and asked a river of questions about raising bees and digging wells and growing vegetables. She didn't wait for answers. She was so happy, she just talked and talked.

When her words finally trickled down and then stopped, Mikala kissed her. Rosie pulled back for a moment and laughed at the surprise of it. Mikala put one hand on the side of her neck and kissed her again. This time Rosie kissed her back, tentatively at first and then with warmth.

"Oh wait," Rosie said, as if she'd just woken up from a dream.

Mikala waited, and as she did, she imagined what it would be like to make love with Rosie. Just like that kiss: immediate, present, rough, and tender. So different from Sarah's out-of-body sexual journeys where, with eyes squeezed tightly shut, she'd go somewhere completely out of reach even as Mikala touched her. And Betty, with all her self-declared sexual liberation, protected herself with a shield of irony, as if making love were the ultimate human comedy.

"You're so beautiful," Mikala said. Her cowgirl eyes were autumn brown, windswept.

"Oh," Rosie said. "Oh."

Mikala watched her face, her struggle to speak, and slowly realized that she'd made a mistake.

Rosie took both of Mikala's hands and said, "Be my friend. Will you?"

It was the sweetest possible way to say no. To say, I'm sorry.

Rosie's guilelessness made Mikala laugh, in spite of the rejection.

Rosie said, "I'm hell on wheels. You really don't want to kiss me."

"Actually, I think I really do."

Then Rosie laughed, too, and hugged Mikala before she got up and walked to the door. She had the grace to just leave without saying more.

Mikala listened to her retreat down the long sets of stairs, imagining each step to be a note played on an unusual drum set, a crazy rhythm, crazier tune. When the sound vibrations no longer reached her ears, she sat down at her keyboard and tried to play the Stairwell Song. Or maybe it would be Sky Lab in Three Movements: Ascending Stairwell, Descending Stairwell, and Polar Tower Solitude.

39

On the first of February, Barney the station manager and Valerie the science manager threw a party. More than half the station's scientists and workers had fallen prey to the virus in January, and while nearly all were recovered, thousands of valuable work hours had been lost. Due to the short summer at the Pole, the window for getting science done was tiny—a handful of weeks each year, and lost time affected the publication of important papers, follow-through on major grants, university careers, the solutions to world problems. Morale at Pole Station was in the toilet. The party was necessary.

Immediately following dinner, the tables in the galley were pushed to the edges of the small room and a sound system was set up. By seven o'clock, the place was packed with dancing bodies, the voices of Dave Matthews, Mos Def, Justin Timberlake, anyone danceable. The mix of people was combustible—a bunch of Pole novices recruited from McMurdo to help finish up the year's work and the season's staff who were tired from sickness and overwork. Just about everyone would be leaving the station in the next week or two, and it showed. Mikala sensed a group instability, as if the South Pole community were a microcosm of a universe on the verge of another big bang. A dense, small, remote cluster about to expand explosively.

Mikala watched the door for Rosie. She felt bruised from the rejection, and kind of foolish for just kissing the woman, making assumptions, acting impulsively. This continent was dangerous. It had rubbed her raw. Still, Rosie had been kind and she wanted her friendship. Tonight she hoped to present Earl like a prize, like an apology, like a gift. *Ta da!* A magician offering the impossible. Earl on a silver platter. The silver platter of the South Pole dome.

She'd found him earlier this evening at dinner, conversing happily with a group of women, as if he'd been on station all season.

"Earl!" she'd cried, squeezing onto the bench next to him. "What—?"

"Dude," Earl said. "How's it goin'?"

"What—? How—?"

"I was just telling these ladies the whole story, although part of my probation is that I'm supposed to keep my trap shut. Ha. What are they gonna do? Fly me out of here again? They're desperate for workers. I'm in the power position here.

"So they kept me in a virtual holding tank at Cheech. Wouldn't release me to the beaches. It just about killed me. But they said I'd signed a contract and they'd make me honor it even if it meant sitting idle in the office for the rest of the season." Earl stomped a booted foot under the table. "On my feet, baby. That's where I land every time. Guess they had a few high-level meetings about me and decided that, in spite of my unsatisfactory performance at McMurdo—uh, ladies, I'll skip those stories, but let's just say I fucked up a few times—they were so desperate here at Pole that they'd send me for heavy labor. Pole Station! Ha. There're suckers who've been working fifteen years at McMurdo who've never gotten to Pole. Besides, man, I love heavy labor."

"It's good to see you," Mikala said and she meant it. The incongruity between his sweet guitar-playing and otherwise boorish presentation gave her hope for the species. "Play some music later?"

"Sure. Yeah. Heard there's a party tonight. Don't I have impeccable timing? Meeting the ladies." He nodded at his tablemates. "Getting ready for some fun." He tossed back a glass of milk, as if fortifying himself.

Mikala had clapped him on the back and said she'd find him later at the party. She spotted him now on the far side of the galley, looking more spruced than usual, his hair neatly tied back with the leather thong, wearing a red plaid shirt and Levis that fit, chatting up a young—too young—woman. She'd be doing him a favor by interrupting. She'd save him from himself, and her from herself—why was she waiting for Rosie to make her appearance?—by suggesting they go up to the Sky Lab, dink around on their instruments for a while.

"Here's the woman I've been looking for." Betty swooped in, took Mikala's hand, and pulled her onto the dance floor.

"I don't dance, actually."

"Yes, you do." Betty sank into an immediate reverie, floating and twirling, entirely out of synch with the house music. She kept a hand like a tether on Mikala.

Giving in—what else was she supposed to do?—Mikala pushed her own hands in her front pockets and shuffled her feet. Okay, so she was dancing. The room smelled of sweat and meatloaf, with a faint overlay of spilled red wine. She caught Earl's eye and he gave her a thumb's up. Mikala rolled her eyes. Earl spread his open hands in front of his chest, as if to say, *Dude! You got that babe under control. What's your problem?*

Yeah, right, Mikala thought. She did know a lot about hippie chicks, but she didn't want this one. She wanted Rosie. But she wasn't going to get her, so use the energy, sublimate the desire, get to work. At least playing some music would distract her, but it was clear Earl wasn't going to leave this party, with its bevy of young women, to play music with her. Maybe tomorrow. Maybe he'd be willing to try out a couple of ideas on his guitar. Her keyboard, a percussion instrument that only played halftones, was frustrating her. The guitar was a rhythm instrument, too, but capable of more shading. She was going to have to get away from the piano to create the texture she wanted.

Mikala started to sink into a familiar despair. The hip hop felt like a harsh light, the drumming like some wall upon which she was beating her head. Somewhere in that head she must have some music of her own. Keep it simple. Maybe something for a brass ensemble. But no, she needed a full palette to capture the nuances of creation. That was the whole point. She wanted to show the Big Bang to be so much more than a bang. She wanted to infuse the work with tenderness, even playfulness. But the whole project felt so far beyond her capabilities.

This was exactly why she should be accepting commissions. They're defined, limited. Write a concerto for a string quartet. Make this poem into a piano sonata. Write a thirty-six-minute solo piece for oboe. But no, Mikala had to adhere to some crazy purity, write only the music in her head, every note dragged from her soul, and no one else's. She couldn't write a note, or even a measure, because somehow, just like the Big Bang itself, the whole thing had to start as some grand singularity, with the pitches, rhythms, sonorities, colors, all realized at once. It was an impossible task. One week to write creation. Did she think she was god?

Betty twirled and swayed in a closed-eye trance, and Mikala left the dance floor without her even noticing. She began making her way over to Earl, pushing through the layers of sounds, from shuffling feet, to light grunting, to off-tune sing-alongs, to the overhead boogie. Bodies exuding all that they exude.

Something clunked her in the head, hard, just above her left ear. She saw a bottle flying away from her face. The bottle was attached to a hairy arm, with a rolled up sleeve, which in turn was attached to a man dancing wildly. She slowly took in the man doing a kind of gallop with his legs and swinging his arms above his head.

It was Marcus Wright. It was Dad. Drunk. Entirely unaware that he'd nearly knocked out someone with his wine bottle. Her temple throbbing, Mikala stumbled to the back of the room, by the kitchen, where Jeffrey sat on a galley table. She hefted herself up and took his plastic cup of wine and gulped. Then she looked for Marcus. There he was, still gripping his wine bottle by the throat, dancing his heart out. This was the man her mother had found irresistible? Now he began a twist, swinging his old butt back and forth, bending his knees gradually until he was crouched, and then gyrating back up again, clearly pleased at his ability to perform this maneuver. A moment later, his index finger shot out, the one on the hand holding the wine bottle, and he pointed it at the ceiling John Travolta style, threw back his head, and exulted in some more body gyrations. She could not discern who his dance partner was, or if he even had one.

Mikala tried to make this image of her father into a story for Pauline and Andy, but it wouldn't go there. The humanity of the man making a fool of himself, expressing joy, *partying*, knocked her harder than his wine bottle had. She looked away.

The music stopped and Mikala realized that Jeffrey was speaking to her, through his hands, which covered his face.

"*What?*" she asked, annoyed. She swallowed the rest of his wine and set the cup on the table.

"She heard it all. Every word."

Mikala knew that *she* was the carpenter he fancied, and *every word* was the radio broadcast from the kitchen. For the past three weeks he'd been obsessing about whether or not she had heard. Mikala had been advising that he use the incident, and her obvious avoidance of him, to move on.

"Did you *hear* me?" Jeffrey asked

"Yes. I'm sorry. Uh, did she say anything to you?"

"Yeah. 'You're an asshole. A complete loser' were her exact words."

Mikala watched Marcus set the wine bottle between his feet on the floor. He mopped his face and neck with a handkerchief. A graduate student clapped him on the shoulder, laughing, and Marcus stooped for the bottle. They both swigged and walked toward Mikala and Jeffrey.

"The thing is, like you've been telling me, it doesn't really matter, right?" Jeffrey said. "I mean, I really love my wife. I guess I was temporarily insane or something. It's just so, you know, *mortifying* to have the deepest part of my libido transmitted to the entire station."

Marcus and the grad student passed right by—Mikala could have touched him—as they entered the kitchen.

"Deepest part?" Mikala asked. She remembered something about a nice ass.

"Yeah, like I was talking about my *desire*." Jeffrey was warming to the subject when Valerie, the science manager, walked up and took Mikala's elbow.

She said, "Hey. Marcus Wright told me that the two of you haven't even met yet. I'm really sorry I didn't facilitate that sooner. It's been the craziest ever season. But come on. I'll introduce you now."

"No. It's okay. I—"

"Actually," Jeffrey said, "we're in the middle of a conversation."

"I guess this is as good a time as any," Mikala said, touching her temple gingerly and sliding off the table.

"Good," Valerie said.

"Come right back," Jeffrey pleaded.

Following Valerie into the kitchen, Mikala spotted an abandoned cup of wine on the butcher block counter and she grabbed it.

Marcus stood next to the big stove, still holding his bottle, talking animatedly with the graduate student and a tall man who Mikala recognized from her flight to the Ice in November. He cradled a camera in his hands, in front of his chest, as though it were a sore body part. Valerie hauled Mikala right up and interrupted. "Marcus. I wanted you to meet Mikala Wilbo. She's the artist-in-residence I told you about, the composer doing a piece on the Big Bang."

He pushed his glasses up his nose and flicked the hair off his forehead. Mikala braced herself for the sarcastic genius sneer, the condescending explanation of cosmology, the I-don't-have-time-for-you explanation.

"That's fucking awesome," he said quietly, giving her his full attention.

She took two swigs from the high-jacked cup of wine.

"No, no, no," he said, reading her wariness. His gray eyes riveted on her gray eyes. "Tell me about it."

Ever since she knew she was coming to the South Pole, she'd rehearsed, in endless fantasies, telling him about her offers of commissions, the couple of mid-sized orchestras that had performed her work, the frankly over-the-top reviews, and Yvonne Beauchamp. Suddenly, though, now face to face with the man, she felt the absurdity of looking for approval from a father she didn't even know.

"I've been thinking of a pretty traditional format," she said, unable to control the quaver in her voice, "to hold the unconventional subject matter. Three movements. One that's pre–Big Bang—the singularity. One that's the Big Bang itself, and then, moments after, you know, the cosmic microwave background. And one for the beginning of the formation of planets and stars."

"*Awesome*," he said again. "That sounds brilliant. Hey, I'd love to show you the telescope, some of our data. Come out to the Dark Sector. Let's talk."

"Okay."

"No, really. I mean it. Look, I'm giving Larry a tour of the scope first thing in the morning. He's doing another piece for the *Antarctic Sun*." He turned to the tall, bald man. "Do you mind if she tags along on your interview?"

"Not at all," Larry said with a confident smile.

"Wonderful. Ten o'clock. So tell me . . . I'm sorry, it was Michelle?"

Mikala folded her arms across her chest, as if Marcus's genius was a burning field of energy that she intended to withstand. "Mikala."

"Right. Mikala." He said her name slowly, as if it had an unusual taste. "Do you have a premiere date for the symphony?"

Symphony? Who said *symphony*?

Luckily, he didn't wait for an answer. He turned to Valerie and said, "Margie would totally love this. You know? Cosmological music. *Awesome*." He held out a hand to Mikala. His palm was warm and sweaty, his fingers precise in their grip. "See you tomorrow then."

Marcus tuned to Valerie and said, "Dance?"

The science manager followed Marcus out to the dance floor, and the adoring grad student trailed behind, leaving Mikala with Larry.

She leaned against Betty's big stove and went to take another slug of wine. The cup was empty. She looked at the kitchen clock. It wasn't even nine yet. Mikala tossed the cup in the big plastic garbage barrel.

"Good shot," Larry said.

"I'm turning in," she told him. "Nice to meet you."

40

Rosie started walking away from the station at eight o'clock. She was supposed to get there first, by eight-thirty, and he'd arrive around nine. The stealth was hardly necessary. Everyone would be at the party. No one would notice their absence. Even better, no one would be at the hut. But Larry had wanted the secrecy.

He'd appeared in the galley this afternoon, having just come in on the day's plane. Rosie was doing the lunch dishes, her arms in sudsy water and her hair in a paper hat. The shock of his tall thinness, there in her kitchen, made her literally gasp. He looked skinnier, his hipbones jutting out from just above the waistband of his jeans, the planes of his face hollowed, as if he'd suffered. Even his hair, which had not been shaved recently and stood in tiny bristles around the perimeter of his head, made him look bereft, like a repentant convict.

She leaned a hip against the stainless steel lip of the sink and waited for what he'd say. It'd been three weeks since she left McMurdo, since he slid the ambiguous note under her door, claiming honesty and asking her to not contact him and yet saying he'd find a way to come to the Pole. Well, here he was. But a lot had happened in the interim. She'd bought land and contacted her family. Tomorrow morning she was flying to McMurdo, and the next day back to the States. She would never again return to this continent.

He said nothing, and finally she couldn't stand the silence. Her scheduled redeployment. The sad yearning in his eyes. His speechlessness. These things combined, combusted, and she said, "Do you know Hotel South Pole?"

He touched her shoulder and shook his head. So she began to describe the hut and the track leading out to it. He glanced around the empty kitchen and cautioned her to speak more quietly. He also suggested that they walk to the hut separately, and he insisted that they forego the mandatory check-out with station officials. All this, and he hadn't even said hello yet. But he touched her shoulder again, slid his hand down to her soapy wrist and squeezed gently.

A series of qualms quaked through her chest. The soles of her feet prickled. But she ignored these sensations.

Now, as she walked toward the horizon, Rosie tried to imagine what it would look like inside the hut. In a landscape like this, it was no wonder four plywood walls, painted black and covered with plastic sheeting, could feel like the most erotic of havens. Even more so when she thought of the way it offered shelter from Mikala's vision of the swirling mass of energy after the Big Bang, time and space exploding into being.

Rosie laughed out loud. The sky was a perfect blue. The snow was firm, a single squeak with each boot step. Suddenly, she got it. This whole continent. The reason scientists flocked here. To many, this landscape meant only fear, the way it could extinguish life so swiftly. But to researchers, it meant the door to other universes, an insight to the beyond. They came to strip themselves of ordinariness so they could see the extraordinary. Like the guy who studied bird shit, endlessly digging through piles of guano so that he might one day glimpse the bird's global journey. Or Alice, who examined the structure of rock, crystal by crystal, so that she might discover a story about earth's cataclysmic history. Or the cosmologists. *Especially* the cosmologists. They spent their days staring at computer monitors, examining long lists of numbers, probably unvarying numbers, searching for some spike or aberration—so that they might understand the origin of the universe.

Antarctic scientists spent not just hours but years, and in some cases decades, examining minute shreds of potential evidence, billions of pieces of data, waiting, waiting, waiting for that one shred or datum that would burst open the mystery package.

That took patience in the extreme. It took a tolerance for boredom. Yet—and here was the thing that suddenly awed Rosie— it also took extraordinary hope. A person couldn't dedicate her entire life, let alone spend huge chunks of it on this heartbreaking continent, looking for one piece of a puzzle, unless she possessed some uncanny investment in the future, an ability to imagine the grand epic. This was the paradox of hope. Science provided the evidence, the facts that supported belief in this beautiful universe. The possibility of home.

There, on the horizon, was her black plywood and plastic sheeting epiphany. She ran the rest of the way and wrapped her hand around the wooden handle, pausing for a moment before pulling the door open.

She hadn't imagined anything nearly as cozy. The small bed had a real mattress and two wool blankets. A lovely window let in a square of bright light at the foot of the bed. A green Coleman stove, sitting on a small wooden table, promised hot liquids.

Rosie used the tin pot to scoop snow from outside and put it on the stove to melt and boil for tea. Then she sat on the bed and bounced.

In the light of the polar expansiveness, she could think clearly about Larry. He was obviously frightened. It struck her as funny how those beautiful long limbs and magnificently sculpted mouth could belong to a man who was afraid to leave home. But how could she judge him? She was afraid to *go* home. Maybe that made them a perfect fit. She longed to feel his entire length against her and she promised herself she'd not miss a moment of their time together tonight. She'd watch him come in the door. Watch him take in the contents of their little fort. Watch him walk the step and a half across the plywood floor to the bed. Watch him kiss her.

She loved the way desire overtook Larry, how one moment he'd be there with all the complexity of his life playing across the features of his face, twitching in his fingers, and then a moment later, how he dwelled completely in his need.

She looked at her watch. Ten minutes.

41

The morning after the party, Mikala sat on the edge of her bed and took three ibuprofen to combat the effects of too much bad wine. Nothing, however, would expunge the memory of her father's warm, sweaty hand in hers, the picture of him dancing ridiculously and drinking wine from the bottle. He was out of the box and she couldn't shove him back in again.

She zipped on all her layers and stepped out of the Hypertat into whiteness. A storm had socked the station. She hesitated just outside the door, knowing she ought to go back to bed until it passed. In fact, an early morning announcement over the public address system ordered everyone to stay in their shelters. Flags and ropes had been planted and strung between the dome and a few key outbuildings, but individuals were strongly discouraged from venturing out.

The storm pleased Mikala. It suited her mood, the howling oblivion, the wind racing so freely across the landscape. She heard Rosie's voice in it, her Antarctic muse, a ribbon of sweetness through the angst of the gale. This gave her courage. She grabbed hold of the rope attached to the Hypertat and stepped into the whiteout.

The series of flagged wands, connected by the rope, guided the way to the dome. They wouldn't have strung a line as far out as the Dark Sector, but maybe the shuttle would be running from the dome and she could catch a ride from there. Hand over hand, Mikala worked her way along the line. The wind blasted about in confused eddies and then passed in long sweeping howls. The dry swirling snow isolated her completely. She could see no other people, no buildings, nothing but white and her own mittens sliding along the line. Every now and then a wand with a red nylon flag appeared, flapping fiercely, announcing that she was still on course.

Mikala stopped to listen and again heard Rosie's voice in the wind. Quite suddenly, the snow-laden air lifted, revealing a dim blue through the clouds. Then a big patch of cloud swept up and away, and there, in the distance, among the cluster of buildings called the Dark Sector, was Marcus's telescope. An instrument welcoming energy from the universe.

Mikala knew that the storm was far from over, that this was just a momentary gasp, the storm's inhalation before its next exhalation. But last night's firsthand experience of those gray eyes and warm hands, set to the music of that angelic voice, overrode all reason. It was time to talk to her father. She let go of the line and started walking across the reach of ice, toward the telescope.

Halfway there, the storm descended again and she could only hope she was walking in a straight line. She could see nothing. She was walking blind. She knew she had to keep going, keep moving, and hold on tight to the picture of her father, his ridiculousness, his humanness, as if she were traveling back in time to the moment when she was half sperm and half egg, just joining. When the veil of storm thinned again, she saw she was nearly there. She walked right up to one of the spindly legs that supported Marcus's two-story instrument and wrapped both mittened hands around it.

The telescope looked nothing like a conventional one. It sat atop the inner of two concentric and mechanically isolated towers so that no vibration would be transmitted from the building to the telescope. Hoisted on the legs of the towers was an irregularly shaped, shiny steel box that supported thirteen antennae, encased in steel tubes, sticking out of its slanted top. Yellow shields, like petals, surrounded the steel body. A big cosmic flower turned to the microwave background radiation.

Mikala entered the building attached to the telescope. She leaned against the inside of the door, breathing and shivering hard, until she felt slightly more composed. Then she climbed the stairs to the second floor, where she found Marcus sitting at a computer, clicking through data.

His shoulders were hunched from fatigue. The hair on the back of his head was all mussed from where he'd slept on it. His shirttails were out, stretched over the paunch. He hove a big sigh, weaved his fingers behind his neck, and stretched. That's when he saw her.

"Hey!" he said, twirling on his office chair. "How'd you get out here? The shuttle isn't running."

"I could ask you the same question." Anger prickled at her scalp.

Oblivious to the edge in her voice, Marcus smiled. "We're so close to first light on the telescope. I don't have a single hour to spare before the end of the season."

"But the storm." As if he were invincible.

He paused, shrugged. Maybe he wondered why she concerned herself with what he did in a storm. Of course she, too, had plowed through an Antarctic whiteout to get where she wanted to be. Like father, like daughter.

She said, "Am I disturbing you?"

His phone rang and he glanced at it, but didn't pick up. "Not at all. I invited you." He used a foot to drag another office chair closer to his and gestured toward it. "Have a seat. Cup of coffee?"

"No. Thanks."

"You know, I think it's really cool that the NSF has this artists-in-residence program. Dialogue between art and science is all too rare. The truth is, science is the new horizon of imagination. Science *is* the new art. It's the study of the universe. What else is there?"

"Your family?" she asked, nodding at the photographs taped along the frame of his monitor. The two boys would be her half-brothers.

"Yep." He smiled at the pictures. "Jerry is seven, Robbie five. That's Margie, my wife."

He took off his glasses and used a shirttail to clean the lenses. When he put them back on, he seemed to look at her more closely, and then scowled slightly. "Your work," he said. "Tell me how I can help. Would you like to see the innards of the telescope?"

He gestured toward an open door leading to a small dark room. Inside were a tangle of intricately arranged bundles of cables and shiny metal boxes, connectors and gauges. The rest of Marcus's lab looked like any makeshift office, with three folding tables serving as desks and several disassembled computers lying about. Half-eaten bags of chips and empty Coke cans littered the floor. Mikala *was* curious about the telescope, and almost let him divert her attention, but when her eyes fell again on the pictures of her half-brothers, she blurted, "I need to ask you a personal question."

Apprehension flickered across his brow. He lifted his hands, palms up.

"Do you remember a woman named Pauline Williams?"

His hands drifted to his thighs. His face slackened with bewilderment, as if he hadn't a clue.

Violent wind shook the building. Mikala looked out the all-white window. She prompted, "What about Redwood Grove?"

"Who are you?" he asked in a whisper, and then cleared his throat, as if the whisper had been an accident.

"I'm Pauline Williams's daughter."

He sat mute and motionless, convincing Mikala that he truly didn't remember anything about Pauline Williams or Redwood Grove. One autumn, a million years ago. One girlfriend, among a hundred. One particularly inconvenient pregnancy, occurring at a time when he needed to run. Surely, though, he would remember other events from that year.

She said, "I know about the bomb and the bank."

Marcus stood up quickly, knocking his office chair behind him, and it rolled across the floor until it stopped against a folding table.

"Pauline says your file is still open. You're still 'wanted.'"

The phone rang again, a grating rhythm of alarm.

"Your name is Mikala?" he asked hoarsely.

She nodded, anger at his obliviousness filling her head.

"Are you really a composer?"

The wind grabbed the building again, shook hard. Mikala actually laughed. Did he think she was an FBI agent disguising herself as a composer? "Of course. What does that have to do with it?"

"I just . . . I just feel. I don't know. Awe."

"*Awe?*"

"You. Here. The South Pole." He spoke with hushed reverence. "Is it really . . . *you?*"

His reaction was confusing. Who did he think she was? "You never contacted Pauline again. After she wrote about being pregnant."

"She asked me not to." He did remember. "She said I would only bring harm if I ever contacted her or you."

"I guess that worked for you."

He felt behind himself for the missing chair. Mikala pointed to where it had rolled. Marcus retrieved it and sat, staring.

He remembered. And suddenly, that made it worse, much worse, than if he had forgotten. A suffocating rage clouded Mikala's head and then burst. "Do you have any idea," she started, "what wreckage you left behind? Do you? Do you have *any* idea? *Lives,* Marcus. People's *lives.* You came flying in one day in October, mouthing off, so fucking sure of yourself. You spent all of, what, four or five months at Redwood Grove and you had more impact on our lives than anyone. For the next thirty-plus years. While you moved on to your fancy-ass education, we covered for you. We lied for you. Do you know, because we were afraid of the hospital, we didn't take Willow in when she broke a leg, and she still limps today? Why? Because we didn't believe in turning people in. Because you were the father of one of our members. That would be *me.*" Mikala realized she was shouting and she couldn't stop. "We lived for what we *believed* in, Marcus, long term, not for one winter or one year. My parents *still* live for what they believe in, right there, at Redwood Grove. *Now, today.* Not just for the moment it seemed like the thing to do. Do you know that Daniel and Sheryl had to change their names, their identities, because they listened to your pretty words and followed you to San Francisco? They asked to come back, after the bank. They *begged* to come back, but we had to say no. Daniel killed himself that summer. Did you know that?" The words were heaving from her core. "Do you remember Elana and Moe's baby girl? Her name was Sarah, Marcus. She was a baby the winter you were at Redwood. Do you remember her? She died three years ago. She died. She died of lymphoma. Slowly and painfully. She was my life. She's been my life for all of it. *All of it. Sarah died.*"

Now Mikala was sobbing. The storm shuddered the small building. Marcus sat watching her. When she quieted, she looked at him, and he nodded. He said, "I know."

"You know about Sarah?"

"No, I don't know about Sarah. But I know I did a lot of damage. Unforgiveable damage. I'm sorry about Sarah."

"Do you even remember her?"

"Yes," Marcus said. "I remember Elana and Moe's baby. I remember Sarah."

Of course Sarah's lymphoma wasn't his fault. But his remembering her felt very important. Fresh tears tore through Mikala.

"Look," he said, as if logic were appropriate for addressing anything. "It seemed to me that staying away was the best thing I could do for Redwood. For Pauline. For you. Coming back in any form, even a telephone call, seemed like it would only bring grief or confusion or even danger."

Mikala found a tissue in a box on his desk and blew her nose. She remained standing.

"Pauline asked me to stay away. But . . . I've wanted . . . I mean, I've wondered . . ."

Wondered. Such a soft word. As if her life was just a dream he once had.

"It seemed like the one thing I could do, not cause trouble for you or her. You're right. The case *is* still open. I doubt anyone is very interested anymore. No one died in the explosion. But I thought the one thing I could do for you was to stay away, given all that happened that summer."

"Maybe you were protecting yourself, too."

He nodded slowly. "Yes, I was afraid. For a lot of reasons."

Mikala hadn't expected this truthfulness. His face sagged and the gray of his eyes softened. He said, "I have two boys now. I can't imagine leaving them fatherless. I know what it means. What happened. What I did."

"I'm not fatherless." She spoke with vehemence. "I had a great childhood. Pauline hooked up with Andy when I was one. He's the best dad possible." Mikala walked away from him, toward the door, and then turned. "Do you regret setting off that bomb?"

The question startled him, and he stood, too. But then he just nodded, as if he got it, got that that explosion went off in the center of her life, that she needed to understand its genesis and conclusion.

"More deeply than you can imagine. I'm not that person, anymore. I want you to know that. I have nightmares to this day. They start in that basement where we built the bomb. Some kid had rich parents who lived in Pacific Heights. We stored the pipe and explosives, everything down by their furnace. We used flashlights to put that thing together. I'm still trying to understand. I think it had something to do with the fact that we *could* build a bomb, the actual chemistry and mechanics of it, and how that know-how translated, in my immature mind, to power.

"Then the explosion itself. Most of my nightmares keep to the basement, as if by returning to that moment of making the bomb, I might understand, or even undo. Sometimes I also dream about walking down the hills of San Francisco, as we carry the bomb to its destination. Only occasionally do the nightmares extend to the bank itself. But when they do, the dream goes way beyond reality. In my dreams, people die. Bodies are strewn all over the bank floor. Blood pools ankle deep. No one died in the real explosion, but a woman did lose her hand. I've never apologized to her."

He looked Mikala in the eye and, his voice husky with feeling, said, "None of this excuses me."

Mikala was disarmed by his candor.

He whispered, "I can't believe it's you." He pulled his wallet out of his back pocket, opened it, and flipped through the cellophane envelopes of pictures. He slid one out and held it out to her. Mikala took the picture. A baby. A red-faced, squalling baby. Mikala as a newborn. She was naked, on her back, her fists clamped shut, and her feet airborne, kicking. The swatch of black hair looked like a wig on the larval creature. It was as if Pauline had purposely chosen the ugliest picture, to keep him at bay. Yet, even in her infant fury, Mikala looked directly into the camera, into the viewer's eyes. On the back, in Pauline's handwriting, were the words, *Baby girl born on August 21, 1969.*

The photograph's corners were rounded and the emulsion cracked from wear. Marcus's hands shook as he reached for the picture after just a few seconds, as if he were worried she might keep it.

"It's you," he whispered. Looking hard at her face, he repeated, "*You.*"

The phone *brrred* across the soundscape of her breath, his *you,* the wind buffeting the temporary building.

42

When Rosie woke up, she was alone. There was the briefest moment when she looked for him, wondered if he'd left already, before she remembered that he hadn't come.

It was late, past ten. Either her watch alarm hadn't gone off or she'd slept through it. She had missed the flight to McMurdo, the first leg of her journey home.

Rosie dressed slowly. She knew she ought to start the Coleman stove to heat some soup for breakfast. At the very least, she should toss back some nuts. It was only a mile to the station, but she had been too keyed up to eat dinner last night, and an infusion of calories would be wise. She didn't feel like eating, though.

She put on her final layers, hoisted her pack, and stepped out of the hut. Bad weather. Really bad weather. Which meant her flight would have been postponed. She still had a chance to make it. She stood on the threshold of Hotel South Pole and considered her options. Stay or leave.

Rosie walked. The sky was lightening by the minute, and the flight would leave as soon as it cleared. She wanted to go home.

A shock of sunlight stabbed through an opening in the cloud cover, reminding Rosie of that similar moment on the plane, when the sun had come in the porthole, just before the crash landing. This window of blue sky was just as temporary as that one had been, and three minutes later the clouds closed up again. She was swathed in white. The snowflakes were tiny desert bits, more like snow dust blown from the surface of the ice than new precipitation coming from the sky, but still thick in their bitterly cold fury. She couldn't see more than a couple of yards ahead of her. Even so, the route, scored by the tracks of dozens of pairs of boots, was easy enough to follow.

Rosie kept walking.

He hadn't come. The words looped through her brain, over and over again, as if looking for a place to burrow into the inner folds. It hadn't occurred to her that he wouldn't come. His longing had been so present, so obvious, just hours earlier, when they talked in the galley. Something must have prevented him. Last night she'd lain awake until three in the morning, waiting and worrying. She'd gotten up and looked out the door maybe a dozen times, thinking she heard someone. The sky had been clear the last time she looked.

Only now, walking back, did she consider the bleak possibility that he might have *decided* to not come.

She trudged on, alone, through the shitty weather. At least she was on a path, a way forward. In spite of the no-show, Rosie still felt that fresh core of sureness in herself. Her land, her family, her new friends, Alice and Mikala, all that. *Still*. And *definitely*.

Today she needed only footsteps.

Tomorrow she was leaving the Ice for good.

Next month she'd see Jed and her mother.

Rosie picked up her pace. It was wicked cold.

43

Alice woke up early in the morning on February 2, having dreamt about walking on the Ferrar Glacier. She was walking alone. The surface of the glacier was littered with Dalai Lama vases. They weren't wrapped in tissue or encased in plastic, like the real one. These vases were out in the open, sitting randomly on the ice. They came in a multitude of styles—water pitchers, tall crystal iris vases, glazed ceramic vases, bulbous stem vases with long throats. In her arms, she carried the biggest one, a Grecian urn adorned with warriors and maidens. Though as big around as Alice, the urn weighed almost nothing, and she carried it easily across the Ferrar Glacier, walking without desire or destination.

She lay in her tent, snuggled deep in the layers of fleece and down, trying to understand the dream. Usually she dreamt just as she thought: literally. Her most extravagant dreams were the block-buster kinds, with armies marching across fields or people evacuating a town about to be hit by a tsunami. They included details she could have gotten straight out of a book or movie. She awoke from most dreams with a headache.

But the Dalai Lama vase dream had a serene quality, despite the extreme setting. It seemed to be an arrow, a signifier. But at what was it pointing? It left her feeling oddly soothed. This was bigger than a proverb, bigger than a spontaneous metaphor. The dream seemed to hover outside her consciousness, as if it wanted admittance but couldn't get past the guard.

Late that morning, Rasmussen and Alice returned to camp for lunch so that they'd be there to meet the helicopter bringing

Robert back from McMurdo. As it descended and touched down, and as Robert hopped out, Alice longed to take his place, to be lifted up and out of this camp. Her three days in McMurdo, where Rasmussen had sent her to do specimen analysis, had only intensified her desire to leave this harsh place. She had almost two weeks left, but enduring it seemed next to impossible. She stood and looked at that pod, topped with a whirlybird, the only way out of here, and wondered how she'd make it through these last few days.

To both her and Rasmussen's surprise, the pilot shut off the engine and the propeller blades slowed. He climbed out of the helo and walked to where they stood in front of the kitchen tent.

"Have a pickup in an hour, two valleys over," he said by way of explanation.

Rasmussen nodded. "Lunch?"

The pilot grunted acquiescence.

Robert, who had shaved off his blond beard and gotten a haircut in town, dragged his duffels to his tent, having hardly said hello, like a schoolboy returning from detention. Alice followed the pilot and Rasmussen into the kitchen tent.

"Girl lost at Pole," the pilot said.

"Huh." Rasmussen scooped some warmed Dinty Moore beef stew onto a plate and handed it to him.

The pilot grimaced at the stew. "She was supposed to be leaving the station today. Never showed up for her flight."

"Happens."

"*Happens?*" Alice asked Rasmussen. "What do you mean, it happens?" She had never before challenged him. He looked at her sharply.

"Big storm," the pilot offered. "Blew for eight hours."

"So the flight was canceled, right?" Alice said. "Why would anyone show up for a flight in a storm? She probably knew it wasn't going anywhere."

Rasmussen watched her carefully. She knew it was her tone. But the two men's indifference annoyed her.

"Yeah, sure," the pilot said. "That's what they figured. But you're supposed to show up anyway. And so they called her boss. She said the girl hadn't been at the party the night before. Or at breakfast. So they checked her living quarters. She wasn't there. No one can find her." He shrugged.

"Yeah," Robert piped up, his voice still scratchy from the virus, as he pushed in the tent entrance. "Everyone in MacTown is all upset because it's one of their cooks."

"Who?" Alice asked.

"Girl named Rosie Moore. Nice kid, apparently. Everyone liked her."

Alice stood, her head pushing into the sloping side of the canvas.

"What's wrong?" Rasmussen asked.

"Take me back to McMurdo," Alice told the pilot. "Please."

"Sit down, Alice."

"She's my friend."

As she pushed out of the tent, she heard Rasmussen say, "Not a damn thing you can do to help her."

Alice ran to her tent and shoved everything—sleeping bag, clothes, pee bottle, toiletries, and the Dalai Lama's vase—into the two orange duffels. She dragged the duffels to the silent helicopter, opened the cargo cage, and hefted in her bags. By the time she clamped the lid and fastened the lock, the three men had emerged from the kitchen tent to watch.

She walked over to Rasmussen and held out a hand. "I have to go."

He ignored her hand. "She's at the South Pole. We have work to do."

This wasn't about logic or reason. She still felt enveloped by the magical field of ice littered with Dalai Lama vases. She saw Rosie waving the white T-shirt like a flag of surrender and saying that she thought she loved him. She heard Rosie's shout-laugh, a joyous sound that came through even in her email messages, as she announced her vision of home sitting on a piece of soil. Then, not twenty-four hours later, that vision had become a reality: twenty-one acres in Montana, with elk and bear and forests and northern lights. If Rosie of the Antarctic, soon to be Rosie of the Bitterroots, didn't survive, no one would.

Alice turned and walked toward the helicopter. Rasmussen grabbed her arm and swung her around. "No one survives a storm at the South Pole, Alice. Use your head."

She shook him loose, climbed into the passenger seat of the helicopter, and waited for the pilot. Fifteen minutes later, they lifted off, banked over Pivot Peak, and headed for the next valley. Alice looked down at the three yellow Scott tents, making their lonely stand in the long, flat, rocky basin. Rasmussen stood in the middle of them, hands dangling at his sides, head back, watching the helicopter disappear.

44

In the dorm, Alice had to push through a gaggle of women, clustered by the door, animatedly discussing Rosie's fate. As if she were gone already.

"Excuse me," Alice said, holding the key out in front of her like a dagger.

They parted quickly, but then one spoke up, possessively, almost accusingly. "This is your room? Rosie didn't have a roommate."

"They've probably already reassigned her room," another sniped.

Someone sniffled back tears.

Alice managed to get in the door and shut it against the women. She pushed the lock button. She couldn't lock out their voices, though, and the thrum of their barely controlled hysteria grated. She needed to think. She needed to search for evidence, something Rosie might have said or done. Alice also knew she had to hold onto the clarity of this morning's dream. That field of pure ice and Dalai Lama vases would help her mind be receptive to the evidence she needed to gather.

It turned out to be much easier than she expected. She began by surveying the room, trying to identify physical clues. Many of Rosie's clothes still hung in the wardrobe. That ridiculous outfit she had worn at Icestock, the tight purple miniskirt and the glittering tube top, had been tossed and left on the floor by her bed. Alice found the married man's T-shirt under Rosie's pillow.

She pulled out the three drawers of the desk and discovered the same rolling pencils and plain sheets of paper. An unwrapped red hard candy still stuck to the side panel of the top drawer interior. Alice sat in the desk chair and glanced at the wastepaper basket where Earl had tried to dump his bag of marijuana. Scraps of white paper covered the bottom.

Only anger—or secrecy—caused someone to tear a note into such bits before throwing them into the wastepaper basket. Alice emptied the scraps onto the desktop. A blue ballpoint scrawl covered most of the pieces. She turned them all face up, arranged the edge pieces along the sides, top, and bottom, using the handwriting to determine the orientation of each piece. It was easy after that.

She yanked open all the desk drawers looking for tape. Nothing. So she braved the clutch of women in the hall. They were still turning over the details of Rosie's plight. This phenomenon had always annoyed Alice, the way people sucked on the particulars of tragedy, as if it were the only way they could experience their own vitality. Only this wasn't a tragedy. It was a problem that needed to be solved. Alice said, "I need some tape. Who has Scotch tape?"

The women exchanged looks meant to convey their disapproval. How could Alice be thinking of Scotch tape, of anything other than Rosie, today? One of them spoke very softly and slowly to counter the tone of Alice's voice and to further point out her selfishness, "Yeah. I have some in my room. Hold on."

A minute later, she handed Alice a tape dispenser, said, "Keep it," and turned back to the group.

Alice returned to the safety of Rosie's room, where she carefully taped the note together.

Dear Rosie,
    I want to let you know that I told Karen. Honesty really is the best policy. I'm leaving today for Siple Dome. Doing a story on the ice cores. I won't be back until after you leave for Pole Station. Under the circumstances, I think it best we don't email one another. It just isn't safe. Once we are stateside, our options will be wide open.

But listen: I'm going to find a way to get to Pole Station before the end of the season.

> Yours, Larry

Alice looked at her watch. It was nearly two o'clock. As she left the room, she had to push through the crowd in the hallway once again. Now at least three of the women were wiping tears from their faces.

Alice said, "Rosie didn't die. She missed a flight."

She heard chuffs of disapproval at her back as she hurried down the hall.

Alice let herself into Rasmussen's Crary Lab office and pulled the station directory across the desk and into her lap. She ran her finger along the list of names, starting with the As and working through the alphabet. Her scientific training served her well. She remained focused, checking every single entry, and didn't let herself feel discouraged, even when she'd gotten as far as the Ts and not seen a single Larry. She moved on to the Us and Vs. Finally, in the Ws, she found a Lawrence Wilder. He was a reporter, working on the *Antarctic Sun*. Just above his name was a Karen Wilder. Galley supervisor, office in Building 155.

Alice punched the number for the station newspaper. A nasally voiced woman answered and Alice asked for Larry. "Oh, he's at Pole, doing a story on that telescope that's about to get first light."

Bingo.

"Oh, thanks," Alice said, trying to sound casual. "His wife is in McMurdo still, though?"

"You mean Karen?" Alice heard confusion in the woman's voice. Why would anyone be asking about his wife? If she'd been slicker, Alice might have thought to say something to the effect of, "Oh, I was going to invite the two of them to a party. I'll just call Karen." Instead, she just hung up.

Alice knew Larry had something to do with Rosie's disappearance. But what? She lay on the linoleum floor of Rasmussen's office and pressed her palms down on the cold tiles.

Linoleum always reminded her of Frank. Frank Two, as Rosie called him. Even their breakup took place in the lab. His wife had come in the day before. She didn't look anything like what Alice would have expected. She looked older than him, her hair in soft roller curls, a sprinkling of moles on one cheek, a squishy church lady kind of body. Her voice was soft, too, and sweet.

"Hi. You must be Alice." She appeared to not have a clue.

Alice nodded.

"I'm Lacey. Frank's wife? I hear wonderful things about you."

"Me too," Alice said, as frightened as she was impressed by her ability to lie spontaneously.

"I'm sure he wouldn't mention it, but today is his birthday." Lacey smiled coyly and held up a brown paper bag. "I made his favorite muffins. Orange pecan."

She was straight out of *Good Housekeeping*. What was Alice supposed to do, take the bag of muffins?

"Is he here?"

"I don't know," Alice said, knowing that he was in the geology library next door, looking up the properties of some obscure feldspar. She was waiting for him herself, having finished reading a difficult paper, thinking a break would be nice.

Lacey seemed so disappointed that Alice felt sorry for her. "You want to wait? Or maybe you could try the library?"

"I don't think he'd want me to wait. I'll just leave them at his, uh, station?" Lacey's chirpiness was wilting.

"That table there is good. I'll make sure he gets them."

"There's enough for everyone!" She was trying to rally.

"Thanks."

Lacey left, and Alice opened the bag of muffins and sniffed. The tangy steam nauseated her a bit, but she didn't have any urge to hurl the muffins at the wall. In fact, she coolly went over to examine some postdoc's fluvial sediment, left under the new Scanning Electron Microscope with a sign posted for others to take a look. When Lacey had been gone fifteen minutes and still Frank hadn't returned, Alice hooked up her laptop to the microscope to make a digital image of the sediment, playing with the magnification and resolution, and then ran a chemical analysis. She had no interest whatsoever in this piece of rock, only in passing some time.

Finally she heard the lab door open and close, but she pretended to be absorbed in examining the digital image of the mineral. A hand on her lower back and an easy, "Hey."

Alice didn't point out the bag of muffins. Not yet.

They often used a study room that had a locking door in the back of the lab. Even so, it was risky because there could be other graduate students in the lab when they emerged. That had happened a few times, and Alice had been gratified Frank hadn't made some inane comment about grading papers together. Alice had thought up and rehearsed a dozen such explanations, but she hadn't ever used any either, owing, she told herself, to a small dose of dignity.

"Come on," he whispered now, and she followed him.

Snapping off the fluorescent lights was a soothing moment, the wrap of darkness, though the linoleum under her thighs was always an icy shock. But then again, the hard floor was restful against her spine, and she liked to listen to the hum of the computers, lulling her off to some dreamland. He was much quicker than he used to be, which suited her fine. Their study breaks were like snacks now, or little naps, innocent and brief.

This time, after they'd finished, while she was still on her back, raising her behind to get her jeans up, and he was straddling her on his knees, zipping his own pants, she said, "Your wife was here a few minutes ago."

"Oh yeah? What'd she want?" No hesitation, very smooth.

"She brought you some muffins for your birthday. Orange pecan. Your favorite."

"Great. I'm hungry. Where are they?"

He was on his feet by now, and Alice scrambled to hers, leading the way out of the study room. She pointed to the bag and left the lab.

The next day, Frank found her in the lab again. He leaned against a wall and folded his arms. She knew what was coming and intentionally got a good, long look at him. His skin was so smooth for a grown man and his black curls were longer than usual, fluffing around his collar, one or two springing down to his eyebrows. Even then, she wanted to hold him and make it better, felt as if she were the one getting away with something, not him.

"You must be upset," he said.

She said nothing.

He snorted softly. "I'm sorry," shaking his head. "I'm really sorry."

She wished she could make herself tell him that she'd known all along, but her silence was all that held the two of them together.

"Look," Frank said in that hushed voice of his. "You're a really sweet girl." He stepped over to her and took her hand. "You're always trying to please everyone." He shook her hand gently and then whispered, "Codependent."

Alice blurted, "What?"

"You're codependent, Alice. You're too nice, work too hard to please. It's getting in your way."

She had rarely looked at his eyes, but she did now, noting first the green and then trying to name the feeling in them. If it had been a test question, she would have written the word *sincerity*. Could that be the right answer? Boredom, too, though. He might have liked it if, the day before, she'd smeared the orange pecan muffins in his face. If she had, she bet they'd be having sex rather than this talk right now. This breaking up had little to do with Lacey and everything to do with Alice's calm.

"You deserve someone who can be there for you." He reached into his pocket and pulled out a small piece of paper on which he'd already written a phone number for a group. "Might help," he said, pressing it into her palm and closing her fingers around it.

Now, lying on the floor of Rasmussen's office, the memory almost amused her. No one could accuse her of any kind of dependence now, co- or otherwise. So far as she could tell, she was entirely unattached. Untethered. Flapping out in the world on her own. Alice patted the tan tiles of linoleum. Same flooring, different continent.

What did this memory have to do with Rosie? Everything.

Triangles were mathematically stable. In human relationships, silence maintained that stability. The only way to free up a side of the triangle, was to break the silence.

Alice decided to visit Karen.

45

Alice stopped outside Karen's closed office door. The facts added up to nothing. Rosie hadn't been seen since dinner last night. She hadn't shown up for her flight this morning. In the meantime, a storm had hit Pole Station.

These were the only facts she had, and none of them had any logical links to the note in her hand. The note was a hunch. A hypothesis. The part of science Alice liked to avoid. She preferred stacking up the data to support or knock down someone else's hypothesis. Today, she had no choice. Rosie was missing and had to be found.

Alice opened the door without knocking. A beautiful woman sat behind a big desk. She stood quickly, but even in her surprise at the intrusion, the woman maintained a measure of poise that unnerved Alice. She was no match for Karen Wilder. Still, she had to proceed.

"Rosie Moore is missing," Alice said. "At the South Pole."

"I heard." Alice saw Karen's eyes graze across her red jacket and NSF badge, noting her grantee status and evaluating how civil she needed to be.

Alice asked, "Is there any news yet?"

Karen shook her head.

"I thought your husband might be able to help locate her."

"Who are you? What are you talking about?" Karen put a hand in her thick, blond hair and combed it back with her fingers.

"Larry is at Pole, right?"

Karen hoisted her wrist and looked at her watch. "I have work to do. I'll have to ask you to leave."

Alice placed the taped note on the desk in front of Karen. The beautiful face spasmed as she read it.

Alice said, "Call your husband. Ask him if he has any idea where Rosie is."

Karen sat back down in her chair. Her hands shook as she picked up the note and read it again. Alice watched her digest the words. She expected wrath. Denials.

Instead, Karen's face softened. She looked Alice right in the eye. She said, "You can't just call Pole."

"*I* can't. But you can. You're a manager."

Karen held the note and thought for a very long time. She again looked Alice in the eye and maybe she saw that Alice wouldn't stop here. She'd take the note wherever she needed to take it. Karen opted for damage control. She nodded slowly and pulled the phone to her. "I'll make the call. You don't have to wait."

"I need to hear you do it."

"What are you implying?"

"That you might let her die."

The venom on Karen's face could have killed a small child. "My husband—" she began in a low voice. Then she stopped herself.

She put the note face down on her desk and called Pole Station Operations. She told the dispatcher, "This is Karen Wilder. I need to talk to Larry." A moment of listening, followed by, "Uh-huh. Of course. I see." She hung up and told Alice, "They don't know where he is and can't go get him right now. Pole Ops needs to stay focused on the search."

Karen placed a couple of fingers on top of the taped note and pulled it toward herself, crumpled it in her hand. Alice grabbed Karen by the wrist. It was the first time in her life she'd forcefully touched a person. She opened Karen's fingers and took the note. She knew how easy it was to forget, entirely forget, the evidence.

Karen didn't struggle. She let Alice take the note. She sat back in her chair, as if comfortable, as if at ease, and said, "Truly, don't you think what you're doing is cruel?"

"If you told them at Pole Station that Larry might have information about Rosie's whereabouts, they'd get him."

"Larry is an editor for the *Antarctic Sun*. He went to Pole to do a story on the South Pole Telescope. He knows nothing about Rosie."

"This note says—"

Karen held up a hand and interrupted. "My marriage has had its challenges. They all do." She glanced at Alice's left hand. "Perhaps you wouldn't know about that. But I'll tell you this: You don't know the first thing about other people's lives. Don't ever think you do."

Alice closed her hand around the kaleidoscope note. "I'm sorry," she said.

"No, you're not," Karen said, coming around from behind her desk. Alice backed up. "People like you—sad, pathetic people like you—love to destroy lives. Because you don't have one. What do you have? You have that wadded piece of paper that you think proves something. My husband—" Again she stopped at those words, sucked in a huge breath, and then went on. "If he left me, he'd lose his job. His marriage. His family. His home. His community. He'd lose *everything*. You don't know what that means. But *he* does. And you know what? Whatever he wrote in that silly little note crumpled in your hot little fist, it doesn't mean a thing. Larry might have moments of heat. But he's not courageous. He'll go up to the line, but he won't cross over it." Karen had worked herself into a steamy soliloquy. Alice wondered if the woman would even notice if she slipped out the door. She put her hand on the doorknob.

Karen did notice. She said, "Yeah, *leave*. And don't ever, *ever* show your pale little face to me again."

Alice shut the door very gently. She hurried away, as if a bomb might go off behind her. When she reached the safety of the hallway, she stopped at the row of computers and sat down at one. Quickly, she fired off an email to Earl Banks, telling him everything she knew. Then she retreated to Rasmussen's office in Crary Lab to wait.

46

I t didn't take long for Rosie to lose her senses.

She hadn't seen a flag in a long time. They were planted to withstand storms, that was the whole point, but the wind today was pretty damn fierce. Maybe they had been uprooted like trees and blasted across the polar plateau. The picture of tangled sticks and red nylon flags flying through space pleased Rosie. Such letting go. Such giving in to the forces.

But . . . maybe this route had never been flagged in the first place. It disturbed her that she couldn't remember this simple fact, that when she tried to focus on remembering, her thoughts tossed about as freely as the flags might have.

Eventually, she forgave the flags—whether they existed or not—for abandoning their posts. They were supposed to guide her, as were her thoughts. But she didn't need them. She would just keep walking forward, following the tracks. Rosie checked her watch. She had been walking for over an hour. Or maybe it had been two hours. She should have gotten there a while ago. She glanced down to make sure she was on course and realized that she was walking across frozen waves of snow, undisturbed by boot tracks.

Okay. The blowing snow had covered them. Forward, that was all. It wasn't that cold today, well over zero. The storm insulated. A blanket. Snug. As long as she walked briskly, her body heat filling the jacket and hat and mittens and boots, she would be fine.

She decided it would help if she faced the facts, admitted that she had been very stupid to come out here without a radio. Larry

284

hadn't wanted them to check out from Pole Ops because then station officials would know they had gone out to the hut together. There would be a written record of the event.

Or, as it turned out, the nonevent.

Thinking of his no-show made her feel more tired and more cold. Alice said all animals mate. They also all die. Maybe biology was a bad guide for life. Ha. Biology *was* life. Still, a person might get more mileage staying focused on Mikala's cosmology, the gorgeous swirling mass of energy, the aching beauty.

Yeah, the aching beauty. In spite of Larry not coming, in spite of Rosie having to say no to Mikala, we all still swirled around in the cosmic soup. Looking for love and beauty.

Rosie fished an energy bar out of her pocket and sucked on it as she walked, warming each bite to make it chewable. She needed water, too, but the only way to get that would be to put snow in her water bottle and melt it against her skin. That didn't seem like a good idea. She was growing tired and getting colder. She needed to keep walking.

She sang—in her imagination only, because opening her mouth would dehydrate and cool her body—every song she remembered from her father's repertoire. Mostly the Dead, of course. But some Janis and Jimi. Even the Beatles and Dylan. Then when she moved on to nursery rhymes, she went ahead and freed her voice, opened her mouth and throat to the elements. She'd be fine, as long as she stayed on her feet, kept walking.

But the cold. It was like knives. Rosie stopped and rolled up a pant leg to see if the knives had drawn blood. Getting the wind pant and fleece pant and long underwear pant all rolled up was difficult, but she managed to find some skin on her shin. She saw no blood.

She carefully pushed all the layers back down over her leg. But as she walked, the sensation of being stabbed intensified. Someone was breaking her joints. She supposed she should return to the station. Oh, but that was what she was doing. Returning to the station.

She really needed to check her skin, though. Her clothes felt so binding and restrictive. She wanted, more than anything, to shed her down parka. She imagined tossing it into the wind, and then her purple fleece jacket, too, and watching the patches of tan and purple fly away, the colors so pretty against the tiny white snow-flakes. She took off a mitten but couldn't get hold of the jacket zipper. Even her hat was stuck on her head, held in place by the strap of the goggles. She was too tired to get out of these difficult clothes.

What she needed was a nap. Why hadn't she thought of that sooner? A little rest. Then she'd get back to the station.

Rosie lay down on the snow. She curled herself up like a potato bug. Her mind was doing a funny thing. It was like a foundering satellite, spinning in its quiet and solitary orbit, receiving no signals whatsoever. Then, occasionally, it would get a signal from the outside and flicker to life. When it did, she'd have a clear thought. Right now that thought was: shelter. Her first season, she'd learned to dig a snow trench for shelter. Snow was excellent insulation. A person could survive for a long time in a snow shelter.

The thing was, when her mind sharpened like this, so did the pain in her limbs and joints. It was a pain so intense she didn't think she could endure it. She certainly couldn't walk with that pain. So she rested. A nice short nap and she'd be good to go.

Then, all at once, the stabs of cold stopped. Rosie unfurled her body and stretched out on the ice, on her back, and looked up into the white spin of snow. A warm syrup ran through her bloodstream. It was lovely. She didn't know when she'd ever felt so comfortable. Nor had she ever seen so much. The bits of blowing ice and snow were stars, the cosmos, creation. Time and space were meaningless. The Big Bang was ongoing. A swirling universe of galaxies and black holes. A whole symphony of cosmic microwaves blasting out from that original dot. How many angels danced on the head of the Big Bang singularity? We all returned to the cosmos. It was heaven.

A lucid moment, or maybe a dream, brought Mikala's voice to her. *Lucky girl,* she had said. *Everyone comes to this continent for a reason. And everyone expects her reason to be met by the continent. That girl saw the heart of Antarctica in a way you or I never will. I wonder if she heard its music, too.*

Rosie smiled. She could tell Mikala, later when she got back to the station, that she had heard Antarctica's music. Rosie swung her arms and legs in big arcs, making a snow angel. She smiled and drifted. The snowflakes hitting her face were warm and lush. A big huge laugh filled her heart. She'd been in flight her whole life. But finally she'd landed. She had only a short distance to go now.

47

While the phone continued to ring, and Marcus held her baby picture, and Mikala tried to figure out what to do next, feet pounded up the stairs. Two women burst into Marcus's lab and one said, "Hey. Have either of you seen Rosie Moore?"

Marcus slid the picture back into his wallet, paying the two women no attention, despite their fluster.

Mikala said, "No. Why?"

"She's missing. Didn't show up for her flight. Not in her Hypertat. Can't find her on station."

The other one added, "We can't really look much until the storm lets up. But we're checking the places we can get to with GPS. No one's been able to reach anyone out here by phone, so we were sent." She paused, and then, "How'd you two get out here?"

"Take me back with you," Mikala said, and she ran to keep up as they stomped back out to their snowmobiles, parked a distance away, because of rules about sound and air disturbances in the Dark Sector. They had left the engines running, and great clouds of exhaust swallowed the machines. Mikala grabbed hold of one of the rescuer's jackets and climbed onto the snowmobile behind her, wrapping her arms tightly around the woman's middle.

The two rescue workers drove slowly, checking their navigation instruments as they moved through the opaque landscape of frozen air. Mikala pressed her ear against the woman's down parka. Her world had gone silent. She didn't hear the wind. She didn't hear the snowmobile engines. Just a dead hush.

When they arrived at the dome entrance, all three women climbed off. The two rescue workers trotted up the corrugated steel passageway to Pole Ops, to get their next assignment, and Mikala hurried to the galley. Pushing open the door, she was glad for the warmth, but silence still enveloped her. She got a cup of coffee and sat at a table. Most Polies remained in their living quarters, but a few had followed the wands and ropes to the galley. Betty was working hard in the kitchen, making muffins and pots of coffee, ladling soup from a big vat. If those who had come to get a bite of lunch talked, if their spoons clinked on their bowls, Mikala didn't hear it.

Marcus still had her baby picture. Rosie was lost in the storm. Like binary stars, those two facts circled one another, trapped together by gravity, barring all other input. Her father. Her muse. One found. One lost.

Mikala couldn't move. She couldn't hear.

At two o'clock, Betty sat down beside her with a cup of coffee. She put an arm around Mikala and laid her head on her shoulder. The touch of another person brought sensation back into Mikala's body. All around her objects, animate and inanimate, sprang to life. People rose from the tables and sat again. The dishwasher sloshed rhythmically. Someone's pencil scratched out words on a crossword puzzle. She wondered what Marcus was doing now, alone out at the Dark Sector.

"The cowgirl," Betty said, her voice husky with emotion. Then she dropped her head in her arms on the table.

Mikala sat vigil, waiting, until Jeffrey appeared before her, out of breath. "God, I need to talk to you guys."

Betty stood up and hugged him. She said, "I know. I know."

"It's my wife," he said.

Mikala and Betty stared at Jeffrey.

"It's true. It turned out to be true. You were right."

"What?" Betty asked in dull disbelief.

"She's having an affair with the guy who fixes her computer." He raised the heel of his hand, but didn't have enough vigor to thump his forehead.

Mikala said, "*Jeffrey.*"

Betty said, "I don't care who your wife is fucking. Rosie is missing."

Jeffrey's shoulders slumped. His mouth fell open. "But—"

Someone whacked Mikala on the back. She looked up into Earl's twitching beard. "Let's go," he said, gripping her arm too hard. "Get up."

Earl took off at a run and, grateful to leave Jeffrey behind, Mikala followed, emerging right with him into the thin blue cloud outside the dome. The weather was clearing.

He spoke in a fast, clipped monotone. "Got an email from Rosie's McMurdo roommate. She says the newspaper editor who's on station knows where she is. I found out where he's housed. Let's go." Earl straddled one of the two snowmobiles left by the search-and-rescue team.

Mikala was about to say that he couldn't just take one of these machines, but the keys were in the ignition and obviously he *could* just take one of them. She climbed on and he shot out, even before she'd gotten a good grip on him. She nearly slid off the back of the seat, but threw an arm around his neck in time.

A moment later, he parked in front of the row of bright blue barrel-shaped shelters. They entered the one farthest out and Earl shouted, "Lawrence Wilder!" at the top of his lungs.

Several grunts and one wheeze replied. Most people were sleeping through the storm. Earl shouted the name again. Two men appeared around the curtains of their cubicles. "What's up?" one asked sleepily. The other said, "Larry's in there," pointing to a curtain.

Earl jerked the curtain aside, obviously hoping he'd find Rosie in Larry's bed. The tall man Mikala had met the night before, at the party, was alone, sitting up, rubbing the top of his stubbly head. Earl said, "Where's Rosie?"

"What?"

"You're having an affair with Rosie. Where is she?"

"What are you talking about?"

"He probably doesn't know she's missing," Mikala said to Earl.

"Missing?" Larry asked.

"Yeah. Gone. *Ka-plooey!*" Earl exploded his hands into the air above his head. Larry flinched. "Alice says you'll have information about that."

"But," he said, "it's storming. We're not supposed to leave our shelters."

"Well, Rosie left hers, apparently. She doesn't seem to be on station."

"But," he stuttered again. "I heard them just a while ago calling her over the public announcement system, telling her to contact Pole Ops."

Earl gave Mikala an is-this-guy-an-idiot look.

Larry looked scared. He placed his hands on either side of his hips, palms down on the thin bed, and pushed himself up slowly, as if precisely deliberate movements would give him control over the situation. His voice was extra deep. "Rosie's so reckless. She's probably doing something crazy."

"Where is she, asshole?"

"Look. I really can't say what—"

"Think harder. She's your girlfriend. Did you see her last night?"

"I'm married. She's not—"

"Don't even start, asshole. I got proof. Just tell me where she is."

"She said she wanted to go out to Hotel South Pole."

"To meet you?"

"No. I mean, like I said, I'm married. She—"

Earl, though a good foot shorter than Larry, took a handful of the front of his T-shirt and said, "When did you last see her, scumbag?"

"Yesterday afternoon," Larry whispered. "She said she wanted to spend a night out at Hotel South Pole. You know, to see what it would be like to sleep out there." He reached for his camera sitting on the desk. "I'll come with you."

Earl took the camera from his hands and hurled it to the plywood floor. Mikala heard a sickening crunch. "You're a motherfucking bad liar, asshole." Earl shoved him so hard, Larry fell back on the bed. "Stay here."

Outside, a few innocent clouds scudded across a blue sky, as if the storm had been a collective delusion. Only a reedy hum, the sound of search-and-rescue teams already on their snowmobiles, scouring the environs, broke the chimera of innocence. Mikala and Earl remounted the purloined machine and set out for Hotel South Pole. Within minutes, they met two snowmobiles coming back from the hut. The approaching vehicles slowed and one driver waved for Earl to stop. When he did, the driver said, "Who are you? Where'd you get the skidoo?"

"We're looking for Rosie."

"Not your job. Anyway, she's not out here. Turn around."

Earl gassed up and roared past the search-and-rescue team. Mikala looked over her shoulder, thinking they might make chase. But they must have decided to not waste precious time they needed for finding Rosie. The team proceeded on back toward the dome.

When Earl reached Hotel South Pole, he didn't even stop. He drove in ever widening circles around the shelter, as if it were a dropped stone and they the ripples. He moved slowly now, and stopped every quarter-circle, so they could look and listen. The storm would have wiped out her tracks if she had gone off the route. But sound waves carry forever in this dry, cold, thin still air. If she were calling for help, the search-and-rescuers on snowmobiles wouldn't have heard her, their whining vehicles obliterating all other sound.

Soon, Mikala and Earl lost sight of Hotel South Pole, but she didn't ask him to go back. They rode and they stopped and they listened. Each time, she willed herself to listen harder, as hard as she had ever been trained to listen. She heard the particles of sunlight zing. She heard the ice crystals loosen with the day's new and tiny zap of warmth. She heard the molecules of air doing their slow dance.

Any moment, she would hear Rosie's cry.

"There," Earl said. He pointed in the distance, to a dark speck on the ice.

48

Rosie lay still and curled on her bed of snow. She looked alarmingly at peace. Right here, at rest on this continent. In this universe.

Earl stopped the snowmobile a good fifteen yards away, as if protecting her from the violence of its wail. They ran to the body and knelt prayerfully on either side of her. While Mikala pulled down Rosie's neck gaiter, Earl yanked off a mitten. He put the pads of his three middle fingers against the carotid artery on her neck.

Mikala closed her eyes and listened. Though Earl was the one making contact, she heard a wet *glub glub*. The slow squeeze and release of a heart.

"Do you have a radio?" Earl asked.

"No."

"You warm her up. I'll go get help."

Earl helped Mikala pull the Therm-a-Rest pad and sleeping bag out of Rosie's pack. They inflated the pad and rolled Rosie onto it. Mikala lay stomach to stomach on top of her friend, her face pushing onto the mat. Rosie's mouth was against her ear. She felt the faint heat of breath. She put her arms around Rosie as best she could and placed one leg between Rosie's legs. Earl fluffed the sleeping bag over them, let it fall on top, and then tucked it all around.

"You'll be okay?"

"Go."

Mikala heard Earl stomp across the snow, the little explosion of igniting gas, the whine of the snowmobile fading away.

She held Rosie. There was a heartbeat. There was breath. There was the Antarctic hum.

And then, there was music. This is what she heard:

49

Alice left the door of Rasmussen's office open and lay on the floor. She waited. Earl was a madman. But she hoped he was the right madman for the job.

Two hours later, at four o'clock, she heard a door slam down the hall. A confusion of voices and excited footsteps. She got up and walked slowly—speed would engender hope—to Crary Lab's nerve center, the library. A crowd had gathered and they were laughing, heads thrown back and throats open. They turned to greet the newcomer. She met all of their eyes at once. A woman she recognized as a penguin researcher slowly nodded, smiling. She said, "Yes."

A man said, "Alive."

Alice put her face in her hands and sobbed. The tears came so fast, they shocked her, and yet they didn't last long, because in the midst of them arose an upwelling of desire. A desire so intense it required action. A desire with a deadline. After all, a human life lasts a few decades, at best. *Alive.*

Seize the day. A straight-forward, three-word directive. Nothing to interpret or figure out. Just something to do.

50

At the top of the hill above Scott Base, Alice looked down on the buildings, puzzling over their lichen green color. The color neither stood out for safety's sake nor camouflaged the buildings for aesthetics. Perhaps the eerie green paint had been on sale or found in some government warehouse. Beyond the cluster of squat buildings, the sea was black, harsh, and cold. Only a few seals lounged on the few shelves of ice that remained this late in the season.

She descended the hill and walked in the front door of the main building. The office to the right of the doorway was empty, but she heard dishes clanging down the hall, so she made her way to the galley.

"Hey!" Her friend from New Year's Eve, the chubby lab tech, approached from the other end of the corridor.

He stopped hesitantly, his stance questioning whether she'd come to Scott Base with the intention of visiting him.

Alice folded her arms and said, "Hi."

"It's great to see you! You back from the mountains? Oh, duh. Obviously you're back. Here you are." His smile broadened. He did think she was here to see him, and she couldn't find the words to tell him otherwise. He said, "I'm off today. Just loafing." That lovely New Zealand accent was a series of fjords jutting into a warm blue sea. Alice didn't know if it was better or worse that she actually liked him. He said, "Hey, want to take a walk?"

"I'm sorry. I can't stay. I was looking for someone."

A not-me look shrouded his face. She said she was sorry again, even though she knew, from being the not-me person enough times, that those words only made it worse. Seizing the day, she said, "I'm looking for Jamie."

"The American biologist?"

"Yes."

"I haven't seen him in a while. Most of the sea ice has melted, so I don't know if he's still even around."

It hadn't occurred to her that he might have flown back to the States already.

"He's gone?"

The man shrugged.

She wished she were the kind of person who could think of at least a gesture of gratitude. The "thank you" she managed sounded cold and final.

"Sure." He hesitated, seemed about to say something more, but she turned and hurried back down the hall and out the door.

Snowflakes swirled in the wind, but patches of blue sky over the sea offered the possibility of fair weather. The Spryte was parked in the same place, in back of the base, and the keys were in the ignition. She climbed into the driver's seat and started the engine. She jammed the steering levers forward and backward, relearning how they worked, and set off down the road, the tracked vehicle lurching and shuddering. Worried that her slow and erratic driving would draw someone's attention, she gave the Spryte more gas and picked up speed. Encased in the steel, her newly formed muscles working the steering levers with increasing ease, the snow flurries insulating her movement, Alice drove to the music of one word: *Alive*.

Crevasses. Whiteouts. Engine failure. None of these possibilities deterred her. Alice drove the Spryte like she was merely on a course in an amusement park, like there were controls that would prevent her from making a fatal error, like operating a lever-steered, tracked vehicle was what she'd been waiting for her entire life. She felt pleasantly reckless.

As she drove, the clouds plummeted to the surface of the ice, swarming around the vehicle, leaving the sky that clairvoyant Antarctic blue. Mount Erebus and Mount Terror floated on the cloud base like mythical mountains, and she drove toward them wondering if she could drive right up their sides.

When she came to the fork in the road, she hesitated. With the sea ice melted, he wouldn't be out by the pressure ridges looking for his seals.

She took the other route, the one leading to his camp. The Scott tents looked lovely through the blowing snow and against the blue sky, their shapes mocking mountains, the yellow storybook bright, all but Jamie's, which was that pale pink one with the radiating Tibetan prayer flags.

He was just coming out of the tent's tube opening, emerging on all fours, and standing unsteadily. He stretched and then noticed the big orange vehicle rolling to the edge of camp. Alice managed a fairly smooth stop, turned off the engine, and jumped down onto the snow. He looked stunned for a moment, but then smiled. She wanted to measure that smile, from one corner of his mouth to the other, wanted a value in centimeters, as if that would be evidence toward an answer to her question.

Jamie wore black wind pants, a brown wool sweater, and nothing on his head, nor any sunglasses. Why him? she wondered. Why not the lab technician? Why not Rasmussen, for that matter? Why did Jamie's male display draw her? She needed a biological answer. She took a few steps toward him, wanting to see his dark gold cougar eyes. His hands, dangling from the cuffs of his sweater, were big and warm-looking. A joke twitched in his cheeks, around the corners of his mouth, as if he waited always to think of something funny. She touched his arm, just to make sure it was really him, and he grabbed her wrist.

"Alice. Everything okay?"

She nodded.

He gestured at the Spryte. "You drove that out here?"

Again she nodded.

He looked at her, took in her pale thinness, and then looked back at the rough polar vehicle and laughed, the visual contrast joke enough. He still held her wrist. "*Say* something. What are you doing out here?" After a long pause, he added, "Sunshine."

She was afraid to talk because she knew the only words she could say would be the exact truth. She said them. "I wanted to see you."

Jamie raised an eyebrow, took a step back.

"Rosie is all right."

"The girl at Pole."

Alice nodded and gulped cold air. "She's alive."

"I know. I've been following the search on the radio. Look. It's freezing out here. I was just boiling some water for coffee. Let me get it. We can talk in my tent. I'd invite you into the kitchen tent, but it's really cramped and uncomfortable, and anyway, Jorge is in there working."

"Okay."

"Be right back."

Alice hugged herself and looked around, while he dipped into the kitchen tent. She was frightened, but only of herself. This landscape was a knife that cut through all pretense. It intoxicated a person with the recklessness of truth.

Jamie came back out of the kitchen tent clutching two thermal mugs, each with a thin drift of steam escaping from the tiny hole on the cup lid. The roasted smell of coffee only intensified the spell. She followed him into the pink tent.

Jamie carefully set the two coffee cups on the tarp-covered snow. He shook out a fleece liner, folded it in half, and motioned for Alice to sit on it. He gave her a sleeping bag for cover. He sat on his empty and flattened duffle and draped another sleeping bag over his shoulders. A dingy pink light wrapped the two of them.

Alice took a sip of the hot coffee. He'd loaded it with sugar and nondairy creamer.

"I have to tell you something," she said.

"Are you okay? You aren't supposed to be back yet, are you?"

"I came back because of Rosie."

"I'm glad she's okay. What happened?"

"I don't know the details yet." She took another slug of the creamy sweet coffee. "But she's alive, and so am I, and so are you."

Jamie laughed, but nervously rather than his usual good-natured moo cow laugh. "How'd you get out of your camp, anyway?"

"I flew out on a helo. Walked to Scott Base. Drove the Spryte here." It was like something in a song, crossing oceans and mountain ranges. No wonder Jamie looked startled. Who wouldn't? "On New Year's Eve I went out to Scott Base to see you."

"Really? Yeah, uh. After that day you and I went to Hutton Cliffs, I got stuck out here in the field camp for over a week. Then when I did make it back to town, I was just swamped and then you went off to the field camp and—"

"I'm trying to tell you something." She had no time for masculine excuses. For hedging. Even for wondering. She would lay out the facts as she saw them. She said, "I know we've had one dinner and one day together. I'm under no illusions."

He laughed, reaching again for humor. "I'm sorry. But the look on your face. I just have to say that you're the most serious woman I've ever met."

"I really like you."

That got his attention. She waited for a new round of equivocation, but he was listening.

"There was a big party at Scott Base that night."

"I heard."

"You did?"

"Sure."

"You heard about New Year's Eve?"

"Alice, it was a huge party. Of course I heard about it."

"I mean about me."

"What about you?"

"I made a mistake."

"Ah! That must be hard for you."

"I had sex with a lab technician by accident."

Jamie was quiet for a long time. Then, "Why are you telling me this?"

"I went out to Scott Base on New Year's Eve to look for you and that's what happened." Alice didn't tell him about the pink drinks. She hated that excuse.

His agitation surprised her. His arms flew in confused expression as he asked, "What kind of thing is that to greet someone with who . . . who . . . well, you know, who you might have something with?"

"I might?"

"Look, Alice. I don't particularly want to hear about your affairs."

"It wasn't an affair. I just thought that maybe you'd heard. Men always talk. And if you *had* heard, I wanted you to know it was an accident. A really stupid accident."

Jamie looked dumbfounded.

"Also, Rasmussen asked me to marry him."

"*Rasmussen?* Jesus. And?"

"He wants me to come to the Ice with him every year."

"Couldn't you do that without *marrying* him? What does this mean about your work? Isn't that sexual harassment?"

"Did you mean that—what you just said—that there might be something between us?"

Never, her mother once told her, *make a man feel like a deer in headlights.*

She said, "Just tell me the truth."

He raised his eyebrows, opened his mouth, shook his head, let out a loud huff of a sigh. There he was in her headlights.

"Wow," he said. "You're like the last of an endangered species. Some pure strain of DNA that will no longer exist ever again."

"Is that good or bad?"

"You scare me," he said quietly.

"I scare me, too."

Jamie shook his head. "Everyone has defenses. But your defense is some kind of complete clarity. Like by being totally authentic, you disarm people."

"I don't mean to disarm you."

"But you have." He grabbed both sides of her head in his big paws and kissed her. Jamie was too clumsy to be tender, and yet his mouth on hers was Antarctic primitive. Wanting him was like wanting wildness itself.

Jamie rocked back and sat on his heels, looking surprised, as if the kiss had been an accident. He said, "You must be a brilliant scientist."

"The thing is," Alice said.

Jamie interrupted, "You're destined for the Nobel."

"I've gone AWOL. I probably have no science career left at all."

"Ah. I have a feeling you know exactly what you're doing, even when you're AWOL."

"The thing is," she continued, "I love you."

He flinched and looked at his watch.

She rose awkwardly to her feet, saying, "I better get back to McMurdo. I want to see how Rosie is."

"Alice," he said, following her out of the tent.

She didn't turn until she got to the driver's door of the Spryte.

He asked, "Does anyone know you took the vehicle?"

"No."

"You can't just drive it back." He glanced at the snowmobile parked next to the kitchen tent. "I could follow you on the skidoo to make sure you make it okay."

"I drove here fine. I can drive back fine." She looked out over his head at the stretch of ice, Mount Erebus, the whole continent. This was her day, and she'd seized it. She jumped up in the driver's seat and started the engine. If she were her mother, she would have botched her departure, ground the gears, lurched dangerously, accidentally thrown it in reverse and plowed into someone's tent. Laughing with sexy peril. But she wasn't her mother. Alice expertly put the vehicle in gear and gently slid it out of the camp, back onto the road toward Scott Base. She didn't look back, not once.

51

When she reached McMurdo, Alice returned to Rasmussen's office in Crary Lab and called her mother. Her mouth, the feel of Jamie's tongue, still burned, the flames licking through her body.

"Mom, I wanted to ask you for advice."

"I had a date last night," her mother reported cheerily.

"That's great. But Mom—"

"With a doctor. And handsome."

"Wonderful."

"You would think."

"Mom?"

"He was fatally boring."

Rosie was alive. She could do anything. Even humor her mother. So she said, "I'm sorry."

"Can you believe that he talked for forty-five minutes about *skin disease*."

"Yuck."

"Yuck is one thing. But the boredom! I thought I would pass out for lack of stimulation. I mean, I've given this guy three dates because of his credentials. He looks so good on paper, on paper and off."

"No sense of humor?" Alice prompted.

"That man can take an hour to drink one martini."

"I wanted to ask you—"

"What that means, Alice, is not that he doesn't like to party, although it means that, too. It means that he can't even finish a drink. Imagine. Let alone finish a sentence. Oh, and he seemed so promising. Well, all that glitters is not gold."

Obviously, Alice thought. The Ferrar Glacier glittered and it was ice. Besides, wasn't gold usually a dull burnished yellow, not glittering at all?

"I guess you can't have everything," Alice told her mother.

"Oh, honey." A long hard sigh. "I should introduce him to you. You'd probably love him. Science and all."

"Dermatology and geology are worlds apart."

"Still. It's that slow way of thinking."

"How old is he?" Alice touched her mouth and looked at her fingers, as if she might find some trace of Jamie on them, while she indulged her mother by falling into the script.

"Age isn't important after you've passed thirty."

"I'm twenty-eight."

"So exacting."

"Will you go out with him again?"

"That's the question, isn't it? I suppose I could tolerate anything if the extenuating circumstances were interesting enough. Oh, why can't they make men who have good jobs *and* are fun?"

Alice said, "I've met a man."

"I guess I could do worse, though. I mean, beggars can't be choosers, can they? A doctor!"

"I've met a man."

A long pause, then, "You're not interested in men."

"Yes, I am."

"There at the North Pole? You've met a man?"

"The South Pole. And actually, I'm thirteen hundred kilometers from the Pole."

Her mother chuckled. "I can picture him. He's perfect for you! He probably chews seal hide to make clothes, am I right?"

"No. But he *is* a seal biologist."

"I thought he was a geologist."

"That's my professor."

"Two men?" Her voice got small, almost frightened.

"I'd like advice." Now silence. "Mom?"

"Honey, men don't work out for women in our family. You're just like me. Remember, the apple never falls far from the tree."

"Actually, the evolution of any species depends on seeds traveling far from their parent trees."

Another long silence, and then, "I've got a whopper today."

"Have you taken your pills?"

"They hardly help."

"You were laughing when I called. About your date with the handsome doctor."

"He's a dermatologist, Alice."

"So?"

"And he's married."

"Oh."

A big inhalation to demonstrate her bravery. Then, "I wish you luck, baby. I wish you all the luck in the world. Go get your Eskimo man."

"He's a Caucasian American and he's a seal biologist."

"Whatever," her mother said, as Jamie's big form filled the office doorway.

Alice hung up on her mother and stood to face him.

"The crazy thing is," Jamie said, all hands and feet, leaning against the doorjamb. "I don't even know you."

52

Betty kept dinner warm and held the galley open an extra hour. People ate heartily, as if they too had almost lost their lives in the storm, and talked in rushed whispers, as if their full voices might break something fragile.

Mikala found a place at the end of a table where she hoped she wouldn't have to talk. There was so much she needed to hold onto: her baby picture in Marcus's wallet, the feel of Rosie's breath in her ear, those first few tender measures of music. She would eat dinner, check on Rosie in the clinic again, and then go up to the Sky Lab to write down this beginning.

As she stood and lifted her tray, Larry Wilder entered the galley. The tall, bald-headedness of him was shocking, the way he carried himself, towering above everyone else, as if blameless. He walked lankily to the stacks of plates and bins of flatware. He filled a plate with food and sat in the last spot at a crowded table, eager, apparently, for company.

Mikala marveled at his composure. Okay, so technically, he'd only broken a date. But you'd think he'd show a bit more remorse about the consequences. He hadn't even stopped by the clinic this afternoon. Rosie was doing fine, rebounding with hot drinks and warm food, a stack of blankets, and a string of friends. Everyone but Larry.

Mikala couldn't help savoring, just a little bit, his cowardice. It was a nice counterpoint to the lovely memory of holding Rosie back to life. A harsh background note that made the music of the moment all the more exquisite.

Now, having eaten, she wanted out of this steamy, low-ceilinged room. She wanted sky. She wanted her pencil and piano. Holding her tray high, she stepped toward the dish dump window.

Earl flew into her field of vision. His hair a mane, his unbelted pants hanging well below the waistband of his shorts, he seemed to explode into everyone's consciousness at once. He stopped in back of Larry, reached around the man and picked up his dinner plate. Earl heaved it to the floor, the wet food splatting and the plate cracking. Then he grabbed Larry by the neck and dragged him off the bench. Larry kicked his long legs and swung his arms, but he couldn't stop Earl from flinging him to the floor, next to his food and broken plate. Earl didn't speak a word. He straddled Larry and grasped his head in his two hands, lifted it and pounded it against the floor.

As men converged to pull him off, Earl stood and jack-knifed his body, to gain maximum force, before unfolding his limbs and kicking Larry in the ribs. It took three men to restrain him. Before they did, he managed to get in another powerful kick to the ribs and one stomp on his crotch.

Earl went quiet, looked serene even, as the men hauled him away. A couple minutes later, medics arrived. Everyone in the galley was still and silent as the medics knelt around Larry, who wasn't moving, and then loaded him onto a stretcher.

Betty was the first to break the silence, breathing, "Jesus, Mary, and Joseph" in a loud hush.

53|

Within minutes of the assault, Rosie and Larry were loaded onto the medevac plane on stretchers. Rosie's health had stabilized and she complained about not being allowed to walk onboard, but Larry, who had broken ribs and head injuries, was unconscious and needed to be transported to better medical facilities as soon as possible. Two Air Guardsmen accompanied Earl, in handcuffs, up the stairs and onto the plane.

Mikala stood near the marker at the geographic South Pole, away from the rest of the crowd, and watched the plane race down the runway. It lifted and soared into the sky. In moments, her muse was gone. She hadn't even gotten to say goodbye.

The wind seemed to follow the plane, its pitch an eerily extended note. High A sharp? Rising to B. Perhaps the Chinese two-stringed violin, the *erhu*.

She felt stripped and defenseless. The very idea of resentment was a waste of time. Mikala turned and looked toward the Dark Sector, where her father's telescope stood on its spider legs, its wings open to the universe. He, Marcus Wright, her father, was just a man, a cosmologist, a former revolutionary. As she began walking toward the telescope she saw, coming toward her, the bobbing purple hat.

They met halfway along the path between the silver dome and the Dark Sector. Marcus's glasses were steamed opaque, and he spoke first. "I want you to know how sorry I am. Words are meaningless, I know. But they're all I have. Please forgive me."

"That was a million years ago," Mikala said.

"Can I do anything, anything at all, to make up for the years?"

"You've been a ghost," she said and touched his arm. "But you're not anymore."

"I'm just so glad," he said, "to have a chance to know you."

She had always imagined that he'd be afraid of her. Or that he might be angry at her intrusion on his life. Never once had she considered that he would be glad for her existence.

"I want you to meet Margie and the boys as soon as possible," he said. "I'm thinking later this month, as soon as we get off the Ice, I'll fly you out to Chicago. Maybe you could stay a few weeks."

Mikala almost laughed. He wasn't just glad, he was *claiming* her.

"I Googled you! You've accomplished so much. And yet so young." He looked quite ready to take genetic credit.

"I already have a family," she said, feeling the need to draw a line.

"Now you have a bigger one."

They stood on the path between the South Pole marker and Marcus's telescope, a vast white place. Yet Mikala's heart was filling fast. "I'd like to see the telescope," she said.

They turned toward the Dark Sector together and launched easily into shop talk, as if continuing a conversation they'd had all their lives.

"I guess one thing I can't get my mind around is the singularity," Mikala said. "The first thing ever in existence was this moment-slash-object, denser than anything imaginable. But how'd *it* get there? And what's the 'there' it got to?"

"Ah! Smart woman. Of course. That's the big question. Some consider it the cosmologist's biggest embarrassment. I won't tell you I have the answer. But," he clapped his mittened hands and said, "we're getting pretty damn close." He leapt into the air and barked *Ha!*

No wonder Mikala thought she could write a symphony about creation. Her father thought he could, or could soon, explain it. Was there a DNA code for arrogance?

"If you really want to understand this," he said excitedly, "we have to discuss quantum cosmology."

They had reached the base of the telescope and Marcus clamped a hand on one of the legs. Mikala looked up at the instrument that was prepared to detect the earliest years of our universe.

"The theory of inflation helps us understand how the universe exploded out of nothingness." Marcus spoke with reverence. "First, there was no sound at all. The initial explosion of matter and energy was utterly silent. It *had* to be: there was nothing through which sound waves could travel, right? But then, in the instant after the Big Bang, there was a quick and powerful expansion or inflation. And now, *now,* the universe could begin to sing!

"Basically, quantum fluctuations rippled, or shook, through the universe, making it resonate like a cosmic organ pipe. So there was one central tone, or wave of sound energy, accompanied by a series of overtones or harmonics."

She heard the organ pipe. She heard the harmonics. "That's what I want to talk about. The sound waves associated with the Big Bang and the cosmic microwave background."

"Of course! Of course! The symphony has already been written for you. If we cosmologists would only finish our work and discover it."

She nodded, listened.

"So, very early on in the universe, this huge amount of radiation from the Big Bang interacted with ordinary matter," Marcus said slowly. "What happened? The matter started to ring like a bell. These sound waves traveled throughout space, and kept on interacting with matter, *changing* it, making it denser in some places, more rarefied in others—a lot like the way in which sound waves compress and rarefy air inside a flute or trumpet. In the data from our telescope, we hope to see the harmonics of those sound waves, those density differences. It's extraordinary, really, how sound waves from the Big Bang rippled across the early universe. And how they set up the galaxies, and the empty spaces between the galaxies, that we have today. A harmonic structure."

She felt the music under her collarbone and at the base of her wrists, as if it were welling there, waiting for release. The full orchestration was *right there*. "Tell me more," she said.

"I'm just so glad," Marcus said again, "to have a chance to know you."

54|

Alice returned to the Pivot Peak camp to finish out the last days of the season. As she flew up the valleys, she looked down on the rock striations, the beautiful layers, the embedded complexity. Rocks are the ultimate timepieces, earth's most accurate clock. If one needed time to be something literal, as Alice did, then rocks were the answer. Antarctic rocks trumped everything. Even human life. *All* life, for that matter. The rocks had been here a long, long time, resting in perfect inert peace, before any creatures came along with their lust and longing.

As the helo descended into the great basin below Pivot Peak, Alice looked out the window at the three yellow tents, the wooden crates of samples stacked in the center of camp, the lone portable toilet. Bits of human desperation scattered like debris on earth's crust. Soon she'd be swinging a pick and stabbing a shovel into that frozen soil. Alice was surprised to realize that some part of her relished the return to hard labor, bitter cold, the slab bed. Rasmussen was right about that part: there was always the work.

When the helicopter touched down, he was standing in front of the kitchen tent, in almost the exact same spot as he'd been when she left, as if he'd not moved these two days. The barren brilliance suited Rasmussen perfectly.

He got her bags out of the cages himself and carried them to her tent. They went right to work that day and worked late into the evening.

At dinner, Robert was sullen. No more jokes and pleas for conversation from him. He looked glazed, his golden curls limp, as if the landscape of rock and ice were fossilizing him. After wolfing down two plates of food, almost angrily, he said, "Bed," and pushed out of the kitchen tent.

Rasmussen insisted that Alice stay for dessert. He assembled the ingredients for the same chocolate pudding he'd made her first night in the field camp. He whipped the powdered chocolate and powdered milk into cold water and set the pan on the Coleman burner. This time he didn't read as he whisked the pudding, but neither did he talk. Alice, who felt especially cold tonight, even wearing her fleece hat and down parka in the tent, watched him cook. He wore only a T-shirt and jeans, but his silence wrapped around him like a blanket. It obviously comforted him. To speak would be like yanking the blanket away.

The pudding thickened and he piled far too much in a clean plastic bowl for her. She cradled the bowl in two hands and looked at the heavy mass. Finally, she said, "Rosie's okay."

He stopped scooping pudding into his mouth and looked up, surprised, as if he'd completely forgotten about Rosie. But then he said, "Good."

"I can't eat this." Alice set the bowl on the canvas cot and stood.

Rasmussen stood, too. He took hold of her shoulders and said, "Stay."

Alice averted her eyes, shook her head.

"You're a crackerjack geologist."

She said, "I know."

"Don't throw it away. Look." Rasmussen took her jaw in his hand. "You're young. A lot of silly things might seem important to you. But what matters most is your work."

Again, she said, "I know."

She was afraid to look at him. His leanness in the navy blue T-shirt and dusty denims. The rock steady face with ageless eyes and mysterious smile lines. What if she never looked away again?

He said, "I've never known you to make rash choices."

Then he put his arms around her and crushed her to him. She might sleep there, with her face pressed against his chest, the mineral smell of his skin. He a cliff and she a cliff dweller. Holed up in the rocky cave of him. Forever.

"I can't," she said and pushed against his chest.

She ran back to her sleep tent and crawled in. There she dug the Dalai Lama's vase out of her duffel and held it in her lap. Slowly she unwrapped the tissue until she got to a hard plastic, well-sealed box. Jennifer said that the vase contained finely ground precious stones which had been mixed with seawater, formed into small balls, and then dried. They had been consecrated, she said, by a bunch of lamas. The sealed plastic box was disappointing. Alice wanted a crumbly earthen vase with a voluptuous shape and maybe a chipped handle. But of course this plastic would be far more enduring. Maybe the Dalai Lama had thought of that.

Quickly, before Rasmussen emerged from the kitchen tent, she stuffed the Dalai Lama's vase in her daypack. She kicked her way out of the Scott tent's tube entrance and examined the pile of field tools. She selected a shovel and a pick, balanced them on her shoulder, and walked away from camp.

Alice hiked for a full hour in the direction of Pivot Peak. The basin in which they were camped was so enormous that it was nearly impossible to get out of sight, but eventually she reached another small ridge and climbed it. She stopped just on the other side, considering, but Jennifer had said to select a place where there was no chance, ever, of the vase being disturbed. Each of the these ridges was formed of glacial moraine, and it was entirely possible that Rasmussen might choose this one to excavate next year. She descended the other side of the ridge and kept walking, feeling her ability to breathe increase with every step away from camp. Even when she determined herself entirely alone, with no view of anything human, she kept walking.

Eventually she came upon a place in which she found three large rocks, gray and edgy, situated in a nearly perfect isosceles triangle. She threw off the pack and began digging in the center of that spot. Bit by bit, she managed to scoop away the surface and then another layer or two of the earth's crust. She dug with an earnest, steady rhythm.

When her pit was about a meter deep, she knelt down to touch the exposed rock layers. Then she gently placed the plastic-encased vase, the contents of which she'd never see, into the hole. Shovelful by shovelful, she heaped the rock and soil back into the hole, burying the Dalai Lama vase. Then she worked meticulously to repair the scar on the earth's skin so that no one would ever know anyone had ever dug there.

Alice stepped onto the burial site and looked up at the mountains and glaciers, the subjects of her life work. Cause and effect ruled geology, the layering of the earth, the formation of its crusty, icy, bubbling hot skin. But here, in Rasmussen's Shangri La of geology, her life had been seized by randomness. The Dalai Lama's vase, friendship with Rosie, the big creature that was Jamie, and most of all, most awesomely reason-bashing of all, was this continent's beauty.

55

It was nearly dusk as Rosie's sky blue '88 Toyota Short Bed bounced down the two-track dirt road leading to her land. She parked in front of the trailer. It wasn't much: tiny with rounded ends, a little dilapidated, white with pale green trim, already getting swallowed by the summer's tall grasses. Just two months ago, the grasses had been bright green, ripe and juicy, their seed clusters tight buds. Now in August, they were golden spikes, scenting the air with their summer decay, reaching halfway up the windows of her trailer.

Rosie climbed down from the truck and paused, facing the mountains, breathing the thin, clean air. A light breeze swept off the slopes of the Bitterroots. Alice had told her that what she faced now was part of the Idaho Batholith, enormous masses of igneous rock that had intruded some two hundred million years ago. At some point, the top of this batholith had slid off to the east, forming the Sapphire Block. The remaining Bitterroots granite had been deeply carved by glaciers. That carving created the beautifully jagged skyline.

The lazy sunlight began giving way to evening, turning the mountains into a purple silhouette against the Montana sky.

As the sun went down, so too did the breeze die, and now Rosie could hear the soft lapping of the stream. She looked in that direction and saw, curling above the alders that lined the stream, a blue strand of smoke.

She walked at first and then ran to the place where the alders thinned before opening into a small golden meadow. There, next to the stream, she found an orange plastic tube tent strung between two trees. A few yards away, a small fire of green twigs smoldered.

"Hey!" she shouted. "Who are you?"

The plastic sides of the tent bustled and bulged. A man emerged and stood, teetering a bit, as if he'd just awakened. He said, "Babe! "

She didn't recognize him at first. Earl's head and face were shaved, and there was dirt caked under his fingernails and in the creases of his skin. He looked old and naked, though he wore a flannel shirt tucked into jeans. He limped badly as he approached her.

Rosie hadn't heard from Earl since they'd flown back to Christchurch together, in the same plane with Larry. She'd gone straight on to the States, Larry went into the hospital, and Earl had been arrested. Now she hugged him hard and said, "God, I've been worried about you! Where've you been? How'd you find me?"

"Larry lived, you know," he said, as if that explained everything.

"Yeah. I know."

"Would have been murder one."

Rosie nodded. "I know. Apparently he's fine."

"You're not still hung up on the fucker, are you?"

Rosie wrapped her arms around herself. When she got off the Ice a year and a half ago, she'd gone directly to Oregon. Max had married and moved to Portland. Her father had surfaced, having called the month before from Anchorage to say he was living there for the time being. Her mother and Jed lived together in a small yellow house, surrounded by overgrown wildflowers, on the edge of Newberg. One climbing rose tackled the left side of the house, its white blossoms spilling onto the weeds below like oversized snowflakes. Jed had opened the door and enclosed her in a bear hug so hard it hurt, but her mother sat at the kitchen table, weeping into her hands, afraid to look. Rosie finally knelt on the kitchen floor and pried her mother's hands from her face.

"You're exactly Rosie," her mother said through sheets of tears. "It's you, exactly."

She hadn't been able to convince her mother to come see her land in Montana. Not until there was a proper house and bed on the place. Rosie said she could stay in a motel in town, but her mother claimed she couldn't leave her job. Jed came, though, right away, and camped for two weeks, right here by the stream. He had a job this summer, building a house in Newberg, and the crew was working seven days a week. Rosie encouraged him to stick with it. He promised he'd come next summer and help her build a cabin.

"No way," Earl bellowed, responding to her long pause. "No way you can have any feelings other than contempt for the asshole. Don't tell me. No, don't tell me you're in *touch* with the scumbag."

"No," Rosie assured him. "I haven't spoken to Larry since the night before the storm, when he said he'd meet me at Hotel South Pole."

Earl nodded emphatically. "Wish I could have finished him off for you."

Rosie didn't want him dead. He'd only been afraid. There had been the possibility of love between them. But he'd chosen his family. The validation of marriage. The storybook hometown of Pocatello. His habitat, the densely layered web of landscape and people, from which he couldn't, or wouldn't, ever extract himself.

He'd been a coward. He'd betrayed her. But he had also helped push her the last stretch home. She'd been going anyway, but the shove, the teeter on the edge of death, had delivered her without any more doubt or hesitation, to the yellow house with the climbing white rose. Her mother and brother. This stream and meadow and these blackening mountains.

"Where've you been?" she asked Earl again. He was a human landmine, she knew that. But he would be forever her friend. If it weren't for him, along with Alice and Mikala, she wouldn't be alive today.

He kicked at his smoky fire, and squatted. "They held me until it was clear that Larry would pull through. Then they had to decide whether or not to charge me with assault. Maybe even attempted murder. Thing was, if they had, it would have been bad publicity for the United States Antarctic Program. They already had one death to explain this year. In the end, I just walked out. I think they sort of let me. Dunno. Anyway, I never got apprehended. I went straight to the first gas station, where I lifted a razor and fresh T-shirt. I used their bathroom to shave everything. You know, so I wouldn't be recognizable. Walked to the pier. Got work on a ship. It took me a whole fucking year and four months, though, to get back to the States. I came straight here, babe."

Earl pulled out a tuft of creek-side grass. "Here's what I'm thinking. You and me. I got it all worked out. You on vocals, me on guitar. Small towns, Rocky Mountain states. You know, the Missoulas and Españolas and Pinecrests. We're gonna be hot."

Rosie laughed. It was tempting. Being on the road. *Singing.*

Earl added, "I loved you, you know."

"You loved Jennifer."

"Yeah. Her, too."

"Hey," Rosie said. "Mikala's Antarctic symphony premieres this Saturday night in Santa Cruz."

Earl looked up, his eyes swirling with that galactic light. He said, "Cool lady. Awesome musician."

"I'm meeting Alice there. Want to come?"

Earl stood, looked Rosie over, like he couldn't quite trust the offer, like she'd held out a million bucks and asked if he wanted them. Then he shouted, "*Hell,* yeah. When do we leave?"

"Actually, I was planning on leaving tonight, right now. I've been staying in town a few days to help a friend tile her floor. I was just stopping by my trailer to make sure everything was in order before heading south. I must have had some kind of premonition about you being here."

Earl grinned. "Give me, like, five minutes."

He dove head first into his tent.

"Grab this for me?" A guitar case appeared at the entrance. Rosie took it and a minute later, Earl emerged with two plastic bags, one stuffed with clothes and the other with his sleeping bag.

He tugged the tent down in a few swift motions, wadded it up, and tucked it under his arm. "Ready."

As they walked in the last light of day across Rosie's land, Earl talked nonstop about the boats he'd worked on and the ports he'd seen. Rosie thought about his hope for a woman with circles under her eyes and ratty hair in the morning, along with the squealing children, and wondered if he had cut those dreams loose. If he were permanently at sea.

"Get in," she said, opening the passenger door to her pickup.

Earl tossed his bags, the tent, and the empty guitar case in the bed of the truck. He cradled his guitar in his lap as Rosie began to drive.

"Listen," Earl said. A series of tender guitar notes mixed with the twilight and road dust.

56

Alice still felt stunned by how effective it had been to seize a day. Jamie had responded within a couple of hours to her declaration of love. It had been an ambivalent response, but a response nonetheless. Then, upon arriving back in the States, she applied for four teaching positions and got offers at all four, including at the University of Washington, where Jamie taught. What would happen if she tried to employ other statements of wisdom from *The Concise Dictionary of American Proverbs* to her personal life? The results could be frighteningly radical.

Of course the true agents of change had been that wild continent and her personal emissary, Rosie of the Antarctic. How glad she'd been to receive the email from Rosie suggesting they meet for the debut of Mikala's symphony at the Cabrillo Festival of Contemporary Music in Santa Cruz. The timing was perfect. She had finished her postdoc work with Rasmussen in the spring and moved, at last, to Seattle in June. She would start at the university in the fall. A road trip would be a fitting celebration to the end of an awkward, at best, year.

Road trip. The phrase tasted like the August sun, sweat, fresh cherries. Like something Rosie would say. Something Rosie would *do*. She hadn't been on a vacation since the failed island trip with her mother a decade ago.

The only thing marring the trip was Alice's inability to reach her mother. While Jamie drove south on Interstate 5, she punched the number every few minutes.

"Maybe she has a boyfriend," Jamie said.

"Her boyfriends last one date, sometimes less."

Jamie laughed and reached a hand out to touch her face. Her cheek was wet. "Oh shit, you're crying."

"I'm just worried."

"You're her daughter, not her mother."

Alice said, "She's all alone," which brought a fresh spate.

"Please stop." Jamie couldn't abide crying. It was nearly to the level of a medical phobia. The funny part was that Alice had never been a crier, had hardly shed a tear since she was six months old. Until that afternoon Rosie was found. Now she cried at the smell of lilacs, the sight of Mount Rainer hovering over Seattle, advertisements on television.

As they crossed over the state line into California, Alice tried unsuccessfully to stop her tears. Jamie swerved into a rest area and jumped out of the car, slamming the door. Not out of anger. Jamie wasn't capable of real anger. But agitation exacerbated his clumsiness.

She stepped out of the car, too, and watched him lope toward the men's room. A year ago, when her mother had met Jamie for the first time, she'd said, "He looks exactly like a llama. For god's sake, Alice. A *llama*." Of course what she hated most was that he lived in Seattle, five thousand kilometers away. When Alice announced that she was accepting the tenure-track job at the University of Washington, her mother managed to get herself hospitalized for two days. She finally relented after the third time she met Jamie, mentioning the llama comparison again, but adding, "At least you won't have competition." She paused and then said, "There's something to be said for brains." Finally, she'd resorted to flirting with Jamie, a desperate bid to win him to the east coast. But there was no taking this man away from the seals and whales of the Pacific Ocean, and Alice herself felt an exhilarating measure of freedom at the continent separating her, at last, from her mother, even as she worried about her.

Alice tried to smile at Jamie as he returned to the car, but she'd never learned how to smile on demand. Jamie laughed at the expression on her face.

"Honestly," she told him. "I have *never* been a crier. My whole life. This is new."

"So you've said." He slid into the driver's seat. "My luck. I finally find a woman who doesn't cry. Only she starts shortly after meeting me."

"Life can be random sometimes," Alice said, dead serious. She dug her cell phone out of her bag and punched her mother's number again.

"Helloooooo!" her mother crooned.

Alice pulled the phone from her face and looked at it. Put it back against her ear. "Mom?"

"Oh, Alice." Obvious disappointment.

"Do you have a new boyfriend, Mom?"

A long tinkling laugh.

"Why haven't you been answering the phone?"

"I went to St. Thomas! There was a deal in the paper. A four-day cruise. It was *heaven.*"

Alice took a deep breath. "You met someone? You answered the phone like you thought it'd be someone . . . exciting."

"Honey, I met about *five* someones."

Alice looked at Jamie, his big mitts on the steering wheel, happily whistling a tune as he drove, head swinging around looking at the mountains with a pure kind of delight.

"*Five,*" Alice said to her mom, letting her win. "Wow. I'm happy for you."

"Well." Here it came, the caveats and accompanying mood dip. "One's in Austin. One's in Miami."

To move the conversation along, Alice did not ask where the other three lived. "This is the twenty-first century, Mom. There are airplanes. It's not like geographical location is that big a deal."

"Not everyone can just up and leave her life for a man, Alice."

Alice's hackles went up. But of course it wasn't where these men lived that kept her mother from them, anyway. She said, "No, I suppose not. I'm in the car and I think I'm losing the signal. So I'll just say goodbye now."

Jamie laughed as Alice clicked off her phone. He said, "So she's okay."

"Apparently. Let's have sex. Can we pull over somewhere?"

It was surprisingly easy to shock him and she loved doing it. His face contorted through two or three emotions before he said, "What is it about you?"

She knew he meant her directness. Her tears. Her brains. Most of all, he meant this lust they couldn't seem to sate.

"Pheromones," she said.

He guffawed. "That's it? Just chemicals?"

"Yes, probably. Don't you think chemicals are a lot more powerful than some cultural construct about romance?"

"You're scary."

Alice smiled. "Please pull over."

"Alice, we can't have sex on the shoulder of Interstate 5." But he did pull into the next rest stop, and they walked beyond the mowed picnic area, into the tall grasses of someone's private land.

She put her arms around his shoulders and neck and squeezed hard, and then they kissed. Jamie lifted her and set her down among the grasses. She yelped as the tiny golden spears jabbed her backside, so he pulled her up again, took off his shirt and laid it out beneath her. The grasses poked right through the fabric, but Alice breathed in the heady pungency of the soil, let the hum of insects loll her to comfort. Road trip. A late summer's day.

Jamie was all mammal in making love, a combination of losing himself entirely and finding his biological core. She didn't mind the lack of sweet words. She needed the honesty of their lovemaking, the animal fact of it.

But afterwards she cried. The sobs racked her whole body as she lay in the sunshine and grasses and soil and insects. She felt so helplessly happy. A terrifying feeling, really. The terror of happiness.

57|

Mikala hung out backstage with Lisa and the rest of the musicians until fifteen minutes before the start of the concert. Then she came into the front of the house and took her seat between Pauline and Andy. But she couldn't sit still. So she excused herself and got up again, thinking she'd see if she could find Rosie and Alice. Both were driving, one from Montana and the other from Washington. She knew Alice would get here on time, but Rosie might have miscalculated. She would be so disappointed if Rosie, her inspiration, didn't hear the premiere.

She couldn't exactly roam around the concert hall looking for them, though. She was the composer, the guest of honor at tonight's performance. So she climbed to the top of the auditorium where there were some unsold seats. She sat in the last row, in a pocket of darkness, and felt glad for the moment alone.

She could see her entire family, sitting in the long row up front. Marcus was leaning all the way across his two sons and Margie to tell Pauline a story. Everyone laughed politely. Everyone except for Andy who sat alone, Mikala's empty seat between him and Pauline.

What most unnerved Mikala was the look of astonishment that had been on her mother's face all afternoon and evening, ever since she first laid eyes on Marcus again. Mikala had braced herself for anger, maybe sarcasm, some kind of solid stance against the man, but Pauline stared at him with . . . *wonder*. Mikala hadn't considered the possibility that seeing him would lessen Pauline's anger, just as it had done hers. It definitely hadn't occurred to her that some of the old attraction might still play on either of them. Andy had been very quiet at dinner and now sat with his hands folded in his lap. Mikala thought she should return to her seat, if only for his sake. Andy, who claimed he'd seen her musical gift when he'd met her at the age of one, who'd given her every musical opportunity in his power to give.

She rose to return to her seat, but it was too late.

Lisa, the first violinist, strode on stage in that endearing way she had of trying to cover her painfully raw shyness by swinging her long blond curls too vigorously. She bowed to the audience, awkward, but with her instrument in her hand, so very present. The audience applauded enthusiastically. If Mikala got up now, she'd be too obvious clomping down the stairs and through the rows to get to her prominent seat.

Instead, she watched Lisa. Such beautiful hands. One set of long fingers held the bridge of her violin. The other set of fingers was busy flipping through the music on her stand. To be touched by the same fingers that played the sweetest violin Mikala had ever heard was nearly unbearable.

She had been managing to bear it, though.

Lisa bid the oboist to play an A for the woodwinds. While those hollow whistles filled the hall, Mikala again searched for her friends. Where *were* they? She began to feel a little frantic. It was as if Rosie were lost in the storm all over again. The concert would begin in moments.

When Lisa was satisfied with the woodwinds' A, she nodded to the oboist to cue the brass section.

At the first sound of those tuba foghorn bellows, and the trumpet seabird squawks, Mikala saw him. In spite of the clean-shaven head and face, the new shirt and tie, he had the same exaggerated jounce in his step, though now with a decided limp and an edge of desperation. No, more than an edge. It had become a full-body plea for help. Earl looked broken. How did he get here, to Santa Cruz, to her premiere? He walked quickly, limping, swinging his head around, searching. She knew it was for her. She almost slid low in her seat, so that she couldn't be found, but then she saw, running along behind him, glancing down at their tickets and then up at the sections and rows, her two friends, Alice and Rosie, followed by a man with big ears, probably Alice's boyfriend.

Earl spotted her. He actually lifted his arm and pointed, saying in much too loud a voice, "*There*." A number of audience members craned their necks and looked up at her—the composer of tonight's premiere—sitting alone in the top of the hall.

He led the way, taking the stairs two at a time, and they all hugged her at once, and then clamored into the seats around her. She had reserved three excellent seats, up front with her family, but there was no time to send them there now, and anyway, there was no place for Earl.

The brass had just finished and the oboist gave the A to the strings. Lisa tucked her violin under her chin and lifted the bow.

"Oh, my god," Rosie said, grabbing Mikala's hand. "Is that *her*? She's gorgeous."

"*Shhh*," Earl said, as if he were the model of classical concert etiquette.

Marin Alsop, director and conductor of the Cabrillo Festival of Contemporary Music, took the stage. Lisa stood and the rest of the orchestra followed her lead. Marin nodded to Lisa, bowed to the audience, and then faced the musicians. She raised her baton.

Mikala thought of the opening notes as a *bip, bip, bip* but actually it was a clicking, audible at first only to the front row, then the next row, the volume rising imperceptibly, but rising. If the piece failed, it would fail catastrophically. She might have miscalculated audience patience, her ability to intrigue without boring. Yes, now she was sure she'd let the singularity of the universe linger for too long. Ah, but the *bips* were loud now, and growing closer and closer together until they morphed into one single, searing note, exactly as Mikala had envisioned. A brilliant transition by the *erhu*. Only the best ears in the house would have been able to say at what moment that had happened, when the particles of music became one wave, one wave with tiny wavelengths.

The wavelengths stretched and the note lowered, and here was the crux, when the other strings took over for the *erhu*. The sound had to evolve seamlessly. It did. Thanks in large part to Lisa on first violin.

The music was beautiful.

Mikala listened to the universe come into being out of the primordial nothingness, bursting with cosmic microwaves. Out of the extreme heat, matter hurled into space. An external explosion of creation. Gravity pulled the matter together and the planets condensed, began swirling in galaxies.

Mikala leaned back in her seat and listened to the formation of earth. The oceans filled with water and the continents shifted. Bits of organic matter evolved, wiggled out of the sea, grew legs and lungs. Antarctica slid to the south, froze over. The cold white polar beauty.

Mikala heard another sound, right next to her. She glanced at Earl. He sat with his hands on his thighs, his mouth open, wholly transported. She put a hand on his back and felt the waves of silent weeping.

58

Rosie couldn't believe she'd almost made them late, but here they were. She was settling into the dark, enjoying their birdlike perch at the top of the hall, happy to have glimpsed Mikala's new girlfriend, when she heard it. The White Salmon minister's hymn. *Her* minister's hymn. Just a few notes of it, tucked away in Mikala's music, but unmistakable, like a nod to the song, a brief embrace of the lovely melody. How did it get in Mikala's symphony?

Then, like the lightest touch, a feathery tickle, she heard another familiar refrain. But from where? The music opened up inside her and she remembered. The cold snow on her back. The spiraling galaxies. The sudden warmth, a pressure against her chest and stomach, between her legs, a human blanket. And then that song.

Until now, she hadn't remembered anything about the time and space between leaving Hotel South Pole and the moment when she'd come to consciousness in the clinic, her head pounding and her joints throbbing, with someone coaxing a cup of hot water to her lips.

The time and space in between, when she'd lain on the snow. She'd heard strange notes and an eerie rhythm, a song of aching beauty that came to rescue her. She heard it again now, a song that carried all the epic hope of that continent. The song that brought her home.

Acknowledgments

Traveling to Antarctica—three times now—has been a dream come true. I am grateful to the National Science Foundation for two Artists & Writers Fellowships, and particularly to Guy Guthridge, whose vision for dialogue between artists, writers, and scientists guided the program for many years. Thank you also to Peregrine Adventures, who took me along as a guest lecturer on the Russian ship, the *Akademik Sergey Vavilov,* for my third trip to the Ice.

For help in crucial Antarctic fact-checking, thank you to Peggy Malloy and Elaine Hood. An anonymous member of the 109th Airlift Wing of the New York Air National Guard reviewed and corrected my plane scenes. Dozens of people in Antarctica were enormously generous with their time and information while I was there, but I especially want to thank Dr. Nils Halverson, Dr. Berry Lyons, Dr. Dave Marchant, Michael Solarz, and Rae Spain.

For musical editing and commentary, thank you to University of California at Berkeley music professor Christy Dana, Andrew Evenson, Emily Evenson, Marcus Bell, and trombonist extraordinaire Pat Mullan, who also composed Mikala's musical thought on page 295. I also wish to thank the Hal Leonard Corporation for granting use of the "Me and Bobby McGee" lyrics. Much of this novel was revised during a Helene Wurlitzer Foundation residency in Taos, and besides being grateful for the time and lovely casita, I particularly appreciated being in residence with two composers. Mark So especially deepened my understanding of creating new music.

For reading and commenting on my manuscript, in some cases several times, I am indebted to Alison Bechdel, Anne Binninger, Laura Bledsoe, Brian Bouldrey, Nancy Boutilier, Elana Dykewomon, Gillian Kendall, Robbie Liben, and Pat Mullan.

For timely and crucial support of various kinds, thank you to Howard Junker and *ZYZZYVA,* Michael Knight of the Helene Wurlitzer Foundation, Tom Fredericks of the Cabrillo Festival of Contemporary Music, Matthew Link, Carol Seajay, Suzanne Case, Kim Stanley Robinson, and Sherman Alexie. Thank you to *Blythe House Quarterly* for publishing the embryonic version of this novel's story. Thank you as well to the Ragdale Foundation for a residency.

Many books were useful in writing this novel, but I would not have wanted to do it without Tony Phillips's *Gateway to the Ice: Christchurch International Airport—Antarctic Air Links from 1955,* a history of flights to Antarctica and the planes that made them, including famous crashes. *The Muse That Sings: Composers Speak about the Creative Process,* a book of interviews by Ann McCutchan, was immensely useful. I am grateful to Esther D. Rothblum, Jacqueline S. Weinstock, and Jessica F. Morris for editing *Women in the Antarctic.*

Working with the University of Wisconsin Press has been a consistent pleasure. Huge thank yous to Raphael Kadushin, Andrea Christofferson, Sheila Leary, Adam Mehring, Nicole Kvale, Katie Malchow, Krista Coulson, and Carla Aspelmeier.

Several generations of telescopes, which look at aspects of the cosmic microwave background radiation and search for clues about the Big Bang, have been built for use at the South Pole. As knowledge and technology become more and more sophisticated, so do the telescopes. For the purposes of my story, I use a generic telescope called the South Pole Telescope. *The Big Bang Symphony* takes place a few years ago when the silver geodesic dome was still in use and the new South Pole Station was being built.

Finally, a word about imagination. While the setting for every scene in this book is drawn from my months of actual, on-the-ice experience, and has been painstakingly researched, I've played wildly with the story and characters. This is a work of fiction. I have aimed to portray a real view of the wonderful communities of people living on the Ice, the habitats and jobs and gorgeously harsh environment. But I've been equally careful to not expose any actual person to the exploits of my tales. The characters who people my story come from my imagination.